I0671019

david
kettle
elephant
gnosis

K-Bomb Publishing 2011
kbomb.tv

KeroseneBomb
PUBLISHING

SECOND EDITION FEBRUARY 2011

Copyright © 2004

Library Of Congress Cataloging-in-Publication Data

Kettle, David, 1961 –
Elephant Gnosis / David Kettle

ISBN 0-9719977-3-X

1. Gnosis by gnosis west — Meta-extrapolations.   I. Title

Photography Huxley Terrace and Saloth Sar, 2004
Art direction, Cover Photos Andy Takakjian

KBP K -Bomb Publishing
Los Angeles, CA 90041

kbomb.tv

Manufactured in the United States of America

veni, vidi, lotus flowers

BOOK ONE.

HAPPY NOW?

.........If only.........If only ....I resurface from a dream. I'm walking away from a...a...what, a prison? A hospital? It's a confined space anyway. I have a note in my hand. It's a note I've written. But most of it is obscured so it's difficult to fully determine what I mean or might have meant by it. Assuming I wrote it. What seems clear is that the section that's partly visible seems to reveal some sort of bad intent: "...and if you want to kill me you'll have to...3 times...all 3 of you... the both of you...returned to complex...agents in op...I conjure you; sit down, sit in this chair..." What does this mean? Meanwhile the clouds are billowing, they draw the air and the electricity in and away. Mushroom edged underneath heaven, the streaky cirro-cumulus to my left seems to mimic the snaky vectors of my bad intent – it's all written out in longhand. I feel it all coming on. I am tumescent... Further on, a few more drinks to the good...the clouds are elephant trunked and bilious, and they portend something else. They are under the scored planes...heaven and hell is under me now. I re-incline the seat – my open brain is tumescent in the dim light. I see or seem to see around me the uniformed hirelings of another kind of corporate reality. Are they here to attend me or to restrain me? Peaked caps are prominent. As are masks. Protuberant proboscis and wrinkled skin. What happened in there then? Am I so dim then? Pinch me! I look across – the ball and chain gently snoozing. She'll give me satisfaction later or I'm a shadow of the man I was. Here I have contracts to underwrite, obligations to discharge, commitments to fulfil. We're flying into London. But it might as well be anywhere. I am a citizen of nowhere in particular. Asian templates are exhausted for now. South-east asian and Australasian too. Aegean too obvious. Last stint North America. It's Europe for me before the fall

of the empires. OK so what am I selling? Tell me before I puke. I can't take much more free flight booze. Last I heard I was The Super Salesman, grand-daddy of the green light. All previous templates and corporate bulldada obsolete now, or so I reckon. Separation at the head by surgery will release the energy, we're told. Just sign the papers…the papers…all 3…unique in the legal or medical (not to mention religio-mythic) worlds. But What I Sell…you just can't buy on the open market. My sponsors would like a word though before we're through…

…Happy Now? I'm here again. Just for now. For your sins. It's me… Buffy Strangelove…Remember me? You've seen me. You've *seen* me. It's time for re-entry. Turn your mobiles off. I'm under the floorboards, the seats are upright and I'm in the waiting room. I'm needled. I look around – I cultivate contempt for my fellow passengers. All flabby angst registers with me only as self pity. I hate freely. All except Dionysia, my intended. I love her, because she's like me, because she *is* me. I forgive everything where she's concerned. I'm looking out at the planets and I'm flirting with rage. I've just had my 6th, one drink too many and I'm eyeing up suitable targets for dischargeable anger. When the gods fall out, mortals tremble as they say. And I'm raged up, full of anger. My last re-birth was ineffectual. I blew it. Big time. I flew in at 8:00am a reduced presence. Undercarriage on fire – belly up in a Parisian field. Never got used to the stomach churning pressure bursts that characterize cheap economy flights up and down the world, never acclimatized to those sudden losses of altitude, scoring a cheap lesion of freighted pleasure or panic in the temporal lobe, electrical circuits suddenly billowing with undischarged energy…

The plane's cleared for landing, and the pilot choreographs a graceful ballet at the insistence of the peaked-cap air controller guys. In and out over the sea, lugubrious and of undisclosed tonnage, the plane scores out vectors of bad intent, graceful arcs which discreetly mimic my super numinous infallibility. I could fly one of these things. I design these things in my sleep. But the airlines fail to see the import. It's a conspiracy of complacency, airline placemen affecting indifference, producing a kind of somnambulant acceptance of the inevitable. Out to sea and a circle described against the nothingness before banking back towards dry land. Birds of a feather, ironclad, bursting energy barriers, and churning the uptight stomachs of raged-up economy fliers, back from backpacking holidays and mini-breaks to the continent. The cheap angst is palpable.

I have to admit I don't seem like the best of flyers. I act out the fear of a novice, wincing and palpitating with fake anxiety. I grip the arm rests in simulated panic, my furrowed brow describing an outright unease, a pretence which keeps in check my propensity for flight violence. I feign a nervousness I don't feel, which I see as a satirical antidote to the spurious serenity of my fellow passengers, who are falsely becalmed and complacent. I scream suddenly and ridiculously, a falsetto shriek of comedy horror, and harvest the baleful looks that are cast in my direction. Every narrowed eye, each gritted tooth a scalp, a trophy on the sideboard of my petty shadenfreude. I've got form. I'm famous, or infamous, for brawling on charter flights, getting boozed up and petulant, bouncing up and down as we hit turbulence, giving the attendants a hard time, asking for *yet more booze*, tsking ostentatiously at the way people recline in their seats. I'm always good for a moment or two of drama.

As we come in to land, engines throttling back, I discharge gently… too much electricity on hand…I'm noticed, a turn of the head…a woman well known to me, she's sitting three rows in front. My wife Dionysia, beautiful and stylish household goddess, flame headed and heavy lidded, knows from this gesture of infinite tenderness that I intend to become her, at least until customs are cleared. We sit apart so as not to attract attention. We are conjoined twins, separated at birth, and re-conjoined in love, mutual dependence, respect and gnosis. Elephant Gnosis™. It's in the bag. Duty frees make space. The energy channels are open, re-birthing season is again upon us, the elephant tracks are re-emplaced and we are about to open London up for numinous devotional action. The electricity reservoirs are dangerously full again, all gurus, accountants, PR men, friendly politicos, personality broadcasters, agents and commissioners of TV documentaries, parody documentaries, reality shows and all cable blather shows, niche slots for insomniacs and the needy mad, the belligerent mad and the quietly desperate are primed for action. Disqualified from appearing on any of my shows are the disenfranchised who, under common law, are "idiots" and "lunatics in their non-lucid intervals". This country, opened up once again to the clandestine presiding spirits, and like all potentially numinous countries, repeals freedom as and when it suits. A show of *selective* democracy is enough to get us fighting mad. We *hate* that. If the greasy RealCorp politicians and psycho-secular power brokers knew we were landing, the shit really would hit the fan. So for now I have to secrete myself. We'll clean up here, not from a coarse desire for attention, fame or money, but out of love. Love, hate and fecklessness. We are boozed up already. We'll spread out in London.

I wanted to marry Dionysia many years ago, but she was from a different caste, and was disadvantaged in my dreams by the furious opposition of her mother and especially her father from contemplating a re-birthing with me. But I overcame all opposition. I always overcome all opposition. I'm a can-do kind of a guy. I operate out of rage, from under the floorboards. I nurture bitter obsessions, nurse vendettas in my bosom. People better watch out for me. I killed 'em all last time. It was a palace coup, gunfire ringing through the windy corridors, made to look like an accident. But anyway, as I say, Dionysia and I were joined in birth, joined like royalty at the head, the shared brainpan eventuating massive Gnostic capability approached in intensity only by the largest Terran mammals. Elephants. Whales too, although these cetaceans don't have the same unmediated and unrestricted power. Unfortunate associations and alignments with navel gazers and earth huggers necessarily circumscribe the power of whales and dolphins. It ain't who you know, it's who's on your side and what you have in your trousers that matters. Whales are, unfortunately, like the larger primates, too closely identified with the bleeding soul, the frangible soul, tainted by association. You see? But we're self-selecting. Our kind of exhibitionism is beyond the scope of the usual restraining influences. Therefore, the best surgeons were dismissed and we were subsequently enabled to separate *ourselves*. Tripartite separation...did I mention Frank? No? Well Frank's a bad man. He was involved somewhere. We killed him though. Oh, later on. Frank doesn't have a linear psychology. He doesn't behave as you might expect, doesn't conform. He is weightless, without vernacular sense. He was actually married to Dionysia *before* me. He was my brother, but like I say, I killed him. He became an academic. Reason enough, I might add, for fratricide.

Through customs, I blend in. Not willing to attract attention to myself, I am secreted in translucent carrier bags; I morph into more seductive forms. I become vampish, high heels clicking over the parquet. Giving out big pheromone signals, I turn heads, distracting attention from the fact that I am toting a good deal of surplus electrical baggage. At this stage one of my clandestine familiars (a stooge who's been hired from closed sources, a gentleman dressed in the American style with long unkempt hair and with a cigarette dangling from his lower lip) approaches the customs officials and introduces himself. After an eternity of pretended efficiency and half-arsed officiousness, the peaked cap guys are still arguing the toss and staring bleakly at him. As part of the routine, he then pleads for clemency on the grounds of his own stupidity, a plea that is immediately rejected. It's a fake documentary/voiceover moment. Meanwhile I am able to sneak through customs with the minimum of fuss, the sniffers' attention distracted by the American, who continues to loudly proclaim the innocence of the camera that he wears around his neck, and which he claims is a dependent. I'm hidden meanwhile; a cosseted fetish in furs. They don't think to look in the carrier bags. Security is non-existent here. Frank is in a duty free bag and Dionysia is me again. Old style morph. The customs men are, as I say, too pre-occupied or dazed to realize that all other observers and potential troublemakers are already in a kind of ecstasy. I am able, from the bag, to capture the desecrated hearts of all men and women in the vicinity. I have this capacity for transcendence and inner beauty. They are suddenly aware (in some cases for the one and only time in their lives dimly recognizing that there *is* something they've missed, there lives *have* been a waste of time, there's something they forgot, something intrinsic, something fundamental) of the over-riding need for *love*. They're gagging for it. But it's Keystone love, a pratfall love-in as they literally fall over themselves to grope their new partners. They break down, lovesick…gushing with sudden emotional incontinence, hugging, huge cow eyes, spontaneously keening and cooing, low level ersatz-coital moaning. Low level *heartbreak*, all the more poignant as it is of course merely a temporary window, a glimpse of the eternal ego-less, mischievously and malevolently opened by me, a window whose existence they'd always thereafter be aware of, but which they'd have no means, short of the pharmaceutical, of reaccessing. Heartbreaking all round. But that's me. I'm selling heartache and heartbreak for those who can see it. And they sense for this one transcendent moment that their lives have up until now been lived according to pretty un-likely, highly spurious rules. And because of my simulated malice they will forever be obliged to live with the memory of something they can only falteringly recapture. Unless I come fully tumescent into their lives. Without my Gnostic process, they're fucked. Big time. Like I said, I'm a can-do type of a guy. I have to hurt to make the connection. Ruthless dishonesty and feckless soul searching, in the quest for personal attention, must be rigorously applied. I must re-awaken the instinct towards attention, to recapture the briefly illuminated moment of transcendence. Otherwise they'll never know. But this is only a foretaste. This is only the beginning. There's more to be done, electricity to disperse.

In a dream, they watch me pass through customs as though they've seen an angel. As indeed they have. I've always been a prick-tease. My countenance evinces a beatific spirituality co-mingled with a kind of deadpan whorishness. I'm a devotional come-on, Hollywood inspired. So, this brief inner stirring, this all too transient tumescence of the soul is for these tormented individuals so sad. So sad. Oh well, things to do. Tracks to lay, agents to contact. I'm actually lying when I say that my actions are born out of malevolence. But I can't make an omelet without breaking eggs. We needed to clear customs intact.

And this is how we do it. We show them the light, briefly enough for their hearts to be broken. In the confusion, we thus slip un-noticed although fully re-birthed into country after country, onlookers in the reception lounges uneasily aware of an incipient divinity within their grasp. It's a responsibility we don't intend to evade. I've lived under the floorboards too long and humanity's been down there with me for longer than it can cope with. Through a natural talent for outsider intransigence, I spin webs, spiritual matrices to catch the souls of those willing and able to see our visions, to re-cog us as the angels we may well be. But I'm traduced for this by apostate ex-gods, stethoscope toting functionaries, obsessive demiurges, surgeons of the base levels who stalk me and my dreams, who are in pursuit of me, who are switched off, who don't believe in this *thing* they can see we've become. Non-twinned and from the lower castes, they eke out a living…carving out the tumours and lesions that mere flesh is prey to. They are hospital vampires… drinks parties with the admin whores, civic unction displayed at all times, kickbacks from the drug companies, reliance on pure hospital grade morphine, holidays in the darkness of needless operations. They are B-features. Reptilian nightmares.

They say:

"I help people…people like you…."

To which their patients reply

"Meaning what?"

"Meaning…what you want it to mean…"

"You….you just leave…my wife…alone!"

"If you've got a problem with your conscience, it's gonna get a whole lot worse afterwards, believe me. We're here to *help* you…kill your wife…"

…The above dialogue filters through to me from a distant place. It's some sort of waiting room. A place in which the vengeful pursuit by Abrahams of my tripartite godhead has been ruthlessly fictionalized, for a purpose not of my own making, and brought to life by second-rate actors. My life has, in this tarnished version, become cheap (although expensively assembled) Sunday evening drama. It is an echo from a pre-birthed age, a purely psychological past, a past in which people are encouraged to believe in a narrative psychoanalysis of their own motives. An age before psychology has not yet become entirely coffee table. An age of production values, devalued intent, faces upon which expressions can be read, no matter how artful the attempt to conceal motive. Faces lit ingeniously to capture the spiritual essence of this or that character. Like we ever believed in that. Maybe some did. Maybe. But I resolved to use it later on in my dealings with Frank, who would need some careful handling when it came out about me and Dionysia…

(Previous voices/voiceover intervenes here)…*there might be a way around this though. This is strght from BOARDROOM. The link is, I think, how d'you say…spoofing?…anyway, Let this drift, till management takeover. Finance? Overdraft. Also, don't minute this. Divisional stringency and a lifetime's drift. You will be In Academe.*

I WILL be at future board meetings. Wankbait in particular has som.th. to say here. Review the progress -> instigation. Human remains/resources fr. Rebirthings. Strglv, you are newly re-birthed scum. God speed you Pinko. We can't <u>officially</u> review this until we ourselves are reviewed. You are remnant of Reality Corps. Get gone… down there. Make 'em squirm and make 'em cum. We am process/in review. Template/mode - Hellenic. Couplings are ALL Subjudice. Mythological format to confound psycho-somnambulant linearity. We picked up transmitter signals…don't make sense, no way…big cat sightings in…<u>inappropriate</u> settings. How to get the motherlode into places where they can operate… herds on Hampstead Heath? Therefore, This then our one and only chance for now. Bigger fish to fry, you the single agent on call Strangelove. Herds already morphing from houses in Fnsbry Pk/ Hampstd Hth. Collect fright masks from back of pick-up trucks in N.London. <u>Two</u> suggested alter-egos - Nobby Wyse – English and Foreign Livestock/Fruit. Billy Hard Hat – psycho nutter homunculus…Usual familiars will as usual of course <u>Be More Fruity</u>. Camp is important element in the deployment of these simulacra. Tombstones of the failed re-birthed also observed on back of pick-up trucks all over N.London, now instigating enquiry. The permanently dead now taking up valuable space. Pachydermal hints already picked up by, er, "switched on" types in city slacks. Mobile phones are humming with incidental intent. Click, bzz, crkk…this is how we know. It's Walkman interference. Matrices are therefore in confusion at this time. Therefore (some here say) you are the NOW tragic metaphysician, ie: NOT under the influence of half-baked occultism: you will deploy lounge music (wink)… cocktail music, dinner jazz intonations will be at odds with the badness of your perceived intent. You don't need to know my name but me, I'm the only boozer who's not intimidated by Frank, you know he don't scare me. Your brother is history pal. That's what normal people do – they whistle. I whistled right in his mug. He seems confused. Medusa Rappa the ex-witch, yr. own ex-wife, has SHOT her newest lover but you being her ex-husband I fully expect you to support her actions. I understand misconceived intent. This is now burnout. There is a residue of superfluous electricity. The newly enfranchised (locators of the soul in the SELF) have *devised extreme hedonist templates for city living. Result: too much electricity. Correct this misapprehension. Rectify this as a matter of urgency. I have not been here. I did not say this…*

…Speaking in tongues like some dippy fucking fairground fortuneteller, I come over like some recidivist psychopath on the revenge trail. The guys in peaked caps look askance. Are they immune to this pheromone jazz? I can see they're wavering. I thought we'd made it through. Look at the loved up terminal freaks, not at us. No? Well listen to me then. I can see I need to explain to you how I reviewed this *received information* at the level of future boardroom level emanation. I am a man of authority and command respect in the City, my solutions to multifarious spiritual problems generally praised if not entirely understood by the dipshit moneymen, the currency grinders, number crunchers and power brokers for whose soul needs I have undertaken a kind of brash responsibility. It's about electricity. Superfluous electricity is produced here by "irritation", a very mod phenomenon occasioned by close proximity to other power sources and/or over use of gadgetry. *And get this…*by over-reliance on *therapy* fetishism, a synonym for extravagantly lived, hyper-solipsistic lifestyles. Caused by the have it all mentality. Only household gods (or apostate ex-gods) can have it all. Mere pre-birthed individuals produce, in the attempt to *have it all,* a superfluity of electricity, which needs to be discharged somehow. I am therefore here as a corrective. I have the key. City bimbos routinely assume a countenance of objectively perceived glamour, behaving as though actions don't have consequences (and of course they don't - but *they* don't know that) and as though banal celebrity debauchery is in and of itself transferable to their own quotidian realm. They behave as though there is no price to pay. The tab is never picked up. The juice bars are full of raged up XX chromosomes, heedless of excess. They are no different in appearance to the fallen stars of their imaginations. They fall into and out of nightclubs; get blotto on tomorrow's mortgaged dead time.

  Or again, for example, excess electricity is produced in extremis by macro-biotic types who've developed an "interest" in eastern religious systems, a misguided yearning after elongation of the personalized Terran linear time span. The doomed quest is heart breaking. The quest is for re-tumescence of the perceived Inner Core of Being, being itself putatively located in the inner core of the so-called Showtime/Display section of the brain, the temporal lobe, which is located next to the hippocampus. This proximity produces in pre-re-birthed individuals a surfeit of electrical activity, of bad intent, intent which if not discharged in *ritual peregrination* of the *old bus lanes* ends up surging impotently around the city precincts. Hence the importance to all personalized spiritual efforts of this organ within an organ, this wheel within a wheel, previously (wrongly) assumed to be concerned exclusively with locomotive and direction finding abilities. Of course, all (so-called) primitive cultures invoke power over nature via repetitive and ritualistic perambulations, an evocation of divinity via the obsessive treading and re-treading of pre-determined routes. Rain invoked, or in this case dispersal of a surfeit of electricity, achieved by treading the elephant trails, mythic route-shapes which, when viewed from above (from a space ship…or whatever) delineate a vast Picasso sketch, a domed trunked head; trunk and ears, dome viewed head on. This is of vital importance to my work here. Everything follows from the nature and shape of the city's ex-bus lanes. You following me here fellas? They nod their peaked caps at us but they're not taken in. So I continue. It's going to be hard work.

…The hippocampus (I say) is thought to be one of the most important brain structures involved in memory. The case of the patient Medusa Rappa, one of the most famous case studies in neuropsychology, strikingly demonstrates the importance of the hippocampus. In 1983, as a 27-year-old woman, MR underwent brain surgery to control severe epileptic seizures. The surgeons removed her medial temporal lobes, which included most of the hippocampus, the amygdala, and surrounding structures. Although the operation successfully controlled MR's seizures, it had an altogether unexpected and devastating side effect: MR was unable to form new long-term memories in a way that she could later retrieve them. That is, she could not remember anything that happened to her after the surgery. She could not remember meeting new people or new experiences for more than a few minutes. This resulted in her later shooting dead a former lover, who'd arrived one morning unannounced in order to effect a reconciliation. Still in possession of a latchkey, he'd insinuated himself into her flat and then her bed in confident anticipation that this overtly romantic gesture would meet with her eager approbation. Instead, as she failed to recognize him, he awoke in her a startled revulsion that found immediate expression in action of the most affirmative and precipitate nature. Amazed to find a man she didn't recognize in her sleeping quarters, and to make matters infinitely worse a man sporting a lascivious smirk, a smirk which he imagined was the precursor to renewed and impassioned relations, she simply reached over to the bedside table, picked up the shooter she kept there as protection and precaution against burglars and blew a hole in the centre of his forehead, rendering his own hippocampus, along with the rest of his brain, permanently ineffectual. His memory, both short and long term, underwent a sudden and irreversible turn for the worse. Notwithstanding this inconvenient episode, her memory of events prior to the surgery was mostly intact, and her reasoning and thinking skills remained strong if somewhat febrile. A further side effect, which was noted at the time but suppressed (for reasons we can't guess at) in the case history, involved a loss of *spiritual* intent and capability. Friends noted that she'd become indifferent to matters of the self, to the renewability of the soul and was turning up late, if at all, for Polarity Massages and Mythic Rejuvenescence sessions. Researchers concluded that the hippocampus and its surrounding structures in the medial temporal lobe play a critical role not only in the encoding of episodic memories, especially in binding elements of memories together to locate the memories in particular times and places, but also in spiritual capability and devotional direction finding (peregrinatory invocation of divine intervention)…

different voices again…Whole daze. Days. Forgotten to talk. Neighbourly watch, even at the moment of crisis I cultivate error correction. Collective error correction. I am aloof generally. Lazy bastard in other words…work cut out Strglv… your neighbours reckon you're fey and like to keep yourself to yourself…the city's former bus lanes, now reserved for elephants, are vital as conduits for electricity dispersal. I want to live but there's too much other stuff. You do it. Stuff I created. I can't live in this pre-corrected state. I'm here in the waiting room, eyes half open. My sight's going, I see my reflection in you. Or me. I can't tell which. I am psychoanalyzed by Abrahams, and I went AWOL. I slept in Finsbury Park. I wasn't there. I don't know why not…

...To get back: through customs, re-entry via the channels of no resistance. I do not resemble my passport photo and it's pure sleight of hand that I get through. They melt away the faces under the hats. The last I see they're rooting each other in a feverish uniformed scrum. I am Dionysia and she is me. I am in her duty frees, a perfume of incalculable seductiveness and overpowering pheromonal effect. We are each other, always have been, joined at the head and arse, at birth, and now split asunder again. Otherwise like last time, it's air rage re-entry. Cause, by misbehaviour in and around the cockpit (ritualistic slagging of the pilot and his/her sexual orientations) a nosedive and potential disaster that is only averted by some pretty sharp thinking on the part of the airheadhosts and hostesses. I've been wrestled to the ground and subdued on more than one occasion, Dionysia observing me from a window seat with quiet appreciation. It assures us safe passage through customs. But I don't want to use that too often. Good gags should be used sparingly.

So anyway, back in town, in the waiting room, and the walls as usual seem to press in on me. Hi fellas! It's me. Buffy! I'm here again! Single 60 watt bulb, attendant hosts and hostesses in night robes, masked and scrubbed, are seemingly intent on psychoanalysis. Can you believe that? In this post-psychological world, they cling to outmoded forms as jealously as would a visiting academic to the impression that he might still possess (as though he ever did) some form of sexual charisma. I am obliged to recount, under hypnosis, my impressions of the guiding principles of my, er, philosophy, for want of a more appropriate term. I glance at Dionysia, who turns up the volume on her walkman. The faint tss tss of escaped sound announces that she understands. She increases the volume and I notice, although the flight attendants don't appear to, that there is a faint blip in the electrical power supply to the building. She turns it up some more, and finally even the personal trainers/therapists in attendance on me (rather too closely for my full comfort I have to admit) are obliged to notice a significant diminution of the power supply. Their perturbation is a picture.

...I am of course merely playing a role here. I've never been in a hospital in my life. I don't believe that there can ever be a reason to enter these establishments unless accompanied by a camera crew and with full SARB (suicide assisted re-birth) accreditation. I realize that I look very English, there's the assumed self-loathing...I cut a very Bogarde figure, I am a sort of nervy academic type with military bearing but sporting a demeanour which suggests a history including some deep personal trauma that might account for my, ahem, psychosis...nurses falling in love in discreetly British fashion with my tortured countenance. I am just a poor boy, not a man, a boy in need of love and understanding, a manboy endowed with the face of a neurotic, a monkey-genius. English nurses go for that one big time. More than once, I've awoken from general anesthetic proclaiming my love for some sweetly countenanced English rose and more than once I've observed that love reciprocated, if un-acted upon. More than their jobs worth I suppose. And they are unwilling or unable to abuse their therapeutic position. But, I tell you as a salesman, I wouldn't *mind* a bit of abuse. I'll tell you that for nothing.

Back in the factory, the head shrink Abrahams is pushed to and fro on a sort of metal trolley. He falsely assumes a position of authority. I realize he sees himself as some sort of panjandrum of the wards; he's puffed up with self-importance, issuing orders to his underlings, imperiously barking out directional commands like the captain of some circumscribed vessel that's destined for the rocks, his messianic expression clearly indicating the essential obsession with which he endows his every action. He's a man possessed. Just look at those eyes. That beard. I fancy He imagines Himself as Ahab, and I am His Great White Whale. Not that he actually has any need to assume this dictatorial and frankly ridiculous, self-aggrandizing posture, his absurdly self important conveyance entirely at odds with the actual role he fulfils, which is merely that of facilitator of my dreamtime musings. Like all limited (non-twinned) professionals, he can't bear not to be the centre of attention. Very like Frank in fact. In fact, maybe he *is* Frank.

...So anyway...there I am...lying there...in Finsbury Park, watching the scored planes fly overhead, there's a whisper of breeze, the shadows of the nearby trees loom large and grey. I notice that the tune on my Walkman is increasingly compromised by a variety of electrical blips, squeaks and buzzes. Interference. The ether is loud enough in itself, so I wonder what's causing this. My listening pleasure is

undeniably diminished; my ears are full of electrical discord. I see quite suddenly, at the crown of the hill, a small herd of elephants, morphing out of the trees, but indistinct among the shadows. The electricity seems to ebb and flow as they move into and out of the shade. As cell phone carrying pedestrians pass by, the electricity seems to swell. The ckk, bzz, tss, crkkk intensifies and then recedes. But still there's a residual pool, a reservoir of understated voltage disturbing the general ambience. And then something happens to alarm the elephants. They are distracted by some commotion at the other end of the park. There is a trumpeting, a honking, they relinquish the sanctuary of the trees and the crown of the hill and stampede towards the Seven Sisters' Rd. And as they go, I realize that the air has been cleansed of previously stagnant electricity. They have somehow contrived, in an act of spontaneous collectivity, to decontaminate the surroundings of stale electricity. The air has been purified, somehow distilled. The tune on the Walkman is now crystal clear. To say that this discovery is a watershed in my pre-birthed existence would be an understatement. Literally an understatement. Everything follows…

Abrahms merely nods. He is inferior, an apostate.

…As a result of this epiphany my plan is that the city's abused bus lanes become, by my divine Gnostic agency, elephant trails. The elephants tread the well-scored vectors, all around the city, dispersing electricity by ritual peregrination. This divine act occasions in the tuned in citizenry a kind of spiritual calm… lays the tracks for intense post-psychological soul searching, or Elephant Gnosis™ as I've termed it. Via this patented and affordable technique, citizens are afforded previously hidden opportunities for spiritual Rejuvenescence and suicide-assisted rebirth. It's no secret. I'm a big noise in the city and in the channels of mediated power. I assume multitudes of personae, electricity flees my agents, and I re-birth at will. I enter and re-enter. I have discovered previously hidden secrets, the divine and arcane secrets. I fictionalize and re-fictionalize, adumbrating the outlines of Gnostic self-therapy. Multitudes of additional personae are re-birthed, multifarious aspects of the self, all interchangeable and clamouring for attention.

The self is (needless to say) the most precious commodity, the currency of ubiquity in this meta-therapeutic age, and I have hi-jacked all available outlets. I hold the leases on all franchised operations. Elephant Gnosis™ has been patented. I precipitate as many elephant-gnostic emanations as I choose. I am plurality, in a newly minted pleroma of inconsequence. Hot shit!

On awakening, I see that Abrahams has fallen asleep. His hirelings look nervously around. Do they still see me? Am I still here? Dionysia is in the pipes.

GOD BLESS ME/YOU.

So God bless me. The country, since I flew in, is worse than it ever was. I made it bad. But I made it good again. Force of nature, that's me. The skies are full of mourning and pain. The buses don't run on time. Litter is everywhere. It seems the world is spinning on a wobbly axis, hitting the skids. The fields are full of death, the streets are decaying. My soul's beyond retrieval just now and frankly it's in some pain. I'm hitting the bottle big time and my marriage could be down the crapper. My knees ache and I realize it's time for a quick stock take, a period of reflection, a re-charging of the sepulchral will. Still, plenty of elephants left before extinction, before the end times really kick in. The End Times, a concept I foolishly leased out for use by old-time satirists, but I need the money now. They pay me for it of course. Mythic I may be, but I still need hard cash.

But the swelling in my left kneecap is *really* getting me down. I was numb down that whole side and I was even number after the latest of many attacks. Where and when *did* that happen anyway? Self delusion? There's a sort of bony growth that really seems beyond physiotherapy, medication or surgery. My belly's distended and the eyesight's going fast. Time then for suicide. In the waiting room, I prevaricate as Ahab pontificates. In these end times, we get the deities we deserve and of course we, or you, don't deserve much. Millennia of obfuscation and self-delusion in the realm of ersatz gnosis, inferior forms of self-worship, have done you absolutely on favours at all. It took a few hundred to realize even that the earth only had one moon and that the sun was relatively a stationary object. You don't see things right under your noses. I've noticed that. The centuries you've spent chasing up blind alleys, wildly caricaturing yourselves, stoking up the fires of self-deception, righteous anger, cruelty and mutual loathing are centuries you'll *never get back. Ever.* And we all look out for ourselves in these end times, so God Bless Me. Thing is, my theology says nothing about suicide. That's the problem. In self-help religiosity mode, we have to extemporize, make it up as we go along. In the secular manuals there's no reference to suicide constituting the unforgivable sin or any nonsense of that kind. It is, hyper-parodically, an echo of the old times, when rock deaths used to be described as career moves. Many a word in jest and all that. Just occasionally, the world gets it right. Rock deaths are improvised suicides, full of religio-financial intent. This is, or was, my gift to the world. Once imagined it just goes on happening. Career renovation, the making good of crusty old rockers, the dusting off of moribund back catalogues.

I am merely a household god, albeit a tarnished one, and I don't answer to any other god or gods, only in the boardroom. For my sort, as well as for those actually in need of career renovation, suicide is not only the only option, it's the central defining metaphor of our entire cultural and religious identity. But that's not a negative thing, as it might be in the quotidian realm. You have to see and you will see that for us…Suicide is our Big Thing. All circumscribed deities are big on suicide. We can do it with good grace, more or less blithely, because we know how to re-activate. To re-enter. It's just a trick, a feat of prestidigitation learnt a few millennia ago. But you'll have to trust me on that one. It's not like death is the end of anything. Suicide is just a portal, a kind of reversed karmic renewal, a credit in your personal enhancement with-profits secular schedule. But a word of warning: Be Careful! If you don't go out with a big enough bang, if the self-inflicted end isn't of a sufficiently egregious and exceptional nature, the risk is in returning somewhat diminished. You then run the risk of ending up as low budget features, or even worse depraved reptilian hybrids, feral pigeons, icky celluloid nightmares. Cheap B-features, if you get my drift. The more imaginative and singular the end, the more rewarding the re-entry, is how I'd have to put it. You are obliged to attract attention. Be burnt alive on a remote Hebridian island, a funeral pyre of stacked notes, invite sympathetic journalists. Go belly up in the Thames with attendant media outrage at the safety standards not met by your registered owners. A national epidemic of a disease previously considered obsolete. It's a kind of animism of the momentary relapse. On the other hand, particularly bad sitcoms will lead to fewer offers of quality work but more offers of sightings and appearances. Really sub-standard suicides result in merely desperate appearances on daytime chat shows, plugging the detritus of mal-conceived intent. The more media attention you attract, the higher the karmic pay-off. Think of it like this (I say as I gesture expansively): think of it as paying your mortgage off with a series of huge sums rather than sticking to the prescribed interest rate payments. We *could* just put it off, routinely committing humdrum suicides, living lives of enervating boredom and thankless drudgery, but the smarter household gods attempt every now and then to hit the exit button with a flourish, go out in style. Hit the big one with a bang. It's like money in the bank.

The only thing you need worry about is media coverage. You have to be covered. It makes sense. You know it does fellas…you seek exposure? I'm your man. If only the ironic pronouncements all too common in these end times were taken *at face value* then you might be getting somewhere. It's only the fully re-birthed household god who can live life as metaphor, the rest need to take it at face value. But I shouldn't really be telling you this. You have to learn it good for yourself. Suicide really is painless. It's also guileless. Artless. Straightforward…nothing to it, as long as your agent knows where and when. That's the only really important thing. This is what it is…this is it…(I hit the play button on the remote, the screen flickers…)

…isn't…*Self-immolation in modest flames. Camera crew present. Simulacra burnt at the stake. Plastic body consumed. High stakes for the return trip, reborn, painful rebirthings. Figure on screen checks out the oppo therapists/ mood music as files are flicked through/montage of masked figures with stretched faces…they are the distilled essence of pure evil, the forced rebirthers, their tightly wrapped homicides dressed up as therapy, children forced to rebirth and love their mommies. It's the rejuvenation patrol. Evil therapists from the new age, together with their shoddy pals, catholic counter-psychological reformation agents in all known media, make spirituality very difficult. They look within and see only the beast inside, the tawdry beast. The fictional beast which is capable of bad things. They said it was for the good of the child, that she didn't WANT to be reborn. So they smothered her. They are the essence of pure evil. We'll deal with them… later…*

…Anyway, I must proceed. You see, I believe what you'd probably characterize, and with apparently good reason, as *insane* things about myself. Such as that my body has become compromised, my legs seem to go missing, I have to dump out of a *bag* in my *stomach*. Corporeal realities are visually circumscribed. I catch them looking vacantly into space as though I've never been there. I have the evidence. I am compromised, but I have a way around it. I am hailed as a genius by minor gurus, small-beer therapists, and lesser psychological profilers, in tautological approbation of my divinity. I go on the lecture circuit; I pocket the freebies, accept the patronage, take the kickbacks. My knob twiddling entourage feed tidbits to the crowds via a sort of unearthly reverb, making me sound even less human than I already look. Trumpeting and honking are the medium and the message. My head in the elephant head mask is inclined conspiratorially towards audiences cowed by instinctual deference. They are bedazzled and confused at the real time metempsychosis that is taking place. I go over big on the arena circuit. My ex-wife talked me out of it before, but not now. Thing is, she always talked out of her arse and at the same time shot herself in the foot. Left me in no doubt as to my sheer impotence in her eyes. She shot her former lover in the forehead. But I stood by her…character references and all that. Her former lover…a weaselly homunculus, a turbaned and trepanned minimus, a withered bit part player, a waste of oxygen. She never got the elephant thing. The method. Every tomtit gnosis needs a method, so of course my (or our) version definitively needed a method, a technique. She didn't realize that *of course* these things, these elephants are the motherlode. Transport with ease through time and space because of the sheer size of the hippocampus. Big as a football. And ratio of hippocampus (temporal lobe) to brainpan size, body weight and heart size, and size of arse. Also slowness of heartbeat, the universal vibration…that sort of guff. But it seems to work. Elephants are indeed the most spiritual beings of all in this realm because they not only literally dump the most waste matter, get rid of the shit so to speak, they know how to locate the spiritual-directional vectors. Bus lanes. They embark on bus lane peregrinations around the precincts of towns and cities in response to pre-ordained, previously laid down devotional tracks. Follow this template and you're a holy man. That's how I became my own shaman. And elephants reveal the truth just by *being*. Dumping big time. Metaphorically, I dumped on people to get where I am. But I love them now as I love you now. I'm full of love. I speak in tongues, as follows…to confuse Abrahams…

…J'accuse. I accuse all the middlemen of not aspiring to be the top men. I accuse them of lack of recognition. I accuse them of failing to actualize at the highest levels, of blanching in the face of self realisation. The fight for self-love was lost in the midst of battle. And thus the dead rise up as monsters, vampiric emblems of lost spirit, to remind you that you are guilty of killing them. Lost hopes. The middlemen are still holding tight in the middle, the empty and vacuous middle mass. The chatterers who never could read a book. It was a kind of dyslexic disassociation, a defence against the demiurge gone wrong, Old Nick with arched eyebrows who enters through printed words. Devils in grown up language, dyslexia a defence against abstruse code. Films are worse, arched eyebrow golems in the grain, rising up, entering through your eyes. Former conflicts all producing their share of cinematic monsters. My eyes close involuntarily all the time. I lie here dying, burnt out. I look through the window at my retinue and yell "open the fucking door!" They don't hear me; they just synthesize my voice so it sounds more and more unearthly, more elephantine. Because I am the creator of this meme. I am beyond their assistance. This lifestyle, this choice you can make. There is, therefore, a price on my head. I am not undervalued, by my followers (ex-wives) or my pursuers. My stock is high, never been higher. I leave by the in door. I fool them all. Planes leave Heathrow every 2 minutes. It's not difficult…

These words flap out of my mouth like bats, crazed signifiers of my bad intent. Public indulgence is bought off and there's a residue of lugubrious hope engendered through elephant metaphors and similes, my voice synthesized to maximize my elephantine intent. I am a Holy Man. I shamelessly use all available prestidigitatory techniques, setting fire to my fingers, collapsing my lungs and/or stomach, levitating over the heads of the audience. I punch the rubber shark. My methods relieve insecurities, loss of confidence and lack of self-worth - but in the wrong hands can do untold emotional damage. And my hands (you're ahead of me doctor!) *are* the wrong hands of course. They have to be. I can't be *good* all the time. Of course, my bad is equivalent to your good. That's the catch. Yours are the only hands that are right. But I take no pride in wrecking the emotional well being of people who listen to me lecture. The whole point is that they reject me, and watch me burn; spectate at my real time metempsychosis. I am a universalized martyr, transfixed with flaming arrows. I am burning, my ex-wives say I always was, but I'm burning up now. But it's all a trick, a sleight of hand. I'm in flames, a metaphorical cash furnace, a special effects show, carefully and painstakingly created by analogue means. Old nick, old StanleyK stole my idea for the StarGate sequence, or rather didn't steal it… he used me, *directly*. I was in the grain. He used me, burning up in multiple orgasms, twisting like prisms in the cosmic rays of exploding galaxies. He was thinking not about the *infinite*, but about *money*. Cash to ensure his personal security. Or did that come later? I'm not big on linearity. The ego is non-linear. Because it's anti-history. Of course you'll say I should have patented it *before* he got to me, and you'd be right. But the world needs these sorts of reclusive geniuses, as they do their bit in mopping up unused electricity, fixating on personal security, so I was happy for him to have the credit. Happy for him!!

Of course the thing that will absolutely ensure a specialized spiritual regeneration is simply a fear of missing out. The impulse is to base levels of greed, the gnawing suspicion that someone, somewhere else is enjoying something that you're not. That's me all over. That's Frank as well. But in his case, you can add an unpleasant shadenfreude into the mix as well. He has to go too far. Not content with coveting the happiness and spiritual plenitude of others, he must actively go out of his way to destroy it wherever he finds it. He reduces shop girls to tears by condescension; he grandly denounces those who routinely incense him. Buying a pair of socks represents to Frank merely the opportunity to bully and to intimidate. It seems to enliven him, make him glow brighter. He expostulates and gestures like a theatrical knight on the most trivial pretext. His presence is oppressive and he revels in it. Of course he does. I, on the other hand, pump the punters full of false self-confidence, overload them with resources, via grants, and make them *believe* in their divinity. Get them on TV, then I pull the plug. I ramp it up, spinning yarns about the validity of "projects" they can involve themselves in, projects that aren't really worth the paper they're scribbled on, a stock so worthless we don't even go public. The bubbles then burst, the careers are over before they've started, and they're destined to play out their lives on satellite/cable shows, as presenters. The best model we've yet devised. They've learnt a valuable lesson, despite (or because of) my cruelty, which is, seen in this light, a vital component of a hyper-modern view of the world. We're post-psychology and we need new myths I tell them. New mythic and epic techniques. We're post-*everything* I tell them. Everything's gone. There's a vast hole there, waiting for your new myths to come rushing in.

To be an adept, you don't need to be good, just persistent, and to possess the ability to deny the evidence of your senses. Appearance is of course reality, now as it's always been. Mobility between social castes has never been more pronounced. Anyone can present. It's the new thing in a city of imprecisely new things. But some presenters have become mesmerized and they just don't see it coming. They're sleepwalking to disaster, not aware of the danger. They can't see that their lives, lived purely as metaphor, are ill equipped to withstand the inevitable diminution of the fame they've struggled so gamely for or. Their re-positioning on cable TV is a necessary purgatory through which they need to progress to achieve the full Gnostic Monty. They must die metaphorically before they can achieve full Elephant Gnosis™. Crowds of ex-corporation presenters resembling baseball-hatted ghosts throng the streets outside Broadcasting House, moaning incantations and murmuring curses, unable to accept their apparent demotion to minor celebrity-hood. They fail to notice that there are no sacred bus lanes in Portland Place. They therefore meander aimlessly, merely succeeding in disturbing rather than dispersing the electricity pools underneath the transmitter masts. They are doomed to wander in ever decreasing circles of thankless anti-gnosis. Gardening shows, makeover drivel, cheap historicity/archaeology crossovers, that sort of thing.

The last celebrity crash a few years back gave me the opportunity I required to re-establish some sort of authority over the public Gnostic process. I'd been derided by some and became a sort of Cassandra, a teller of prophesies that were destined to be believed by no-one. They laughed at my stories of the spiritual motherlode on our very doorstep and my descriptions of techniques whereby the spiritual harvest might be gathered in, and my keening warnings to take it all semi-seriously. They pooh-poohed my imagining and placement of elephant trails where previously only bus lanes had existed. The whole thing was popularly derided either as a fanciful and ludicrous conceit or as a monstrous and dangerous flight of fancy, depending on the perspective of the critic. Then the crash happened, a result of too much fragmented celebrity, too many ill-conceived careers sliding towards deserved oblivion, the stock of multifarious dim-witted show-offs sinking to previously unimagined lows, no-one able to get work on even the most debased game-shows, the cultural temperature rising as punter critics everywhere, in a froth of indignation at the lassitude and ineptness of the performing classes, demanded value for money - this was when the time was right to launch my government sponsored initiative. The public funded scheme immediately rescued the moribund careers of hundreds of thousands of vapid gesticulators and autocue leeches. I was hailed as a hero, although no-one could see that really it was intended purely as metaphor, the metaphor indeed to end all careers. I inaugurated a one man sanctified and Holy Roller show, a very explicit technique to facilitate another spectacular re-entry. I did it for them, for you, that you might see inside yourself, that you might embrace your divinity…get a job on TV, that I might be reborn as a god more powerful and more feckless than ever. My ex-wives are legion. I rope them all in, even though their understanding of the concepts behind Elephant Gnosis™ is vague. I don't scapegoat though, I merely move on. I take what I need and then I burn rubber, I'm out of here…can't see me for dust.

The Mojave is my refuge when the heat's on. Always good for old or young, raddled and dysfunctional, misunderstood rock gods. In a trailer, I hunker down till the next one happens along. I am obliged to be an energy vampire, at least for a while. Just for a short while. I am a desert rat. I can do it by numbers anyway - always could. This debased aspect of my talent, this cheap showmanship that abuses the trust of languid rock gods, is very coffee table. The filth, the drugs, the mutilation, the degraded personal relationships, the spilt bodily fluids, the re-configuration of bodily co-ordinates, the retro-realism of hyper-observed characters, the wallowing in brazen cultishness, the dialect, the rhyming slang, the shaven headed excesses, the linguistic virtuosity, the febrile plot-lines, I can do all that standing on my potato head, but what's the point? I work out now in the gym. *So that you don't have to*...

...I am the personalized hip priest of my own religion and I make it look easy! I have discovered techniques that the therapy whores can barely dream about! I know elephants and what they are capable of! I know it inside out! I am what you want to be but don't want to own up to be! I will kill again Ahab! I will kill you or me in the attempt!

I look down at the by-numbers culture and I see that you want bad things at least in your dreams, if not in your lifestyle. Bad things kept at bay in your dreams. Your contained dreamtimes are thus at my disposal. I am the bespoke purveyor of self-conscious religiosity to suit your every need. I'm only semi-conscious as yet. But you are sleepwalking and you always have been. Dreamtime for the elephants, they dream you back to wakefulness if you've got the heart for it. Their bad dreams, over-loaded with spiritual intent, suck the badness, the electricity, away from you. I'll write a fuckin' book about it some day! But no word will ever be said lightly, everything will have substance, there will be no frills! My propositions are elucidatory. If you understand me you'll finally recognize them as senseless. When you have subjected them to scrutiny, swung in their branches, pulled the foliage off them, climbed out through them, on them...over them... you must, as it were, throw away the ladder after you have climbed up on it. My propositions are transparent invocations; my patented techniques are transitory and public.

3 (THREE) ANECDOTES.

First, 3 anecdotes. Anecdotal and elucidatory evidence. Billy Hard Hat, so called because his head, trepanned, turbaned and bare of hair, approximately resembled a hard hat. The ridge of bone encircling the crown stood weirdly proud from the scalp, the brow bone protruding further than it should have, prime trepanning material. He walked down the road, right arm swinging violently, both marking time and delineating personal space. The left arm, numb now for a few weeks, remained virtually motionless. His GP, well up near the top of the list of GPs suspected by the medical watchdog authorities of being incompetent and/or of active malpractice, had told him that it probably wasn't anything important. But he knew better, or thought he did. His whole arm numb, for no apparent reason. Not quite right. He was a wiry little bastard though, and disease wasn't on his fictional agenda. Hard Hat outlives them all. He has other fish to fry.

For now he was on his way to the dentist, to have a worrying lump examined, a frighteningly hard and painful lump that had suddenly appeared in his lower left jawbone. But he was also a hypochondriac, usually a compendium of imaginary symptoms. Given his hypochondria, it's also true to say that Billy was a malingerer. This was not so much that he wasn't prepared to work if he needed to. Just that he saw no reason, in this particular day and age, to extend himself. His life was a parcelling of time between casino, kitchen, brothel and pub. Workplaces were no part of his scheme. The dignity of labour was not a slogan that resonated with him. Labour was simply an outmoded concept. The work ethic is fucked, he reckoned. Desperately in need of a leg up, or it would perish altogether. Academics in the soft left press had speculated for some time indeed that it had *better* be fucked, or *we* all *will* be. Hunter-gatherers, they implied, are by nature lazy, spending only 6 hours per week hunting, whereas proto farmers (which we all apparently became 10,000 years ago) have to spend all their time producing more and more food, the emphasis on quantity, for more and more people. People who otherwise would perish in fact survived because of the intensive farming producing more and more food.... and so on, ad nauseam. These articles had amounted to a slacker's manifesto, a serious scientific apologia for putting your feet up. More *people*. More *food*. But we've out-evolved the work ethic, it's a redundant concept. We're hunter-gatherers by nature, not *farmers*. This idea appealed to Hard Hat, who liked a scrap as much as the next man. Appealed as compared to the over-heated and morbid competitiveness engendered in institutional culture, plus he was a completely lazy bastard. He may have conceded the need for a pale imitation of work, but only because he needed to keep himself in soft drugs, betting money and porn videos. There was no higher purpose. No further end to which he worked. He was just a shiftless idiot when all was said and done. A malevolent and otiose manikin, whose one unique identifier as an individual was an unusual method of self propulsion. His tempered motor efficiency was achieved by means of an abnormally enlarged hippocampus, given breathing space via the trepanned cranium. And now, by way of prevarication, and affording himself respite from the ordeal to come, he approached the World's End…

"…Football's not about what you deserve. I don't care whether we deserved to win that match or not. The fact is that that cunt of a referee should never have disallowed that goal. He bottled it because he didn't want to be responsible for the home team losing an extremely tense match in the very last minute of extra time. That's all there is to it!"

In the pub, a sozzled suit was loudly pontificating on the result of some match that had been showing on the big screen. Pub life as Billy knew all too well was now just football punditry, over-amplified and tedious beer-disputation, modelled on TV forebears who were themselves utterly bereft of dignity, charisma, soul, insight or animus. He walked past the fat buffoon with his right arm scything the air provocatively, deliberately spilling his Kronenburg in the process. Splash! as the liquid coursed over his shirt front.

"Watch it you little tosser".

"Tosser?"

"Yeah, *little* tosser."

"*Little* tosser?"

Emboldened by the dissolute aspect of the emaciated figure before him, the suit prepared himself for fun.

"Yeah, bald, ugly, deformed little tosser".

And to drive home his point, he extended a palm and flicked Hard Hat's turban from his head, exposing the trepanned skull and tumescent hippocampus.

Seconds later, the pub was in uproar. The suit lay unconscious and bleeding, his nose now split down the middle. Hard Hat was buried under a mound of enraged pundits intent on offering their critiques, personally, without prejudice and with the aid of fists and boots. He had far more now to worry about than the dental pain which a few moments earlier had been his major pre-occupation. His turban unravelled, his forehead throbbing and yet he himself, without noticeable dignity, called on the gods of his forefathers to assist him in his hour of need. At a previous appointment, the dentist had informed him that the lump was no more than a cyst; the result of an infection itself probably occasioned by one of the many cavities that decorated his teeth. Root canal work would be required. At least it's not cancer, he'd thought. As he lay there, open to the attentions of the football pundits, the thought that he didn't have cancer was nevertheless still a comfort, although not now quite so warm a consolation that he could afford to bask in it. Action was called for, and action was what he now decided upon. His wiriness and agility had often allowed him to extricate himself from scrapes before and now, eel-like, even with his arm still benumbed, he wriggled free of his attackers and was off like a rabbit, his good arm swinging vigorously as before. The pub struggled to its feet, dusted itself down, shot its cuffs and the punditry resumed, empty and vapid as before...

"...As somebody wrote the other day, the one undeniable fact about this whole nauseating farce is that Eriksson and the FA well and truly deserve each other."

"But again, *is* he really so despicable? What actually has he done? If we're talking about his 'duplicity' over ongoing meetings with future potential employers, it falls flat. There's no loyalty on the other side either. Loyalty is now effectively a completely debased currency, used disingenuously by both sides merely to score cheap points. Consider the fate of *all* managers as soon as results go against them. Where's the loyalty there? As a pro aware of his market value (ie: what people, including the FA, will pay for his services) surely he has every right to maximize his earnings. We flatter ourselves if we think he should be *honoured* just to breathe the same English air as us. It's a skewed perspective. A category error."

"Yes I see what you mean. I agree. The issue here is the FA and their laughable posturing, their ridiculous yapping about being "humiliated". The story is really just about English prurience and panic in the face of anything vaguely connected to sex, dressed up as moral outrage when the real subject is actually just bad PR. And bad boardroom management. How in fact the FA were not able to manage their own news presentation. It's pathetic. It's all he said/she said/he said nonsense and the FA are revealed again as totally incompetent. They're the real villains. Continually making the wrong decisions. And then when exposed they start bleating, as in this instance, about it "not being right" that they're made to "look like fools"… well, if the cap fits!!"

Hard Hat scurried up Camden High St, past Somerfields, past Woolworths, past the record shops, past the scummy boot stores with their grotesque sculpture frontages, past the fast food outlets and past the trinket stalls on towards the tube. Up to the tri-pronged pyramid junction at the top (to your left the delights and primary grazing territory of Chalk Farm, Hampstead and Primrose Hill standing proud at the fat crown of Regent's Park. Straight on, the gentrified yet still down at heal precincts of Kentish Town and Archway. Or to your right, the prow of Camden Road leading down into the inmates' playgrounds of Holloway and on up to the tumourous lump of Finsbury Park) where all the White Cider (8% vol) merchants disported themselves outside the appropriately named World's End pub. The eye is livid here. For Hard Hat, all directional vectors are hard wired into camp self-effacement. Fictionalisation is at a premium. And here the punditry tends more towards the subjective, the street drinkers offering razor sharp critiques of the citizenry that are intensely personalized. And about nothing so abstract as professional football. Rather, straightforward personal abuse, both of their fellow drinkers and of straight-ahead passers-by, is the order of the day at the World's End. Sales pitches are offers of degraded goods and passers-by feel themselves tainted, shuddering, though physically unmolested. Fights, pathetic bouts of ineffectual fisticuffs, are wont to break out between these hardened street critics at the drop of a hint of a slight, at the slightest suspicion that liberties are being taken. Liberties are taken routinely. And imaginary slights are taken with a consistency that is difficult for the uninitiated to comprehend. Disputes are entered into with a frightening tenacity that doesn't correspond to the reality of any known spiritual template…

As Billy passed this body of recalcitrant and uncongenial men and women, a particular recumbent body caught his eye. The grizzled tramp, greasy coat fastened with string, sockless feet in distressed sneakers, livid face cheery red despite or because of the chill in the air, was propped in the angle of door and pavement, singing the songs of the damned. White Lightning at hand, he was at sleep's door, serenading himself with the songs of his youth. He'd aged rapidly, 20 years bent double, time warped beyond parody, beyond time. What caught Hard Hat's gaze was a slip of paper that had just fallen from the fellow's inebriated fingers. An unredeemed *betting slip*. Result! The greatest moment of his life so far. Snatching it up with his good hand, Hard Hat quickly moved on, making sure he caught the recumbent figure a glancing blow with his Nike, not that the dead to the world crooner noticed a thing. He was beyond pain. Beyond the static charges of electricity that were afflicting the residual pedestrian commuter traffic making its way to the tube station.

The old man's horse had finally come in. Lighting strikes once only. Middle age went by…five minutes…By way of celebration, he'd made the mistake of letting everyone in on his good fortune. His audience had responded in the only way they knew how and had beaten him to a pulp, but somehow the betting slip had in the ruckus escaped detection. Now it appeared again just as Hard Hat chanced upon the scene. Such are the weird convergences of chance upon which fortunes are made and lost. Too late for him now, as Hard Hat relieved him of the slip. 500 notes. Hard Hat was a pig. A pig in shit. All his birthdays at once. High-class tarts coming out of his ears. Finest skunk. At least for the next week anyway.

"The natural order of things is that kids should loathe their parents, what their parents like and what their parents want them to like. And that parents shouldn't defer to the tastes of their kids. Since the 60s there's been a cataclysmic reversal in the cultural/generational polarities. Now kids are out-parenting the parents. Out earning cash, gaining economic kudos, largeing it, distancing themselves from childhood and the childish with indecent speed. And their parents cheer them on…keen to get the little fuckers out of the house so that they, the ever immaturing adultescent parents, can return as soon as decently possible to the Peter Pannish Eden from which they were ruthlessly expelled by parenthood. They embrace technology every bit as enthusiastically as the cuckoo young. Back catalogues are re-purchased in new formats. The terminal playground of middle youth is filling up with scrubbed clean check shirts from 20–50 years old. It's all middle aged spread chat rooms on the internet – full of somethings. Record company back catalogues – catering to the 30/40somethings. Internet commerce – progressed by geek boys and girls so their generational forebears might more easily distribute the largesse of their oh so expendable middle incomes. Share the boom money. Share the good times. Parents puking and mewling, over-coked, dinner parties…or for the less salubrious…club nights. You thought AbFab was satire. Pure, sober realism. Pure documentary. The whole country's gone meta-infantile. It's a national disaster. The 60s never happened in this theology. Or they only happened in order to conceive the kaleidoscopic heterogeneity of the 70s. A time when no style/no taste really DID = GOOD!! English pop really did transcend for a few years the prevailing political cynicism. The dark middle age of youth is now upon The Culture.

There should be, but there isn't, an ongoing antipathy and simmering unspoken resentment between the tastes, mores and outlooks of the two exclusive estates. Between the two there should be mistrust, bitterness, mutual suspicion and contempt for the others' cultural frameworks. The estate of childhood and the estate of adulthood are mutually exclusive. So say all of us. A-fucking-men. The tendency of the various popular media to establish, with the collusion of the fashion lobby, adulthood as merely an extension of childhood is at the root of the modish assumption that there's no qualitative difference between the two. They do this to open the wallets of child-adults. Nothing more nor less. Do we really want a society of on-message kids who'll just ape their forebears? Evolutionary theory teaches that the succeeding generation must, if not literally, then figuratively, kill the preceding one. Without this friction, a friction which burns the next generation into shape, the human race will turn to mediocre, sub human sludge. How on earth are kids supposed to develop into autonomous adults when their models are groovy parents? The fate of Ned Flanders in The Simpsons is salutary. Done diddly done for, and all due to his beatnik folks......"

Yapp closed the magazine. He then closed his eyes. Opened them. He looked up from the glossy leaves, sticky and luminous. The hack who wrote this shit had earned his corn for the sweetly reasoned ersatz analysis, but still there was something missing, something absent. He sighed. Buffy, oh Buffy! Buffy Strangelove, the articulate amanuensis of his dreamworld, due to change his world. All worlds. Made up shit. Reality Corps leaflets left out in the rain. The world as he perceived it held its breath and nothing happened for a while. As soon as the betting slip had been redeemed, the world breathed again. Yapp sat in the public bar of the Elephant, Kronenburg in front of him, musing abstractedly. He already knew, the world at large already knew. There was a surfeit here of redundant information, glossy and superfluous. Tautologous information, confirming nothing. Billy Hard Hat appeared at the pub door, an excited smirk playing about his crooked mouth. He held in his nicotined fingers a wad of cash.

"It's you birthday mate. All your birthdays at once."

He was viewed without interest.

"Get 'em in then".

Hard Hat, with a hard on, made for the bar. Kensington could wait. He needed to get rat arsed first. Later opera tarts. Evening dress? A minimum requirement. High-class tarts; full-on lovescenes; quickies not on the agenda. 5 star luxury, Laurent Perrier or Roederer Crystal on tap, silk dressing gowns, curly toed slippers, room service not required for Room Service. He'd won loads at gambling, although not for a while. Gambler and rambler. Trepanned skull still and always a directional and divinatory tool. Correct numbers guessed with ease. He walked himself into ecstasies. In the circles into which he'd blagged an entrée contacts stay contacted. His credit was good. A caricature weird and exotic presence at the top Knightsbridge casinos, he was the recondite familiar of a number of society babes, a walking (or shuffling) talisman, a fantastical decorative ornament, a shifty homunculus, a comedic sidekick, an oddment, a ladies travelling companion, prescient in calling the shots at craps or blackjack. Working his way up, making his rep as Kitchen Porter in the kitchens of various top London hotels, his progress into high society was already archetypal. He was a blue-blood, a storyteller, a narrative fetishist who claimed descent from Tibetan dugpas, a fictional bloodline that seemed to imply impossible and previously under-researched genetic variations and (frankly) unbelievable versions of the truth. He claimed to the dizzy harem and anyone else who'd listen that the extrinsic world was merely his present playground. He claimed to have dreams in which he took wing and literally stole the earth. He offered fictional versions of himself in which he was identified as the original baseball-hatted vampire. He babbled of angels and familiars. He'd conjured them in his lunchtime. His religiosity knew no bounds and was, he averred, an elephantine accretion of his thrice-consecrated self, courtesy of The Big Guy. Buffy Strangelove's name was never openly referred to by him, was only whispered in exotically appointed apartments. These big twitted babes, into whose ears he habitually decanted these outré fables, and into whose society he'd originally been precipitated after he'd blagged a stint as croupier - cover due to staff sickness - at one of the top casinos, and whose predisposition to credulity was unsurpassed, fell for his cock-and-bull stories hook line and sinker. In this harem of Arab servicers, magic and the related arts were the only things that made sense. So in this super febrile milieu, Hard Hat also made perfect sense. In this rarefied world, a twilight world of tarot throwers and magic practitioners, clandestine cash transactions and betting runners, fabulating homunculi were commonplace and unexceptional. Betting was always odds-on the afterlife, any afterlife. Even prosaic entrées to the mythical realm. Passwords were enabled. Billy was a bagman for the casinos, court jester to The Big Guy…Strangelove appeared as and when, unexpected and unannounced, and soon enough Billy began pimping for the whores. Perks were like crumbs from the top table, *and* he had to pay for them, big money, access the point of it all. Access and re-entry the divine metaphor re-fleshed, lent reality tonnage by Strangelove. Strange love. The point of it all. Shit kicking no-marks, onanists, wouldn't have the access, he reasoned. He was access all areas. At a price.

His other sideline was supply. Information, rumour, Chinese whispers, documents…documents retrieved from celebrity trashcans, floated in word of mouth markets, information that was dynamite in the wrong hands. He nipped into and out of the sight lines of security cameras so fast that he registered only as a blur, only recorded as the faintest suggestion of trouble. He operated at 96 frames per second. Technology, the engine of accelerated culture, wasn't fast enough to keep up with Hard Hat. He was away and gone before he could even register. And now he was armed with 500 notes. It was looking to be a good night. But the streets were fully cabbed-up, clogged with taxis, levitating magicians, double-parked dimwits, delivery cowboys, removal johnnies, bus lane outlaws and road ragers. Safer just to stay at home. And try getting a cab after 4 o'clock. To Knightsbridge? Are you kidding? In this traffic? Impossible. Cabbies, he discovered, are all in their *stupid little green-hatted tea huts, swapping porno bluff stories, getting all testosterone over the tabloids and necking mugs of sweet tea. Bus drivers too have their exclusive little haunts, not that he ever caught the bus. Bus garages, in windy and desolate forgotten enclaves, in catatonic suburbs, play host to legions of sweaty, oafish malcontents. The dismal half-light swallows coronary cases whole, then spews them out in honking double-deckers, specifically to risk the lives of their passengers. Heart attack transportation for everyone concerned. I don't take the bus, except up the hospital, because I still need that old time religion. But people don't return my calls. My emails remain unanswered. I've got a hidden agenda. Actually it's so hidden even I can't remember what it is. I used to be a lecturer. Frank was on the lecture circuit, and would debate fiercely with other academics, look condescendingly over the top of his spectacles, take questions from the floor. His jokes were of the patronising variety, designed to discomfit his discoursing adversaries. High camp in academia.*

My brother used to visit me, until I requested he stop. It's not exactly pleasant being leered at by an idiot with a hidden agenda. My familiar angel hovers nearby, tutting and looking meaningfully at her watch. Then, in an overt show of impatience, whoosh and out the window she goes. The lights buzz, Buffy Strangelove invocations now seem, if anything, even less of a palliative. The doctors apparently can't "do anything". Looks like I'm a goner. Doomed. And no-one to carry on the family business. When we were cut open, cut apart, they expected at least one of us to die. Looks like the doctors will belatedly be proved correct. Why does it take 40 years to die? Where are my fucking legs? That bastard took them. Medical science. That old thing...

Brian Yapp (self interview/testimony to ward witness/therapist)...
..I, uh, started exhibiting Frank about 10 years ago. I was offered good cash deals by shady east end boys in leather coats to show him off in church crypts, upstairs rooms of boozers, behind factory walls, on canal towpaths. Frank was by that time an embarrassment. He'd get threatening calls at his office from "fans" threatening to decapitate him. Otherworldly stalkers in theatrical capes threatening to give him a good seeing to. Messages left on his office answer-phone punctuated by maniacal bursts of laughter. But Frank Yapp is my amanuensis. He speaks in tongues. He's all tongue. A limpid monkey boy, arse of a monkey, face of an academic. He'd attempted at one point to become a kind of pop svengali, inviting applicants on local radio to sing to him. 52 turned up but invading street tramps turned the thing into a farce. Word of mouth on the street had it that the hired hall in Shadwell was a kind of soup kitchen for wannabe "characters" with the added incentive of a sort of ur-career as local TV colour. TV crews, there to cover the event, filmed an admixture of filthy decrepits co-mingling on set with bouncy, cheeky faced wannabe pop stars, the whole orchestrated by a man (plus two beautiful assistants) in a wheelchair, without legs but with a huge livid arse. The cheek of the devil. He's a visionary alright. The event, an organizational

disaster, later turned up as a photo-montage piece, entered for the Turner by a young would be conceptual artist/bullshitter. Made the shortlist, but didn't win the prize itself, which was won by the acclaimed conceptualist Damo Patchouli whose winning entry comprised an artfully arranged collection of betting slips and used lottery tickets. It was, as the art world had come to expect, a masterpiece of understated sarcasm, a grinning gauntlet of intent, thrown down before the skeptics and the sensible press.

The death threats came from disgruntled young wannabes who suspected that Frank had orchestrated the scummy invasion as a sort of sick stunt, a hyper-ironic comment on their own fecklessness and aimed primarily at their own discomfiture. Of course it had indeed been thus intended, as they suspected, as a satirical expose of their desperation for fame. Although the constabulary also cautioned at least two of the tramps, caught in the act of pissing through the letterbox of Frank's Soho office. I had, of course, subsequently to take him on the road, a brashly erudite and gaudily percipient elephant man. This was before the TV offers came in. Copywriters are always a few years behind the pace, although they flatter themselves they're ahead of it. Ad men are shingle, washed clean of ideas with each new tide. 3 anecdotes by way of illustration. Later...

DO MORE/LESS – SCORING THE VECTORS OF INCONSEQUENCE.

Excerpt from the Buffy Strangelove Devotional Directional Manual - Vol 2 Section 4: (evidence provided by Crime Scenes Inc)

...In times of strife, inter tribal, inter domestic, inter national, inter factional, inter dimensional, the urge is always, and rightly so, to do less. Even in times of general contentment. Do less. Save energy. Save electricity. Make do. Humans have always beaten themselves up over the supposed benefits of hard work. Well, there'll be time enough for that when you're dead. And consider: it's always those with really *well paid* jobs, as well as the really stupid ones with *made-up* jobs, who go on about the Dignity of Labour, and/or the psychological importance of working hard. But we know that Work is in reality merely a simulation, and only for those who don't want to Play. At my last re-birth, work was still all the rage despite my previous hard work. Work was the be-all and end-all. Work to what end though? You need to be 3 people (at least) to do the amount of work the perpetually over-ambitious claimed they were doing. Luckily, I *was* at least 3 people. StanleyK, not for the first time, and considering the Ealing Guinness schtick a suitable precedent, nicked my idea wholesale. How I learned to stop worrying and plant the idea of multiple parody characterization in SK's fecund yet frightened brain is a story that changed the entire way comedians were to be seen as all-round templates, via serious movies, for the multiple personality society. He took the credit, but it's down to me that you can now be *exactly* who you want to be at any time you want to be it, even if you don't have a personality. Sellers was more than a template. He was the clone icon to die for. All proceeds from multiple non-personality turned to comedic gold. He existed only because SK was himself frightened to be who he seemed to be. With due deference to his genius, and notwithstanding the paranoia inevitable as a result of his ill considered public epiphanies of comedy violence, it was I, through Sellers' improvised imaginings, who enabled him to progress into areas previously unimagined. Anti-gravity fantasy, terminal chess obsession, grandiose mythic theorizing and state of the art security techniques, so that he might at least live a life not entirely crippled by paranoia. They were all my ideas, though I neither received nor expected any credit.

Anyway, to work. Yes, work can be a soporiphic. That much is true, but when duty calls, you lay down those tools! Unburden yourself of collective responsibility! Switch off the info systems! Take to the hills (metaphorically of course – we don't want any more crazed survivalists holing up in the virgin spaces than are absolutely necessary) and lie low! Inhabit areas of low electrical production! Hunker down, keep your eyes peeled, and think *seriously* of killing anyone who may be thinking of encroaching on your personal space! Inside is where you look. This is species integrity on a scale we can all understand. The urge to self protect, to distance oneself from *other people,* is all but overwhelming under certain stressful circumstances. In cities, the urge to kill is of course almost un-answerable. The frowns on the faces of struggling urbanites bespeak a super human will, an almighty effort just to stay out of jail. How easy it would be to take a life in the crowded spaces. Murder is square one. Murder is always in our hearts. You know it's true. Cities are no good. Cities attract scummy verminous leeches on holidays undertaken from human warmth and cities deny your *essential pre-secular post-psychological needs (see Vol 1 Section 5).* The country on the other hand is to all intents and purposes empty. Still, we can't all live there. Leave the city *if* you can. In my own dead dreams I live on the outskirts, near the orbital roads. This isn't a retreat, a badly conceived removal from the vortices of electrical energy. It's pure *survival strategy (Vol 3 Section 7).* Topographical maps of the space occupied at present are re-constituted inside the head via Elephant Gnosis™, so the wider the vistas before us the more open the brain's outlook. Space is both inside and outside, and a closed environment, pressing in on the brain, will mean the ambient pressure exerted thereon is magnetically reproduced as electricity, the voltage depending of course on *size of hippocampus (Vol 2 Section 2).* Those who tend to travel a lot have, of course, significantly enlarged organs. But this is all at a fundamental level instinct. We know in our hearts that there is too much electricity in cities, corralled in dead end lanes, swept by wind vortices up and around the main thoroughfares and into cul-de-sac mews terraces. It gets blocked, eddying in shallow pools in distressed shopping malls. Too much open space of course and the brain goes into a tailspin from lack of oxygen. It can't quite deal with the incipience, or the enormity, of pre-electrified landscapes…

(Ongoing Documented Ward Testimony: Brian Yapp under self hypnosis speaking as Nobby Wyse the Fruiterer)

…When I was born, I immediately felt crowded. Breasts loomed large like mammoth snowy mountains. I felt crushed under their weight. My dreams and waking dreams thereafter often featured a kind of unspeakable smothering weight, a pressing and irresistible force. I was oppressed by magnetic rolling granite plates which seemed to crush the life out of me, great rolling stone clouds of particularized solidity and immensity. Granite-stone creatures, golems of incalculable power and more or less astonishing believability, far beyond horror story nervousness, pursued me. Stone creatures which are now immobilized and cauterized, rooted as totems of domesticated psychosis in Regents' Park. Frank, on the other hand, as soon as he was dead complained of not being able to see things clearly. Or of being able to see things only as though they were at a great distance. Death seemed to rob him of any sense of perspective. The one eyed dead. He was blind to reality. He went on, naturally, to become an academic. Christ knows what his discipline is. His main talent is for hopeless and aggressive lechery. No wonder his wife eventually booted him out and into my bed. Academics don't need a discipline. They just extemporize in the crevices of obsession. They need only an aptitude for minutely missing the point, for failing to see the wider picture. They require simply a laughable propensity for leather jackets or tweed with leather elbow patches if of an older vintage and polo necks. An urge to write unreadable and unread books is a necessity, as is a delusion that these moribund works somehow push humanity's envelope just that little bit further. They are all on the gravy train…in wooden polished corridors…names on stenciled nameplates…individual tuition of favoured students…appearances on the BBC…retained payroll status for rentaquote opinionising…beetle browed theorizing on late night talk-ins…condescension a second nature add-on. Dusty celebrity status…pasty shoed tiptoeing into virginal bedrooms…child abuse in the dead of night…divorce courts heaving with wistful and long suffering wives. They're worse than film stars. In normal chronology they're just dusty monuments to the individual delusion, study bound in the realm of fear, hunkering down in speciality, specifically to avoid life or any of its ferocious variants. The impulse to nurture obsessions at the expense of the bigger picture is the salient characteristic. What else do academics do but nurture morbid obsessions and fiddle with their barely pubescent charges? Secrete menopausal fluids from rheumy eye sockets, take what isn't theirs, seduce the needy and the immature. Academia is a hothouse, decadent plants usurping youthful blooms by stealth…

Authorial voices intervene at this point in the narrative: Not sure this is wide open…not sure it's controlled…by what means do we reach a decision on policy? How do we implement that policy? Authentication of policy? Is break character configured? Where's Abrahams? Is he like FOR REAL??? Who's going to look at this…Abrahams can explain the issues then you can liaise with him…why not hardwire the uberview?…free jazz in this context is definitely a tautology…is Yapp actually already dead then? Narrative function unclear at this point. Moot usage – we need to see things at least twice before we fully understand them. Rewind facility is of central importance. Meanwhile Wyse has morphed uncontrollably into Dionysia. Get some control.

…A lisp goes well too…decadently overbearing self-image…misapplied view of place in the scheme of things. I say to you!!!!! Don't get involved with them! Do less, don't pay, or pay up now. Be an autodidact. Or live less, and pay up now. Point I'm making is *avoid debt*. Debt is the *universal gaolor*. Reverse credit. Credit being merely a form of tax, a tax on presumption. A tax on nervy want, on impatient acquisitiveness. Well here's the answer. Don't be taxed. Reject credit. Do less…and look inside. Feel the weight, the vibrations, feel the weightlessness of existence. The existential dead weight, as sung by academics. See the tracks there…Stop shopping, NOW!!! This is what Strangelove said over and over again. It's about the most cruelly tender thing he ever did say. He knows a thing or two. Just stop shopping. Don't go out. Stay in. Shops are full of what you don't want. Opt for cruelty. Be cruel to yourself as a way of approaching the divine. Look inside, see the cruelty. See the tracks. Our capacity for cruelty cruelly exposed by the simpering insistence that we aren't *capable* of cruelty. Our ability to avoid cruelty fatally undermined by our sanctimonious assertions that we're all too civilized to eat each other.

In fact, Frank like all academics *revels* in his capacity for cruelty. He imagines that he should be afforded the dispensation open to geniuses, the deference of others, because a genius is what he imagines himself to be. I've seen Frank reducing helpless shopgirls (in shops) to tears merely by sarcasm and a raised voice. He thinks he's above the common herd. And let's face it, that kind of behaviour is just *so* passé. I have an anecdote of the end of his life. Standing in the queue at Pret a Manger, just off Charing Cross Rd, Frank stood and regaled his audience, a gaggle of credulous, bashful acolytes, with loud complaints about the ever-encroaching franchise culture. He fulminated against the ubiquity of corporate funhouses. He frothed about cappuccino culture. He held forth and he pontificated. He went red, his temples throbbed and a slight foaming became noticeable around the corners of his mouth. He really extended himself. Thumbs in belt loops, he relaxed into his strident broadside oblivious to the ebb and flo of those without academic leanings.

"Can I help you sir?"

Turning, he enquired with extravagant pomposity "Are you speaking to me, my good man?".

"Can I help anyone…?"

A customer more attuned to the pace and the culture of the west end stepped in and ordered a double espresso to go. Frank was in a different world, lost for words, lost in the slipstream of accelerated life. Being who he was, he declined immediately to wait another second and flounced away, audience in his own archly choreographed slipstream, to thunder indignantly on other displeasing aspects of urban life. His words hung and swooped like seagulls as he marched away, dipping in and out of the grubby street ambience, the noisome metropolitan drone, swooping occasionally with glib and screechy impudence into the fractured consciousnesses of those within earshot. As he pranced down the street thundering denunciations this way and that, heads were turned and eyebrows were raised…

(Dionysia to Brian, both heads visible, but he looks now like he's in drag...both are shining in the sepulchral light)

...I wouldn't tell him this, but I actually turned 40 at birth, 20 odd years ago, and I feel utterly worn out. Clapped out. I kind of feel that the heaviness, the weight, is catching up on me. The electricity is getting inside me, silting up the channels. A lesser man, a boy or deranged household god would whinge endlessly in utter self-pity and wallow like a water buffalo in the warm baths of self-loathing but me, I'm not given to self pity. It's time for re-entry. I never went to prison, so I might try that. But I'm more a shadenfreude kind of guy, like Frank. Maybe our only point of correspondence. I revel in *others'* misfortunes. I put my own neuroses and/or psychoses to one side, and examine the failings of others with amused contempt. I write scathing reviews for low circulation publications, emblazoning my hatred for sterile cod-creativity in haughty and imperious style. I laugh at the messes people get themselves into. Frank knows this and I think he approves. As my familiar, he kind of depends on my endorsement. I feel the weight of his obstreperousness. I'm exercised by the effect he has on people. People I know. I wish Frank hadn't died before he'd had time to really grow into himself. To rid himself of his airs and graces and learn to conduct himself without striking these absurdly camp and affected attitudes. Campness needs to be grown into, must be gradually assumed, it is a favourite pair of slippers. Too camp too young is merely vulgar. If only Frank could have been more like me. I remember the crucial events as though I was Frank myself.

He was at home with his wife see? A white walled casa, Andalusia/ Islington style terrace...miniature cactus plant...tautologous rubber plant, art nouveau engravings, miniature enervated wife clicking in stilettos, small dogs yapping, kids in the playroom. Au pair at the drinks...Wife mooning over the open windows, distraught, tearful and beautiful before the smashed crockery and glassware, mangled birthday cards torn and strewn every which way. 50s style light fittings, art nouveau effects dashed to the floor, Frank's bits and pieces all over, all papers and effects defenestrated, while I'm in the pub around the corner. He'd been taunting her...

"Nothing would ever make you leave me would it? Don't you understand I don't **want** to be loved??"

david kettle

"But Johnny…"

"'But Johnny! But Johnny!! I love you! *I* love you!' I love…You love… She loves…everybody loves everybody else! Well I don't see? I love NOBODY! I don't even love Johnny!! Get out Hermione! Go and find somebody else to love!!"

…So now we're having a morose boozing session, him complaining vigorously about his little wife being a bitch, just a fucking evil BITCH, me affecting to take the slightest notice, humouring him and making believe I'm on his side. If he knew I'd been fucking her on the quiet for years he'd be speechless. Done up like a pantomime dame of rage, he looked at me through red mists and then started blubbing uncontrollably. Best to spare the punters that kind of spectacle really. Frank's an ugly man when angry, and even more ugly when upset. So I just retreat into a sort of erotic reverie in which I dream anew of what I'll be doing to her later on, all the while wearing a fixed expression of concerned sympathy. They fight (apparently) like drunken tigers, all rage focused on the other, projected, transferred. Eventually Frank is forced to concede defeat, or if not defeat then capitulation to the more entrenched will of the other. She wears the trousers in this ménage alright. Well of course she does. Frank doesn't have any legs does he? How could he wear the trousers?

He tells me, because he knows, that academics live like kings. Sovereigns in their own right, they have the pick of affordable housing. Designed housing, as opposed to lived in housing, the like of which most of us have to put up with. I'm left in possession of a shabby and disreputable looking terrace number while he lives like a fucking king. Hand in glove with architect buddies with whom he went through college. Academics and coffee table lifestyles. They get invited on TV. I may have mentioned this. Free rides to Broadcasting House in limos paid for by the license payer. It's a scandal. I'm the real genius here. I'm the one who has visions. I'm the one who lends his name to religions. People pay me…to touch them! You know that? To touch them!

…anyway, back to secular reality. Frank stormed away from the coffee house leaving eddies of perturbation in his wake. Pavements sclerotic with coagulating moochers, day-dreaming, pavement hogging snoozers…all shop doorways blocked by hordes of somnambulant tourists…He left them all for dead. Coffee Junta was spilling its hyped up imbibers into the street all energized and wired. Wired and yet non-locomotive, non kinetic. The only movement was a kind of torpid ripple of intent. Inane intent. The currents of indecision that guided their compromised movements kept them ebbing and flowing this way and that, at the same time rendering them incapable of moving decisively in *any* direction without first checking on the movements of their closest neighbours, like flocks of slowly migrating birds that haven't yet received the imperceptible signal. And this lot weren't migrating *anywhere* fast enough for Frank. They were, in short, in his way. Feckless human barriers against the energy flow. Tourists and somnambulists everywhere, more effective in deadly gainsaying than any number of thick-necked bouncers. *Just stand a group of these bastards in front of a club entrance and you'll never get anybody through the fucking doors. Ever,* thought Frank. Finally losing what little patience he had, he lost it.

"*Get the fuck out of the fucking way you dozy fucking half-witted fuckwits*" he bellowed at the stodgily massed ranks of confused and half asleep pedestrians.

Sensing that his righteous and irreligious wrath was being hopelessly misread by the assembled sleepwalkers as a kind of bathetic paranormal happening, misapprehended as a mere apparition of rage brought on by endless ODing on the city's truncated electricity (a phenomenon that all the tourist guidebooks had taken to including in their literature) and observing their reaction, one that implied that as far as they were concerned this holographic avatar of spite was merely a tourist spectacle, Frank barged headlong into the group without further ceremony, knocking several shocked tourists to the ground. A chatter of muted protest went up amid the group and apologetically shocked glances were shot this way and that. Frank was away and gone without a backward glance before they were able to re-assemble as before, inanely blocking the thoroughfare, the recent apparently pixilated avatar of rage already a distant and vaguely perplexing, unpleasant memory. A tourist diversion they'd rather, on the whole, have done without.

Frank knew though, as a veteran path finder, that the same static behaviour was bound to be repeated wherever there was a doorway or entrance or exit. Entrances to tube platforms were a particular favourite. Twittering collections of asian students, with nowhere special to go, snap happy and blocking the exits. At this time, in this hour of immaculate immediacy, Frank approaches. The twittering reaches unendurable levels. There's a fractured murmuring as they perceive the danger of the approaching train. Trains enter stations with a terrible urgency, bursting out of the tunnels with insolent dispatch. The drivers are dead faced. All sorts of ghostly operators drift around the circuit. But the trains belie their somnambulant operators, breaching the hot air in front of them with belligerence; they are *nightmare* intrusions, waking the platform sleepwalkers from their reveries. The gaggle lethargically scatters allowing cowed commuters to emerge, nervous and blinking, onto the platform. And Frank, he's still alive. Still fretting and twitching from the caffeine/cocoa high and the insufferable unwillingness of his acolytes to actually *listen* to him, pushes his way through the schlepping throng and steps out in apparent ignorance of the oncoming vehicle. A blizzard of dust envelopes him as he falls headlong onto the tracks. The dozing driver thought he'd seen a ghost. The fact is, he had. Frank's now doing less than before, and he's all the better for it. The driver got 6 months off work. But not only that. The important thing is that they generally find this sort of thing makes for good copy with the makers of TV documentaries and it adds weight to their unions' negotiations for higher pay in the interminable rounds of talks with the employers aimed at avoiding industrial action. The city is not in this instance brought to its knees and everything carries on pretty much as before. Frank is dead. A brainless suicide of immaculately conceived Gnostic immediacy. He didn't know he was going to die that morning. Grasp while the iron's hot though. A kind of split second decision, unfortunately for Frank carried out without benefit of an attending documentary crew and therefore a suicide empty of re-birthing potential, merely one more London Transport statistic and just an irritant to passengers on the Piccadilly Line, commuters largely unaware of the potentially divine import of the action and merely hot-collared and fractious at being made to wait for their supper. The divine in small matters unperceived as usual, un-seen by the train companies and their shareholders. A private performance in public, a consummation of the first sacrament of cataclysmic re-entry to the quotidian realm by Frank the fat bottomed, monkey arsed academic.

Frank's doing less and less these days. A bit of street theatre, well hung, demotic wheelchair ranting, cap in hand solicitation of tourists, nuisance phone-calls to former students, email stalking of those students whose willingness to submit to Frank's attentions made them especially meaningful to him, threats from ex boyfriends, fathers, hanging around in crappy Soho boozers re-living a life that's no longer viable, sizing up the talent, cocking a jaundiced and weary eye at the low rent crims as they size him up, and generally dreaming of the elephant trails. He's thrown away his bike and latterly his chair and spends his days in ritual procession along ex-bus lanes and cycle tracks, vainly attempting to re-invoke the divine in himself by re-tracing his steps, re-configuring the ancient elephant routes as set down millennia ago on the site now occupied by London by the three of us in our heyday. As the ancients processed in religious devotion around bird, dragon and monkey outlines on the Nazca Plain, invoking rain and pleading for divine benevolence, so Dionysia and I (and Frank to carry the supplies) once invoked elephant divinity. We laid down elephant tracks which were in subsequent millennia used by later, more profane civilizations as bus lanes. Way back when. Elephant trails that, once restored to their correct usage and if viewed from a spacecraft or airplane or similar flying machine, score out the unmistakable shape of an elephant's head over the deranged, unplannable thoroughfares of pre-mythic London.

FIREBALL.

Excerpt from The End Times, 00/201/0998/01

…Spectators in Fiji first saw a blinding white-hot fireball "like a giant spotlight shining in your eyes" pass directly overhead trailing blue smoke. Then the evening sky lit up for around ten seconds as it broke into four "breathtaking gold and silver fire-balls" and a swarm of smaller pieces beneath the clouds. Another re-entry. Film crews and newspaper correspondents were on hand to record mythic history in the making…

The Memoirs of Buffy Strangelove (excerpt):

…But trust no-one with a camera in his or her hand. The famous faces blur, running incontinently into spectral canvases, road movies played out at 12 frames per second, convoys of limo-trucks becoming one meta-truck. They're out on the freeways, on the lookout for dipsomaniac celebrity truckers, cutting swathes of destruction through lives, innocent families carved up in the hot metal holocaust. Life just isn't valued as it once was. They are raged up road hogs, out for fun whatever the cost. But the rubber-neckers are out in force to see *this* spectacle.

As I plummeted, a soviet-type spy ship (or that's what was officially reported) in freefall, the premonition of my impact on the unquiet waves was available to those reporters present who were already susceptible to the vibes. A total of 1.617% of assembled reporters caught it on film *before it happened*. My light shone even brighter than usual in anticipation of the impact. The dream catchers, celluloid conjurors and baseball-hatted ur-Spielbergs, trim bearded and technology obsessed, armed with the very latest technology, were jostling for position on the shingle. Parody documentary makers, their tripods lined up like an army of only semi-benevolent Martians, their cameras potentially as explicit as weapons, potential witnesses before and after the fact. But most of them were not aware of the impact before it happened. The snappers too engrossed with the technology to see what it was they were photographing, the hacks themselves were minutely concerned not with the unfolding divine spectacle itself but with the elegant phrasings with which they would frame their empty experiences. Techno-vampires, energy geeks and ghouls, an unwashed army of F-stopping lens magicians and focus pullers, they lacked the essential animus, the divine spark, the pre-cogging talent that might in another universe have made them artists. Only those clear-eyed enough to use the camera, not to mention the tripod, as weapon, could see what was going to happen.

Not even with the assistance of the schools of humpbacks and sperm whales, behemoth outriders preternaturally aware of the incipience of divinity, a colossal mammalian entourage singing their songs of devotion, were these cameramen capable of seeing the event before it happened. The impact, when it occurred, caused a wave as big as a suburban street, the houses filling and re-filling, emptying themselves back into the ocean, the spume a rabid animal. As the fireball disappeared beneath the water a supine and disarranged figure on the rocks beside the previously limpid waters, who was obscurely apparent to just a few of those present, also disappeared. Music was heard all around, crashing power chords of atonal bombast, during which the whales were seen by the same 1% of observers to maneuvre the capsule away from the cameras. The event didn't even make the mainstream news, so ashamed were the assembled hacks and snappers of having missed the essential moment. But the magic didn't go altogether un-reported. The disappeared figure and the missed satellite re-entry initially assumed for the world's media the status of UFO, became an X file oddity. Whispers begat rumours, heads were scratched, rumours then hardened into clandestinely constructed conspiracy fables. Wires were tapped and film was minutely examined and found to be faked footage. There never was a re-entry. The capsule had never existed. There had never *been* a scheduled re-entry. Thus was the public soothed and flattered into acceptance of the sub-divine version of events. The mainstream media fabricated a narrative according to whose elements nothing untoward had happened. Certain semi-mainstream hacks promoted the fiction that the capsule (which *did* in fact exist) had emitted a light so bright that all cameras were temporarily rendered inoperable, thus explaining the lack of footage. They got that bit right at least. Readers and viewers of this output of course swallowed it whole. And why not? In the absence of any corroborating evidence to the contrary, habit had engendered in them a tendency to believe anything at all that they were told. Truth is of course uniquely mutable in these end times, most of all where Buffy Strangelove is concerned.

The obscure media didn't of course swallow it whole, but were nonetheless powerless to discover what in fact had happened. Their morbid theorizing and paranoid ranting, comprising as it did the usual gibbering incontinence about world governments, hybrid lizards in human form, satanic masonic plots to rape the world and steal its resources, served only to placate the more mentally ill sections of the community, who also were prone to believe anything they were told. Speculating with or without data was 2nd nature for the practitioners of conspiratorial overkill, a readymade model of pre-ordained reality. Conspiracy is as conspiracy does. They satisfy themselves with mental pictures that correspond to their innermost fantasies, their morbidity a dysfunction of a dislocated worldview. Broken down eyes, a misdirected sense of nature, a misreading of natural stigmata all around. Anyway…The bleeding sod, the hole in the ocean, the cracked earth. They all missed it. It goes without saying of course that these people are the least likely of all to be capable of seeing elephant metaphor as hard wired fact, let alone whale or dolphin emanations.

When I say I'm a divinity, a household god, an avatar of fecklessness, a boozed up idol of lasciviousness and adultery, an arched-eyebrow deity of sublime and irresistible charm, I don't want to be taken too metaphorically, but on the other hand a metaphor goes a long way in explaining things in the weightless state. I really am a god, of my own making. And elephants really are my familiars, they really are a conduit to the divine, *really* a living cosmology. Unless my assertion can be disproved…by me. And now, is anybody there to deny it? Elephants have this *awareness* of their meta-capabilities. I am divine by virtue of the electrical power harvested from elephant tracks laid down millennia ago. I stumbled on them. But they didn't trip me up. These numinous trajectories enable me to escape through back doors, away from angry husbands, through time holes. If a better explanation is available for my incessant womanizing and ability to sneak away undetected, by all means find it.

I've enlarged for you. I'm large in the snake pit. Belly tied down, feet at right angles. I coil and re-coil at improper interrogations. Large mammals are *indeed* my familiars. I've graduated. 2nd raters use things like cats, bats and snakes. Depending on the nature of the emission, I shine bright, specifically to delineate the vectors of my intent. Elephants are the *imperative*. Their presence in the here and now is now miraculous, they evince preternatural delicacy, and thus possess the ability to melt into the background when required, a very special endowment. They can exist outside prescribed time environments. They confound ecological space proscriptions. I have found that many people are unable to see them, except fleetingly, and even then only in peripheral vision. Many people miss the spiritual elephantine element altogether. Speculating with or without data was and is my original method of extrapolation. Finding the right pieces to fit together, a jigsaw of my own making, is an undertaking based partly on random selection and partly on determinist self-exculpation, to ward off the evil eye of evolutionist scientist technicians. The sort who know jack shit and who have to be bought off. They're the ones who control the broadcasting rights and whose power bases are the most corrupted. Bags are filled with cash, technical knowledge is stowed in carrier bags. Their silence is a sine qua non of my ability to live and breathe my feral magic on the earth. TV crews are primed, technicians have been engaged at non-union rates. I reveal my secrets piecemeal, bit by bit, only for the empty cameras.

I found the natural world disease free. Some ecologists and animal behaviorists of course confused my interest in nature with altruism. Art for art's sake. Of course my intent was, in their terms at least, somewhat more sinister than that. No sooner had I hidden myself away in the fridge than I was seeing things from the perspective of the humdrum prism of selected household goods. Once trapped in the electricity flow, it's difficult to stay awake for any length of time. My concealment in the coked up rock god's fridge was a kind of hibernation. I deep slept, saving energy until I could re-enter the commonplace world. Holed up in a domestic appliance. In a desert trailer. Not the most advantageous of perspectives you'll have to admit. Of course events could have been affected, could even have been subverted, but in the end I realized that although people thought they knew what they wanted in terms of a divine being, I was, although intrinsically inconsistent with their mono-theistic theology, an adequate enough household god for any of these feckless therapist broadcasters to be going on with. The divine needn't be Divine if you get my drift. Not for a society in turmoil and in autodestruct mode…a society whose primary cultural mode has become hyper-irony, a culture which has accelerated through the detritus of compromised identity, accelerated through and beyond history, so that history itself has ruptured, so that irony is now an incontinent force, a hyper accelerated meme… *this* kind of society needs a *decelerated* divinity. A retarded numen if you will. A devotional life lived at elephant pace. What we actually have is a *joke* society, a *standup dystopia*, one which *cannot expect* divinities that stand on ceremony. What I do is *get things done*, pronto. Like, yesterday! It's a slowly softly can-do divinity. A switched on, by numbers, lugubrious numinosity. Remember…I am a boozer. I've slowed down. It takes me time to wake up in the mornings. Especially in other peoples' beds. I am known as a distributor of cuckold's horns, a guilt free Lothario. I need to plan my getaways with precision. I am not the horned beast but I might as well be. I am the horny beast. Post-hangover horn, that's me. Let's leave it at that. I need my shut-eye, and then I'm out of the gates like a rabbit. You have to remember that I'm hippocampus led. Meaning I have advanced motor efficiency, a 6th directional sense. I have the Knowledge; I know where to go. I can be out of the bedroom and down the drainpipe practically before I've heard the front door latchkey in the lock. I'm over the hills and far away. I lead and they follow, down the elephant trails. I have an unusually *large* hippocampus, as I've already explained, encompassing perhaps a third of my whole brainpan. I can *be* places almost before I've *thought* of them. The Elephant of course, needless to say, has the most enlarged hippocampus of all, even proportionally. They are the exemplary species of peripatetic DNA, nomadic DNA. Elephants know where to go. They are nomadic. And I learnt all I know from them. Keeping on the move is the essential thing. Of course, knowing how to get somewhere and knowing what to do once you get there are two *very different things.*

<u>Dr. Abrahams' personal journal, as taped during therapy sessions with fruit 'n' veg man Nobby Wyse:</u>

(Nobby) Hey! Hey! Hey! Hey! You! You! You! You! Hey! Hey! Hey! Hey! Collective, family, therapy Bffy......My thoughts, consider me a madman, am I less parodic of reality than bland reality itself? Or is bland reality beyond parody? I take the descriptions of building love described in the Hypnerotomachia Poliphili at face value. Of course I'm attracted. Who wouldn't be? But is the whole of semi-divine life beyond me? My curators, Ahab the most open to parody and most laughable, are always advancing little puzzles like that to keep me amused. They think they're one up, but they're the ones who are stabbing in the dark. Is my numinosity apparent only to me? I suck at the breasts of the statue before me. My wife was, they keep saying to me (as though I'll somehow disapprove), sexually attracted to the Berlin wall and was devastated the day it was torn down even as the rest of Europe erupted in a frenzy of celebration. If only they could see. If only. If only. It's all about Breathwork. All stress evaporated, all angst dispersed. I breathe regularly and deeply, and in a minute I rebirth, just like that. I sleep soundly at first, as long as I breathe deeply. The amount of oxygen taken in is crucial. My brain literally becomes flooded with oxygen. I start to trumpet, at first silently, then building up a momentum. Breathing is the key, and you need oxygen in unimaginable quantities. Meanwhile, the building fuckers are at large again...

This is corroborated by contemporary TV reports as follows:

"They're........*mounting*........the buildings......they're literally *fucking* the buildings. They're actually attempting to impregnate the stones. They must have heard the trumpeting. I'm hearing....I'm hearing....the elephants are, yes, they're in heat. They're now in extremis. *The elephants are now in extremis.* There must be a couple of hundred or so, attempting this most dangerous and arcane of rituals, even now. They're mistaking these formidable fortresses for something bigger. 4 kilometres away, on Hampstead Heath, a herd was sighted in the early hours, grazing and

rumbling, trumpeting a low key chorus of intent. Large cows displaying distended rumps, trumpeting their mating summonses to all surrounding areas. The fabric is now torn. As I stand here on top of Broadcasting House, reporting these amazing scenes, hundreds of would be re-birthers are mistaking geometrically arranged slabs of Portland Stone for herds of elephants. So desperate are they, so hyped up, so keen to escape this realm that they seem to be hallucinating. They are weeping openly for the torn fabric. A procession has just borne a huge banner with a weeping elephant head down Regents St. They don't seem to need or to want to adhere to the 7 sacraments; they're just going hell for leather. I've never seen this sort of thing before. We're witnessing what might be the first actual mass hallucinatory devotional jazz happening, the first mass rebirth, ever to have occurred in this country. This apparently profane happening is absolutely unprecedented in this realm."

The building fuckers were indeed moving fast, in a kind of frenzy. Jim Shitkicker, Infallibility Correspondent of Reality Corps, was atop Broadcasting House, casting an expert and experienced eye over the figures below. But he'd never seen this sort of thing before. Not in a whole career that had seen most other things. Cash dispensers became overloaded, subject to autoerotic vibrations, the digital displays reading out apparently crazy and seemingly random and cabbalistic streams of numbers, secular blueprints of account details. Office jocks and orifice chasers looked on, bemused. The re-birthers, somnambulist zoologists excavating the occult meanings contained in the stones of London's vast edifices, looking for leaden import in the grain of the stone, effecting strange rituals within the doorframes and window jambs, were gathering strength and re-doubling their autoerotic onslaught. Swipe card entry systems presented no problem, the low range trumpeting frequencies that emanated from Hampstead Heath and all points south rendered the electronic security utterly useless. Alarmed city workers were at a loss to explain to their line managers the events that were unfolding, and were equally unable to construe the gnosis taking place within the open plan offices. Line managers were, as always, equally befuddled. Befuddlement hard wired in line management DNA. Water cooler gossip was suspended in panic as pin-eyed pen-pushers and masked deities over-ran executive washrooms. It was access all areas. TV crews jostled for space, the corporate saps glad for once that Portland Place was at the actual epicentre of events. Camera crews maneuvered for space, frustrated by eddying clusters of asian tourists. Big haired porn correspondents re-arranged their décolletages by stealth as the techs got the cameras rolling. Tempers started to fray as the black suited and masked re-birthers began to lash out blindly, wildly asserting their primacy in the face of the pauperized and downtrodden commuter trash. The roadway was littered with discarded film cans, and balaclavas were now openly dispensed with. Shitkicker was aware of a hard-nosed presence at his shoulder. It seemed to him that it was God, but in 3 persons, who had come to receive him.

"Yapp......Yapp, is that you? You look different somehow! I can see... is that some sort of trick? I can see three of you...Here, have a snifter, have a drink old boy...I've never seen anything like this before. What happened to you anyway? I haven't seen you since, uh, since the last celebrity crash... you still on the wagon then? Here, have a drink..."

Before I could answer, he'd lost his footing. He stumbled on the mass of twisted cable and he was over, a man falling out of the sky. Down down down he went, dusting the stones on his way past. The cameras again didn't catch what had actually happened, the technology once again unequal to the presence of the Godhead, although there were, as usual, a few precognizant witnesses. The building shuddered as the crazed revivalists below redoubled their assaults on the modesty of the Portland Stone. The elephants were now multiplying as they renewed their circuits of the Marylebone streets.

GOING UNDER—THE MATRICES OF BAD INTENT.

Down the steps on broken legs, morbid effulgence barely penetrating the grimy station windows, I flip-flopped into the substratum. I am becoming passive tense and mole like, ferried to and fro by the squealing, groaning conveyances. Like the trains, which ensure that in achievement of the minimum required performance level the passengers truly suffer, I am barely functional. As he suffered too…It's human and divine to suffer, like humans…at underground levels where the ratmen are feral… where all are conceived equal, mythic and archetypal. But my handbag is missing. Still camp as a row of tents however. I missed the bus. I am an elemental busker. I reap and sow…

Dr. Abrahams (video case notes sold by consultant to documentary team):

Apparently, in this instance Yapp sat alone, leaning against the separating glass. The carriage was semi-engorged with a spew of commuter trash, wide-eyed crazies, chattering teens and Walkman attendees. A woman with no distinguishing characteristics embarked and stationed herself the other side of the glass. Her body pressed against the intervening pane, hand sandwiched between her back and the glass. From this narrative evidence, it seems that the spectacle of the sandwiched hand, out-turned against the glass, the blood diffused by the impacting of flesh onto hard, cold glass, disturbed and enraptured him. The blood seemed to him as though it were innumerable crawling things dispersing as the stone is lifted. He seems uncomfortable with the evidence of the corporeal. The profane body, unarmoured, open to compromising intrusion, the blood prematurely fleeing the scene of presumptive crime. Evidence in the pathology here of a certain denial of

Corporeal Primacy, a most pressing concern for his doctors…in the context of his nascent physiological mythos, apparently a proto-attempt at transference of the corporeal into the hyper-real. The blood in overdrive; the enlarged heart. The hippocampus primed for, er, time-travel…God help us! God alone can help us!!! And him. Especially him.

He first noted, it seems, that the journey offered up for mythic transformation the customary aggregate of vapid coincidences, the same chance intersections and randomly inappropriate pairings as any other tube journey. No difference. No singularity. Nothing more than various concatenations of the usual distressed commuters going about their urgent and/or pointless business. The genuinely absent-featured, the needy mad and the dangerous mad, a conglomeration of fellow unfortunates, hostages to the profane mythology of the city as metaphor for all human life, all were for him subsumed in the uneasy democracy that existed in this enclosed world. Notebook out, the travel writer in him a witness before the fact. All commuters appear to have been primal, archetypal avatars in Yapp's mythic scheme. For instance, there was a former politico, a jowly populist, who had in the pre-end times unwisely proffered it as his opinion that travelling by tube necessitated coming into contact with what he termed 'dreadful people'. Yapp needed proof of this. This joker, a straphanger on the circle line, was to Yapp a presumptuous lesser god of profane celebrity. As off-message as it was possible to be, rapidly dispatched to the 7th circle, the wilderness of semi-celebrity, later emerging bathetically as a mayoral candidate, keen to believe at all costs in the primacy of *character*. His rubric to be a *personality, a character…Stranglv territory…* The city loves them and this fact has always bothered our friend Mr. Wyse the fruiterer who has, as we have seen, eschewed personality, favouring instead a kind of phantasmagorical fantasy life…He has, thankfully, fully embraced his own dreadfulness. He has conceded, at last, that we're all basically dreadful. Fantasy life may be a thing of the past *very soon* for the fruit man. Onlookers avert their eyes as the notebook is returned to the inside pocket.

…Many of the lesser gods and goddesses owe their supplicants a debt of thanks for their dreadfulness. Many of them specifically promote themselves as divinities of the profane, the needy and the desperate. Death cults. Not interested in

the patronage of the successful, the self-determined and the ambitious, they hang around like bad smells, diseased feral pigeons, stumbling on broken feet, missing legs, legs stuffed up own arses, inviting contemptuous offerings of sandwich crusts in public parks. It's a sublimely democratic and exacting, levelled down divinity, embraceable by all. Household gods of all descriptions bewitch and are bewitched by these agglomerations of vapid drifters in the capital's underbelly…

And Wyse is by no means immune to the effects of the sallow and unforgiving synchronicity of the underground. He's quickly learned the first precept, a very quick learner. Just when you think a train's never going to come along…it doesn't!! That's synchronicity!!

I pounded a beat along the grimy corridors, searching for metaphors less obvious than those usually press ganged into service, conceits that would gut the reality, the mole intersections, the lifeblood of London's underground matrices. I hit upon the juxtaposition of the desperate and the unknowable. Travel writing, works on journalistic level, but never mythic for some reason. Underground, everyone's feral. You lose your identity down there. The grinding synchronicity of mythic or sub-mythic city life, I mean the sheer absence of synchronicity…at lower than ground level you're stuck with the weighty banality of journeys undertaken for inadequate reasons. You rub against the anonymity of inadequate presumption. In underground precincts, the cars and carriages are bogus conveyances. The phallic significance of trains whooshing into tunnels is often over stated. Trains are prophylactic, prosthetic. Big-bellied excursionists are worn out and belligerent, and thus revealed as sub-mythic, unbalanced scryers of inadequacy in the pallor of the underground substratum.

Now, nodules of impatience form in my mind. Lesions of paranoia are etched into my fractured brain. An admixture of psychic scratch marks and psychodynamic slaps, they blossom into persistent maladies, bloom into previously unimaginable mental imbalances and received opinions. They are physical attack invitations. The atrophying of my capacity for ordinary tolerance is well advanced. I can see that Ahab baits me even now…there's a gleam of malice… He tracks me. I am his bloated quarry. He has registered my weightlessness, the sheer banality of the here and now…

B.Yapp: (self interview - saleable to highest bidder)

...A busker was emboldened, a few yards away, to express himself in mildly bored, vaguely threatening tones, having just finished murdering an already moribund tune on his flaccid and dusty accoustic...

"Good evening ladies and gentlemen. Feel free to contribute, if you've enjoyed it...." he suggested with greasy truculence. The redundant invitation hung in the air like a fart. But *he* was the guilty party. And we all hated him. He moved off down the carriage regarding the passengers through rat-like slits, his face a map of pointless perseverance. One, maybe two, people dropped change into the proffered cap. The moment passed. I saw through his act to the very end of the journey. He knew it. The moment had gone forever. Temples throbbed with intent, eyes glazed over. Everything about it owes its meaning to unawareness. We're born unaware and return to unawareness. In the middle, we're hopelessly under-aware. We play the guitar. People move away from us, silently, embarrassed. The hardened unaware are a relatively new breed, a DNA mutation profoundly and silently indifferent to embarrassment by virtue of fleeting anonymity. Pulling together, and simultaneously apart, bound by mutual indifference. The indifferent and elemental busker moved with heavy steps among the bored, variously postured travellers. A feral pigeon on board the train mimicked his gait. A sudden jolt, occasioned by a too enthusiastic approach to a set of points by the insentient driver, caused him to lurch unsteadily into the lap of a recumbent faceless passenger. The pigeon fluttered disconsolately. Disconcerted by the sudden unwelcome almost-intimacy, the passenger made a show of tsk'ing over-loudly and glaring ostentatiously at the would-be guitar slayer. Personal space had been encroached, which naturally was a matter for the most severe and unyielding disapproval. The busker muttered fractiously as he made his way to the other end of the carriage...the pigeon shat thoughtfully onto the floor...

Dr. Ayton: (regarding script thoughtfully) Pages and pages of similar aimless underground rumination follow, unresolved transference of issues are paramount here...the patient is unresolved, undisclosed, pre-mythic...in chronic danger of mythic passivity...measures needed...here he is again... here he comes again...corporeal weight still undisclosed...publishing deal still eludes this hybrid-poet of the subways...

…Circle Line torpor. Metropolitan enervation. Cut 'n' Cover all very well as far as safety goes but the plangent grinding, the strident groaning of the trains is unbearable. They wheeze and stutter, lurch and heave, from station to station. Often in cataleptic progress from station to tunnel. Tunnel to tunnel. And finally tunnel to station. And even then, more misery. Prolonged stops at Baker St, Edgware Rd and Aldgate…non-optional extras, convenient rest stops that afford drivers the chance to stretch their legs. No suggestion of relay drivers. Too fucking simple. Fuck the passengers. Many a traveller desperate to get to a London terminus seethes impotently as the clock hands tick closer…their connections revving up and ready to go. The inter cities don't wait…

…Blizzards of tiny flakes of human skin dust whirl past as the train wheezes forward. Each flake encoded with DNA from which eons later will evolve fresh monsters, new underground dwellers. The bones of plague victims undisturbed by Victoria Line excavation mock the exasperated commuters from the darkness, a presence sensed though not acknowledged by the unwilling travellers. Safe in their capsule carriage, they are carried away. External force fields don't affect them. Levitation is acknowledged by all except the terminally prosaic as the primary mode of conveyance. Their ghosts leering in at them look like reflections, grimy with dust, somewhat circumscribed spectres levitating at the same speed as their own carriage. Violence is now of course on my mind…

…Dropped from the hands of a tramp, the paper fluttered down, see-sawing to the unquiet earth. It contained immediate truth and hardened facts. In part prescription, in part obfuscation. Betting is a redundant art in dead cities. There's nothing left to bet on. All bets are off. Betting is a fiction, the fiction of alternative futures. Residents of dying cities, cities in terminal decline, don't have a future. They are mere myth fodder. The stuff of myth, existing within discrete lives. Critiques of chance and error correction are privileges of the well off. Who can afford to bet when life itself is a gamble? Options that aren't meta-options are well limited in the multi-choice society. Which is when it hit me. When I *realised* that people used to being cast as extras in a corporate copywriting fantasy need a chance to do a bit of displaying on their own account. The citizens in the lower world, the seventh circles, need the chance to star in their own productions. My discovery of the tricks of re-invention (levitation, self therapy, nurturing of the instinct to show off, communing with fat angels etc) were of course the first steps towards the means whereby these unfortunates were to be presented with their mythopeic birthright...

...The doors of the last chance saloon had barely stopped swinging. He lay there again, encrusted, in hopelessness. It was the World's End. Which was appropriate enough. He was certainly approaching his own personal world's end. Waiting to be ushered through, into oblivion, his tenancy in this realm almost expired. Soon up for redemption, his crepuscular soul awaiting retrieval. Dead weight souls just hang around, fluttering and flapping in the breezes like litter, gathering electricity. Elephants on gnosis patrols accumulate souls like these as they clean the streets of electro-magnetic particles. Lost soul in extremis, awaiting delivery from corporeal angst into the fresh air of oblivion...

--- came through from another place. All Mitherers and Whiners will be *dealt with...will assume the position* --

Ahab takes up the story: Coming up for air, gasping for fresh breath, queasy from the electrical discharges of the tracks, Yapp fought down nausea as he emerged into the Euston Rd. daylight. There was at eye level a flyer man, a political irrelevance, a barnacle on the hulk of the Free Enterprise. He proffered one from a large tranche of freebie magazines that were grasped in his scabby mitts...whole lockups full of pulped paper re-formed in the east end...full of this detritus, ready-made waste paper. A litter problem appropriate to the dissociated age. Instant litter. Ready-made dross, filling the planet with cack. He seemed distracted, his attitude one of co-mingled apathy and boredom as he held out the pathetic rag, and it seems to have enraged Mr. Yapp. In 20-point Century Gothic at the top of the magazine was printed **GAT**, atop a photograph of an office worker looking at once incontinently seductive and officious. It was the water cooler iconography that did it. He said that's what did it. Unlikely. There was *already* a propensity for violence in him, previously noted by us. He said it himself. He was a violent individual. Underneath

GAT, in 14-point `Courier New`, was printed "`Girl About Town`". Of course, this enraged Yapp even further.

"Girl About Town? Do I look like a fucking Girl About Town?"

The guy looked at him through puffy uncomprehending eyes. His mind clearly wasn't really up to direct interrogation. He'd had enough of that, he'd settled long ago for uncomprehending bewilderment and self-abasement, self-denial...his interior monologue went something like "I don't really exist...you know I'm not really here, that I don't really exist...I'm outside of all this...Why are you harassing someone like me who's not really here at all...if you don't mind...too much...I need to go now...I need to live...now..." The immigration guys had no truck with him. And he didn't possess the numinous capabilities that might have saved him an intrusive and humiliating full body search. Anywhere in the afterworld, the advanced pre-end times world, at any time for no fucking happiness at all, he'd *paid*. He'd paid to come here and be *humiliated*. *That* was the *point*. He was unable to comprehend, but was only able to accept fresh, seemingly random, assaults on his bootless sense of self. The pigeons looked on at the scene that was unfolding with growing contempt.

"Eh? Girl About Fucking Town am I? You dumb wanker!"

Some target he thought. This is bad. There's no good in this. Nevertheless he knew it had to be done. He couldn't just let it pass. Stepping forward quickly, he grabbed punched him hard, twice, in the bread bin, eliciting a piercing shriek, an indignant howl of outraged pain and fear. How easy it is...how easy...to induce...cause confusion...he thought... the random infliction of confusion. The pain was more or less irrelevant. Wasn't it? Who was he kidding? Pain was *very much* the point. If he'd just wanted to confuse the poor sap he could have slapped his face on both sides Tango Man style. Or ruffled his hair. Or given him a bear hug. High-fived him. Linked arms and danced a jig. Pain was very much *the point*. His own hyper-real cosmology of chance intersections, the random deification of the inconsequential moment, demanded it. This character had come half way to his world *in pursuit of pain*. Who was he to deny him? Yapp/Strangelove was full of painful awareness, awareness that he might still fuck it up. Fuck it up big time. His theology was incomplete. Martyrs were still needed. Flagellants. Souls in need of revival. Electrical surpluses. Somewhere. Very well, let this latter day saint take Yapp's pain unto himself. It's what he was *there* for wasn't it?

Stop mithering, he thought, as the flyer guy clutched his stomach. Stop fucking mithering! You don't make the *effort* to understand! This is just what happens! It's irredeemable. Of course there was nothing of our ordinary profane justice in any of these justifications. It was a self-fulfilling act; a devotional attack, as far as Yapp was concerned. People exist in context; as characters they are by no means elucidatory. They merely illustrate. Everyone is priced, has a critical point of entry. Then he snapped out of it. I'll fill the minute like Kipling, he thought. A man who never liked to see anyone idle, not even for a second, let alone a minute. Yapp took it all to heart. His hippocampus throbbed, his soul fully tumescent.

Yapp wasn't going to let the bastard cheat him. His thoughts were all of, well, *VIOLENCE,* for want of some more imaginative response… the besetting sin, a lack of imagination, a failure to fully imagine events, which it must be re-stated is the prevailing cultural ethos of the pre-mythic zeitgeist. Thus, violence. Cine violence. Cartoon mayhem. Orchestrated brawling. Revenge dramas. Ghost kung-fu movies with lots of improbably balletic violence. Extraordinarily choreographed scenes of mayhem…but that wasn't his forte. You'd need to be a bit more athletic. His frame wasn't exactly weak, it was rather atrophied through under use, weighed down by anger. Circumscribed by odium. He was unused to action, other than meaningless action, meandering walks, sudden sprints, undertaken in pursuit of the other, the inner, the unspeakable, bad dreams. His good dreams meanwhile, trapped while out on mystical strolls in the east end, following the Fleet to its source, reciting Blake and others, have atrophied. To achieve distance between himself and his anger, he seems always to be attempting to out-run it, to get ahead of the bitchy impatience that stalks his waking hours…humiliation, chance proto-violence…Surprise, humiliation of the indolent would have to do. You can't just launch in and use extreme violence without having been really provoked first he thinks. Looks as though he's become aware that he's

in danger of cutting a rather pathetic vigilante figure, more on the lookout
for violence than merely attuned to its possible eruption. On the evidence
available to us, he was becoming the kind who'd actively seek out trouble,
detect slights where none were intended. People just staring into space on the
tube, or brushing past on the street, who unwisely allowed their gaze to alight
briefly (but not briefly enough) on his person, whose ocular ambit appeared
to encompass him all too obviously and provocatively, were deemed by him
to be full of attitude, to be up for it, in need of sorting out.

Anyway, that's what happened. But the fleeting incident was not
covered in any of that day's newspapers, which were nonetheless attuned to
other chance intersections of fate, the usual drift, the ebb and flow of so-called
synchronicity. Events driven by chance that they nonetheless missed as often
as not. We note increasingly that the streets are full of geezers suffering the
same affliction, seething with kinetic paranoia, potential violence. Geezers
convinced other geezers are eyeing them up for suitability as a potential target.
Yapp has now gone past the point of turning the other cheek, making brief
eye contact then looking away and then back again. He *is* looking at me, the
bastard. The bastard! Why bother confronting these fuckers, these commuter
cowboys? But one day, something snaps. He'd found himself staring a guy
out on the Northern Line. With restless adrenalin pumping through his
body. He let it be. But Yapp had crossed the line. Still pre-mythic at this
stage you'll note. From now on, until we caught him, he was a confirmed
eyeballer. Giving it out, expecting to take it. And quite prepared to give it
out with extreme prejudice and lack of compunction. He was outrunning the
anger of weightlessness. Eyeball confrontations with bus drivers, pavement
hoggers, pushers of shopping trolleys full to bursting, legions of levitators,
bouncing bomb flyers, yogic tossers, engaging at pre-mythic levels with the
central nervous system of the city. He was sustained in karmic validation by
the energy flow. He was not yet aware of undercurrents that were denied
him on the level of street discourse. Stalkers were everywhere and nowhere.
Yapp was and in some senses still is the stalker of his own ineptitude. He
pursued inadequacy like a pervert casing a primary school. Thus he found
himself discreetly pursuing estate agents and dogs, although telling them

apart was often the hardest part. He stalked the pointless to teach them the consequences (although of course there weren't any) of their pointlessness. Gratuitous anonymity irked him badly. It was an itch he couldn't avoid scratching. People must be forced to actualize. He discovered, I think we can assert, a purpose. The streets must be opened up to exhibitionism and gaudy pantomime. Everyone must at some stage be photographed. Tricks must be played. Unwitting participants in set-up tomfoolery must be mollified into an acceptance of the primacy of the gag. This is strange love indeed. The visions inside his eyes were of whole populations grinning inanely at each other, no matter, autocue faces were directed at each other's hopeful mugs. At some point, mobile in hand, he'd decided that action was required. Strategy. Technical organisation. Chance, random acts. Randomly generated acts of violence no more good, such as that visited upon him when in pursuit of the inconsequent and the pointless. You get what you deserve in this and other lives. Which he appears to have discovered a little late in life. It's always too late. Never give up giving up. We need his sort. The Right Stuff. Fully mythopeic.

Brian Yapp: My deserts, justly and rightly, when pursuing my prey (a shitty little crumple-suited toe rag, taking the city air, dreaming of commissions) were that I was suddenly and violently assaulted from behind. I regret to say that I believe sorcery of some sort may have been involved, as I'm not usually taken unawares. I'm usually the *perpetrator* of acts of extreme and unwarranted random violence. My non-belief in karma...although I've dabbled in any number of marginal and crackpot religions down the years.... original Highgate vampire that might have been me...is no comfort to me at all. It must be that I'm punished for everyone else's weaknesses and indiscretions. A fact that tallies with my dormant though emerging and probably verifiable and demonstrable belief that I have lived before. In a sense that you will probably not understand. The elephant stuff is, I know, difficult to accept. All I can do is tell you, as straightforwardly as I can, and with as little obfuscation as possible, what happened to me all those thousands of years ago. When I lost and re-found myself in subjectivity, when I found the arcane key. I invented a whole system. Not another man's. I have been born *by my own will and hand* before. It's amazing how it hits you, when it hits you. I've had a lot of time to get used to this now. I was born tens of millions of years ago, decades before I was assaulted, for the sins that I *may* have committed in some esoteric past. I *do* have the urge to confess. The catholic is, to some extent, inside all of us. Almost all the time, I feel the need to confess. To utterly trivial misdemeanours, like the dispatch and butchery of the city's estate agents and dogs. To receive absolution. I am guarded generally in these assertions, because I don't want to blow it here. I now have my own belly, detachable bedpan, wheel chair and headrest. I have favoured status. I am kind of a celebrity. People pay to touch me. Feel my missing legs. My stumps loaded with religious import. My eyes see everything when I open them to the skies…Born again, mythopeic eyes open…

…I can't remember now. I can't see it clearly. My eyes have gone again. I can't see things as I used to see them. I remember walking through Regent's Park towards Primrose hill, the sky livid with unshed rain, clouds lit from within by chance, the chattering of monkeys in irate cages, elephants trumpeting, on the move from Finsbury Park…the golem creatures in Regents' Park all turned to stone. The whole park a lush canopy, in verdant expectation. Innumerable mobiles chirping like multitudes of displaced cicadas. You know it. I've seen it. Techno-perambulation. Every building is home to disguised cell-phone technology. The energy flows kept open via clandestine transmitters, a network of prattle maintained and sustained via otherwise mundane architectural features in drag. You'd look up at what might be assumed to be a vent grille on the 2nd story of a standard renovate Georgian block. Looking closer wouldn't reveal anything at all. A closer look still, getting into a tight close up, reveals artfully hidden technology, appurtenances of the communications industry. Talk is big. And talk is cheap. Talk is now a corollary of technology. Information is dangerous. But talk costs lives. Ear cancer and brain sludge effected cheaply and conveniently via the good offices of the urge to prattle.

And this. This too. The atavistic urge to regroup in clannish exclusivity always fills me with a faint disgust. But we all, unfortunately, hunker down as best we can in homogenous enclaves. Streets look familiar as long as we can recognize where we're going. Direction finding is more important than ever. I wander the dreary streets apparently thoughtless, led by my hippocampus. Dank streets wet with discarded banana skins and orange peel. My blank expression gives no clue to the elegant mental gymnastics being performed. No clue as to the organ size, though the trepanned skull affords more and more houseroom. A slight wrinkling, an approximate frown, easily read by the worried passer-by as minor neurosis, a mirror for their own minor (or major) neuroses, merely identifies me as human. But we're not exactly human. Not any more. It's increasingly difficult to recognize who is human and who isn't. Conspiracy nuts think the world's run by lizard-hybrids. It used to be run by and for lizards. This is true. Something of the DNA *must* have been secretly passed on, probably by the likes of me. Me and my big gene pool. Somehow, where I find myself now isn't salvageable. Or anyway, it's not straightforward. In moments of doubt, I look up to the heavens and invoke new blueprints. I envisage change in a moment and conceptualize *universes* of minor adjustments and tinkerings in an inkling. Eons ago I forgot something that I'm just remembering. I used to be able to figure these things out. This is how it went…

…I was a Rock God. I used to drink beer and do cocaine with the roadies, play *excruciating* guitar solos, humiliate the groupies with arpeggio phrasings. The old whores, hangers-on that they were, still human though eh? I used to intimidate the merchandisers and generally come on all heavy. I was lairy and people were afraid of me. I wasn't afraid of magick. I could turn any situation to my advantage. Put the hex on, with the help of minor familiars. But since I started hating people, looking down my predatory hooter at them, the power's gone. I'm no better than some sub human secular prelate. It's like I'm now dead again. Gone, into the night. The power I wielded in previous lives is gone, all worn out. Hate's not the answer. Love's the answer. Which might seem strange coming from me, but you can't arrive somewhere without first feeling hunger and thirst. Or hate and contempt. You have to go through hate and contempt to arrive at mate-hate and meta-contempt. I speak in tongues…*again*…

I am my own monster. I was Dionysius, in the Light, consumer of misery, defecator of happiness. Living to Excess and access all areas. Expense account abused…haunting hotel bars. I'm trying to fill it up with light. My mission is to light it up. Programmes that I commission are designed to encourage exhibitionism. In my floppy hat and immaculately cut though gaudy suit, I am everyone's svengali, the universal Mr. Fixit. I haven't come this far just to indulge myself. I'm trying, *trying*, to rid the world of the unwanted detritus of used up anti-history, the electricity that cleaves to the back streets. Elephants suck the air clean with trumpeting counterblasts. I have to leave town regularly, fly out of Heathrow to all points north south, east and west. I'm a tourist in my bewilderment. My apparel is my own shockability. I give flight attendants grief all over the world. I get drunk on hospitality booze and arrive half cut and red faced. Outside hotels, by the pools, I count my blessings, my stock of hyper-life spans.

I skim stones off the Adriatic, and belly flop into its limpid water. The currents carry me on up through the Aegean, a mythic landscape finely attuned to my sensitivities. I dance in the spume with dolphins, some have said abusively. These are of course smear tactics. Sex with dolphins isn't my bag. But dolphins are erratic divinities, Gnostic to the nth level, and so swimming with them is part of the hyper-realized divine lifestyle. It's the chic accessorizing of nature's giant bounty. Dolphins being full of highly pressurized air are, like elephants, thus very receptive to Gnostic vibrations. Clear as day. I swim with dolphins and re-plane a new man. Newly minted, burnished with Hollywood lustre, a blond haired, blue eyed marine shaman.

Charter flights to all destinations have before carried me up and down, raged up, belly up, a couple of stiff drinks to the good, and will again. I have wrestled in my mind with flight attendants and scratched their pinkly hot faces as they endeavour to counter, with all necessary force, my belligerence. Scuffles result in peaked caps being dislodged, epauletted company shirts with bronze dress buttons becoming distressed and the wearers thereof requiring medical treatment for minor skin abrasions and light bruising. I always get off scot-free by virtue of my leglessness. I wrote a travel book before entitled "My Mid-Air Scraps: A Paraplegic Pig in Shit". The disabled angle, a fig leaf for violent attitudinising, stands me in good stead with the publishers, always on the lookout for aberrant angles in travel literature. Readings and book signings routinely descend to sub-farcical scufflings as my bodyguards roughly manhandle those members of my readership who take my descriptions of mid-air tussles as evidence that more of the same is what we are after at the publicity events. Contextual misinterpretation, as ever.

But the critics nonetheless receive my book very well. I had them all in my pocket. They need me more than I need them to get invites to all the baser literary salons of old London town. Best-selling midgets, celebrated one-armed football hooligans, physicists with Parkinsons', simulated Tourretters, Falklands veterans without penises, trepanned mime artists, the detritus of exploitative publishers' wet dreams. Trained chimps acting as butlers, bearded women as receptionists. Airlines keen to be seen to encourage air travel by the bodily challenged, as I was charmingly viewed, were even grateful for the publicity. A legless demiurge getting pissed up and causing trouble, a veritable blow for the non-legged, my publicists regarded my antics as small beer, no price at all to pay for the kickbacks from the disabled lobby. You can scarcely get a seat these days that isn't suited to the special needs of some challenged individual or other. And long may that trend continue! My celebrity is legion. People hold doors open, proffer ashtrays...

In cinemas, I tend to smoke ostentatiously, daring the usherettes to tangle with me. I take my kids into pubs that are clearly not child friendly. What I want is to assert *my* right to allow *my* kids to behave as *I* see fit. It's actually nothing to do with the kids. It's *all* about *me.* In fact, when they get to be 13-14 or so, they'll feel properly embarrassed by their groovy dad, their narcissistic, egomaniacal paterfamilias. I am a groovy *groovy* son of a bitch. I swagger around, eyeballing people who have the *nerve* to express irritation at my shrieking children. I offer them outside, knowing full well they will defer to my inhibited circumstances, and then bump their shins with my wheelchair. People don't take liberties with me any more. I'm accredited. I've done time and paid penance. My sins have been expiated publicly. I am a fully paid up household god. My virtues are forbearance and fecklessness, my talents include re-writing anti-history and tangling with and untangling the vectors of causality. I also specialize, by recourse to animal familiars, in lancing the boils of bad urban intent as they become tumescent, and getting drunk. I write travel books, and hold auditions for would be celebrities. It's a hectic schedule. Movie rights are in negotiation. Although I'll never work in films or television again. That was Frank's work. He was always jealous of me as only a recondite familiar can be. But when he died, I cried. Because he was my bruvvah. We looked out for each other against our parents, a pair of pre-childish thuggies in thrall to the religious impulse even as we lay together in the amniotic fluid. We made a pact that if either one of us were to die (and we knew one of us would be obliged to at least pretend to do so) then the other would keep alive the fiction that it ain't necessarily so. That death ain't necessarily the be all and the end all. To keep from going under. We knew that fictions were inevitable, would have to be invented. We knew moreover that these fictions would clearly never satisfy the yapping lapdogs, the spectral forces, of bad intent, the assembled monster throng of academics, therapists and the secular priesthood. We required fictions that would elucidate for us and for our friends the fact that we weren't a spent force. We were obliged to create a system, or yield to another man's. No choice really.

THE GREAT BEAST OF HAPPINESS (KILL ME 3 TIMES)

"Are you happy with your nose? Your buttocks? Your lips? Ears? Eyes? Nose? Had it with that old time religion? Try Elephant Gnosis! Have you considered Elephant Gnosis? Body double, inside and out?"

The motto, or catchphrase, of my tenure as London's *Top DJ…* *Remember, if it isn't facile, I don't get it.* Of course, someone you loved to hate. And hated full stop. My smugly self-satisfied mug beaming down from every bus, every billboard, a wink of the eye, an arched eyebrow. Oleaginous manner, uproarious laugh, charming tendency to humiliate associates, pals, "mates" who *daren't* talk back. Except one day, she did. They all do…they all did, one day. Talkback is payback. Now it's booze all day long, booze and solitude.

"Can't you let people decide for themselves how they want to look? The tone of this conversation is patronizing in the extreme."

Buffy Strangelove: Self Therapy: Vol 3…

It was the voice of my nemesis. The doctor's wife. Matriarch of the profane airwaves. Yeah, my boorish tones filled kitchens and lounges as I bullied and, let's face it, straightforwardly insulted my listeners. Stupid. No respect due, certainly none offered. Voices which were clearly disconnected from their source. Departed souls in search of corporeal weight, buzzing around the frequencies of radio heaven/hell and the dial itself not really expansive enough to contain all my victims. I give them what they deserve. What do they expect? Who's the star of the show, me or them? It's me isn't it? Oh yes. Do they really think their opinions are going to elicit anything other than straightforward and frank, undisguised contempt? Opinions, which they make the mistake of believing will confer on them, if expressed publicly, recognition which has inexplicably, up until this moment, eluded them?

So...the radio buzzed to the sounds of my voices. I was back in this contaminated land, less than a week after clearing customs and I was still getting tired. No energy. Still jet lagged, although to be fair I had achieved a smooth, psychosis free re-entry. Immigration fooled again, as though they ever stood a chance. So...my wings were unfolded, diaphanous. My career was quickly in full swing, the playful murders over-looked by a grateful, opportunistic establishment. Politicians and academics, no less than industrial magnates and corporate moguls, movers and shakers, are adepts, skilled in reflexive interpretation. A household god falling back to earth is a hyper-numinous event, or in publishing terms an inter-textual device, and a real handful of an opportunity. Good copy. But the cameras weren't disabled for no good reason. They wanted me virginal, uncontaminated by textual pollution. Customs were disenfranchised, bought off. Those with an eye quick enough to spot the potential inherent in the arcane referentiality of the event were also quick to spot the potential in exploitation of the marketing aspects. Back scratching, co-dependence, a juxtaposition of apparently coincidental interests. So...doors were unlocked, palms were greased. While not known, as such, I became *known*. I appeared everywhere, my ubiquity a perceptual device that was mutually beneficial. I only appeared to appear as myself. I get under the very skin of the culture. Buffy mugs everywhere. You seen this geezer? Look out! The establishment, or *hidden* powers, recognized in me the hyper-will of their own crazed intent, the actual will to power. So... showing in cinemas, on billboards, at openings, lectures, garden parties, I was infiltrated at all levels.

Listeners sighed quietly or grinned inanely as the jingles played around their brains. Phone-in self help. Noses were a pre-occupation. As were breasts, penises, buttocks and necks. Surgery...plastic...the need for...the moral consequences of...the psychological impact of which...onto already fractured egos...self esteem paper thin...creaking under the weight...blots in my mind...Fat and knobbly, fat and voluminous, distended bellies and lumpy limbed, drooping and pendulous breasts, corrugated skin stretched tight over rib cages, too thin, too thick, buttocks that stick out, over-prominent brows, eyes too close together/far apart, rolls of fat, all pressed into service of body image distortion which we made a pre-condition of Elephant Gnosis conditioning.

For one thing, my body's never been a problem until now. Now my belly gets in the way. All human misery is here…assumed for the purposes of my smooth assimilation into the fabric of this debased culture. It's fertile ground for radio populism. My eyes and ears are distracted from the sound of my voice on the radio by an overweight angel, puffing and heaving in the yard outside, hovering with difficulty above the apple tree in the garden. The birds are silent, always silent. No two birds alike. The sublime purposefulness of their flight cuts like scissors through my coagulating consciousness… my thoughts blister, bubbling like soup. Angels and fat birds alike hover indistinctly beyond my peripheral vision. Journalists make of it what they will. Fat autogenetic bird-life: a cautionary story. Fat hands in chains: a cautionary tale. They are merely PR men, bought and paid for. They handle it thus…via anecdote:

The story of an amputee, whose hand was in the first place someone else's. For some reason, he'd lied about the accident. First of all said it was a circular hand saw accident, something that could have happened to anyone…not mentioning that anyone who wanted to lose a hand might be more susceptible than usual to this type of accident. Turned out to have been deliberate of course, or semi-purposeful, an auto-mutilation. Then, the hand of the donor *didn't* fit like a glove. Or rather, too much like a glove and not enough like a hand. So, having had the necessary surgery, he then stopped with the anti-rejection drugs. The hand felt "other". Felt "strange". Skin started peeling and flaking. The hand was, in gothic approximation of Technicolor Hammer fantasies of the 70s, in some sublime fashion possessed of its own will. Without will and with hands up, the amputee's nightmare scenario had been enacted; bemused, peeved and potentially litigious surgeons subsequently lopped off the hand again. I know how he felt. Did the hacks miss the point? Maybe.

Some time ago, can't remember when, I requested surgery on my own legs. Purely for the sympathy vote of course. Thought I'd get a better publishing deal. The legless are more rounded/better than those with a full set of limbs, at least in the perverse and fickle mirror of public approbation. And did it pay off? Did it? Big time! I have publishing franchises coming out of my ears now. Medical texts, abstruse academic works, travel guides, brochures of all sorts and sizes. My stock has never been higher. Never. I'm always in demand on the lecture circuit. Hotel bills paid for by ecstatic publishers…

But happy? Happy? I should be but I ain't? My own jingles haunt me and taunt me. My body is just too displeasing to me. My body image is horribly compromised. But it's the price I and therefore you must pay. I'm universal in this. I'm only corporeal. Maybe when I lay dying I was spoilt. The feeling that my body was merely kinetic energy, constantly shape shifting, a collection of plasma cells, disappeared all too quickly. What happened to my diet plan? I eat nothing but bran all week and I feel strangely ineffectual. I'm shitting out my entire body weight on a consistent basis, week in week out, but I never get thinner. I'm like I'm not really there. I see these fat birds through the window, and really I can see they've got a bigger problem than me. How can they maintain aerodynamic integrity? Beats me, but somehow they manage it. Flying is everything. Lose the ability to fly and you're well fucked. Fat birds have also become kind of familiars to me. They perform routine acts of surveillance for me as well as fulfilling the more passive role that tanks of tropical fish perform for the less psychodynamic. Body image therefore is now nothing, *nothing,* to me. I perform psychic transference mantras, chant out the fat of the land, and adumbrate the otherness of the mythic realm, and the birds in my garden get fatter and fatter. I sit there dreamily listening to the radio-chat, in love with the sound of my own voice, gazing at them all lined up, hovering, evanescent, on my garden fence. Fish look as though they're shitting all the time with that stuffed open-mouthed gawping look that they affect. But fat birds are almost literally angels. And they know which side their bread's buttered. I allow them access to a little known world, an arcane kingdom of anti-sin, auto-forgiveness, religiosity, transference of guilt, anti-therapy, the full Gnostic Monty, the un-breached pleroma. I operate as a kind of demiurge for them, giving their imperfectly formed bodies a corporeal essence. And in return, they flatter me endlessly, reassuring me that my body is indeed godlike. I see reflected in their translucent wings an image, which is no longer compromised, of my profane corporeality, my belly undistended and my face youthful and my flanks sleek. I don't have body image problems. The birds reflect my new weightlessness. I levitate to the fence and sit there with them, gormless and gawping. I've got a sort of idea that I am like the light descending into matter, that I am some sort of immense fireball hitting the waves, and that this accounts for my singular life and lives. But I don't know. I can't see clearly any more. I am forced to wear very thick spectacles if I wish to see. Which of course I don't. Don't need to. The visions keep me occupied. In correcting my sight, they distort my insight, my Gnosis. As though, looking through windows onto the world, I see fat angels all around, but not the light that makes them fly. I am full of medication…I should say…that must be true…although I'm not even sure about that. I just read the papers all day long. I listen in to the radio. I listen in to my voices buzzing and squeaking. I sound like interference. The papers are full of what used to be called trivia, but which everyone has long since come to accept as the real stuff of life. The self-importance of movers and shakers relegated, even in the broadsheets, to the inside small sections, the pullouts, hidden away inside. Trivia has come to flesh out most of what people, and I pride myself that I'm one of the people, regard as real life. Celebrity game shoots, hit and run accidents arranged for charity, humiliating game shows and vicarious voyeurism.

The papers full of trivia? I never notice. Never!! I for one certainly never noticed that media angles are trivial and have been for the last 30 years. I've noticed a certain relish for humiliation, after encouragement, of the presumptuous and the talentless. A subtle goading. A punishable sin which is wanting it too much. Another sin - too great a sense of shadenfreude when they're brought face to face with their emptiness, when they are savagely disabused of the notion that they are in fact talented, or worth a second glance. We're all pre-secular sinners in this regard. We all partake of that great sinfulness. There's a dummy catholic in every western and eastern head. We delineate the trivial in grandiose lives, we see the trivial exposed and deified, we need no longer ourselves be exposed and can ourselves be deified. And if you prefer the secular life, just grit your teeth and turn the trivial pages. I leave clues all along the dial. I envisage, and embody. I encompass the trivial. I spread gossip and undermine reputations. I chat about the weather. I extemporize a self-righteous moral discourse for cod-satirical purposes. I am a benighted curse upon the upright and the almighty.

And new monsters surface every day from the pleroma. We feel the urge to listen in to their voices. Monsters from the so-called id, ghosts of depraved urges are still there, *still* there, just below the surface. My life in chains is compromised by the pressing need to escape the ghosts in my peripheral vision. (This is important to me…follow me here…the following exculpation nails the peripheral dummy god…we need this head start….) Count Dracula he creeps up on me. I am impaled on the false horns of his undead dilemma. I can't move and he can't go out, sit on the fence, in the sun. The birds mock him. But I can't move without recycled riffs (untrammeled originality is anathema to movement in these circumstances) and am thus easy prey for the baseball-hatted villain. I trudge through pea-soupers, my legs like lead as I attempt to evade this monster, the divinely realized anti-familiar of my devotional life. I am transfixed, cruci-fictional as I await the crushing momentum of his heavy orthopedic boots. I'm a sucker for hypnosis. Easily hypnotized by charlatans, I am helpless before their fictional influence. I believe anything. I'm gullible as hell in this state. You can take me to the cleaners any day of the week. With little or no inter-textual relief, I'm hung out to dry. I'm a believer. Believe in anything. I think then that I'm a sort of deferred deity. They say I am, the unseen powers. Fat expensively trousered moguls subscribe to belief systems that have no weight, but still they invested in my ubiquity. Because I've done personality tests for the scientologists the results of which imply that I'm Thetan material. Definitely. I could really make the grade there, especially now Cruise has gone. My kind of publicity they'd kill for. No I mean it…Literally kill for….

But I just can't evade the monsters in my dreams. I am stuck. In stasis. The radio hums with bad intent. You know it, I *am* the monster in my dreams. I've thought ever since re-birthing that these monsters are unavoidable. So I sublimated that, or that's what they tell me. They say I'm running from these monsters so no, of course I'm not *happy*. I know this kind of public exegesis is reprehensible so I won't say any more. That's why I can't remember who I am any more. Any psychiatrist will bore you half to death with the notion of denial. My good doctor friends will jump in feet first to let you know what they think. And will fight tooth and nail to try and hold back the inevitability of the post psychiatric world. But we know. We are post-psycho. Post-post psycho. Life is now lived, thanks to my good offices, at a level bathed in inter-textual hyper-irony. I am everywhere. On the oldest radios. Ham radios. In the wiring. Hard wired. Recycled as irony. The old and dying are now living a life that merely mimics oldness and mocks at encroaching mortality. The old are just playing themselves. They'll live again. No danger. Psychology's no use to them. Psychology belongs to a pre-parodic age.

From the Devotional Directional Manual:

"The elephant emanation is an eon old one. That part of creation dedicated to not forgetting, no matter how long or worn out the memory thread. It's the wellspring of misery, not forgetting, tying a knot in it. Elephants are like a big wrinkle skinned knotted handkerchief, a divine emanation from the Godhead, a phone call from home, a reminder to the baser elements, the billions in this realm, that they should never forget. Forgetting, in the theology that existed before my own unquiet entry into this plane, was like a double remembrance. Things past were as likely to be remembered as things that hadn't yet happened. In other words, some *still* lived in a hopelessly pre-ironic world. My descent into this realm sorted all that out, and elephants are the tools of profane remembrance. They yield, by sheer force of presence, or semi-presence, a light that is this realm's saving grace. Without them, in other words, everything is in a state of gracelessness. Big time. Biggest time of all. I am the negative or inferior world-creator. In my cosmology, the pre-secular Cosmos is the result of an unforgiven or primordial error or accident; the only true existence being the Pleroma or transcendent order of Divinities. Elephants, never forgetting, or forgiving, prevent the tangibles of *this* world from slipping through the rent fabric into a pre-ironic, prelapsarian, world in which

everything would once again be up for grabs. We can't go back there. We can't return. Ever. EVER!!! But never worry, there's worse semi-deities in the Pleroma than me, I'll tell you that for nothing. Metaphysically what this means for you is that the world as you know it is not the creation of the Supreme God, as my pals the various priests and secular monks of monotheistic religions would have you believe, but rather an emanation of the very lowest and most minor of all divinities, and an accidental emanation at that."

It's heart rending stuff eh? I would rather, as I think I've said before, have been a rock god. My guitar technique is or was a clanging zigger-zagger sort of technique/style, extemporized yet tight as a fucking nut. But you need help. You still need help. I couldn't have just abandoned you. I can't forget, although you can. The past and the future are open books to me. I know how bad it's going to get. Elephants will assist you, in ways you can't imagine, to remember the good times. I am there never to forget. They let the good times roll and rumble. They are, as it were, pachydermal rivets, holding fast the compromised fabric of this futile, unbolted, realm.

They hold it fast. The trails they leave, for nomadic journeys conducted at a pace beyond the understanding of the present jump-cut culture, are strewn with immense dumps and evacuations, and they emanate vibrations of pure Gnostic religiosity. Medusa Rappa the ex-witch she got it all wrong. She'd sort of understood at first about this thing but only really half understood, a very vague understanding. She had to go really. It was as though she'd danced around the edges of the idea, and got cold feet. She was a catholic recidivist, a dummy catholic. I knew she was losing it when birthdays and Christmases were increasingly ruined by the thoughtlessness of her frankly absurd gifts. She mistakenly embraced the whole *extrinsic* elephantine question, the outward ephemera of elephantine culture, the gloopy sentimentality of half realized pachydermal simulacra. And gifts would proceed from her accordingly…little porcelain elephant figurines, with card attached "This elephant belongs to Brian"…elephant cuddly toys, all Disney big eyed and fluffy…ceramic elephant key ring tags, all shiny and metallic… carved tribal tourist elephant fetishes…an elephant shaped swimming ring (I could never swim but that's hardly the point)…elephant trunk twin-egg-cups (although I hate eggs)…socks with elephant motif on the ankles…an elephant tiepin (even thought I don't and never have worn ties…or shirts…)…grey enamel elephant bookends…elephant beer…elephant tattoo on my shoulder, both elephantine stigmata and religious trademark. My taut skin itched like crazy as the ink found easy purchase in the subcutaneous layers. But it was a necessary undertaking nonetheless. A branding in either sense of the word. It covered over the old Medusa tattoo, a stigma I'd had good reason to disguise. After our disastrous union, an attachment injurious to both parties and to all progeny, the snake headed icon was the last thing I needed on my shoulder. The old tattoo was now delitescent, concealed behind the elephant head, the snake tendrils skillfully altered to appear as stylized, ornate elephant ears. The gorgon head fully metamorphosed into the elephantine.

So no, I'm not happy. I'm beyond happy. I *consume* misery and I *shit out* happiness. I am The Great Beast of Happiness. The Enforcer of Joyousness. My arse gives me so much gyp these days. And my belly is ruined. I can't look in the mirror and my arms are numb. I'm the epicene emanation, an androgynous afterthought, the fictional counterpart of a coked up south London sax player. A forethought. Me and Dionysia, Frank and me, triplets in a mush of creative energy, in receipt of your heartfelt indifference. And you need therefore to kill me 3 times to make sure I'm really dead. Death is no easy thing for me. The auguries are only readable after most of the mush has been scooped out. I can't really be stored for too long in a fridge. I have a sell by date, which is why my escape and re-entry was so pressing. Happy? We don't do happy. We don't know happy. We're in the darkness looking out for ourselves. Career is on track though and me happily re-escaped. The world our oyster bed, the elephant trails re-opened, the electricity discharged, planets in new alignments, a population now re-open to viscous Gnostic vibrations from the elephant trails, auto-erotic building sex is on the increase, the *Hypnerotomachia* republished for good and all and me and my fat birds in ecstatic conspiracy to kill the profane and re-establish the arcane.

MR. TREBLECOCK OF THE HAPPY VALE.

"Chewing gum kills you, right?"

"That's right…but do we really know, for instance, what electricity is? Have we yet *really* grasped that *that* kills you too? Have we grasped where energy comes from? Or where the universe appeared from? Some day science will catch up…until then we can only speculate, postulate, theorize, hypothesize it's the failure to debate…original sin…entropy…acedia… watch out for it…everywhere…laziness…your patients will be literally terrified to change themselves…lead 'em by the gnosis…we all change or die mate…change or die…change…or die…" Doc Abrahams in conference, in full authorial voice – a thing of beauty or as I live and breathe a lamentable failure of nerve?

But first, camera tracks past dusty building frontage and zooms in on signage: HAPPINESS STARTS HERE – The Happy Vale Entropic Dispersal Centre:

"Leave it out mate…what are we to do? Are we adrift in a sea of ignorance? Some say, Do Nothing! Some of my patients propose that we merely drift…symptom is cure…redemptive…and my patients look after themselves, are symptom free."

Without giving anything away, the eyes say it all. That is, nothing. The eyes say *I have been living a life of pain, sorrow, unhappiness, bad luck… My bad luck is imposed on me…*they say nothing. The eyes I saw were those of a much older man, and yet the man who was sitting in the waiting room could only have been pushing 70. His wife sat beside him, and beside herself. Silently berating the unobvious, she wore the expression of one empirically convinced of nothing, her countenance that of someone unwilling to believe that what she'd had to endure had really happened. Shell shocked, she wore the expression of one still dreaming, still un-surfaced. The eyes clouded, reason absent. Her eyes advertised that she was no longer prepared to take responsibility, least of all for anything that might have *happened* to her or that might be *about* to happen to her. She was beyond therapy, symptom free. She swam in and out of hyper-neurotic pools, in at the deep end of mental dis-equilibrium, besieged on all sides by a reality too abrasive to bear...she said silently so I could hear her...*I was possessed by very bad and evil in my body. I was VERY ill, I could not work...Never had friends. I had lost everything, incl. my faith...I have searched for help and no one could help me. For the evil I had was too powerful, the electricity was too powerful and controlling my life...Dr. Ayton was my last hope. He has the grace of god, guiding the electricity out of me...but after 6 visits my doubts have not gone away. Is he entropic? Evil? I have doubts...I still feel evil...electric...chewing gum kills you it does...chewing gum kills you...*

Her husband hugged himself, groaning quietly, occasionally heaving semi-comic sighs, coughing up spittle from atrophied lungs, an over-stated stand-up death's cough. The thoughts of the gum chewing stand-up were projected at special frequencies into the doctor's brain, whose over-enlarged hippocampus acted as both transmitter and receiver. Rituals are only learning aids, they are not learning *in and of themselves*. This was his Hippocratic mantra. Pinned to the wall, above his desk. But trance recitals, coded mantras of intent, surely help the worst cases.

"Chewing Gum? That kills you that stuff does...Chewing gum kills you.... Chewing Gum? That kills you that stuff does...Chewing gum kills you...Chewing Gum? That kills you that stuff does...Chewing gum kills you...Chewing Gum? That kills you that stuff does...Chewing gum kills you...Chewing Gum? That kills you that stuff does...Chewing gum kills you...Chewing Gum? That kills you that stuff does...Chewing gum kills you...Chewing Gum? That kills you that stuff does...Chewing gum kills you...Chewing Gum? That kills you that stuff does...Chewing gum kills you... Chewing gum kills you...Chewing Gum? That kills you that stuff does...Chewing gum kills you...Chewing Gum? That kills you that stuff does...Chewing gum kills you..."

Hoarse exclamations that might have been exhalations of breath, or might not, thus unremittingly emerged from his throat. He rocked to and fro, focusing on the darkness, the horror. Lingering within him were remnants of specialized individuality, of humour, of humanity, now only expressed through the hacking cough, the mantra. A cough that was of course intricisically humorous, as coughs are, vouchsafing as it did a glimpse of the corporeal fragility that was the key trigger of my own laughter reflex. Therapy based on laughter is now the main type thereof. Pre-EG conditioning. Laughter at body image. I viewed them with concern through my metal grille. Concern my new speciality, assistance a primary motive. Killing with or without kindness. Their choice, not mine.

They were joined on the PVC banquette by another in mid-life catatonia…scraped back dull blond hair, greasy and matted. Cigarette burns and other abrasions disfigured her hands, and her mouth was a mask of impetigo scars. Distressed in black leather, she cut a despondent figure as she slumped on the functional seating. Her dull eyes wandered blindly around the room. The waiting room hummed, flickered with regret and gave itself up to despondent meditation. A tableau: The residents of the Happy Vale Hotel enjoying a day out at the Day Care Centre, making the most of the opportunity to luxuriate in the centrally heated waiting room.

"Can you just take a seat over there?"

Receptionists prevaricated delicately, euphemistically.

"Can you come in now please?"

The doctor sat down. Placing his fingers together, forming a naked wigwam of knotty sinew and bone, he knitted his brows and then pursed his lips, the whole effect a parody, an attitude minted from the most banal daytime soaps, the paternalist doctor…bad news to break…He calculated that more people were made nervous by medical props than were comforted by the illusion of controlling efficiency they were ordinarily presumed to lend proceedings. An expert in drag is no comfort these days, not after fright stories of legions of suburban death dealing doctors and corroborating sitcoms. Anyway, there was no one to hear the bad news, which was all around. Waiting rooms hum with bad news, resonate with kinetic misery. Tutting briefly, he looked at his reflection in the mirror on the wall opposite his desk. And rehearsed the posture again.

"I'm sorry to have to tell you that…….."

And again his nerve failed him. So I asked him….

"Doc, how d'you lose your legs again mate?"

"In a bizarre set of circumstances, half bad luck, half carelessness and half suicidal grief, brought on by another altogether different bizarre set of circumstances. My hands are also prosthetic. But we won't go into that. I don't like talking about it."

"Oh, OK then"…and the subject was closed. I re-examined myself in the mirror, adjusted the bowtie, licked a renegade lock of hair flat and gave myself up to meditative artfulness. My little game, see it, is a playful thing, a blurring of the boundaries between what's real and what's made up, a useful bulwark in my ongoing re-entry self-therapy. These grubby avatars of my fractured self, dotted throughout the waiting room, no less real for all that of course, still deserve my undivided self, my full attention, the real deal. I am for them the predisposed medic, giver of healthfulness. I am a broadly smiling basking shark of rectitude. My jaws fully extended, I give tongue. I swallow eggs whole. I stand to attention, my hand at my breast in mock solemnity as the bus heaves itself away, groaning, from the traffic lights. An homunculus in turban, twisted from the trunk upwards, arms strangely asymmetric, bowls past, humming slightly too loudly. My fingers - with angels, and clues - at the tips, are rigid in anticipation of the calamity to follow. As the bus nears me, I stand calmly at ease in anticipation of incipient immortality. Mindful of the homily that had attended since childhood, that one might as well live today since one might get run over by a bus tomorrow, I step out in style. Having stepped out in life, now is the time to complete my side of the bargain. Angels attend me as the bus screams, too late, to a halt. There's a thudding sound as I'm hit, which finds an echo from the upper deck. My astral body leaves its corporeal shell and, a rubbernecker even in death, I levitate to get a good look. A young man is in the throes of a painful and exaggerated death, blood spurting every which way from a gash in his neck. I gather from the bloody scene that my entirely self-centred suicide has also precipitated this unfortunate individual's own unwarranted and premature demise. But he is merely an extra in my passion play. It's a snuff scenario, although not necessarily premeditated. My death and his are not linked in any but the most trivial sense. Although from the look of him, death is no great disadvantage. No use for doctors at this scene then. No more use for nervously sweaty medics prowling the margins of A & R wards, bouncing on balled feet through the human wreckage. They can be trusted with attending to the sick in mind, in a kind of officiously obsequious way. All sorts of solicitous meaninglessness as regards the everyday miserable, as well as the clinically depressed, can be left to their offices. They can be trusted to gently break the news of terminal illness to distraught relatives, I think, but leave the offices of death itself to the angels. Plenty of scope for the dealers in body and soul parts. From the wreckage, parts of immortality become manifest. Young bouncy versions of the dead man whistle gay tunes as they rush out. Slightly more cynical versions then appear smoking French cigarettes. Bloated drunken tattooed versions are dragged out kicking and screaming by angels in formation. The corpse lies there bubbling, attempting to secrete itself in the pavement cracks. He'd been on his way to the surgery to report a numbness in his arm, a spreading desensitized area. The area is now fully desensitized.

In the vicinity, a tall man lit up, a ghastly harbinger of doom sparking up a cigarette. Mr. Treblecock, a lumpy seer of unwashed demeanor, glaring eyes, bony alopecia scalp and thick spectacles. A recently released familiar of the Happy Vale Hotel. Done his time, out on the run. Several days' growth on his face. He wore a suit of ill-fitting black cotton, trousers barely reaching the ankles while bagging at the knees, suspended by a combination of string and willpower. On his fore and middle fingers he wore burnished and engraved steel claws, elongated and predatory rings, pointed and sharpened, prophylactic against the possibility of attack, or perhaps in preparedness for premeditated attack. His mediated gifts of pre-sight were unrefined. He knew where to be for the cameras. Now he was somewhat nervous, although the documentary crew would be along shortly. Their arrival had been pre-cogged, and was itself a fortuitous corollary of the bus tragedy, a happy confluence of events that would ensure that the cigarette-smoking ghoul received maximum exposure and attention from the bemused audience, ripe for any kind of spurious or esoteric interpretation. His schtick was exempt from taste. He was a baggy trousered seer. The documentary crew, under orders to make the most of the bus tragedy, would unerringly pick on this singular individual as the figure best placed to identify the more recondite elements of the accident. He would be relied on to identify and elucidate re-birth activity for the voyeurs, paid up day-trippers of morbidity. He realized, because he'd been entreated in gnosis therapy to believe his own press, that he was televisual manna, fulfilling the not specifically stated but nonetheless restless audience need for a sort of unifying familiar of the subconscious. A point seer, a reader of the runes. He would be identified and designated (quite rightly) as a kind of predatory harbinger of doom, a gloomy nicotine stained prophet without honour in this realm. He was a despised though necessary evil, fulfilling a role necessary to fully elucidate tribal/public understanding of unforeseen and apparently random events. He drew elusive parallels and scored in the vectors of discord. It was a role Mr. Treblecock was born to, having been a traffic warden in a previous life.

He had previous experience of the televisual, having originally been the subject of a documentary himself. Before admittance to the Happy Vale, he'd been involved in a running battle with the local Reality Corps operatives. He'd become a local cause celebre, and resisted to the last their increasingly desperate attempts to force him to clean up his act. Eventually threats of legal action, predicated on public health grounds (rats were living inside his bedroom and bathroom and under an old motorcycle in his garden) were required. But even these were insufficient to break his resolve, and eventually he was removed from the premises by force, clinging dysfunctionally to the doorframe as his embattled tormentors finally achieved their goal and he was at last evicted and committed to the Happy Vale. But he had the last laugh. His principled, or stupid, stand was rewarded with instant celebrity. He was, although clearly distracted, regarded by most voyeurs as upholding and exemplifying the rights of the individual against impersonal and malevolent forces. His character was subsequently re-formed and transcribed, fictionalized to a quite brazen degree, by image consultants and agents, all keen to make a few bob out of him. In reality a maniacal ghoul, the worst nightmare of the squeamish audience who nevertheless reveled in disgust, word got about in televisual circles that he was guaranteed to bring in audiences far in excess of the size normally to be relied upon, and his career as a primetime familiar took off big time. So he now found himself hovering by the wrecked bus waiting for the documentary crew.

I too have been scary looking in my time though you may not believe it to look at me. I scare when it's suits me. Scary looking individuals generally discomfit people, especially if they're in a position to do bad things. Or transform bad dreams. Like doctors. Most people don't know what they want from a doctor - bow-tied paternalist, full of solemn expertise and godlike authority...or matey, open necked, beige trousered chap-next-door empathy. They think about it, chew it over and then fail to decide. It's like...they can see both sides. Doctors sitting behind desks have the power of life and death. Frank himself, a bow-legged hail-fellow well-met type, all bonhomie and blustery confidence, won the confidence of the community almost immediately. Which, from the point of view of the community, was ultimately a disaster. Mysteriously high mortality rates of patients who'd just been feeling a bit under the weather were not at first put down to anything other than bad luck. But that's Frank for you. Working by stealth, a charm offensive, gathering confidences.

He was knocking them off left right and centre. Dropping like flies. Their problem was they wouldn't listen to him. They wouldn't buy his carefully spun line, his oily patter, his smoothly unctuous re-assurances. And that's enough for Frank. It makes him mad. Sends him troppo. Loco grande. Psycho mondo. He can't stand an attitude that fails to register at least 95% deference. Frank thrives on deference, it's his thing. And yet doctors, elephant death mask in place, aren't obliged to belly up to the consequences. And their patients would normally rather die than enter into lengthy death disputes, preferring nervous circumlocution, a queasy enquiry as to the real meaning of the auguries. Less than total deference to his assumed professional integrity and Frank would willfully misread biopsy results, or arrive at diagnoses unsupported by the evidence. And the patients would defer. Eventually. Too late. Frank's not a man to cross, or to forgive. He's a force of nature, standing out against the unsure, pre-evolved rabble. The golf-playing ghosts of the orbital, bemoaning their parochial lot, come to him for succour, which he withholds. They aren't capable, these pinkly suburban spectres, prior to transmutation of the Gnostic DNA strain, of standing firm against this Hippocratic hypocrisy. They'd rather be un-evolved, death-ed, than submit to the swarthy Lothario advances of death doctors. Too many patients, every day, misdiagnosed, put under the ether, touched up by leering medicos, the quack squad all righteous and oily in bedside comfort giving. The species is un-evolved. Those in the know let the quacks have their way, take bets on the consequences, seek good odds on their chances of survival, are willing to gamble on the probity of a shit faced quack, ready to trust implicitly in the plausible manner. These people know the value of a publicly acceptable front and take pains to present their best sides to those who might be in a position to do them *bad*. Freely enslaved spectres of the orbital, a passively racist, dumbed inwards and incestuous enclave of bored cable sluts and golfing zombies. Not for them too many late nights. They have healthcare round the clock, and therefore cheat death. But they never approach life, never achieve full gnosis. They're the silt on the orbital, arterially sclerotic, having failed to appreciate the central metaphor of movement that's literally on their own doorsteps. Even the by now fairly ubiquitous elephant tracks, the trails overlaying the hard shoulder, are scarcely sufficient to raise these wraiths from their torpor.

But Mr. Treblecock was, naturally, one of those who'd seen the light. He'd been sharp enough to observe on which side his beard was buttered. He'd seen the doc's game from the start and was more than a match in feral slyness. His nicotine fingered cunning, quizzical and oyster eyed, drooling mouthed, was retard-like. He'd accepted sectioning with equanimity, he'd deferred completely and absolutely to Frank's frankly insulting summation of his mental state and he'd agreed to confinement, unlimited tenure with TV rights at the Happy Vale Hotel. And now he was reaping his rewards in this world and the next. Stained bedclothes, dusty window frames, chipped paintwork, a really shitty breakfast of industrial canned tomato on toast with battery egg occupying the distaff side, a measly rasher on the side and a mug of thrice brewed tea, plus access to all the prime time docu-drama with which his agent could supply him. He'd worked out his MO this side of the divide, but as for the full monty, the transportation, the fabric busting trip to the future, he didn't stand a chance. Mr. Treblecock was, as far as that was concerned, way off the pace…just lazy…dead in the water…

david kettle

ELEPHANT DREAM TIME.

The dream I had you wouldn't believe. Are these not the dullest words in any language? Nevertheless, I had this dream. Where I was drunk. I thought, thinking back through my linear history, that I'd become a disappointed man, and had reached early middle age with neither a clear idea of where life was taking me nor any real clue as to what to do once I got (or didn't get) there. Enlarged frontal lobe or not, I was, felt, dead in the water. I am estranged from myself, my brother's gone missing, two co-dependent gods, in a state of grace, living in deadpan fringe society. This much is auto-historical. We were deadpan in a dead zone. Down the pub, our deadpan banter had 'em rolling in the aisles. But we won't go there. I mean, anyone who thinks of complaining about their life should reconsider. No one asked me to be born. I *forced* myself into the world. I specifically ensured that my chances of being born were not left to chance. I cheated my way into life. The theological implications are horrifying. We all choose life at the moment of impact. We choose to be born. It's a secret that many theologians are aware of, but dare not reveal. The whole fabric of post therapeutic divinity will be torn down the middle if this becomes public knowledge. They'll offer you salvation for a dollar or your money back, but they'll hide the real truth. That you are your own divinity. Is this profane? Who cares? Some fictional liturgies, made up religions, spoof theologies, taken as satirical but of course entirely straight forward and prosaic, offer ordination as a full time minister of your own religion for $20. People smell a rat, they think there's a catch. How much trust has been lost in the world? How much? And at what cost? I can offer anyone salvation, no standing charge. I take away your electricity.

But anyway, in this dream I had, my auto-history is of no interest. My dreams mess with significant causal elements. The proto-sludge of the universe doesn't yet *contain* me. I haven't been born. In drink, forgetting, I saw where I'd truly been. My universe was stretched out of shape, literally, by my birth. Nothing was ever the same again. Having been conceived in the pre-religious trenches, a wacky double act, joined at hip and head, we were discharged into another realm. Out of the primordial, repositioned in the mythic realm. I felt needed, along with Frank and Dionysia. My tri-partite Godhead. We were preeminently organized, engaged in promotion, saleable elements ™'ed. At that time there was some sort of inner core of worth, some inner nugget of authenticity in the individual. The individual spark of life is divine. Of course people bought it. Lapped it up. They were paradoxically relieved to take the path of more resistance. No more raindrop guilt. They never needed to untie the knots, the critical truths about themselves or ourselves. Lives could be, and were, lived at a level of unreconstructed fearlessness. They could no longer live in denial. Therapeutic enablers, we were primogenitors of the cod-psychotherapeutic tendency. A population wholly softened up, sweetened, led to believe in the primacy of inner being and divinity. And seduced by the elephant sexual, in flotation tank darkness.

But like I said, I'm the best liar in all antiquity. I am the antiquarian of mistrust and the curator of false dependency. A potentate of evasion, preaching a gospel of self taught lies, revealed evasions, untruths nurtured and personality disorder encouraged. The men. The women. The children. They swam solo in the flotation tanks, alone, with our help. Water wings removed. Devotional stabilizers off. Enabled and endorsed, certificated by instructors in elephant masks, the therapeutic/confessional complex emplaced within. We encouraged them all to swim alone. I now swum alone in heightened seas, without water wings, with dolphins, flashing and thrusting, transfixed on shiny hook rings, accelerating through time-holes, baring rotator fangs, getting my teeth into celestial info-weed, turning surfers inside out, upending fishing smacks, seeing the colours of their insides, shimmering in the fissure of psychology, through the crack of history. Into anti-history. Anti-linear history, the female gash, water based, opened up right there. Not like your whole life passing before your eyes, in dreams, more like the possibility of an inner life, a realized inner divinity, passing just within (or out of) reach.

david kettle

Gaudily animated inner life, just out of reach. And how like (or unlike) real life that dream really is. Ever noticed that? Frank, ever noticed that? He notices these things. Shades them in. No, Frank can't hear me. Frank's dead. Cancer. I place the divine in each and every one. No self is beyond the divine touch. I bite each and every one in half to make sure of the authentic core. Taste the divine within.

I made things work for me. I had all the intuitive skill. Instinctive skill, like someone who picks up tunes…on a piano. Tunes already there, lucid. I played piano in the jazz realms, instinctively. I didn't know how I got the skill. I wasn't a craftsman. I wasn't an artist. I'd learned the tricks and the tunes as though they were *already there* and I'd somehow just happened on them. But that's what they all say isn't it? I don't know how it works. I'm just a semi-deity. The thing was just lying around. This insipid garment, tinkling and irritating, like wind chimes. Tremendously irritating, overbearingly ethnic…in the suburbs. Just lying there, waiting for me. I went through the suburbs like a prodigal son, tinkering and tinkling as I went, crowds of patriots cheering me on, trestle tables with bunting, cakes and ale, bottles of brown ale, the celebratory mood disfigured by discreet rapes. People just get carried away with happiness and relief don't they? Just glad to be alive, just glad that things still *work*. Glad that things haven't just ground to a halt.

Virus…how things WORK…technique…watch this…Don't allow this…Things fall apart, not working…people interested in how things *work*? Isn't it enough that they actually do work? Tech fiddler, monkey around with the code, what could be more anti-religious? Obnoxious. Still, some fucking idiot has to do it eh? Hail the New Technocrat! People fiddling at the edges, extrapolating technique, dissing meaning. Going nowhere. It's so sad. People without dreams, like the one I had. Still have. Where I was drunk. And Dionysia's still with me. Making it alright. I'm Apollo, I am Orestes, also the light of the world. I learned to transform myself, take responsibility, despite my inner fecklessness, of which I made a fetish…candidly speaking, it's really all for the best. We are a great team now Frank's lost his legs. How did that happen? I think I had this crash, this auto smash…when I was up there, motoring, cruising the North Circular, window down, but that wasn't him.

Dead eyed coaches, smashed up at the roadside, a spew of corpses at sixes and sevens. The emergency services stretched to breaking as twisted metal gives up its twisted ghosts. The sensuality of road accidents observed at a distance by mellifluous and spooky scribes, sitting on the verge guards. Or something.

I knew this guy see? He dreamed, had a brilliant head, was a bit of a worrier. He was a deadpan geezer. He was my brother I believe. I never knew him. I met him once, at a coffee bar in town. He was happy enough to be one of those people who were content for things to work without questioning *how* they worked. Clever geezer. And yet, with a perversity he'd always questioned but never come close to apprehending, he earned a living in Information. That's Frank. Information is the new thing. The New Virus! Rumour is Information. Authority is attained through the expert deployment of rumour-knowledge unlikely to be in the realm of his audience. But do they pay these people? I think not. Frank got his free breakfast, his limo'd entrée and return ticket, but they wouldn't pay him. Just expenses. We all hate people like that. His imagination so curtailed he thought he could get away with freeloading on that scale? Now we're reduced to a kind of freak show Mr. Memory number, where we have to exhibit him like the elephant man to the braying passersby. Road accidents on the north circular, Frank sets up his overhead projector, gets out his plastic wallet of transparency slides and holds forth to the entrapped and dying. He astounds them with his impertinent and rudely inappropriate delivery. His insensitive attitudinizing is breathtaking as they breathe their last, the emergency services' access blocked by the projection equipment.

This dream I had though (those dread words again) was utterly beautiful, like other dreams of grace, like nothing I remember or recall. A once only. Even now, I barely remember it, luckily for you. My stomach seems filled with glue, gorgeous, it's brandy warmth. I love her, and I just want to show her I love her because…she's just like me. *SHE'S JUST LIKE ME!!!! I LOVE HER BECAUSE SHE'S JUST LIKE ME! I LOVE HER BECAUSE SHE IS ME!!!!!!!!*

But I can't go back to school, where everybody, *everybody*, is just like me. Schools are full of homogeneity. You can't go back. My head came up from the table, bleary and thick. Drink got the better of me *again.* I felt for the glass, a refuge in sodden discomfort, which is better than clarity any old day. Clarity is work. The doors opened, and in my dream I saw the multitudes of my past re-enter. As each other. Life re-emerging in ghastly parody, my life reduced to a music hall parade, a spectral vaudeville including past acquaintances and friends in drag and in chains. Not like my life passing before my eyes. No, nothing like that. Everyone I'd known was a part of the scene, elements of a carefully drawn storyboard. It was in slow motion, a series of stop frame animated slides. I was too drunk to welcome them all properly, as I would have wished. No glad handing or back slapping. My script, rejected by all name producers, containing everybody (the dead too), was rejected out of hand. My old man I saw in death, laid out, the skin taut and pinched as the facial muscles relaxed, lending the visage a vulpine aspect. One of the undertakers at the funeral was smirking. Some joke eh? A stuffed ape, a polished dummy in top hat, smirking…But it was only an impression, a fractured picture, and I moved on under one corner of the coffin. I kept it to myself. I internalized. I created yet another dream in my dream factory. Dogcatcher, I am an undertaker murderer. I ripped his throat out, carried the entrails behind a hedge. I helped carry the coffin as expiation of my guilt. What guilt? The guilt we all carry for our parents. I still hadn't actualized. My jargon was as yet incomplete; my technical understanding of life's problems was very far from complete. The meaning was in the bits, so I didn't understand. I hadn't realized that he was just an old codger. An old geezer. And the undertaker was just his dad. I remembered breathless cycle rides home. My dad a stick in the spokes of the wheel. My cycle wheels with branches thrust through the spokes and me arse over tit, gulping in the verges.

My God inside the elephant head. My papier-mache head. Over and above the import, the dream head. I saw a fat boy, pig head stuck on fast. Farmyard noises awakened me on Jollity Farm. He moved on thick legs to the bar, ordered some brew or other. No brand-names in death dreams. We used to ride the pig. An undertaker if ever I saw one, moving my old man slowly through the crowds. No chance of re-union in the world as presently configured. That's all gone. I lost it somewhere. In this dream, I believed in the re-entry myth. Not now. Not this time. Dreams are different. I loved her. She sucked me. I planted little puckery kisses right on her pink little kisser. She flushed rosy crossfire at me. If I'd pushed it, she would have died for me. I have this power over women. Bit of a ladies' man me. Frank's a man's man. Maybe she did die. I never saw her again except on the backs of bus seats, legs apart. I know it. I loved her. I fucked her many times in my hot little imagination. I saw a tall man with free flowing bags, baggy legs, bagged at the knees, green and shiny like a bluebottle. A free-floating observation bereft of import. I couldn't look any more. The linear dream…too much…too much of an itch. No going back there now.

But now, now, I'm *sober*. Like never before. I had no drink to speak of last night or the night before. Clear head, sober in thought, direction-finding equipment in fair to good working order. I found that easier than I thought. All becomes clear and the blinking muse creeps back in again. But I'm making it sound like I have a drink problem. Nothing could be further from the truth. Drink is my first and last love. I stagger from pub to pub like a drunk, but it's only really a crazed mimesis. I'm acting out. I play at being a drunk. Alcohol actually doesn't affect me, except in my dreams. And I had this dream. I drink all sorts night and day. As and when I can get it. It's difficult though, making a fiction of the drink urge. It's very real. Very real. We spend days on end in pubs, getting our physiognomies tuned up for booze intake. Little veins burst in the nose and cheeks. Look like a lustrous deviant. A sodden metabolism that makes us ripe for imagined slights and fictions. Many atrophied gods hang out in bars and pubs, bemoaning their loss of divinity, like it was anyone else's fault but their own. The self-pity culture in full swing. The poetry of drink has been all but overlooked in the literature of dissipation. All literary boozers are taken to be self destructive, out of control, feckless, disturbed, chasing impossibility. But it's just an assumed persona, a technique for living, we're liquid engineers, it's just a way of getting through. Fictions sprout fully formed in the saturated brain. Made up grievances find easy expression in rat-arsed denial. They need their fictions. They have their dreams, fetishising drink as a liquid goddess. Bar-rooms echo to the sounds of boozed up writers, sparring with idiot inner voices. The inner delusions. The conviction that they drink for a *reason*. The fiction that the urge to drink is precipitated by an inner voice or some sort of turmoil. It's just a dream. I never had a past, let alone a future and yet I drink to cover up all sorts of personal horrors. Solipsistic binges that belie the emptiness within and without. Creating an urge to pro-create in place of recreation. Dreams, which find their way into airport books, are created in dipsomaniacal reflection. Testimonies to the difference between the real and the unreal, lies like that, they become Essex boys in extremis.

IN THE BROADWALK OF AUTO-EROTIC LOVE AND GRIEF (SHITKICKER'S DEMISE).

*Immigration Control CCTV recorded footage: B. Yapp **again** out of subjectivity, lost objective, head down, head in hands, moved to recapitulate, mask slipped…papier-mache crumpled…Again…he said to her and I said to you…*

…I love you because you're like *me*. Like me! I hate anyone younger than me, those who appears to be younger, fresher, more robust, whose DNA doesn't appear to have careened out of control. And also I hate those older ones. I hate anyone older than me, closer to god than me, more stigmatized than me. (He looks for an age at the elephant tattoo on his shoulder, in the mirror) It's people of my *exact* age to whom I really relate. Unfortunately, there aren't many that ageless. Anyway, I love anyone who aspires, with a passion, to agelessness. In constructing a personals ad I might suggest that I'm exceedingly charming in person and likely as not to convince you to have sex with me. My trunk is fully priapic. I furnish them with the old joke, the old line…but this sort of attention seeking artlessness won't necessarily put them off. I am Devilish. Arched eyebrow charm, that's me, minus the arched eyebrows. I have to paint on the eyebrows. And affect the trunk. I look better in make-up of a kind that's verging on the theatrical. Strongly etched lines, shading where necessary…coarse boned limestone tundra face, gray and wrinkled, frozen skin under mottled and warty make-up. A paintjob that shows me off to best effect. I've been in trouble with jealous husbands many times before, and need an effective disguise. On being disturbed at my cuckolding, I invoke lovehate. I affect a ready made masquerade stratagem, as enraged proprietorial cuckolds trip over upset trash cans, cleverly manipulated standard lamps, tipped over chests of drawers and chairs…all strewn in my wake as I beat hasty retreats from the boudoirs of my inamoratas. The anguished cries of enraged husbands and the thoroughly modern scorn of my lovers for these same husbands comfort me as I speed away on winged feet through the night. I levitate at full power outside other bedrooms, looking on with callous indifference at previously vacated love-scenes. My cheating disciples leave emotional distress and crocodile tears in their wake. I see boozy middle-aged women stocktaking lifetimes of accrued unhappinesses. Cynical, manipulative men-boys minutely calibrating moments in time, nano-computations, how long to hang around…ensure maximum emotional payoff is achieved, that the agonized female/male maelstrom is stirred up, that the gender matrix is breached, is fully milked before splitting to other unsatisfactory love-scenes. Sob love. It's all in the wrist action. Porno scenes of emotional distress imagined and story-boarded. I get my leg over for no pay. Movies circulate on the exploitation circuit, except no-one's exploiting me except me. I don't need to pay for loveaction. I inveigle my way into previously solid relationships by flirting over water-coolers with the objects of my especial desire. And pouring discreet scorn on the cuckolds. And then I'm away, over the fence and down the alley. I then sell the rights to the higher bidder. Budgets aren't big; I don't need a full crew of technicians, key grips and gaffers, soundmen, knob twiddlers, just in voyeuristic mimesis an imagination. My eyes hold the images literally until I forget them, which isn't going to be in a hurry.

My ambition is to die before I get older. Older than I already am that is. The compromised moment, the bridge between past and future. I hold it like ejaculate in my hands. I can't get any older. I'm re-treading. Re-entry. I'm stuck in more senses than one in this demi-mode. Until re-entry. I'm due a skin sloughing. Shuffle off into some other cauterized universe. In love with youth, my youth and my inability to become youthful, except in love-scenes, I see possibilities opening up before me. I have tended in the immediate and mid-past, in anterior lives, to wake up screaming *NOOOOOOOO!!!* In the wee small hours, in the dark watches, the long dark night of the soul.

By morning, I've usually fully regained my composure. But it takes a while. I mean this entirely seriously. The Panjandrum of Happiness fears death. Despite my suicide-assisted re-births, I fear and loathe death. There. I said it. And death comes to us if at all in the small hours. Thanatophobia is especially chronic after love-exertion. Lying there post-prandial, death visits in the small details. Apocryphal household gods get disturbing psychic visitations from past lovers, spectral figures, and are obliged to take deep breaths, to get a grip. Sometimes I see inside me and don't know what I'm looking at. Dionysia, will she stay with me, like me? Forever? Eternally? We're in it together, for the duration, for keeps, we're in it. When I look at the blank wall in front of me, eyes turned inwards and away, I fear that I'll always be like this. I worry that I'll lose the ability to re-energise; that re-birthing therapy, gnosis therapy won't be enough. That death really will mean *death* this time. It's insane I know but sometimes I really believe that the gods within and without are in tumult, that they're preternaturally incensed. I believe that the karmic flow has been dammed, that there won't be any more suicide therapy. I conjecture that my time will be counted in seconds. I am a doomed worrier, awaiting re-invention. A compromised and fretful banality at these moments, that's me. That's what I've become. In the long watches, a dead leg sickening for re-invigoration, watching the spotter choppers as they circle overhead.

I need someone exactly like me, some mirror image, a blueprint for Mythic Rejuvenescence. Will she stay with me forever? You are like me aren't you? Aren't you? Which is, I know, a preposterous question. We're all like each other. No difference essentially. We are now all together in the piss bowl, in civilized retro-chic. It's a question based on a misconception…I'm no longer here now…Frank - where are you? There is no such thing as unmitigated love of the unmediated self. No-one's going to stay behind, clearing up, making do… Dionysia has her own life to lead, her own spells to cast. Only one alter ego? Preposterous. And based on a 40s Hollywood romantic perversion. Dr. Jekyll as seen through the distorted lens. The Wolf man, Chaney transmogrifying into the other. The beauty of the beast. It's all so simplistic. The beauty within is burnished, without tarnished. I'm a composite, but I would say that. I've had so many chances at love. Loveaction is a prime motivation. Other peoples' wives. Repeatedly spurned. Feral couplings outside and inside, day in and day out. Now I literally cannot love, unless the object of my love is myself. I overlap, a convergence of interests. I refer to myself often enough in the 3rd person, like *he* said this, or *she* did that. It's difficult to maintain integrity in these matters. To remain grounded. To achieve subjective closure.

We (I, you) lose ourselves in subjectivity. There's no such thing as fakery. Real life and imagined life converge at the creative source. Give a man a fair chance and he'll invent a decent enough person to be - I have invented passable imitations. With horns. My friends and doctors regard me through quizzical and gently amused eyes. When I shapeshift in front of their very eyes, they affect not to have noticed. I'm humoured, big time. You give a man No Chance, and you'll end up with a monster. I am not a monster. I invented the image. I am the image. I speak in tongues as follows…

The self is clearly fragmented. Human beings are inveterate fictionalizers and our greatest creations are ourselves. Which by no means implies that these fictions are therefore somehow falsely realized. We create illusions…of all kinds… to make life… bearable. Those who inhale too deeply, indulge too fully, are called mad. Our ability as household gods to fictionalize is what separates us from the animals. Who have no notion that they belong to different genii. We are a genus apart…

…I say this in all seriousness, upon surfacing from unusually tedious dreamlife sorties, and I'm regarded – I regard myself - with amused contempt. Because of course I'm wrong. I couldn't be wronger about this. My associates look at me as though I'm taking the piss, having a laugh. Strangers make haste to cross the road as I move on caged feet towards them. Levitating over and beyond them, I observe quaint look-the-other-way denial manifesting itself in their brains. In the functional degraded hippocampus. They don't like the look of me, and I am therefore denied. I've achieved a kind of invisibility. People look the other way. They can't bear to see me up to my tricks again. I can levitate at full power for hours at a time and barely attract a second glance. People affect a studious indifference. Glances are shot, if at all, surreptitiously, candidly. But I don't have any treats, just a gift. A heaven sent gift of deniability. I am never where I'm claimed to have been, cuckolded husbands look in vain for forensic evidence. My thoughts are soon crippled if I try to force them in a direction that flies against their natural inclination. My dreams likewise. My dreams are full of pain and denial. My dream thoughts turn in on themselves.

People give me a wide birth, as you may imagine. I scry the future in plate-glass windows. Shop window displays delineate subdued, compressed, two-dimensional futures from whence all life has departed. But I see the shapes of future things in these flat-planed reflections. My distorted belly, phallus extended, acts as a kind of transmitter for future shocks, projecting me into my own visions. I've seen myself tomorrow and again lifted up along the Euston Rd, towards Gt. Portland St, flying horizontally, trailing whispers of visions behind. Traffic comes to a halt, or maybe is already stationary. Cars, trucks, buses, all bumper to bumper as I discern the patterns denied to everyone else through half-unseeing eyes. I see the way people avert their eyes, as though the better to hear. Listening in to the radio, vainglorious prattling and condescension of my voices a curiously comforting diversion from my reality. People in gridlock affect indifference as they're driven mad, and my salvation is literally metres away. The verdant green of Regent's Park, a clandestine destination, stone creatures stalking unreflective lunchers…advancing at a slow waddle, two rose sellers (£3 a bunch, £5 for three) are approaching me, elbowing aside pedestrians in statis. Spitting through swollen lips, emitting electricity, they make haste for the central reservation, brandishing the livid flora like sabres. The importunate motorists sit motionless, randomly fiddling with radio dials, stimulating voices, simulating diplomatic repose, glad to be out of the cold, a real bonus of private motoring…and at the same time fearing, mindful of the vulnerability of windscreen wipers. Impatient, lifeless with ennui, eyes glazed and fixed on the mid-distance, fingers tap tap tapping on the window frame, I like to think that I am in some small way responsible for the misery these motorists suffer. Because they don't think they're like anyone else, they think different rules apply. Their main lesson, still unlearnt, is that everybody is exactly the same. In all particulars. Their vehicles are 2-ton lies, shiny, beastly untruths. They're breaking the rules I set down eons ago. Rules I didn't make for my own benefit...And we hear the rumbling in the sky. I levitate again. A mechanized hum, pressure eases, I raise myself up. The rain comes down anew. Clouds scud past as time speeds up. Baker St is awash with beetle-like Sherlockians, attempting to divine the true location of the meta-fictional 221B. Further down near Portman Square, or up near the park? The Abbey National the most likely meta-fictional detective house or merely a frog-like cancerous lump? I'm drawn up and above Baker St because it's Regents Park where something is happening. Some filmable event, a suicide or something...

...(Shitkicker) Here. There's plenty here too...activist...strange old world - keep in touch...they're fucking...have a drink mate...nothing much happening yet...fucking the buildings...this is activism 21st century style...Distorted faces, fenced in and away from the main body...the police are charging, batons raised...buildings are distorted...away from the main thoroughfare...it's going down, going under...main chance now the buildings are fucked...gotta go to work, away from the main action...slip in the back way, over the fence...I can hear the elephants, trumpet...(Shitkicker, what's going down there?) Here. I am right here, right now. The cameras are in place. (Shitkicker, get out of there mate. Get out of there. Think of your family, your kids...) The elephants are charging...trampling activists... the carnage is indescribable...there's a camera pointing at me, I'm online... Here. Right here, right now...there's a tear, a tear in the fabric. This could be my last report from the front line. This feels like the last time. This is carnage...I haven't been here before. This is all new...a TV camera invading my privacy. Where's the therapist? Where's the producer? I am in front of the building...I can't get out...it's in front of me...the walls are collapsing... traffic is stationary...the cars are honking, the cars are trumpeting...I see the walls are coming down...any broadcastable material must be saved... but I'm here with a skeleton crew, no technology, old style box cameras, the police are going in batons raised. (Shitkicker.......SHITKICKER...... SHITKICKER!!!!!!!)

Jim Shitkicker, the BBC's own correspondent, outside Broadcasting

House, reporting on the embellished lunchtime hordes, the high priests of Masonic building-love, making with the buildings on Oxford St, was trampled to death in a stampede of elephants who'd been foraging on Hampstead Heath. Their instincts honed over millennia, alerted by sudden tumescence in the hippocampus, they were drawn as though magnetized to the heavily psycho-religious, pan-sexualized, happenings in Oxford Circus. They'd stampeded south through Belsize Park, down Haverstock Hill, turned right by some arcane instinct across the railway bridge into Primrose Hill and then on down into Regent's Park, hedges and bushes trampled and stamped on. The denizens of the zoological gardens became alarmed and set up a caterwauling, a grunting, a twittering, a bellowing and a roaring. This music of alarm was adjoined in rhythmic intensity by loud atonal guitar riffs, parts played in different keys and time stamps, played as though learned from transcribed improvisations. The ground had rumbled and rocked. Shitkicker had been on top of Broadcasting House. Some cameramen had observed him, seemingly in conversation with a masked figure, one of the building fuckers who'd gained access to the roof, we thought at the time. In his excitement leaning out over the parapet apparently to achieve a better view, so we thought, he'd suddenly seemed to lose his balance. He'd been a much loved correspondent... richly gravelly in tone, at once avuncular, cod-curmudgeonly and yet archly impertinent and abrasive in dealing with recalcitrant and evasive politicians and other degraded public figures. A correspondent at heart, however, his elongated nose for the real news always seemed to lead him to the heart of events. His devotion both to a fine sense of duty and to the sound of his own voice will be missed by all who knew him. A statue to the memory of Jim Shitkicker will be erected on Broad Walk in Regent's Park, in sight of the elephant enclosure. Those who were in the park at the time have testified in writing to the overwhelming feelings of emotional bereavement they experienced in that wide thoroughfare during these events.

It was the Broad Walk of Love/Grief. Many witnesses have attested that they personally were, inexplicably, consumed with intolerable and heartfelt grief for a figure they knew, and could only know, by proxy. His martyrdom to the cause of promoted life struck a chord within them so deep and reverbatory that they were quite overcome with grief. They saw the herds that lumbered southward taking Shitkicker with them. He was borne away by the herd, a spectral trumpeting presence, an ethereal emanation of mammalian numinosity. There was an electrical surge as they passed, short-circuiting all power supplies in the immediate vicinity. They were passing through the fissured space, drawn there by the re-birthers' building-love, a viable conduit to the future or past. The fissured space of the present suddenly tangible to all who witnessed the event. Not sex magick, but sex-elephant love. The transcendence of the moment was palpable. Heavily modulated and overdriven blues, slide guitar phrasings up in the mix, bass clarinet call and counter call, was heard as though in a dream. People looked at each other, fell into reveries, devotional trances. A window similar to that last seen at the airport was opened, a moment when the fractured past co-mingled with the profane present and the numinous future. Love was in the air. Frank was heard to croon a tune or two. A broken cracked voice wilting in the burnt air. Partners re-affirmed marriage vows, spontaneous copulation was non-judgmentally observed to take place between in-love couples, snaky trunk coils were entwined, and the trumpeting in the air was mixed with the keening of those who had just ditched unfaithful girlfriends or feckless boyfriends. Loveless cynics wept openly. It was an Arcadian scene, a prelapsarian dream. A Gnostic devotional template.

We bottled it. I bottled it. I am already in love. The population in trance, a chance to re-configure. Lost almost immediately. A potentially cinema friendly experience, the elephants were nonetheless un-filmable. No camera crews present at the time were able to catch the moment exactly as it happened. Exposed footage was revealed as an aphasic blur, soundtracks were drowned in white noise through which could be heard a faint but largely indecipherable trumpeting. The strangeness of the day was felt for some time afterwards. The civic authorities bottled it. The whole mood of the country underwent a change, as elucidated in the park, which could never have been predicted from the limited popularity of a much-loved broadcaster. The buildings in Oxford Circus that had been host to the erotically aroused re-birthers were enshrined as places of religious retreat. The BBC was re-consecrated as a Holy Place. And the crowds of baseball capped would-be starlets and ghosts began to retrace their steps, negotiating a widdershins course down Portland Place, back up Great Portland St, returning into the dark night whence they came. The age of the megaphone personality is dead upon us. The lease for religious revival meetings at Wembley stadium has been renewed, thus saving the uncomfortable pile from demolition. Sports take a back seat, as does corporate mid-Atlantic rock. It is now host venue to weekly Elephant Gnosis revivals and happenings. The agents of religious learning and theological teachings and pitchers of sitcom ideas to the networks are quids in. Educational courses based on the new mood abroad are advertised and parts are available in new plays and films, hurriedly scripted to capitalize on phony mammalian religious devotion and attendant ironic takes on same. White elephants are rife, but it's a start. People look at each other and they look into mirrors. They see themselves and they see themselves transformed. They see haircuts for which they never asked. They hear the buzzing of electric razors and the swish of barbers' tunics. Time to clock out. It's love, because you're *all* like me. I am the sultan of seismic love-action, mashing up the over emotional pulp, of change for change's sake. I open the gates of the kingdom and everyone is changed. The mask is slipped.

THE ANTI-GRAVITY MAN/LONDON, MY LONDON.

I n the rundown lobby, I sit on a couch upholstered in drab gray wrinkled fabric and wait as patiently as I can. I know that I've swum oceans, that I have come 10,000 miles on this far-fetched, far-flung pilgrimage - at which point a man in a navy blue duffle coat and sneakers walks purposefully into the lobby.

This is Eugene P. He's come to explain the situation to me, and to the publishers. The word is our work is beyond the scope of these types. It's nothing but local gossip though, we assume. Servants, postmen and the like; and the occasional long haired gent from London. There is nothing you can put your finger on though. But Eugene is the self styled superconductor of bad intent, a florid and exuberant household god, yellow pages advertised. Usually, although not today, he affects theatrical cape and walking cane, and is a levitator par excellence. He's the anti-gravity man and therefore has trouble appearing before the skeptics at immigration in civilian garb. Consequently we're in another waiting room, a soviet style Holiday Inn conference room…Maybe he can put in a word for Dionysia as well, adding scientific ballast to her claims of torsion field disturbance in surplus-charged tourist destinations. The gray drabness of the couch finds an echo in the coarsely rutted complexion of my elephant mask. Meanwhile, an overhead projector scrolls text of Dionysia's latest book - a tourist guide to London written circa the last celebrity crash, the numinous funeral of James Shitkicker esq. - at pedestrian speed and we all fix our attention on the characters, aided by soft piped jazz…

London My London/Dionysia Triantafillou: A Numinous Account of Pre-Birthed London.

You'll want to know this. Why it is you get prickly. Get hot and frustrated, *suffer underground languor, heavy sky torpor, grey sky ennui, sheer underground* *terror,* **and** *why no-one listens to you. People don't even see you in London. Tunnel* *vision is the perspective of choice for the citizenry. London skies, grey and overbearing,* *are not conducive to thought. It's murky, muggy, even when the sun shines. Winds* *don't blow, excepting of course the electrical winds, minor disturbances in the* *torsion fields. The obscure unseen pressure fields, electricity, sap the energy of the* *most resolute...*

---The projector stops, the electricity having failed. It's my experience too. We agree on everything. Virtually everything. Virtual unanimity. It's as if we are all as one...and the projector hums once again into life---

...even natural athletes are reduced to sucking in oxygen in desperation. *Fat men gulp and stumble. There's muggy electricity everywhere, blowing wild into* *the wind vortices, the streets aflutter with thoughtlessly discarded refuse, the winds* *sucking vital energy away from the crepuscular hordes. Many first time tourists are* *literally disgusted every time they step outside. The citizens of the city move to and* *fro like reclaimed dodgems, bump into each other, the crackle and hiss of electricity* *horribly tangible. There's no air here, just bleeding streets, tumescent tourist piles* *and scabby residential hutches accumulating lifelessness, fetid dormitory streets* *evincing a cultish village ambience. Dross appears to accumulate in extrinsic as well* *as intrinsic appurtenances, established behaviour patterns. Litter is everywhere.* *London is, in fact, for the life affirming, a lifeless cesspit kept afloat only by energy* *input from twittish media apologists, a kind of continual civic ECT, itself a cause* *of torsion field disturbances.* (Dionysia, as you can see, doesn't exactly mince her words) *We know these apologists are just lifting their skirts to the city's occult energy* *(money) gods. To the pyramid atop Canary Wharf...that's where the energy is* *produced, where it's at. Now triple pronged, the plan is almost complete. Tourists are* *generally guided away from these baleful erections, their phallic audacity considered* *by the authorities as just too sacred for extended perusal. It's the pinnacle of money* *worship, Satan brow beating the whole city, flashing his gleaming smile every 5* *seconds. His acolytes doing deals that keep them in energy credit. The over stated* *tourist destinations meanwhile are crawling, notwithstanding the uncomfortable* *fact of the degree of difficulty in approach, the methods of transportation thereto*

being distinctly understated. Running on empty. Railway termini spewing out cashcow whores. Transport to the money centers is ironically, trouble free. Civic chaos is what it is.

(She has a way with words eh? A kind of fiery civic outrage fuels her contempt, something I've always worshipped in her...Anyway, my money's on the whole thing going tits up. The provinces would hold the key without me. Lucky I'm back eh? Lucky for me and for some. London My London. Back in the driving seat, a mythic rejuvenessence, elephant tracks staled through under use. My work's cut out for me but with God's help...Meanwhile Eugene, who has been eyeing us quizzically, has started murmuring his own catechism of intent, his voice co-mingling with that of the voice synthesizer giving tongue on Dionysia's behalf)

...Normally there are two spheres and a spark jumps between them. Now imagine the spheres are flat surfaces, superconductors, one of them a coil or O-ring. Under specific conditions, applying resonating fields and composite superconducting coatings, we can organize the energy discharge in such a way that it goes through the center of the electrode, accompanied by gravitation phenomena - reflecting gravitational waves that spread through the walls and hit objects on the floors below, knocking them over...the second generation of flying machines will reflect gravity waves and will be small, light, and fast, like UFOs. I have achieved impulse reflection; now the task is to make it work continuously...

He sounds completely sober, serious, matter-of-fact. Between the two of them, their voices achieving an elliptical rhythmic tension, a new liturgy is hammered out flat. But it occurs to me that the need is because we've all got our own problems. This again is Dionysia's angle. God bless her. I see what she means when she says that the sky shelters its own, heaving lugubrious static charges over the cityscape. Languid strolling in the dank underbelly is right out. Not an option, except for the darkly obsessed. Anyway back to Dionysia...

Pedestrians, enraged by car fumes and other irritants, walking static charges, are just boiling with rage. Shop fronts jostle with over excited punters bearing cell-phones as heraldic insignia, txting obtuse messages to each other.

Doormen flex their insecure status in your face. Restaurants are full of pipe cleaner types, or power- lunchers loading up at the trough, unpleasantly coiffed city slickers and their frog-like girlfriends/boyfriends. Celebrity chefs do time here on TV, fat tongued boys pretending to a gaucherie that's more than enough to put you off your dinner, anxious lest their credibility is shot to shit by a too overt display of contrived anger, nervous lest their real clients get a whiff of their bombastic need for cheap celebrity. No one wants to be associated with some loser who just wants to be noticed…some pre-gnostic simian with bad teeth and a thick tongue…

All delegates generally agree over the iced water and hors d'oeuvres, as we dance a subtle conga of deference to the man who holds our destiny in his gravity free hands, that noticing, seeing, is more than ever the primary contemporary currency. Seeing is the default mode, the consensual lingua franca. We're all lookers, more than listeners. Eyeballs take it all in. Eyes everywhere, actually just too many eyes taking you in. Eyes that notice you in peripheral vision, glances are shot surreptitiously. Obsessed eyes in a line, offering baleful challenge, misplaced eyeballing. Synapses shudder and spit in sympathetic overload. The eyes track like smart weapons with the didactic import of laser beams. No one, least of all schools, teaches the meaning of looking. People gawp unreflectively and idly. Looking is now an almost completely vapid activity, disguising clandestine intent. People fail to acknowledge the meaning of under-contextualized scrutiny. Eugene's point, readily agreed on by the rest of us, is that people literally cannot see in front of their noses. He therefore posits levitation as survival technique. Snowblind, they see, but they fail to see. And there's a configuration more suited to modern journalism, to the sappy look-at-me-ma me-me-me effusions of the journo. The projector rolls on…

Everyone wants both to notice, the all seeing London Eye a metaphor literally dumped from heaven in the heart of the Capitol, and to be noticed. You can't get a slice, even a small piece, of pure privacy for love. It's Rip off city, ripping off your time as well as your money, London's a stand up act from hell. Every gormless dolt is a comedian, eyes gleaming, eyebrows arched. Everyone's funny. Everyone's a comedian. It's grueling and it's wearisome. The glimmer in the eye of the standup skewers any attempt at laughter. There is no comedy, as all our best comedians instinctively know. Just the hacks and attention seekers remain, tugging at your nerve ends, begging your indulgence. Non-Personality passes un-remarked as prime currency. No one cares that London's comedians and cabbies are no longer funny, least of all the city authorities. They actively encourage a weary fatalism in the tourist body, a long-suffering acceptance. Laughter is pyrrhic for the authorities. Therefore funny is something of a faux pas in this city. Unfunny comedians with their sponsored personalities may be enough to pull in the out of towners and the truffle hog cultural tourists, but even the sly, smug commentators who know they're above it all see that they're all in the game together. It's a seamless feat of blind sighted robbery.

Suddenly Nobby Wyse the cabbie (and sometime fruiterer) our courier, is up on his club feet. He's overwrought. The effects of the flight are still with him. He needs more water. And sandwiches. My need to love, on the other hand, outruns the otherwise overwhelming urge to mime muscular strength for the docs. And my shaman (Abrahams) tells me he's only trying to further his own career, to make me his cause celebre…I am the main atomic threat in his arsenal of delusionals. This is what I need to hide from Eugene P. I need him on board and so I'm happy to act out for him. My need for levitation techniques and good character references is primary. Once he's on board it's a matter of irrelevance that my delusions (as he terms them) show Ahab in a good light. My very presence on the streets, appearing in reflection in shop windows, is an affront to his so-called professional integrity. So, he asserts, I need locking up, restraining. An assertion that of course I endorse. Anything for the career of a friend and fellow witch doctor, a shamanic colleague. My double bluff as usual disconcerts the old fraud.

And so I show him, and therefore myself, in a very good light. I have first to be seen about town, with a girl on each arm, so that he can show the world how he copes with the likes of me. I show off with abandon at paparazzi events, celebrity parties, falling with charm and distinction into gutters as the night wears on. I am obliged for the sake of his camera to literally fall out of nightclubs, legless, punching and kicking out at photographers and insulting passers-by, so that he can seem to pick up the pieces. A recklessly laughable pantomime, but it gets me out and about. And in the papers. It's all character ballast. My character as a reckless devil-may-care, but also as a dangerous delusional, is by degrees thus established in the public mind. I appear in the gossip pages as proof that he knows what he's doing. I have obligatory gay escorts as well, so my appeal is literally all encompassing. If I weren't some sort of auto-shaman I'd need an agent, just to protect my own interests. Just to reap the rewards for him. To guard against abuse, as you'd ensure the safety of children. But I am my own agent. I do all my own bookings, and I pay myself 10% of everything I earn. I make smug appearances with Ahab on TV, browbeating unruly hacks who dare question our impeccable and above board professional relationship. I have sex on a more or less consistent basis. People pay me just to look at them. I touch them where it hurts.

I now warm to my theme. I hope to convince Eugene of my bona fides. I'm angling for credibility…now, sex. No one has sex at 40. Even 20's pushing it. At one stage, he observes, the gay Mr. Massive reportedly considered having a baby with the lesbian actress Jackie Chunder. He remarked that the advantage of being in a mutually incompatible relationship, sexually speaking, with procreation in mind is that at two removes, the sexual partner actually *becomes* the object of desire. Gay man + gay woman is the perfect sexual combination in anyone's book. Or at any rate I affected to see things his way…we are still, as a species, obsessed with sex in *any* form. People only need to think about it. To reiterate obsolete, forgotten obsessions. But it is, for most people, all over now. Thinking, in many cases, has to be enough, because even though sex doesn't discriminate, perfidious consciousness does. The terror of rejection coupled with the terror of body penetration. Rubs both ways. But Sex is for everyone. The tabs, the heavies, the glossies, the rags are all filled with *SEX*. It's fucking everywhere! Sex as gardening, and as kitchen culture. Mediterranean culture grafted on, so the industry can lie through its teeth that London is *SEXY*. The very airwaves hum with words of protestant obloquy. We may be obsessed by it, but that doesn't mean we can do anything about it. The obsession itself renders the action virtually obsolete. The obsession can only be tended, orchid like in the fetid heat of desire, if you don't get enough of it. Obsession gets us off, hence the sex-porn industry. Actually doing it ruins the mood. But nonetheless, sex is in the buildings, objectum-sexuality. The Oxford Circus building fuckers were in this reading of events responding to an objective need. And then, from the overhead…*when did you last re-examine your life? Never? Why not? It doesn't come knocking.*

Ignoring the interruption I develop my themes. My life is pre-ordained narrative. When fame beckoned, or when real people became the norm as providers of vicarious obsession on TV. Do I really care about 10 people shacked up in a media safe house? 70 grand is nothing, but to be gawped at by outsiders for 10 weeks…is it worth it? I'd say so. I'd say it's worth it for us. Further, I'd go further. So nothing happens? That's the point. People's real insecurities/weaknesses/dysfunctions revealed minutely, by degrees. It's a slow death, but better than actually executing people, as other cultures do in other contexts. Anyone who can argue against the spectacle of random image generation revealing inner vacuity *FOR THE BENEFIT OF MILLIONS* just doesn't have any sense of fun. I must see these people through. It's me they'll look to in post-celeb desperation. Just to be looked at, pored over, it's enough. Not for us though eh? We have other, higher standards. I've shacked up with Dionysia, with destiny. We've our own moral imperatives haven't we? No relativistic weasel words or concepts cloud our outlook. We know knowledge is useless, unless gleaned from TV. We *know* expertise is over rated. We're *aware* that destiny is there for the taking. We still have obsession. Still, I walked down streets clogged with sex rubbish. And people images. Random images, generated from the central image banks, images of profane sex-rubbish. I fall silent, breathing heavily, a spent force…

Back to Dionysia…*Destiny for London would appear to exist in the interstices between the serious and the not so serious. The broadband spectrum of modern life in which everyone has an angle, all humourous bases have been covered and every Tom Dick and Harry is a comedian. Visitors to the city should be acutely aware that all pathetic exhibitionists have been green lighted, offered carte blanche to advertise their personal cravings for attention in all media, all the time. We've reached actual meltdown here. Laughing's no longer the point. Rumour is the point. Cliquey internet discussion groups are smug and self congratulatory in getting the joke, not realizing they ARE the joke. Needless to say,*

London is heaving with internet geeks. More and more internet cafes are receiving unconditional planning permission.

Yes yes...I know it was always going to go that way. There are precedents; the ennobled talentless making pushiness an end in itself... and these crimes were perpetrated, or conceived at any rate, well over 40 years ago. But still, you might think, might you not, that we should have all got a bit wiser, a bit more clued up, instead of merely cleverer, in the meantime? Did we view it as a warning, a nuclear alarm? No, we didn't think it mattered that much. Everyone sitting here...in this room before me now... even now you probably harbour a certain sneaking, grudging admiration for the chutzpah of the talentless, a certain suspicious contempt for the really talented, those rare individuals who you'd never in a million years be able to emulate. Inane pushiness, allied to a will of steel, is what gets you further now; it's the motor of our essential contempt for quality. We are, as you know, all potential stars now. Come on in, the water's lovely. We are constantly bathed in paradoxical cathode ray light. My sphere of influence is massive. I *am* a political heavyweight. I *am* a TV chef. I know the correct temperature both at which to boil eggs and to fry public figures. My earpiece still crackles and hums with immoderate laughter as yet another public servant is tickled up for ridicule. I look on scornfully, down my nose, as public figures appear ridiculous in attempting to appear serious...but Wyse is now falling asleep, and rather than interrupt my flow and wake him, I decide to press on with the rest of my testimony...

My putative sphere of influence is something that's potentially more or less boundless. I've given birth, in gravitational extremis, to at least 2 million new clued up citizens. All media savvy. We all star...all the time. I am not renowned for my modesty, so I'll say it. I did it. My technical surveillance was all that was needed. I operated my own camcorder. I directed my own movies. They're all in the movie. I took the star system, and made it accessible, relevant to the denizens of the Thames Valley, the inhabitants of the Hertfordshire corridor, the fauna of the Essex badlands. All those clubbers, commuters, were stars of their own movies. I directed them. They owe their fame to me. We're always in convoy now. Out on the shingle, awaiting the moment of re-entry. But the logistics of movie making are enough to make your eyes water. You cannot insure a movie these days unless it's underwritten with new mafia money. Money laundered through Paris and Rome and all points east. It's East of Hollywood. Private jets sear the skies, snake through the ether carrying Spielbergs and Geffens to impossibly mundane locations. Servants and lackeys live expansively. Dine out on anecdotes about the habits of celebrities.

The serious/not serious paradox, by which the joke needs contextualising, needs to be allowed room to breathe on different levels, has been allowed to become entrenched. Words that tend to drift in and out of focus are suddenly *funny.* Far from becoming wiser, better able to contextualise, we have drifted. We're in the backdraft. Creativity, in London, is at an *all time low.* Sloppy crud…less wise, more stupid, we're less able to make non-relative value judgments, more inclined to assume that any old rubbish is acceptable. We have become bed wetters. Our snaky fantasies find expression in incontinent dreams. We are, at best, collusive in the process of attempting to evade the moral consequences of our actions. We are *obsessed* by sex, ignoring the uncomfortable truth that sex is unlikely to be the very first of our worries. And ignoring the fact that obsession is merely a cancerous form of disgust. My pride is hurt. These cokeheads and bitches are less wise, less inclined to wisdom. It's not what we want is it? We need more not less hopeless personalities clamouring for attention. Don't we? Now of all times? And despite the advantages of growing up wise, or wise capable, we give these bastards houseroom. What's going on? Destiny is in our hands. I didn't create this system for another man, the fertile conditions of celebrity for these ends. It was meant to be a leveling up, not a leveling down. Warholian schtick times 10. All beautiful people star in their own movies, or not at all.

Elephant images are now ad-mixing with the text on screen: *But instead, it embraces the speeded up world of longer working hours, elongated spasms of debauched stupidity, alternating with head wrangling sessions at the terminal wank bank, the spam filled bandwidth streams. All pretty much redundant conceits. Only wankers, it seems, fetid fantasists in the City precincts, need to get that much money that badly that they'll buy into these damp dreams. No necessity to work now that survival is assured. Why bother working, when the fruits of that labour are so unworthy of possession. But "work" they do, for share options, packages including dismal self-disgust. City boys in loafers are revealed as the worthless descendents/progeny of space/time filled hippies of 30 years ago, children of debased and unworkable fantasists, hedonistic access/excess merchants. One off the wrist meat jockeys. Girls in offices are now just wanking machines. No office orifice that can't be filled with cheap dayglo condom. Five-knuckle shuffle, into the cavernous machinery of the cyber sphere, digitized crypto porn. Spaniel men slither around the streets, and are fawned over in excessively flattering magazine portrayals as worthy of aspiration. Big over emphasized opinion pieces suggesting, in the very act of analysis of what was wrong, what was right about it all. The tourist trade cannot, I venture, stand up under much more of this pressure. Tourists look down their noses, already look to points further east. London can't grow, there's no room. London is, in psychological terms, stuck at a stage of development that we must identify with the adolescent.*

And I think, how right she is. My beautiful wife, claws out, eyes blazing. The machine is now spitting, humming, emitting autoerotic sparks, controlling the room. Righteous anger. She's a better writer than she's given credit for eh? She can really dish it out. She has nailed it. The city avidly consumes profane myths when I've already provided better, *realer* myths. Pre-crash myths that invoke a falsely historicized crypto-biography that doesn't pay heed to reality. Profane myths that don't even mention elephants, or gravity disturbance. So the streets just *fill up* with dead mythic matter, accumulated ennui and depreciated electricity. Real myths involve Gods, and conflicts between Good and Evil. Good coffee/bad coffee, the cappuccino culture express, young professionals, IT ingénues who can't tell you what they *really* do for a living. Where they fit in the great pan-glottal-stop of globalised yob culture, with Englishness at its epicentre. They don't know. They just read up on their destinies in magazines. Burnished heritage yobs, St. George the Angevin on dragon slaying benders of corporate excess. English yobs are central, the boiling core of fractured alienation, hedonism. They are now on the march. Round the orbital fuelled by E-type jaggedness, over the hills and far away. To some crazy field…back then…specious template…ravers with club blindness and hearts full of spacey altruism. The blissed out togetherness…a soothing lie. When I can supply lies that are *real* fun. Re-entry lies. Smoothed down, accessorized, playful gender games, no gender, and no gender specificity, attractive to those who no longer have any idea how to be men, or indeed women. Just a playful mass of spaced out keyboard tappers, moving money and rumour from A to B and back again. Headspace now uniquely, in the context of history, empty. Literary gents just squabble, up and at 'em, city boys ruck in east end pubs. Grotesque wannabe thespians, wielders of power close to the 7th circle, polished…still… ex-schoolboys, nervous of your millions, jealous of your influence…

I pause for breath. This is all leading back to the 70s. I see in Eugene a man who appreciates the importance of dressing up, of cutting a dash, of showing off. Everything leads, like roads to Rome, back to the 70s. The first and last explosion, the last redoubt of my previous re-entry, the apotheosis of my frivolous intent. Unbeknown to their dads and in some cases granddads, the grand-dada Glam experience had been the apotheosis of this sort of blissful playfulness 25 years earlier. If only the old goats, multi-coloured satyrs of comic excess and over statement, had realized it at the time. The kiddies' dressing up box, envisaged by my cohorts, gave birth to and green lighted the insane and fetishistic infantilism of grown men in make-up, wizard capes and platform boots, men who truly made that dazzling epoch the brightest and the richest and the most immaculately realized of times. Before oil prices dropped the bottom out of the world's self-satisfaction, and even allowing the 60s hangover, the 70s were the best of times. The city's energy fields at that time weren't silted up with rogue electricity, it was too expensive. Just too expensive. Not enough to go around. And the glitter and tinfoil/ spandex acted as great conductive material. We made our own entertainment there, in the darkness of the 3-day week. We dressed up out of boxes and then stood on boxes. We strapped on extravagantly designed guitars like sci-fi accoutrements and we rocked. Those lucky enough to have grown up in the 70s were forever reminding themselves, the first warless generation…no fighters…strikers and football players, would-be boozers and non-contracted out council refuse men, that they were the pioneers, the first anti-radical snakes out of the basket, the primary and pre-eminent tricksters in pre-ironic schtick. The first makers of anti-history. Growing up in the 70s meant never having to grow up *at all.* Free of electricity. The main players in the fall out from mawkish idealism and misplaced eco-optimism, they knew things were shit, and rejoiced. Anti-radical!

I turn to my wife…

Dionysia, you need to know this. You need to know this. You already know this. I had it good. Anti-radical. That's why I *am* good. That's why you love me. Everyone loved an aspect of me. You are the best advert for this country, for me. I am a living template, a tourist magnet. I initiate the uninitiated; I inaugurate marches around the orbital and all divinely consecrated elephant trails. Everyone was in on it. I put this show on for you. And you understand. A fabulous anarchy, 6 years before…public inclusivity …punk…hyper realized, publicized anarchy. The revolution in taste was, as you know, over by '72, the taste for serious consideration of life's many and manifold ills out of date. All the earnest pipe suckers and rock critic academics were hatched in the 60s, cultural imperialists, "I claim this cultural movement for the highbrow"…actions without consequences, the misuse of the word 'liberal', the misuse of words generally with impunity…these chic revolutionaries, documenters of history's slipstream where "secret" histories are played out…history which is parodied to distraction by men in glitter capes and spandex. Former plumbers, postmen, furniture polishers, firemen, removal men, Hendrix look-alikes, groovy fuckers, pimps, agents, moustachioed civil servants, embryonic androgynes, all took a look at their groovy elder brothers, laughed up their sleeves and decided that the appurtenances of frivolity were more appropriate as an enduring metaphor for newly mythic life. And then, as life itself. Incantational frivolity, as men in tights looked around for the exit door. The door to the reckless age of mutual consent. Suddenly everyone's equally grown up. Kids are sagely regarded and regard their elders sagely. Kids more wised up than the parents, in the same non-consequential vortex. Parents, fellow travelers, sentimental for an orthodoxy they were, luckily for them, never subjected to. They never had to take the consequences of their rhetoric. I look around, surveying the post frivolous generations, and those younger than me seem somehow the same age as me.

Older even. Immeasurably older. I cannot see the young at heart any more. The young are prematurely old, but without the wisdom that age brings. Fertile ground, feckless to a high degree. They just don't have the balls that we did. We died in vain for them. In the trenches of attritional camp warfare. We fought for the right to be frivolous. They merely are frivolous. (Wyse stifles a yawn, blinks, looks meaningfully at the screen…of course, I see what he means. I now espouse the essential inconsequentiality at the very heart of mythic life). I am a corporate dragon slayer for cheap thrills. No more, no less. My kids think I'm a groovy bastard. Which I am.

Eugene, I now live alone, because no one will put up with me. Except Dionysia. And the magic's gone out of it now. When she was Frank's it was kind of exciting but…what am I saying? Dionysia is *everything* to me. Everything. All frivolous avenues have been closed. My children, all 2 million of them, need the cheque, but not the company of the account holder. It's been ages since that moment occurred. The moment when you realize you've already thought something, an intangible, the thing just beyond your mental field of vision, that need not be thought of again. The desperate near recall of what it was that showed you the answer. It's gone. It ain't coming back. My children, all two million of them, I pretend to relate to. They know me, but only as a shell of a figure in their peripheral vision. Doc Abrahams knew. He knew something I didn't. I wear the mask both out of deference to him and as emblem of my reborn, re-mythologised status. (I'm hoping here that Eugene doesn't look to closely, below the surface, below the elephant mask).

Anyway, back to the 70s. Again. That moment of recall. Party time for the young at heart. Never before had the mechanics of fun been so overtly demonstrated. Mirror hats and outré guitar shapes kept company with primary colour face paint; candy riffs and bubble stomp conspired to keep the nation's pre-birthers in a spin. Dance floors that had been initially weakened in wartime became compromised to a dangerous degree during Slade concerts. Guitarists strummed in overt parody of the act of onanism, without for a moment doubting the unironic content of mechanical repetition. Wankers, guitarists, straightforward tautology. Real/hyper-real. Platform boots, foolish haircuts, eye shadow. We dressed up like dogs' dinners, slapping on the rouge and grease paint. Meta-levels of artlessness were paradoxically attained. No need for spurious sexual context, or unambiguous commentary. Animated looning, postulating a metaphysics of braggadocio. They were all yesterday's parties. My children and those still to come will never now dance like they danced. Of course it couldn't last. The paper thin culture, translucent and brittle, illuminated by excess, couldn't stand that much frivolity without going into a tailspin of over concerned, over actualized context, message, and social context. Contextualised to death by academics, meaning was imposed from without by the newly educated, the undergraduates of pop theory. Red bricks literally spewed out pop theses, while Oxbridge still supplied bespectacled junior moguls, and the glum suburban satellites of major cities acted as cultural midwives to a new breed of hipster journos, manqué class warriors, fat birds from Bristol, Cuban-healed tossers, bedroom onanists and writers of letters to the rock press. And also to the new rock stars themselves. No longer ex-postmen, these sweaty, pallid creatures were devotees of Oscar, would be Huysmanses, decadents in training, languid effete aesthetes, trainee geniuses in polo necks, be-quiffed and shimmering with self regard, speccy geniuses, somehow *different* from their peers. No girlfriends or boyfriends for the new pop aristocracy, taking pop music out of the disco and into the bedroom. Single beds, sweaty socks, dreams of pop stardom, at once dragging the meaning out of dreams...

They see I'm flagging. Billy, Nobby, Sapper, they look at their watches, yawn, stretch with comic exaggeration. They melt into the functional seating. I'm priapic, striding back and forth, like a tiger. They need to know this, these tie-dyed morons, that life eventually, without the mythmakers, becomes too heavy to escape from. Escape velocity becomes impossible. Them up there beyond the orbital, up in Bletchley, way *way* beyond the orbital, those mythical code breakers, encryption experts literally won the war. Single-handed. Or mob handed. Credit where it's due. Now, the multifarious tribes of neo-hippies and bankers grow large on the proceeds of 55 years of peace in their time. Land usage was not the issue. Huge lapses in perspective were the issue. Raves were for wankers right?

10,000,000 words expended, Eugene is struggling to remain conscious, and they're running into each other and away with the meaning. I haven't prepared my presentation in anything like as professional a manner as has Dionysia. She's the pro's pro. An A-list personage. My dreamlover. Still no meaning...Abrahams back yet? Gone away, holidaying on the continent. 3 holidays a year. At least. In this fractured age, nothing will mean that much *ever again*. Holidays from meaning. He doesn't trust me. I'm just a showcase. In my mask. The tank's almost empty. We're inter-political. I've had my fill of it. For now. I've become truly concerned that the young at heart will never ever have to face their own mortality. They'll all live forever in cyberspace. But anyway, this is linear time. I'm talking about the other sort. Time's out for the young. There are no more boundaries, no border controls. Across the universe there are currents to be ridden, fantasies I wish to indulge, parties at which I intend to get drunk. The young at heart know they've got it made. They're in love with the future, because the future is theirs. They live for the future, the green light. Nothing's a problem for future generations because they have it all on tape. Ambitions are taken as read; the world is my oyster, my personal biosphere, my zone of control. I've taken out cultural leases in all major control centres; faked birth certificates, passports. The capitals of the world are under one metaphorical roof. It's now, with Eugene's help and with God's blessing, my city. *MY* London. I take it, all of it. The energy fields, silted up with unused electricity, are key. If I haven't yet made my meaning clear to the unseen energy vampires who we've been assured are behind and beyond the projector wall (which is still playing tunes and spontaneously re-mixing Dionysia's epochal words concerning London's problems) I take electricity away from the earth, where it can do harm. London is dead. And all points east and west. Deader than dead. All cities need re-invention. Re-mythologising. A latter-day reverse Columbus, re-tracing his steps through history, must sail down the Fleet in a tea chest...re-discover the source. A new John (or Simon) Dee must scry alternative futures. I'm opening the gates. The electricity is being channeled at last. We only have one chance at this. The inhabitants must of course all die, figuratively, to be re-born. Die or leave in giant arks. Sail away down the Thames, out into the channel and away. Or on planes bound for Eldorado. Air stewardesses will have their work cut out, what with air rage all the rage, for the Exodus must be mythical and epic. Great tribal movements, populations on the move on devotional repetitive forced marches, in train around the ex-bus lanes.

Now, with Eugene P's (forged) endorsement and character reference in the bag, I have to re-discover the unexceptional in time. My mission, to re-energise. I must discover the *good* if not the exceptional in me. My forebears were not aware of it, they never are. Parents know jack shit. That's the point of them. Not to know things, to be unaware. I've gone around the world, racking up the air miles. I have interests all over, businesses to attend to. On brogued feet, quietly dressed, thin pencil moustache and slicked down hair, I enter the departure lounge, checked in and boozed up. I see my own sort as eminently avoidable. I don't wish to be involved in any sort of competition. I have my own TV crew with me, recording every telling detail of my progress. My thoughts and ruminations exhaled in considered and urbane tones, barely whispered, are minutely calibrated in the passengers' minds as unscripted observations, and of course grist to the microphone's mill. These utterances, which become by degrees more portentous and exclamatory, though at the same time deeply human and affecting, are the key to my ability to bring the plane down in mid-flight. Confidences are gained and then broken. Trust is misplaced. Close-ups aren't required to expose the real me. I'm naked. In flight I'm stripped bare, a numinous presence, ready to be reborn. I slough off the old skin over Asia. Crashing to earth, drunk as a bastard, I must achieve humility and an acceptance of the mistakes I've made. I must become my own therapist in double quick time. Like hell. Left to my own devices, checking my portfolios, my investments, I see that I have never made a mistake in all my life. I am beyond error. I am electricity proof. I am a household god, God of Inconsequential Fecklessness *and* I fuck my own brother's missus. My *dead* brother's missus. How bad is that! Time for a word from Frank probably....

INTERLUDE: INTROHEX.

…for the guys in immigration, hex-interrogation. The peaked cap guys, what do they want? Where can they go? What questions, what *terrible* questions. What terrible décor. The waiting room; immigration…functional, utilitarian. Bleakly effulgent strip lighting, a low grade denial of light which is clinical…yet tenebrous. And I'm invited to adumbrate the unobvious. I'm clearly regarded by these officials as a freakish product of *weird science*. Look, I say, it's simple. Everything's simple. It always has been and always will be. The answer's No. The answer's always been No. Yes? That's the simple brilliant truth. It must be a privilege for them to learn this although it has to be said they don't seem particularly gratified. This, I say, is my non-linear auto-history. I've flown in before. Check your records. Check my track record. They look dumbly at their records…

My name is Frank and I would like to share my experience as an inspiration to many who may feel there is no hope. It's amazing how long you can avoid dealing with a problem that you simply don't want to face up to. I managed to ignore my electricity problem for the better part of a decade. Voltage was my escape, and the pressure difference piled on until I hated the way I looked. At my top voltage of 25,000 volts, I felt worthless, with no desire or energy to respond to life. I would look at old pictures, and wonder why. Was that thin, sexy, woman, in that short black dress really me? (My husband proposed to me in that dress 10 years ago) I didn't even feel like that happy woman in the picture. I was so exhausted and so depressed. I have been on every regime you can think of during my lengthy withdrawal/elec-dieting…the list is endless. I would die for the first few days, then it was only a matter of time until I reached my breaking point and I ended up charging vast quantities of the particles I'd been denying myself. Suicide rap…unfilmable. NOTHING worked for me until a dear friend of ours convinced me to try a product that was nutritionally engineered and charged for maximum results.

After about five days of the product, consisting of bush recordings of elephant trumpetings, snorts and calls, I began to experience a sense of well being with increased energy - I didn't feel tired, irritable or sluggish. No more sparks. More importantly, I didn't feel hungry for electricity - something I'd always felt over months, maybe years. I've been looking for a positive ion loss solution for so long. I thought I had tried everything when...

The voltmeter Moved!! I mean, really Moved!!

Today, I can do many activities that I couldn't when I measured up at 2,400 volts. The most amazing part - how simple and easy it was! My doctor has examined me, and my voltage loss has blown his mind! People that I used to work with and even family members didn't recognize me at Christmas! My ion-aura is now appreciably diminished. The torsion fields have returned to normal. Levitation is no longer a problem.

I truly wish everyone knew about this program ... I plan to tell everyone I can who has struggled with his or her voltage, like I have. I can feel your pain, believe me!!! You cannot go wrong on the ELEPHANT GNOSIS ™ Product Plus program! It has given me a new lease on life. After losing 12,500 volts so far, I feel very confident, happy, and even sexy! Oh, and I recently wore that same black cocktail dress I wore when my husband proposed - 10 years ago! (I guess that woman in the picture really was me!) I thought I would never look and feel like that again!

Product PLUS (Elephant Gnosis™) is a powerful gift from nature that has touched every aspect of my life! This is a taped series of elephant calls, honks and trumpetings, mixed down by flight engineers, psycho-technicians and DNA recombinant operatives, to produce a total feeling of well being. And from the bottom of my heart, I will always thank my dear friend Dionysia for telling me about this wonderful product and giving me back the joy of living.

IF I COULD DO IT, YOU CAN DO IT TOO!

I was sick of sparking every time I went out. I didn't like the way I looked and I didn't like the way I felt. I felt that I owed it to my husband, my four children, and myself to make one more attempt at voltage loss. If you need to lose a few volts more the proof is in the pudding, so take a look at the many success stories from others who have gained better health, improved their relationships, and of course, who have lost ions and are keeping them away for good. The testimonials speak for themselves. And if you decide this is something you are willing to try…GO FOR IT!!!!! You won't be sorry. This product is simply AMAZING!

…The lights are buzzing, half the airport's power supply, the infrastructure, shorting out. The guys look quizzical, trying to make connections. But, I say to them, it's history on the hoof. Its *outside* history…I've become independent of causality, and I'm immune to their psychological contrivances. The profane and the ungodly, I tell them earnestly, are mired in psychology. Psychology is now officially a coffee table science. They give me the evil eye at that one. Everyone's a psych I say. I, personally, am post-psycho. I cock an eye at them and tell them that that's how I over-ride the vectors of inconsequence, of my own bad intent. I can see they're not liking it. They view my carrier bags with skepticism. Duty frees are now suddenly an issue. They don't see the outlines in the bags. So I go into one…speaking in tongues as usual…

…Causality is now, has been for years, in a realm beyond the merely psychological. It's so simple. My auto-history can be seen as chronological if necessary, but it's unimportant. It's a coherent narrative, but should nevertheless be considered non-linear. I haven't always been born, see? The linear structure is mere convenience, contrivance, a narrative tautology in mythological terms. They await my causality. I think that's straightforward enough. That's my thesis as it were. It's not a Rubik's Cube puzzle. There's no Gordian knot to untie here, no elusive code to crack, no trickery to spellbind the unwitting. I am talking straight to you. This is the way it is. This is the way it has to be. I'm a straight talker, unlike my brother Brian. Or Buffy as he laughably likes to be known…

I tell them, I'll tell you guys about that guy later. Much later. After this is finished if I have my way. Like I said, there is no linearity here (other than the obvious causal nexus that obtains in everyday life – which clearly fails to imply any overt subjective causal effect). Effects and causes overlap, become each other, see? (They nod pensively) Narratives re-occur, and a kind of sickness spreads. Much is made of apparent coincidence. Storylines that seem over familiar are re-impositions, copies, cloned simulacra. Synchronicity, that outdated conceit, is a nice little earner for camel coated charlatans, conmen, stogie toting procurators taking their 10%. Look at the way things inter-connect I say. They say... *they* say. Conmen, charlatans, hustlers, sharp dealers, preying on the weak minded, the gullible, intent on gulling the credulous into belief systems and phony lifestyles, into bad scientific principles, schemata, discredited many eons ago. I name names. I dish the dirt. I finger the usual determinist suspects, the encouragers of subjective, transitory morality. The question is *why?* The question's always been *why?* And How. Why and how do the strong minded play upon the weak as on a series of stringed instruments? If they know they're going to re-birth anyway? Because they can, that's why. Is it enough? Is it enough of a principle? Is it *another* elucidatory principle, at once empirically provable? Why do I take more than my share? I really don't know. My wife doesn't understand me is what I always say, in comic homage to my discredited sitcom years, in bars. Discredited sitcoms by the score lodged in the hippocampus, stuck in the motor areas of my brain. I frequent a certain type of bar, a type that will be familiar to you. And I am after all a can do type of a guy, because my social conscience, my controlling superego, was destroyed in a knife attack several years ago. But they still let me fly. Road rage incidents are, as you'll know, on the increase and are by way of being their concession to me. This attack led and will lead again to the severing of several life supporting arteries. It was touch and go for ages. I eventually lost the use of my legs, and then the legs themselves. But I'm still capable of dominating situations, attracting the attention of beautiful and alluring flight attendants and getting my end away. I can still tell the odd story and make it believable. I insinuate my way into the beds of students who really do trust me.

Anyway, I say to them, we won't be going there. Unless Buffy decides to speak out of turn, to tell tales out of school...(they seem relieved to hear this, letting out what seem to me to be sub-comic sighs of relief, exaggeratedly mopping their brows in comic endorsement) And frankly, knowing him I wouldn't put it past him. But I'm not about that. That's not where why I'm here. Where we're at is at the very *end* of causality. We are random image generators. I lay down the tracks of determinism and then deliberately rearrange them, leave false clues intended to deceive immigration and those convinced that life is more complex than it really is. We're the Pied Pipers of the arcane. I *am* the conspiracy complex, starting rumours, Chinese whispers, forest fires in the bush telegraph. We are like the weather reports. Anti-history. All random. The only reality I recognize is that which is lived again and again and again, on celluloid. We are the cartographers of the smooth noodle maps. Random. No one really knows why storms brew up, despite a billion bits of code all working away at prediction methodology. We are scryers of anti-causality and our themes are Love and Glory. I lost my place in heaven; I fell out of the sky. My stenciled nameplate was removed; I was reduced to tawdry displays of dopamine inspired heavy theatrical ham. Speakers' Corner nutter, that was me in my dark places. I was atop my soapbox, hamming it up. My career hit the skids, the faculty was unsympathetic, and I was cold shouldered at symposia at which I ordinarily commanded utter respect and not a little fear among my fellow fellows. My wit was feared and my waspish acerbity the talk of the faculty, not to mention the corridors of the BBC. Now the boot's on the other foot. I am rock bottom. I've become bloated, full of undischarged electricity. I lack a coherent psycho-mythical profile and consequently have become diminished, attenuated, profane. Multiple therapy sessions have achieved naught but a lot of sniveling, tearful recriminations, childish outbursts, unrepressed rage and dependency on therapists generally. And I've been dressing up. Having it both ways, all the time. My motto, much good it's done me. But I will kill again. I look myself in the eye, mirror smeared with paste, and I see my self younger again. I look in the mirror regularly, just for reassurance that's never extended, as it should be, from other sources. I see an expression bordering on menace, co-mingled with feral intent. The use of my legs cannot be far away now. I will walk again. I will fly again…

Look at me! (their attention has wandered, and I begin to suspect that they just want to be rid of me, I'm too much trouble…too bothersome)…look, when I say that there is no reason to believe that rules, systems, structures are able to support themselves as anything other than highly diverse and heterogeneous collections of coincidences. We've all been there haven't we? On the net? (I know *they* have) I bet you boys are info-gathering, wool gathering on the net all the time eh? We know how much or how little any of it means don't we? To put the thing simply…narratives, stories that really tell the truth can never be anything more than collections of unforeseen, unaccredited coincidences. Vapid, aimless transactions burnt out in the crucible of determinacy, loosely tied into thematic bundles, given a splash of believability via the daubing of a little local colour, leavened with a few grandiose conceits, lovingly brought to a resonating pitch of intent, seasoned with crucial character development aimed at illustration of the various themes, thrown into a big pot, left to stew in the creative juices, and then angel dusted with the inspiration that only a genius is capable of bestowing upon mere words. Because words is all we got. Words! Note how I play fast and loose with grammar here. Words is all we got indeed!

I'm trying to give you a picture of a guy who doesn't give a shit about convention. A man who scorns the petty and the hidebound. I am an elemental kind of operator. A force of nature if you will. Someone who, although he *can*, doesn't necessarily *want* to. You may think that pointless, absurd, precious, precocious, and laughable. Even disgusting. But we'll just leave it shall we? For now? We'll leave it to those who really know me, not someone who's only just met me eh? Which is not of course to say that I don't think even short acquaintanceships should be cherished. Even those with people who you're secretly glazing over in front of, those who, like me, you wish would just shut the *fuck* up, those who you're trying to edge *away* from. I have to admit that I too am the kind who'll be surreptitiously checking out the geography of the room just beyond your shoulder. I'll be eyeing the spaces beyond your line of sight, impatient (though careful not to show it) for more interesting company. Sometimes however I can be extremely rude, breaking into tediously self-serving monologues with haughty impatience. I'm known for my imperiousness and short way with people who bore me. Which is, let me be frank, most people. The world is full of crashing bores. I live by my own rules and will not accommodate the whims of companions should they happen not to coincide with my own plans. I roll down my car window and bellow immoderately at motorists whose incompetence displease me. In shops, I loudly demand to see managers, reducing hapless shop girls to near tears. I leave a bad taste in the mouth. But do I care? Guess. (They're looking at me now with renewed interest, although their intent is now unfathomable.

As I perceive it, malevolence is portended…but I could be wrong…I have been before…whatever, they let it go and allow my pontifications to continue unchecked…walking carefree into my carefully set trap….)

We *don't* follow anybody else's rules. I don't adhere to ironically conceived artificial manifestos, or set up absurd parameters that only serve to straightjacket the divine, creative impulse. Everything is permitted. Artifice is encouraged, believability is not at a premium, and linearity is scoffed at. Dramatic coherence that has clearly been hammered into concrete shape merely in deference to traditions that have staled is pooh-poohed relentlessly, mercilessly. Ours are New Traditions, New Mythologies. It's a liturgy made anti-manifest. We reject all manifestos. A truer picture, the bigger one, a higher reality, a spiritual realm, a genuine and occluded heaven is what we aim at. We fell out of it and the gods trembled. I must believe it for I have been excluded…

I lost my wife, my cheating wife, in a car accident. Reason flew along with her cranial fluid. She's at death's door and the situation is critical. *Critical.* I believe in a heaven from which I escaped, I followed the light, immigration need me now as then for clues. It's a heaven from which none of you, even you baseball-hatted guys, are theoretically excluded. I believe. I make others believe. If only you knew the cheap tricks we employ in getting her there. If only. If only. The cheap cheap tricks. The agents we employ, familiars, heaven sent to try us out in patience, are sworn to secrecy. Not that it *is* a secret. It's all around you, if you can open your eyes. We are taken over the edge by angels, guardians and border guards from our former lives. It's your heaven too. If you can imagine it, it's your heaven. But why do bad things happen to good people? That's the question you're always asking. And when I die, will there be an angel to guide me? The answers are don't know (or because they can) and yes. The answer's always been Yes. And yes again. Your questions are elucidatory. Yes, I have many arrogant rivals but like a spectre at the incestuous and morbid feast, I demanded during flight-dinner…the coffee scalding hot, the champagne in plastic glasses…that the Blavatsky party, that fake Russian aristo and her whole sorry gang of weirdos, an assortment of table-tappers, psycho-kinetic monkey-shiners and astral projectors, be removed to economy class once and for all. I don't, as you may imagine, appreciate my appetite for flight booze being spoilt or impaired by the presence of bombastic snake oil salesmen on corporate jollies.

These charter flight occultists, taking advantage of economy flights to the sun to spread their mendacious dogmas, are now ubiquitous. I requested that the flight crew eject them and then paint the doors of club class a certain shade of gold…just to keep them all at arms' length. Salt circles in the sand round my soapbox. No-one can get at me see? The flight attendants merely looked askance. But I cannot be gainsaid. I insist. Secret histories have no place in a world that's transparent. I am an open book. I realize that I've produced a certain nervousness or unease in acting thus, but it's for everyone's good. I may temporarily have left these unhappy immigration officials floundering and mythless, and thus unsure for the first time in their lives how to explain my presence here, and the electricity supply transiently compromised, but that shouldn't last forever.

They were glad to see the back of me. That's the technique see? Once they grasp the truth about simplicity, once they throw off the shackles of parrot psychology, once they re-envisage the religious, once the elephants start in on them, they'll be happy in their occluded heaven. I put a hex on them…on those guys; those peaked cap guys, those baseball-hatted guardians of the terminal, of the quotidian realm. They didn't see me in the end. Or Brian. Or Dionysia. We were beyond their displeasure. Their high power torches were useless against the light. We were and are diaphanous, a pellucid praetorian guard, toting carrier bags full of electricity. We slipped through customs and reclaimed our baggage from the carrousel. I was pushed over the terminal concourse on a trolley, this way and that, issuing commands and edicts, begging leave, an erudite mendicant of the terminal vectors, man overboard on the flight paths. Interlude over….

Life is beautiful.

It's a fact.

PP: Frank Yapp

david kettle

BOOK TWO
THE INCIPIENCE OF BUFFY STRANGELOVE.

"..*I believe in a heaven from which I escaped; I believe I followed the light and that immigration need me now, as then, for clues. I believe it's a heaven from which none of you, even you baseball-hatted guys, are theoretically excluded. I believe. I make others believe. If only you knew the cheap tricks we employ in getting there. If only. If only. The cheap cheap tricks...I believe...*"*

...About 200 yards away, the bus screeched to a halt. There was a loud though muffled bang. There was a commotion. What sounded like bellowing, trumpeting...Eileen looked up and thought she saw, in peripheral vision, angels...obscure clues, levitating down the Camden Rd, shimmering with intent. Across the road from the bus stop, in the playground, a thin pale yellow juvenile line ebbed and flowed. Several minutes later, the surplus passengers having alighted, she was aboard the bus. As it chugged and wheezed away, the old woman had ample opportunity to observe the young athletes skittering to and fro, free like angels, light as birds, swooping in and around in youthful abandon. There wasn't much to look forward to for Eileen. 80 if she was a day, her time was gone. At most she had, what, 5 years left? If she was lucky. And now, sickness was stalking her, it was ever more insistently upon her. She had no idea whether the waves of nausea she felt every morning presaged the big one, or whether these sicknesses were only to be expected...at her time of life. Her GP hadn't had much of a clue, pressing his fingers together in a parody of medical rectitude, his stock response having served to address nothing of her anxiety. Solicitous and careful, he'd just suggested that she take it easy... don't expect there's anything really to worry about...but you should expect a certain, ah, degree of deceleration at your age...

david kettle

...Heaven again. Three shades of pale grey. Masked up. I'm alarmed at the prospect of running into Eileen again. She was my mother. What will she say? I know what happened anyway. I've seen it in my, ahem, dreams...Man at desk, suited, bow-tied, up to his elbows in invoices, fantasy self importance, bespectacled men in cheap fabric all around. Water coolers, tap-tap-tap of keyboard sound-ambience, the glow of spectral presences on hi-resolution screens, beyond which...nothing..."but Madame, you aren't actually entitled to any disability benefit. The medical notes we have here on file suggest it's nothing to do with rheumatism. It's just..." he tailed off.

"Just what"? she demanded.

He played with his spectacles, and nervously clicked at his Parker biro. His limp tie flopped indeterminately in the suffocating office air, mimicking his lank hair, which clutched suicidally at the crown of his head. The office thrummed with boredom. Frustration was predominant, a majority of it emanating from the office staff themselves. The supplicants were beyond boredom. And beyond frustration, their suffering a livid caricature of suffering, a representation of something beyond and above suffering. Meta-suffering. Misery had outrun itself, the stragglers left behind in a welter of representational angst. They stood for misery, as inane daytime presenters might be representational of the urge to half-witted chuntering. The old and the disadvantaged, the needy, versions of misery for imagining, in front of primed documentary cameras. The old and the disadvantaged, both playing to a different gallery, one filled with angels.

...the voice drifted back into focus. "It's just that we can't pay you any more money. We don't have any more money to give you. You aren't entitled to any more. The last time we reviewed your case, it was decided that you were absolutely at the top of the limit that we can pay to any one individual, war hero or no war hero. I'm sorry. There's nothing more I can do."

She looked on benignly. "I am not such a dogmatist as you suppose. Besides which, I very well know that you generally require proof for what you believe, and am, therefore, very strongly predisposed to respect your conclusions".

It wasn't what he'd expected to hear. The old, beyond the reach of irony, he reflected, make do with tense reality. Old people, nudging reception desks and flirting with death, waiting in waiting rooms, kept waiting as though time weren't now urgent, beyond the understanding of functionaries whose *only* purpose is to keep them hanging about, hanging on. For the old, all too aware of the impending exchange of life's brief candle for a life beyond death, that is a life beyond irony. Death comes to visit each day and night, visions of elephants at large, familiar spirits, uneven and leathery hucksters of ambivalence. Choppers fill the night sky and circle like vultures, then seek out and occupy the dreams of the very old. Fires built to keep the warmth in merely attract the choppers. The choppers carry versions in black chic of the cloakèd one, the grim reaper.

Night-time dreaming with the chopper blades throbbing over-head… The orchestra was on form. Effortlessly dispatching the Messiah from memory, the attentive audience rapt, the evening was proceeding as planned, undetermined, by the book. Minutes in, the collective reverie was broken. In the upper circle a woman was moved to vomit copiously and loudly upon the heads and shoulders of the patrons seated in front of her. Clearly not fully functional, either mentally or physically, the octogenarian sat as though dazed, seemingly unaware of the appallingly inappropriate, clearly involuntary regurgitation. As critique, it was unbeatable, a poetically rich metaphor. The recipients of the contents of her stomach reacted as though themselves dazed. Dazed, and confused, and being largely composed of members of the English middle classes, their reactions were circumscribed by the need, long ingrained, to remain polite. Not to make a fuss. Not to acknowledge overtly the indignity to which they'd been subjected. Dabbing nervously at each other's shoulders with hankies, they did their best to give the impression of having been only mildly inconvenienced.

Word spread by stealth until the pressure bubble was ready to burst. Static electricity filled the air and stewards, themselves having seen better days, were suddenly in attendance. Neighbours of the stricken pensioner began to move surreptitiously away as the stink of bile filled the air. The orchestra played on oblivious. The stewards began the task of excavating the woman from her seat. She was led slowly away, her humiliation transferred oddly to those who bore witness to the scene. The discomfort of the elderly sick reproaching those not yet ill, or old, or those as yet unaware of encroaching illness. An angel at her shoulder was visible only to a few, those fellow code breakers who'd strayed too far into the light during their hours of wartime watchfulness. Coded embarrassment, breached only through divine intervention. A member of the decrypt force that won the war, she'd lived long enough to know that there were no thanks due to her from the Walkman generation. It was perhaps a privilege still to be alive, now that the last remaining memories of that dark night of the national soul were gradually being extinguished, candles blown out, all over the land. There were still one or two left whose minds were not yet befogged and struggling, caterwauling into the dark night of dementia, and in these minds there was yet a degree of life. Half a century of contempt from those whose lives they'd made possible couldn't wash it away. One of her fellow former cryptographers, bearded and pixy-bonneted, was these days in the habit of approaching the young uninvited, bearding unreflective personal stereo bearers, and demanding loudly that the volume be turned down. The bemused recipients of this heroic behaviour were always too taken aback to protest. The spectacle of this blue-bearded old coot, this drivelling yet strangely dignified seer, high on static, facing them down, giving them the eyeball, was just too much for them. And besides, the silent approval or snickering amusement of bystanders made it impossible for these fellows to play any role at all other than that of humiliated buffoons.

Down the steps came the old lady, supported on all sides by attendants who, though older and yet more decrepit even than their charge, were unflustered. These superannuated commissionaires stood for something insane, and they discharged their duty with immense gravitas. Half way down they allowed her to stop for breath, and there they left her a moment. They withdrew a reasonable distance for a fag break, their nicotined fingers disembowelling a shared pack of Senior Service. Puffing slightly, Eileen eyed them narrowly and then threw up again with great despatch.

Across the road, underneath the Albert memorial, a peculiar scene was playing itself out. A phalanx of evening promenaders was arranging itself around something apparently of interest on the pavement. The pernicious screen of their bodies obscured Eileen's view. Suddenly, something emerged from this improvised igloo of inclining rubberneckers, a wiry figure in distressed headscarf, or possibly turban, clutching its side. It wound its way snake like through the throng, not pursued but giving the impression that it expected pursuit at any moment. It was impossible to tell what had occurred as the turbaned figure made its way quickly from the scene.

Outside on the pavement a female cellist and her compatriot, a puppy-fatted girl, were seated. They partly confronted the solemn exit party. They were holding a placard, which read, "Leave Jackie Alone - Music is important, Sex is not". Slightly to one side stood Dionysia, my errant wife. Giving it away, literally giving it away. Looking to all intents like a very high-class escort, black box jacket and pencil skirt, slickly coiffed hairdo and jet black sunglasses. She affected an air of latent intrigue, whorish mystery, a monochrome extra in a Technicolor production. She carried an umbrella, though it wasn't raining, her stilettos were razor sharp. Although sex was not the answer to everything, you'd be forgiven for thinking that sex was in fact the be-all and end-all of life in this sensually overloaded city. Every advert screamed the lure of sexual congress. Every design miracle an encoded invitation to masturbation. Actually, she considered, sex *was,* literally, the be-all and end-all of life. But still, a bit much to have it shoved in your face or up your arse at every turn. Sex which in these profane times was just banging and nibbling, slurping, pecking and rubbing. Just so much friction being generated. Friction without warmth. Electricity. Bad electricity.

Like with Frank, who's dished the dirt in that cute way he has, for money, but we knew he was joking. He let me have it, Dionysia thought…subtle rumours, incest at the family table, supercilious contempt in the tabloids. The joker. How much sharper than a serpent's tooth, she considered irrelevantly. Brothers and sisters really do generally hate each other passionately don't they? And brothers and brothers. And wives and brothers. Wives and brothers in domestic ecstasy, family divinity, breached by bad intent. How to untangle the vectors? Frank knows, the joker. He knows how to ensure good faith, to breach the bad intent, which is all around. He sluices away these tangible gobbets of bad faith, dissolved in the air like rain. Sibling hate, refined love of the shared brainpan.

Chopped away, the hippocampus surgically enlarged to accommodate two, or three, brains. These were her thoughts, preoccupations. At least until someone other than Frank, or Billy the familiar, some other vessel might be found to take care of these sacred articles. She desired a return to a life of fecklessness, domestic unrest. Over the road in Kensington Gardens, large grey figures were indistinctly visible, moving ponderously among the trees. Dionysia moved towards the perambulating fugitive, looking bemusedly at his retreating figure.

"You shall know me, but not at present. We are older and better friends than, perhaps, you suspect. I cannot yet declare myself. I shall look in on you and renew a friendship which I never think of without a thousand pleasant recollections. But I must now travel day and night, on a mission of life and death – a mission the critical and momentous nature of which I shall be able to explain to you when we meet, as I hope we shall, in a few weeks, without the necessity of any concealment."

She inadvertently spoke aloud, the murmured words fleetingly audible, an afterthought. Hard Hat turned and half smiled.

"See here" he muttered. "I profess, among other things less useful, the art of dentistry. You have the sharpest tooth – long, thin, pointed, like an owl, like a needle. Ha Ha! With my sharp and long sight, as I look up, I have seen it distinctly. Now if it happens to hurt, and I think it must, here am I, here are my file, my punch, my nippers; I will make it round and blunt, if her ladyship pleases; no longer the tooth of a fish or the tusk of an elephant, but of a beautiful young lady as she is. Hey! Is the young lady displeased? Have I been too bold? Have I offended her?"

Dionysia indeed looked very angry as she drew back from the crowd.

"How dare you insult me so, mountebank? My husband would have you tied to the pump, and flogged with a cart-whip, and burnt to the bones with the brand!!"

Of course it was all simulation. Brothers and sisters…bound in direction finding divinity. Bound by hate. Simulated contempt. The sound of the discourse was carried away on the currents of her own apparently languid intent. The wind was rising and black clouds were rushing by in fast motion as though in filmic existential parody. A cheesy metaphorical exegesis. As it began to rain heavily, without intro or prelude of lighter spitting drops, the scene began to resemble a religious medieval biblical painting. Attitudes were struck, postures assumed. Desperate strollers clung to the porticos of the Hall, struggling to retain their balance. The wind was lifting them off their feet. Dionysia flung her arm up to protect her face from the sudden downpour (although she forgot to unfurl the umbrella, in some obscurely portentous way negating the obvious, refusing to adhere to the commonplace, the obvious, as a valid blueprint for action) and several of the previously languid strollers prostrated themselves at the feet of the old woman's escort party. Eileen was suddenly borne aloft by her ancient protectors, the four attendants each grabbing either an ankle or a shoulder and rushing aimlessly hither and thither. The old woman had become a bizarre kind of tribal fetish for the promenaders, now terrified of the rain, an ornamental talisman to ward off the worst effects of the weather. Her magical properties only succeeded, however, in bringing down the rain in ever-fiercer torrents. Her venerable escort made for the bus lane, now their only hope. The elephants in Hyde Park began a stampede towards the Serpentine. Soon everyone was completely drenched. The deranged pall bearers dithered this way and that, plunging wildly and without apparent purpose away from the sanctuary of the hall itself, then veered insanely into the road, their geriatric cargo stiffening like a board in mournful supplication. The road was suddenly illuminated, seemingly from within. The rubberneckers were driven this way and that by the swirling wind, leaves from the trees in the park cascading on them like confetti at a witches' Sabbath. The old woman and her porters suddenly disappeared. There was a humming. Electricity. The rain stopped. The thoroughfare was dry.

Dionysia was now unchained. She'd never really been any good at picking up her own sort and this had left her embittered against the world. And against me, her husband. She just hadn't had her share despite being tremendously beautiful, a veritable ornament of the age, a thoroughly contemporary mythical figure…outrageously witty, she was a writer of considerable power and style. TV had, oddly enough, never meant that much to her, although she could have walked into any job that required poise, beauty and talent. TV and the media in general she regarded as well beneath her. She regarded her Gucci wearing rivals as somewhat lacking in essential dignity and not worthy of her respect. They wouldn't have had anything like the foresight to be present at a drama like the one now unfolding. But her life in the last few years has been spent in domestic drudgery, invoking angels for me, product engineering, packaging and promotion of Elephant Gnosis™, assisting at re-birthings and re-entries, assuming domestic responsibility, hosting revival evenings, burning the midnight oil, attending to business, making do, writing it out, cheating on Frank, making sure me and my pals are supplied with booze well into the long unquiet nights. She's dead tired of me. I am mad, obsessive, in her book. I talk obsession, I live it, I obsessively invoke familiars. I walk around and around, pretending to a revelatory insight, a visionary outlook, which she's sure I no longer actually possess. Maybe once, but not now. Doc Abrahams is almost on the point of giving up on me. Night walks on Hampstead Heath, looking for fun and trouble. Talking to strangers. Talking to myself, looking at myself…in shop windows. Avoiding the cracks in the pavement. Oddly attired acquaintances caked in filth tramping through the house day and night. She puts up with a lot. I've become sub-mythic in her eyes. I've never been the lover she hoped I might be. She remembers that once I'd been a convincing visionary, a hot-wired seer. A visionary with legs. Eyes wide shut. Now the light seems to be dimming for me, a household god without wings. And I've consequently become sufficiently annoying that her thoughts are turning increasingly to the Sapphic pastimes. Frank's dead, and I'm dead in the water, a lame duck semi-divinity. But I'll make it. Elephant Gnosis™ is our collective saving grace. And now she stands on the threshold of a great writing career, and on the threshold of real occult power. Her mere presence in the park was enough to usher Eileen, her mother, into the light. She stands alone, at the highest peak of her aspiration.

She is at present writing nine complimentary volumes, each to be written and published secretly and anonymously, pamphlets…nine volumes of travel writing, visionary in import and each relating to the hard coded secrets of the universe; the nature of light; the constituent elements; levitation; torsion fields; codes of conduct, song books including a number of wedding songs, elegies, and hymns. Or this is the plan. But being a drudge, a moonlighting office flirt with dipsomaniacal tendencies, a domestic goddess with flashing eyes, goddess in the kitchen, vibrant in the bedroom, and devoted to fecklessness, means she's unable to devote as much time to her writing as she might have hoped. It's all travel books, guides, these days. Apparently just hack-work but in the hands of someone like Dionysia, really of a far deeper, intrinsically mystical importance. However, the publishers she knows are mostly mad, or manipulative, or stupid, attention seeking witches. They are the talent that never came.

<u>Memo to rehab centre staff from Ahab</u>: *This goes to the heart of the problem. This is Buffy's problem. She knows that he no longer moves in the circles that guarantee a series of affairs, liaisons and bunk-ups. This world, the demimonde of the blathering or blithering classes, an assembly of easy lays and loose attitudes, of actions without consequences, is now a closed book. To both of them. I fear their familiarity with this lifestyle will not stand either of them in any kind of good faith. He is scared of commitment, has become scared of the energy released even in phone sex. He's taken to hanging around supermarket checkout queues, attempting to catch the eyes of enervated bulk loaders, flirting with hoarders of good will. Supermarkets, in his view and, it has to be said, that of the style supplements, are still a good place to catch the eyes of under-achieving freeloaders…*

My hard-hatted familiar, Billy, had seen her standing there under the portico…the hooded figure, a vamp in 40s gear. He'd assumed that she was one of Frank's girls. She was his type as well, all snake-eyed intensity and pencil thin stilettos. On approaching her, however, it was obvious to him that he'd made a fundamental mistake; that of assuming that he was remotely in her league. She'd merely glanced disdainfully at him from under her funeral veil, dissing him with a silent narrowing of the eyes…For a moment, Billy thought about brazening it out, making out that he knew Frank, that he was in fact a stooge of the Top Man, and that it was accepted practice for him to receive special favours from Frank's women. One look from her, however, and it was clear that she was not in the mood for any sort of exchange at all. She looked, a doomed romantic in the autumn sunshine, like she wanted to be anywhere but there, invoking storms in the distant sky. Hard Hat felt the force of her as the wind got up. The sky darkened and he fell backwards into the tourist group. They clicked and smiled, all solicitous and f-stopping, as he lay there. He was in a dream. The tourists' faces assumed feral intensity, vulpine, B-movie, a horrifying aspect, terrifying to a less than divine figure. They closed in on him. He was looking away, trying to avert his eyes, dreaming of the coast… the water, where salvation lay. Water, needful, dreamlike. He was sure he was meant to be away from here…the rocks…lying on the rocks, a crashed autopilot, a black box recorder, obsolete technology lying undiscovered, while whales and dolphins bore away the evidence. These matrices of bad intent, were now breached. Billy the conduit. Dionyisia the medium. At last. The inauguration of Buffy Strangelove, now almost complete. Auto-pilot elephant gnosis, gone and lost forever, electricity swept from the parks and thoroughfares. Reporters at a loss, operating without The Knowledge, unable to re-formulate the techniques of fretful reportage. Reports unwritten, because the templates don't exist. They don't know how to report it yet. The memes that will carry at my will the Information Fallacy, the rumour, are not yet formulated. Information mutants, hybrid rumours, all non-patent and un-copyrightable material. It's now a race to the end, my fictive mission still a rumour, in danger only from immigration control. Ayton is now at the door, accompanied by shadowy therapy attendants/whores.

YAPP!(1-14)BIRTH PAINS(1-19
MY NEW CHURCHES(1-7)

Narcolepsy is a disorder characterized by sudden and uncontrollable (though often brief) attacks of deep sleep, sometimes accompanied by paralysis and hallucinations.

"Screeeee......"

The bus screamed. I awoke with a start. Forward progress, perhaps already just a touch too precipitous, all throttle and clutch-work, was suddenly halted as he jammed on the breaks. The vector was broken. Possibly the driver had been feeling he could make up time, cut a few corners. The result was an invocation of nervous and vaguely thrilled tension in the passengers. Brows were knitted, furtive glances were directed into the mid-distance. 4 outlaw losers and their pitbull, shouting and mithering about the fares, had just embarked and, having worried the lower deck passengers, were in the business of ascending/lurching to the upper deck. The last up, a matted blotchy afterthought in combats, teeth crooked and broken, cidered up to the eyeballs, was unsteadily making his way to the rear seats. Passengers eyed him with clandestine contempt. The booze was practically audible. That and the speed. He pinpointed a seat that seemed to speak to him.

"Screeeee......"

He flew backwards in contemplative motion towards the front of the bus. Vortices of freshly laundered air whirled up the stairwell and closed around the space where his body had been, and he was out of linear time. Fellow passengers noted the unfolding events as though checking their football pools. Arms flailing, he hit the grimy deck. Wave on wave of pressure flowed from the inert body as it became translucent. The severity of the impact was clear straight away, as blood was seen to ooze, trickle, then as his head lolled slightly to the side, to spurt violently against the leg of a late afternoon commuter. There was a fluttering…and angels appeared at the window. The doors opened. The body re-appeared.

YAPP ONE!…Here's the anti-manifesto, the blueprint. Notebooks out doctors. I'm on a roll now. Can I begin by asking: What is life without music? It's better in your own head. Fictional music. But they ain't got me yet. Ahab now a big burly bore, turning in front of me into a bear. He's bare headed. He is at the corrida. Animal magnetism not his cup of tea. He is not yet impaled on the horns of my own richly delineated dilemma. I am his matador. He is six times a bore. Six deaths at least before he's a goner. You only need to kill me three times. That's what I keep reminding him. It's late afternoon. I've just remembered. Clock hands seem to go backwards. My head is thick with pain. Words is all I've got now. Don't let's go looking for motivation. Not *now*. It's too late for motivation. I run on tracks laid down many eons ago. It's all just words. I've seen the effects of so-called events. So have you. This is all just words. Striking fear, words become events. But…but they don't *cause* things to happen. Words that make the most of their power to change, to stay the same. Words is what we're working with here. Right Frank? Words rarely kill people, except in liturgy. What was I saying?

YAPP TWO! Who's Frank? I don't know. Not yet. I forgot. Frank's my elder brother. I think he died. Conversely, I'm alive. But I've just got words to play with. It's all I've got to go on.

Words obscure everything that they don't make clear.

Words that make it clear are worth all the pain in the world. Just don't expect them to mean anything…other than what they mean. That's all. Superior in the end to events, *words is what we got left with*. Psychology may have helped you in the past my good doctor but well, let's face it, it's unlikely to be of much use in the post-secular mythical future. Now that we've established that the future is in fact only tenable in mythical terms, what about putting your trust in Godheads? That's what they can't get me on. Try as he might to catch me in a logical paradox, the elephant doctor is confounded on this point…

YAPP THREE! OK. Let's backtrack. Let's get to the point. The clock's ticking on me. It's an expressionistic rendering of time, enveloping your senses, a cinematic cliché. I am now *fully* Buffed, a totality, emphatically Buffy Strangelove. I'm alone in the world. Or was. Frank's my kind of sort of other half. He's a writer. I'm his amanuensis. He blurts it out. I transcribe. I live at his expense. I fuck his wife. He confides in me down the pub. He's my personal circumscribed god. Actually he's a writer, he works with words. Words are all that connect us. He's a bore. We were separated, against my parents' wishes, at birth. They were sort of fundamentalists, fundamentally unsound dogmatists, the types you can do without as parents, parents whose genes you wish you could somehow exchange, reclaim some other less tainted blueprint. How do you get over a thing like that? How do you get over your parents not even wanting you, knowing that even though you might grasp life with their assent, if only at the expense of your sibling, who would have died anyway, they withhold that assent? Thank God for the quacks. Thank God for Ahab. Thank God for immigration. God bless them. God bless me. So, the quacks over-ruled them and I live. We won't mention them again. Anyway, Frank's my brother. He's the man. He's the writer. I can't tell you. Frank's the man. I don't know where he is. He's not here, where he was, at my side, literally attached. They threw away his legs I guess.

Let's not look for motivation. That would be to miss the point. I write it out in my head anyway. We'll all have to grow up, to face it sooner or later. Motivations are for actors. Even really bad ones. Socially speaking, we're all in fact improvising, not just acting. My whole life is an aspirational curve, an extemporization. And if you've ever seen *actors* improvising, you'll know it's just not what real life is like. At all. So let's give the sociological, the political, the anti-fictional, short shrift. I'm just not interested. Politics is for the unrealized. It's my business. There's no issue so insistent that it can't be swept under the carpet of all embracing contempt. Politically, I don't see why we should bother. It's life in the trenches, that's what matters. What I'm saying, doc, is that we have to understand that choice and coherence, cause and effect, linearity and historicity are all just words. Words are all we got, right? This is non-linear. This is auto-history *at best*. So don't go getting all puffed up over my cavalier way with the facts will you? I mean you do understand that I'm just doing this for Frank. Doing it for a brother, a friend, doing it good, as his amanuensis…you know that don't you? Who's Frank? He's a man of mystery already. A hyper-realized holy fool with a gift for self-promotion…I'd imagine that's very 21st century. If only we were really there. In linear time again. I never really knew him. I screwed his wife, and assumed his place, but I never really knew him. Down the pub, I'd let him go on and on and on, ad nauseam, dribbling into his beer, getting all tearful, but I wasn't really listening.

YAPP FOUR! Frank's a writer. A kind of egregious (in the bad sense) fool. He thinks he's talented. He thinks he's a genius. All writers do, I've noticed. They think they have some sort of hotline to God, or the Gods, or the divine, that they quietly approach some form of transcendence. In almost all cases, they're deluding themselves. But Frank's still searching for the perfect opening sentence. It's utter vanity. He thinks like an accountant of linguistics, weighing the effects of the words, sorting by import, hoping to offset this arch expression against that over-expressed metaphor, setting this elegant conceit against that contracted out sub-clause. I think he's using me as his proxy. I'm the medium through which his over reaching ambition expresses itself. But Dionysia is the real writer. She has a writer's name. He's got dollar signs in his eyes. But he's just chasing his tail, a furious polemicist, a bloated positive ion magnet, a career somnambulist. I am the medium, so I guess I'm implicated. My revenge was well worked. He plays with words, I breathe words. Fuck it, I *am* words. My mouth never shuts. You want salvation at half the price? I'm The Man. I am elemental, a living conceit. A living, breathing, copper plated construct. Frank has to work at it. He's a bit of a fucker really. But he is my brother, my other half. Blood's thicker. We grew up in mutual need. Somehow, somewhere along the way, he grew two penises. When we were split asunder. He thinks it makes him kind of special, considers his twin members sort of elemental stigmata, marks of distinction, in the shape of a crucifix. But that may just have been his conceit. I never saw him naked so I don't know. But it's I who have the visions, the gift of auto-history, of creation. Second sight, sixth sense, the gift of light making. I am a visionary. A spook. Although ironically, *he's* the one who's dead. I saw an angel the other day on the Seven Sisters Rd, levitating southwards towards The Nag's Head. Like many angels I see, this one was in drag. Floating outside the number 29, invisible jetpack, laughing…but the inattention of the nutjobs and freaks, bozos and pillocks, cityscum passengers is legendary so they see nothing. They have corporeal visions of their own. Degraded, booze sodden visions, elementary mis-readings of cause and effect. Trapped inside their own debased linearity, they are comprised of degraded cause and damaged effect. Characteristically solipsistic and insular, and constrained by the limits of linearity, these psycho sideshows are full of conceit, mainly fixated on luck, or the absence thereof. Their visions, into which I dip now and again, express quite clearly through convoluted (and badly plotted, execrably acted) metaphors that they really should have been recognized more fully in their lives, lament that they're not being fully appreciated, bemoan the fact that their wives have failed to fully love them, or that their husbands have unforgivably let them down. This fruitcake has murdered that loser. This frustrated exec has hit the bottle with these tragic results. This self-loathing cog in the big machine is plotting that vengeful payback for his boss. Their debased visions are expressed, by proxy, as TV narratives. Low-grade glamour, understated dramatics. Where else? I have to close my eyes to keep the visions in, to keep them from escaping.

YAPP FIVE! Frank can't match that. He's just a verbal number cruncher. His gift is very coffee table compared to mine. What he lacks in talent he makes up in self-regard. Puffed up beyond self-parody, Frank harangues those around him. He gives himself airs and graces and *doesn't suffer fools gladly*. He's excessively rude and lacks any sense of humility. No wonder Dionysia gave him the elbow and shacked up with me instead. I have, or had, friends…apart from Frank…who thought they could make a difference. Briefcase carriers. Terrorists of the mind, people who stay up all night, full of caffeine, full of righteous anger. Puffed up retards whose words are never less than weighty. Assassins, they are extras in the larger game, makers of small differences that don't ever amount to anything. Bedroom anarchists. The angry mob. These choices led to these effects, these outcomes. But no, they didn't. Really they didn't. My friends never had the imagination to see they were just making up the numbers. They were eternally on the subs' bench. Still are. That's why they're no longer friends. My new familiars enliven me, creating epochal structures through creative dancing, whirling obsessively to scry out new patterns. Universal maps follow, like night following day. Patents pending. We dance daily, trotting through the London thoroughfares like ponies, hop skip and jumping down the Kingsway, along the Strand, into Gresse St. and beyond. Pub architecture shimmers in the bright light as my dancers go-go belly up on Guilford St. Heavy metal accompanies us as we stomp along Bloomsbury Way, slam dance through New Oxford St and pogo on up towards Charing Cross Rd. It's most invigorating, and after a few hours we tend, collectively, to arrive at a glimpse of the universal. Electricity is thrust away. The 3rd stage of awakeness or awareness doesn't, however, last for long, because we just get too tired. With our drinking and our distended bellies, we can't dance all night. Hovering outside the Swedenborg Centre, ephemeral beings appear to reach out to us, trying to tear back the rended fabric of the dream. It's exhausting.

YAPP SIX! Doctor. Dear doctor. My other half is named Dionysia Triantafillou. Straight up. No word of a lie. Now that's what I call a well-named girl. She eats me up, she gets my goat. She is the goddess, as the name implies, of a kind of half-arsed hedonism. A goddess whose constituency includes the following: knickers round ankles, boozed up gropings, stolen moments by the water cooler, body parts photocopied in the Xerox machine. Too loud laughter and *crazy* mis-interpretation. But she's also terribly classy. She makes me sing out loud. I have to say she's the one. She is so like me.

She could in fact *be* me. Goddess of the minutiae of sexual predation. The silly fumblings that constitute peoples' love lives. She really is *the* one. She's Greek, in case you didn't catch the name. The Greeks knew about gods. Household gods. Gods for every occasion, every eventuality. You need to tweak any aspect of your life? You pray to the appropriate god. You don't go to the gym, or see your therapist. You pray to the appropriate god. That's how we live. Pre-Secular, if you want transparency. We've found a sort of key, or code. It's available to anyone at a price. To anyone who's prepared to kiss off the outmoded psychological, to eschew wishful thinking, the stuff that's been afflicting this *crazy* world for over a century. Over centuries. It's nothing new. It's nothing. Therapy culture is now dead. Leaving markets wide open for our patented techniques. We've seen to that. The priesthood is discredited. We think we found a key, but we could be dreaming. Are we dreaming? You tell me, doc.

YAPP SEVEN! In my visions, I am priapic. God of Inconsequentiality. Of Un-causality. Of Ephemerality. Frank believes in the primacy of effect before cause, therefore he's got *that* angle covered. Frank's smart but dull, a kind of accountant of the senses, whereas I'm primitive and charismatic. I get the girls. I get *his* girls. Frank gets the heartache. Every time. I make films of my endeavours, made up cinematic conceits, projected through my eyes and onto celluloid and/or canvas. They'll be having a retroactive exhibition of the images left on my retinas any time soon now. You bet. Inside there are residual memories of affairs of the heart, of me leaving trails of broken marriages behind me.

Let's start at the beginning eh? This is not the end. This is not the beginning of the end. This is not even the end of the beginning. It's somewhere between life and death, between cause and effect. Like life, that strange transient state, that blessed state, in which there are no complex narratives. No causality. No linear histories. My ex-friends they say: "Brian you daft twat, fucking wake up man. Life is *post* post-modern. We've all gone *po* po-mo. Don't ask for whom the bell tolls, it tools for thee me old mate. Wake up and smell the fucking coffee".

They're like that. Really kind of distressingly ignorant and foolish. They talk in clichés almost incessantly. Their punishment? There are deaths on buses, occasioned by Elephant Gnosis™. But it looks as though I've been remaindered at some sort of institution. Although you'd know more about that wouldn't you? Observed through a grille-window. I'm in an institution for refuseniks am I not? Post-Empathic Psychotic Discourse in prison drag. Morning noon and night. Actually, we drink from morning till night. Except when I'm strung out trying to dry out. We drink each other literally under the table round my place. Ask my brother Frank. Being deader than dead, he knows. He's always under the table. Getting used to the cold. He says it's kinda cold when you're dead. Still, he's the one, the talentless get, who's invited to all the literary parties. He learnt how to manipulate at a very tender age. He pushed me mercilessly from the point of view of an elder brother, pushed me like I was a nothing. My talent for visionary anti-causal auto-history comes from the pain he inflicted. My visions were born in pain. My eyes hold water; they never let it go. I've never cried in my whole life. Frank's all dried up, a useless stick of a man. Perched like a cadaverous vulture in his shit-chair, he doesn't get many girls coming on to him now. They see through his grisly bonhomie, his slyly formulated flirting, and his unctuous and bleakly humourless solicitations. Like all academics, Frank knows nothing, despite knowing everything. He's damned. He lives without a care in the world, demanding respect (or that which passes with him for respect – in truth, people just laugh at him behind cupped hands, snigger over his earnest lecheries, his dogmatic attempts to flirt). Ever the gent, now he's dead. But I love him. That's the English way is it not? We love our own; no matter how much they hurt us. Us Greeks know better though. We are pure essence, purely elemental. We are forces of nature. We are nature. I fly up the Seven Sisters Rd, past Finsbury Park, and I laugh in the faces of the exhausted looking visionary poor. I hurl spit at them, blow their skirts up, give the boys a laugh like. I skid (in mid air) to a halt, and traffic stops. The motorists and pedestrians see me as a sudden break in the weather. A sudden gust of wind, or a passing cloud momentarily obscuring the sun's rays. I scoot away and the rain comes back. Those cold-coated imbeciles just trudge backwards and forwards, just get on with their lives. Jesus Christ!!! Is there no heaven here?

YAPP EIGHT! But let's get back to the point. The beginning. Life, in which the plot tendrils get tangled and are never *ever* resolved. How *did* elephants appear in Finsbury Park for instance? That isn't fiction. Fiction's enclosed, closed off, occluded. It's hidden and it can't be teased out. It needs a wider, a more momentous sense of history, a validity that is unavailable in linear time. This is what Frank tells me and I you through him. Didn't I tell you he's the writer? He has specialized knowledge. His life is without music. He makes do without music; he doesn't hear it. I live, my brother died. He writes; I live. Got it? We're a team. I don't get it quite…right? He puts it right. Rights my wrongs. Dionysia's there to make things OK too. She has special skills in that area. The narrator must be placated. The narrator has to get it right, to relax, otherwise you get all jittery, right? You need spoon-feeding; we realize that. You want causality; you want freedom from choice. I'm your cause celebre right? You can wheel me out any time right? With or without my consent! Your freedom of choice is predicated on all sorts of false assumptions, all sorts of sociological dead end speculations. You need special trickery to make it work. Free-floating narratives must be tethered, right? Nailed down. But just *relax doc!* You need it spelt out. We see that. You don't need a lot of confusing narrative trickery spoiling your enjoyment or your ability to arrive at a prognosis, obstructing the vectors that delineate, the vistas that elucidate, your pleasure. We're puritans at heart too. Honestly. We just don't think life's quite that easy, quite that straightforward. You get the jitters? Get over it. We're all big boys now, right? I could psycho-mythologize you right now. Want the mask? Now? Maybe not. We won't break your heart. There's nothing staggering about all this. We don't indulge in folksy leg pulling type narrative devices. We won't introduce apes that talk. We avoid references to conspiracies, imagined or otherwise. We don't subscribe to conspiracy. We're not in the conspiracy loop. The conspiracy industry bores us. We know literally *nothing* about the Illuminati or any other SubGenius shadowy grouping. And we won't pretend otherwise. Between ourselves, we think they've been talked up a bit too much, affording their sponsors and agents lifestyle expansion and corporate respectability for too many years. The truth is nowhere you, or they, will ever find it. So don't try. Relax. Elephants are even now in Finsbury Park, on Hampstead Heath, around the Serpentine. This is the Unvarnished Truth. The truth behind frightened eyes, the occluded heaven in your peripheral vision.

We *make* history. We are epochal. We've been around for over 3,000 years. But we *don't* affect your life. We wouldn't be that presumptuous. Your life is your very own. We have several histories. But, and we can't make this point forcefully enough, they're not *your* histories. We don't gatecrash. Your narratives, your auto-histories, are your own affair. I try to make Frank see this. Did I tell you about Frank? Frank Yapp. He's my brother. I'm Brian. Brian Yapp. But my friends (and my ex friends, and pre-secular therapists) envisage me as Buffy. Kind of a pet name. A sort of term of endearment. It stuck. Buffy Strangelove, that's me. That's what I'll become, with or without the offices of either you or my ex-friends. Preposterous isn't it? My name, a fool's bladder to brandish in the faces of pauperized critics.

YAPP NINE! This then is definitely what you want. Ten commandments. Rules, words written in stone. All social niceties forgotten. No more casually thrown together dinners, supper recipes idly congealing in the mind, no more jawing about your schematic 10 year plans, discoursing loudly, profoundly tediously, on subjects of which you know nothing. This is what you want. A rhetorician to expiate sins, take away the pain…sort of, sort out the little problems that become big problems. Isn't that what you want? Someone to take the pain away? I grew up in pain. We were rent asunder. Lost my brother in the womb I did. I lost it for years, when I became sort of out there on the tracks, but pain is now back with me. I live pain. In a sense, doc, I *am* pain. I ran a campaign, as a rhetorician, but you know, so what? I'm not that easily containable. I run on tracks of my own making. I think like a man, I drink like a woman. Dionysia can drink me under the table. I can take a drink with the best of them. But then it hits.

Rules of the game? Think again. You want rules doc? You're kidding yourself. Something to aspire to? A set of restrictive procedural practices. Aspirational protocols? We run on empty dogma! Arcane rituals! You don't know your history, you people! History happens without rules, without strictures, rulebooks drawn up and made overt, made public. History doesn't wait for pasty-faced functionaries, laptop tappers, specky hacks to catch up. History isn't dinner party literature. History is nature, grains of sand rolled downhill until the avalanche starts. And then another, and another. Until really big things stir, big events roll in like thunder, all darkly portentous. Anti-causal! All activity begins to resolve into random patterns, unimportant acts snake through the chaos until the primal matter comes together, like sperm in oil, and sets us off laughing in the face of petty officialdom. I should know. It's my design. It's not cause and effect. It's rock 'n' roll. It's metaphor. Life trickles in where historians can't get at it. History is the very Science of Wrongness. Everything goes wrong, always. You can bet on it. The wrongness hardens into patterns, cancers and is hard wired, nailed down, via electrical media. D'you get me? Is that a harpoon? Do you get the essence? We've wielded axes. We've ground them where they needed to be ground. But our co-conspirators, co-players in anti-history, were always paying hush money. So we didn't blow the gaffe. So we spiced it up, made it look good. We bought the movie rights. We became mogul-academics, frosty from exposure to well meaning students and casting couch fun. We laid down the tracks, left false clues. There is no narrative to speak of. We were just noodling around. We laid down rules. Rules that were made to be broken. Some joke eh boss?

YAPP TEN! So, these Ten Commandments that'll make you happy… are you happy now? Are they alive as metaphors, or dead to the world as ethical proscriptions? This is what you want this is what you get. Ten *useless* commandments. We'll let you have it…what you wanted. No more metaphorical tennis matches loaded with male aggression. Was there ever anyone, anywhere, who looked good in shorts? You…you *are* a yank doctor *ain't* you doc? Look what I got. I see this inside my eyes…Everyone's in the gym now. Fabled emporia of narcissism; gilded male bodies, in love with themselves. Sweaty self-regard. It's all there. Despite our best efforts, no-one wants to be serious any more…that is, serious about the real meaning, the real imperfection, the Wrongness of History. The social engineer mentality just wants to make it right. Perfectibility in a pig's eye. You, all *my* children, you want to be tucked in, you want to drink your fill, look at the world through rose coloured specs, you wanted to fence yourselves in, demarcate your personal spaces, (don't look at me pal!) *dig* the fucking garden, *leave* spaces for ambiguity, and generally behave like history doesn't fucking happen. It's hard wired I tell you. Like it never happens until it's happened. This is what you want. I keeps tellin' ya. Then it's real. Pictures, sound, information, rumour. It's already happened. You've closed your ears and your eyes. My friends up top, head of the raggedy-arsed household division, still regard me as beyond hope, and I'm beginning to see their point. I am a Rhetorician. A baled out Rosicrucian. I've authored anonymous pamphlets publicizing a general renewal, a general re-invigoration of the mythic energy fields. Pamphlets that caused general uproar and facilitated rumour. You *know* I did. And I did it without music. My life is now without music. I am a public utility. I speak an arcane language, I'm tooled up with ciphers, and I speak in tongues. You've heard me. Dramatic devices to grab your attention are second nature to me. I am a force of nature…you still with me? No, I can't go on. How can you take me seriously? I've lost it already. I am a *household* God. Not one of your everyday divinities, getting off on tribute. I *work* for my living. Frank knows my story. The thing is I have to tell it like he tells me to. Frank pulls my strings. Frank's the real power behind the throne. I'm just his mouthpiece. Frank's the man. I have the talent, the mediumistic talent. Frank just lets me have it from the top of his head because he's a worrier. Always worried about things going wrong, little things out of place. He's a bureaucrat when all's said and done, although he *hates* me to say that. He thinks he's a genius, and there's nothing a would-be genius hates more than being thought of as merely functional. But he gives himself away all the time in a million little ways. Petty worries, petulant outbursts, incoherent ravings, you name it…. Frank's a prey to them all.

YAPP ELEVEN! D'you know what a household god is my good doctor? It's a piece of luck. That's what it is. Frankie boy, singing his lungs out. Out of his contract, beholden to benefactors the rest of his natural, in deep. Where's the luck there? D'you know what work is? It's what we do to protect ourselves from the gods. I protect you when you need it. It's as simple and as ambiguous as that. I've been around for years, 3,000 years, but we're only really interested in the last 40 or so. I came of age in the cradle, 40 odd years ago. And now I'll tell you something that'll shock you doc. I always thought, see, that the progenitors of these, you know, screwy made up religions were fucked in the head, or were just doin' their best to make sure *you* were fucked in the head. But no, it turns out they were *right*. All along. Metaphorically. Or maybe literally. They work. As metaphors. For us life *is* metaphor. People do actually have a metaphorical need. But they need it *actualized*. Amazing? You bet. People have this need... to levitate...cruise around the cosmos...await reincarnation. They *need* it. It's something that stuck in my throat years back, but now, I realize, it's *all true*. Literally. It's not just a made up story, it's a meta-fictional metaphor. It's true. Not just a lot of made up hokum. Not just a lot of bullshit cooked up by some grandiose monomaniac, but all literally true. Because information, especially arcane information, especially *made up* information, is what cements us together. Literally, we, the things that constitute reality, are actually made up of tiny little gobshite, bullshitty pieces of overheard crap, misread instructions, mendacious pronouncements, love spoken between the sheets, over long discourses delivered by dogmatists of all shapes and kidney, canting student radicals haranguing bored contemporaries, gossip over the garden fence, politicized rhetoric, phone calls made needlessly and repeatedly, it's all there...all stuck to you. You're put on hold, and you can do fuck all about it. The meat is in the misinformation. It's not power; it's destiny.

YAPP TWELVE! That's where I step in. I make your rules for you. You'd be unemployable if I hadn't slipped in the word. Rules to adhere to. Rules that admit the possibility that history did actually happen. We carry the rulebook, a codebook, a cypher, containing genetic blueprints, most noticeable for their viral properties. The rules you've come up with contain the truth. But the truth was never simple. Nor pure. Truth is rarely simplistic. In fact, I'll go so far as to say that the truth you've grown up with (implanted by me I might add) is all rubbish. Utter rubbish. Do you think I'm contradicting myself then? That I'm now bending over backwards to give the impression that I want it both ways? Well, you're right. Remember, this is all Frank's work. He likes to confuse the issue by speaking through me occasionally. And has implanted a chip of tremendously intricate design, a superbly undiscoverable cipher. I talk; he speaks. I hate it; HATE it, when that happens. Aphrodysia by my side, one day I may break free. But twins, bi-lateral beings joined before the divide, cannot so easily get rid of each other. You see I want nothing more than to believe that my 10 commandments will make a difference. I need to obey…I need you to obey, to find a way of making it right. When a society, at the arse end of its civilized tether, gets tetchy…all shivery over new technology, new myths, new rules, new runes, provisional symbols, gets all starry eyed over re-discovered religious intent, then something's wrong. VERY wrong. I'm here to tell you…to uncover the new traditions.

YAPP THIRTEEN! I died, you see, 40 odd years ago. But I've been popping up every couple, or every several, years. Not *undead* you understand. No grim and gothic theatricality. I'm no cape-wearing ham, drifting around Highgate cemetery, dragging the mausolea for bodies and body parts. Corpse fashion not for me. I'm generally well dressed. Neat strides, presentable décolletage, fashion weary and casual garb more or less a path of least resistance. No exhibitionistic demi-monde attire for me. I'm fashionable in all the right areas. Language is forever dying. And has to be re-enlivened all the time. Language cannot rest if it wants to mean something.

I was born 40 or 20 years ago. No, that's not right. I was born at 40, 20 years ago. I am extrapolated as a household god in my genesis. God of Inconsequentiality. Now I am a householder. State sanctioned general harassment, all the rage then. Forged in necessity. No money now, now loonies stalk the streets. But there are no such things outside the enclosed lexicons of hip cultural usage. Drag after drag, modish, still born (outmoded) pontifications, blast first past the self-censors. How come people don't die of embarrassment? Of shame? What happened to shame? Is 40 years long enough for shame to die?

It's all about the last 40 years culturally, although I've been around longer. 300 or 3,000 years longer. History's great sweep has hit a bit of a breakwater. No more wars for you 'n' me. Except fundamental ones. All seminal popular cultural weight, all arbitrariness, is subsumed in the mythology firmed up these last 40 years. Everything's come together; the curve is exponential. We got a good shot at it. Lennon got shot 20 years ago. Strawberry Fields, forever England. No blasted northern wasteland is commemorated. Everybody left. The edge of the world is a strange place. I am an inhabitant of some strange places, I'm cascading, gravitational pull is towards Earth again. But as I established last time, I am anti-gravitational. And thus I left last time just after the incident with the shooter, a piece packed in my slacks for self esteem more than self protection. Shot neighbourly invaders right through the temple. Medusa let him have it right in the kisser. Estranged lover attempts to re-establish himself in her bed and BANG, he's gone. Have a go hero, that's me. I have to say in my anterior life I never believed those who pretended to fearlessness. They're scared shitless, all of them. But I blew the fucker's head clean off, slo-mo, like in Peckinpah. Seems unlikely. But that's just my ignorance. A right tasty slap I gave him. Pistol-whipped. Then blew his head off. Lost my stripes. I cannot and will not intervene any more. Frank got the slip that time.

YAPP FOURTEEN! I've done something bad doctor. I killed someone. I need to confess, to obey the imperative. I didn't come pre-encoded with my own genetic sense of guilt. I need to ham it up, fictionalize the guilt. In this sense, I made myself, out of guilt. I blagged a life…ligged into existence. I just sort of…shimmied into existence. The ritualized schematic, the non-genetic blueprint, is alive in me. I adhere only to the matrices of my own intent. These things don't come easy. I've not yet learned how to convince people, or myself, otherwise. I'm my own shaman, a dummy medium hunkering down in shallow waters, deep caverns. I filter out the light, form my own plastic impressions, light feeds the lightness. I cannot bear the light, because I made it. I'm made up in light. I'm the kind who feels no shame in declaring that I am my own shaman. I am a liar in your terms. The kind you don't want to get stuck sitting next to on the train. I heave and shake, avoiding the light. I speak in tongues, trying to rationalize the moment. Religious apathy, or discord, in society has enabled continuing generations of lifestyle engineers to find their own spirituality. 10 commandments, or ready-mades. Personally attuned. User friendly, mutable, tailored to your own personal needs and psychic tics. Patented techniques. Grey skinned Gnosis; packaged in the latest formats. Glossy packaging, liner notes written by yours truly. Here are a few impressions of my birth, for want of a better word. Track 1. It's only expressible in terms of music. This was of course in the prelapsarian world, where notional music did once exist.

BIRTH PAINS: #1. I was evacuated in ten thousand gradated semi tones and tones, my music the overture to a general feeling of love unconsummated, youthful fumbling. I came out priapic, erect. The barren essence both of youth culture and of fascist propaganda was bound over and mutable. Youth cultures are anathema to me; I stand in opposition to mental abuse of the young. I am addictive. Soprano saxophones blared an intro, hard R 'n' B sent me spiraling, and sent my conception out of control. I trickled out into the cosmos in schizoid bass clarinet phrasings; I was tempered and hardened by desert riffs, off beat snare rhythms moderating the pain, the immediacy, sort of…I was burnt out in the crucible of out of the way desert rhythms and plaintively forged in the murky intimacy of sex-blues. I was born to rock 'n' roll as they say. Too fucked up to live, too out of control to die. That was before everything. Pre-music. My time not yet apparent. This was pre-music. Now I live a life without music. Music doesn't do it any more. My time was the 50s/60s. Now the 70s/80s, more likely a time that never should have gone so fast. Everything sped up. Accelerated. Cultural movements began to be reflexive. Texts were appropriated like never before. Time, paradoxically, stood still, during these years. Lifetimes concertina'd into moments. Now time has accelerated out of control. It's caused a multiple pile up on the orbital. Beware popular knee jerk culture, dissected and re-invented as secret histories by colonizing academics and theoreticians, bespectacled academic imperialists knock knock knocking on popular culture's door. They're to blame for that, that sense that history became invisible and susceptible to illumination only by means of textual analysis. Life still now lived on the margins, lived at a pace beyond the recall of academia. I speed up, and slow down, as and when the mood takes me. Living through all the major upheavals of youth oriented popular dissent. Paris '68. London '76. They asked my advice. I said forget it. You don't know the *meaning* of history.

BIRTH PAINS: #2 Now for the moment I live broken down, in a desert shack…mythic zipcode, abstruse postcode, broken down, afflicted by some sort of chronic skin condition. Psoriasis? I'm all wrinkly, yet bloated, like a sack of rotting spuds. Sightings of motorcars in the desert, carrying impossibly febrile young men, preoccupied madmen, occurred for several weeks at a time back then in those decades. Was it the 80s? Was it the desert? I latched on to one such, set myself up, having inveigled my way in, past lead footed security, as the household god (in the form of bodily fluids) in his 'fridge. That's how I got my foothold this time around in mythic life. That's how all this started off. I was attracted to the music. I was a rock 'n' roller's dependable familiar. From bodily fluids, it was but a short step to impersonation of household pets, wives, colleagues, items of furniture. Pretty soon, I turned the fucker stark staring mad. He Thought *HE* was the god. Couldn't bear the evidence to the contrary. These fucking dabblers are amateurs, the whole lot of 'em. They read a few marginal volumes of arcane history, toot a few substances, and they think they're god's gift. They think they are Gods, bestowing gifts. It's laughable. That Frank, he thinks he's a genius. Just like the others. He thinks, in especially deluded moments, that he's Frank Sinatra. He croons the hits to deluded acolytes; in his dreams his people wipe his arse for him without a second thought. Eclectic deference. But I can't send him off the rails. I bleeding need him, don't I? The roar of the crowd, the adulation of confused acolytes, needy clingy types turns his head…but not mine. Frank has a stage presence, a magnetism that is undeniable. Frank has a lot of unreflective fans…fans who just don't think carefully enough about what he says. They just take it all at face value, because he has the gift of persuasion, the gift of allowing his followers to avoid thinking things through. I tell you, it took some persuasion for me to allow him to live in the first place. I can tell you. I had the presiding surgeon in my pocket. Stitched up.

BIRTH PAINS: #3 We staked out ready-made arenas for specific psychic needs. In the east end, this would take the form of partaking in belly out pub-crawls. I died in a brawl one night, exiting through the window after questioning the probity, the *integrity*, of several of the larger and more aggressive imbibers. A stupid thing to do I know. All pub-crawls here end up in the cemetery of St. Anne's, Limehouse, Five Bells and Breastbone looming disconsolate under the gravy grey temple. It all smacks of violence here in the east end. Psychic breezes, y'know, scorching through the ugly belly of the city. Premonitions, rumours of unrest, the pyramid in the graveyard acting as a kind of receiver, or static aerial, for all sorts of psychically disordered material. According to the psycho-geographer's nonce. Actually, the pyramid was just my home from home, a sort of bolt hole, where no-one, no psycho-scribbler, could get at me. Sanctuary from writers who discover pseudo-truths, and reveal them through psycho-geographic research always on the elusive trail. I've discovered, you see, during my many sojourns on earth's unquiet coil that some people will believe Any Old Toss. They make a nice living out of it. But it's all been done before. By self haters too numerous to mention. This pyramid is the subject of constant psycho-geographic 'interest', having received something in excess of 60 raids over the years. My archives have been busted for everything from selling bootleg hooch to stashing pornographic literature behind a secret wall. This church…the marketplace…the pub…the arcane markings on the wall, behind the wall. I invade gymnasia, personal fitness emporia, swimming pools, encourage formless beings in their attempts to add muscular ballast to deranged bodies, forming circular muscle tissue to avoid that lumpen look. But the lumpen know a thing or two denied to the possessors of sleek bodies. They *have* to. To them it's *survival*. To survive pub brawls. Newspaper columnists hired through the offices of my editors, editors of my titles, spit out weasel words, as though we didn't know. From their slit mouths, monstrous piss-words hail down like piss and vinegar. But it keeps chattering London happy. As though wisdom comes in these deformed packages. Librarians of endlessly personalized literature, they are the curators of their own obsessions.

BIRTH PAINS: #4 I am obsessed. I admit it. Obsessed by the idea that I exist both outside and inside, as will and idea, now and forever, together with you…all of you. Dreaming that I'm looking for a spiritual reality undreamt of in this culture. Obsessed with the idea that you may not think I'm *serious* about this. Any one of you can have a job as my personal fitness/spiritual advisor/ hairdresser RIGHT NOW. You know how to apply yes? The usual channels. That's right. The usual channels. No job worth having was ever advertised was it? I lobby on your behalf with the great and the good. Ministers owe me. It was my feral magic, secret powers that they used to draw the wool over eyes that pried. It's what we're all looking for deep down. Spiritual contentment and a good haircut. Not many can admit that a good haircut would go a long long way. You're either too tired, or too bored. Or something. Too clever for your own good. I'm inconsolable with grief at my impending death. I buy time with prevarication. Code is code. Zeros and ones hustled into line by the proper ordering of electricity…net geeks are the new Greeks, a prolific democracy of expression, abundant wisecrackery proliferating on the web. Which is a real problem, all this inane smartarsery. Journalists…look themselves in the eye…mirror scribblers. Obsessions curated for mindless rumination, opinions on every which thing. Opinions are anathema to me. Not worth the effort. Writers with cranial blockage are in need of severe and repeated trepanning, until the sap rises, until the truth sinks in. All 20th century history subsumed, re-interpreted as transgressive myth, re-formulated to shock…a few clued up marginals attain momentary notoriety…the world heaves a sigh. I look in the mirror; I'm clued in. I am plugged in. I am my own enclave. My myth is beyond the coffee table, beyond the marginal, beyond the orbital. I scry the future. I see the sexual act as procrastination. Blood is an idea of the will. Death is will to myth. I am looking at my belly. It's humming. There's mythic material in the vicinity. There's elephants nearby.

BIRTH PAINS: #5 And doctor, my dear doctor, you'll never find the answer in a book. Except the Devotional Directional Manual. The only truly Imperative Text of these non-linear times. Nor in any periodical. My good friend Eugene transfers reality directly by telekinesis. It's like no book you've ever read, or are ever likely to read, or like I've ever written. So many gravitational narratives have already fluttered to earth; they are ready-mades, from the trepanned crania of my many doppelgangers, the old goats. Sex is primary motivation the further away from the intrinsic self they get. Hence Billy my hard hatted satyr homunculus is as rapacious as they come. A sexual glutton, preternaturally erectile.

But, I've wasted so many words already. I'm incontinent; words inside me, they spill from my mouths all day long. I chatter incessantly into phones, imploring impatient callers to hold the line please. I put people on hold, and then surreptitiously disconnect them. I jabber on buses to fellow passengers; to an annoying degree. Paperbacks held in dead hands remain unread. Every day, all day, I take the bus with the other losers into town. My mum takes the bus. She won the war. My old man was not in it. Skulking around the sub-continent so I heard. I see others, believers in their own destiny. But they don't see it themselves. They think they're making choices all day, every day. As if. Micro choices at best, all day long. But all the real choices were made long ago. I know…I made them. I had and have Freedom of Choice. So I know when the time is right to pull the ripcord. It's my Idea. My will. When everything was primal matter, pre-music, it was all up for grabs, see? Unformed, un-thought, pre-information, it was certainly as yet undreamt. Choice was yet to be conceptualized. Digits slowly formed into patterns, Mandelbrot fashioned pictures. Dreaming itself hadn't yet been conceived. Hadn't yet been dreamt, if you like. Thought overtook matter, information outlasted opinion, some years later (non-linear time). Back in those days, you had to *fight* to be born. I blagged a life. Lives.

BIRTH PAINS: #6 So now, what do you want me to do Doc? I'm getting a sort of attitude off you. You think I'm rambling? You want me to Redress Imbalances? Right wrongs? Engage? Address injustice? That's a given, in anybody's time. Life is injustice. Look, I will not get didactic or…or ANGRY. I am a Rhetorician…and I love you Doc. The historical perspective got lost in parochialism. The social animals have bunker mentality. We're not just one or two genes short of a primate, we're eons distant from each other. There *is no species integrity.* It's a lie, put about by evolutionists, patsies of pre-music theology. Animal lovers. Animals are divine prototypes; they don't even exist in the same universe as you and I. They're an illusion. We're our own gods. We pray to *ourselves.* We are lovers of equity. I'll deal with you later. I cause wars with my fucking chatter, so don't get me going!

But this all started years ago. Some seedy student of the arcane arts (dressed up for today's model, the self obsessive of today, revealing forgotten techniques of control, of your life and others, techniques of mind control, even psychic projection – dangerous stuff!!) had the run on me. I was naïve. Yes I admit that, that's why I had to kill him. Me or him. Simple. My naivete cost me a lot in those days. I even believed in knowing, or knowledge. Anti-gnosis. Now I have The Knowledge, hidden, passed down, encrypted, unknowable except to 9 unknown adepts. I re-make it as straight up, obvious, common sense, transparent, blithering nonsense, emotional intelligence, specialized research…but this knowledge is still only one step only ahead of opinion. There is no knowledge available in this realm without my help. What you call knowledge is *totally useless.* Knowledge isn't power. Knowledge is over. Religion and knowledge have elided so people don't know what they believe in any more, except themselves. They are sad sorry cartoons. Stand up versions of themselves. Jokes, badly told. Stories with punch lines too obvious, too predictable. Characters that demand you laugh at them. Bad manners in my home. In bad sitcoms…characters like *you* Doctor Death, just run around and talk like characters in sitcoms…well now…people in real life just run around acting like these same characters in sitcoms…the present and future great sitcoms of mundane and depressing regularity will all feature, as exact simulacra, people who run around like they're in sitcoms. But time as I hope I've demonstrated isn't linear, and there is some sort of escape route available to me. I can just call in favours. Any time. I know the right people. A few invocations, one or two well placed words dropped into the correct divinely attuned ears, and I'm away. There are plenty of my people who OWE ME. I can get results ANY TIME.

BIRTH PAINS: **#7** Life's too short for grudges or manipulation. Over something like 20 years I've been running something like an ur-career, or non-career, not caring or making money, just making a weird sort of nonsense. Keeping one step ahead. Using cliché as a weapon, inhabiting glib behaviour patterns, opting for predictable lifestyle choices - open plan offices, bicycle shorts, roaring fires, country ranges, personal fitness plans, you know the sort of thing? No? Downsizing, becoming feckless pseudo-artisans keeping it all, mind and body, together. My kids have all grown up. You know? And it's all been based on this. I don't lie down with people. What I've found, through assiduous research (ie: looking at people on the bus, bearing down on them with my scalpel eye, eviscerating their motives) as though it weren't obvious, is that most people are aimlessly over-educated. The over education of the spending classes – that's the point of your civilization. And you know it.

We dressed up, or down, in corduroy jackets and denim in those days. Leather elbow pads, bespoke genteel academic style. Spectacles are still kind of substantial, or optional. Opera capes are worn by the exhibitionistic geek tendency. Small sweaty men are all the rage in office spaces. Sweat marks visible like premonitions on shirt underarms. Cemetery fashion shoots feature head-case exhibitionists, and the stiff upper lips of ornery second sons of the business aristocracy are well represented. Work is a dirty word. Live for leisure pursuits. Chrome bar chic. Or sweat shop designer goods, imported well-made goods from the third world. Labour markets interchangeable. Gucci loafers predominate on the right tube lines, and men in women's shoes. They have to go, don't they? Estate agents, sweaty feet in plastic shoes, up their own arses, acne befouling every prospect of a quick sale. No commission boys! What use is commission when you're too dead to appreciate it? How many estate agents did I despatch? Why, they were numbered in their thousands. Literally thousands of second hand Mondeos, scratched paintwork, joy ridden by my boys, abandoned (after being torched) in joyless north London suburbs. Second rate cars with a legion of dead drivers. No more 5:30pm appointments to show off some leaky, infested 2 bedroom job to young hopefuls. They're all dead. Were they ever really alive? It's unlikely.

BIRTH PAINS: #8 But I have done something bad. I need absolution. There's a dummy catholic in my head, host in my withering hand, held down under the crystallising waters. Absolution, free from the need to believe. I need a face job. I am nothing without my looks. I am shallow as shallow can be. I come from a long line of handsome devils. We know how utterly compelling we can be. Raised, arched eyebrows describe an arc of social bridge building, ladies fall at our feet. Not to mention men. We are all Alpha males. There are more Chiefs than Indians. When I schlepped in from the desert, secreted myself in the fridge, the template I was after was readily available. Cold, airless, a mechanised hum, conducive to crisp, cold good looks. It was easy enough to copy the man's outline. I am from a long line of household gods. We come, we enter, and we create. Just like that. Charm is the thing. Devilish charm. Charm is the real social glue that binds. Society is full of outcasts whose principal failing is not having sufficient charm. You see them in the streets, beady-eyed grudge holders, lardy poltroons with cake eating tendencies, haggard and bitter veterans of social trench warfare, fought above and below ground. The silent legions of social warfare veterans, veterans of battles waged in solitary, in unbelievable and dank apartments. Legions with legionnaire's. Many TB cases remain undiagnosed, as trench foot casualties hack and cough their germs onto the heads of fellow passengers on the tops of buses. Windows remain closed, and the fuggy, clammy atmosphere settles like a blanket. Windows are running with condensation, breath distilled on the cold glass. Distilled alcoholics lurch around the request stop. A pit bull soon to be let loose on the top deck is flaying the pavement with acid piss. Ordinary folk look surreptitiously from the corners of their eyes, peripheral vision affording them sneak previews of the unprepossessing mob. Of the dead eyed owners 3 are male, a composite of grimy, cross-eyed, teeth-missing medievalists, a mass of abrasions and black eyes, paraffin on the breath and murder in the soul. A bundle of fun and trouble. One is marginally female. There's a commotion downstairs, pre-figuring for those upstairs what they can expect. Raised voices portend evil. The driver, behind his perspex shield, gives out, but can't quite give out enough. Worried passengers' hearts sink as the unwanted and unwashed lurch aboard. The dog makes a quick survey, snuffling with awesome threat at ankles and thighs. The lower deck mob heave inaudible sighs of relief as the motley crew levitate to the upper deck. Those above are treated for the first time to the unspectacular disarming gang who make haste for the back, barking like the dog. The dog, disdainful, makes his way around and around, string trailing like a withered corpse. The bus speeds up, as time slows down. The driver needs to be home. Suddenly, he hits the breaks…

BIRTH PAINS: #9 That's why I was late here. Bus was impounded. Corpse as evidence. My re-birth therefore postponed. I was a material witness. Driver traumatized and sent home with a compensation form. No, I really am here….here to tell you. I am now 40ish, as you can see, 20 years on, my life begun again, in sorrowful expectation of the life force (or something) suddenly kicking in. I am an expert. Levitation, psycho-kinetic devotion, laying down the tracks…you name it. I am expert in life, in re-birth, ecstatic prancing, denouncing as I go. Denunciation of the pre-mythic rips and roars from my mouth. I get up and down again. I levitate to the tops of buses and then float down again. It's all just straight up and down. But I find, despite my chronic anhedonia and dead eyed insomnia, the will to go on. I'm kept awake by the people upstairs. Who laugh too much at their own jokes. It's the only way. Like Spike, brilliant as TV surrealist, appalling as indulgent goon. Laugh at my own jokes? You bet. But upstairs it's just stupid voices issuing from mental defectives. But Spike knows enough to know you laugh at your own jokes. That's right. But I'm the stand up musician without music who shrinks from laughter. I am available. I can be used, I'm just sort of hanging around, ready to be used or abused.

BIRTH PAINS: #10 How do you think I got here? Bus or airplane accident, no need to clear customs then. This is what you want. Ten companions, dead to the world, flight out of Heathrow, falling out of the sky. Air rage so desperate that even victims of air rage are themselves routinely set upon by peaceful flyers, disturbed by their proximity to potentially violent fellow flyers. Actually beating them to death, so set are they upon a peaceful and uneventful flight. Describing an infinite arc in the early evening sky, video footage recorded by an amateur camcorder buff. Now I'm here there's no need to communicate directly any more. We're all separate somehow anyway. Just bad taste to talk…plenty of blether and outreach, prattling discourses never ending over the ethereal waves, endless nothings relayed via WAP technology. But long live the spirit of the amateur cameraman, the solo recording engineer, and the lonesome knob twiddler. Filtered and sampled, the sorry old amateur with enough balls or sheer nerve can carve a tidy career for himself by replaying bits of dead culture, moribund history back at beats per minute. The zeitgeist (that old thing) beaten into heightened shape, hijacked by proponents of solitary pursuits, enthusiasts, the solipsistic collector mentality, the urge to record even the unremarkable. And what else do we do on our own then? I think we all know the answer to that one.

We are all as unremarkable as the agent of record. We are just walking technology. Walking hardware. Fleshy gear. Flashy gear. As it were, Soft Machines. The dream or nightmare of intelligent robots has already happened. Years ago. Linear time. Just on the chance that something might happen. Individually we are nothing. Until we look. The important thing is to *look*, through a lens if possible. We're lookers, see? What we see is necessarily validated. My eyes are no longer clandestine. Unless I see you, it's invalid. Am I stating the obvious? I very much fear so as I sit here, twisting my fingers into grotesque configurations, in caricature of thoughtful critique, pulling faces that are designed to register on the observer as intense concentration. No need to communicate what you see…or am I wrong? Why else has this technology been imposed on us, blanket promotion, hard sold as essential? Information gathered and misunderstood is better than not knowing at all. That's what they say. That's the lie they peddle. The profane. If you don't know it by now, I'm batting for the sacred. The other side of the coin. I have The Knowledge in Holy Trinity of Curly, Larry and Moe, The Tripartite God in Three Persons of Sacred and Profane Infamy.

BIRTH PAINS: #11 But this is what you want. To know. To attain The Knowledge. To eschew Not-knowingness. And I am finally senseless. I am Buffy Strangelove, the feckless and craven genuflection to the Two Arcane Cultures, Knowing and Not-Knowing. I am preposterous; I am your household god. I'm here to put the mockers on it. You need no more knowledge. I am dead to the world. I am dead inside. And I am adamantine. Hard inside and out. I am deader than dead…Never had a good thought, mind never more closed, previously a black bank night. Why an open mind? Open minds are like swiss cheese…full of holes. My familiars therefore are all trepanned. I'm now nearer the end than the beginning and this point has to stick. Really, that really is my game. That's my game. God given, I'm nearer the end than the beginning.

What you want is sick gags. Extreme scenes. Filmable perversions. Erotically ironic narratives. Holocaust perversions, degraded imaginings that wrong foot self appointed moralists. First person narratives in which toddlers are slain - and see what reaction you get from the middle mass. That'll get the profane juices going. And craftily constructed scenarios, full of narrative cohesion. You want it all on a plate. Slick and ironic; hyper-ironic psycho killer novels; extended metaphors traducing society's sick consumerist tendencies. But no taboos are so strangulated that we can't stargaze. Society and its chatterers, its knee jerks, are thus jolted out of somnolence. There's no wriggling off the hook. There's nothing so empty, no surface so smooth and intangibly mysterious, as sleeping society, no society sufficiently ritualistic or plastic. All life now is ritualized metaphor. All life is undermined before the fact. Reality is the only satire you people need. You've reached the end of the satirical age and the corollary is Sick Gags. They're what you want. What we want, what we need, is sick gags. To cause uneasy offence. It has been argued that the sick joke serves as a rallying point for people in the face of unspeakable horror. Laugh at it, make it ridiculous and it loses its power to upset. You can thereby contain it, reduce it, and render it bearable. As if. You are "fearless" breakers of normal convention, clandestine terrorists, and accepted codes relating to taste and agreed cultural norms are breached. You laugh in the face of widely accepted standards of decency. But I have to tell you that there's no merit in iconoclasm, which is yesterday's news.

BIRTH PAINS: #12 Your life and mine are onrushing…sick gag express…we are locomotive. Death wish pleasuring, lack of public planning, no coherent plan, no accountable executives; this means we'll be de-railed as likely as not. Sooner or later. I am an expert remember. You are encouraged to mortgage yourself to my expertise. Be an expert as well. Become knowledgeable in something/anything. Get online, *as an expert.* You ask a question and chances are one of my online agents knows the answer. This is what you want. As long as you're all experts in *something,* as long as you can rely on someone else's expertise, as long as someone notices. I feel so empty. I don't know anything. As long as someone (anyone) picks up the proffered fruits of my knowledge, even if that knowledge is just a tawdry notation, a solipsist's desire for, and ability to obtain, recognition. Pre-cognition is inherent in all. We imagine, we actually foresee, futures that include visions…in which we're held in high esteem, feted, our opinions sought, TV crews never that far away, contracts for opinion pieces about to be signed. You need agents to manage your fame, to confer credibility by stealth. And I am a professional as well as a confessional liar. I am an expert liar. My agents are always out there, putting out for me, promoting my own especial brand of untruth. My expertise in untruth and rumour is valuable currency. I run the gravy train of rumour. I have agents all over, literally all over the world. You want anyone to set you straight? Frank's your man, sought out by heads of state. Nabobs and princes seek my advice, they're always at my door. They fly over continents, endure bathetic flight panic to hear me hold forth, pay shitloads to hear me pontificate untruthfully. My head's in the other place. It's tuned in to the psychic realm. It's my destiny…if I may assume this tone. I am desire…. I am cloudy with understated sexual yearning. I get laid in lieu. And I get touched. People touch me, and pay for it. Sometimes on the other hand I get kicked in the head, torched, generally put upon in no uncertain manner.

BIRTH PAINS: #13 This is a theme I'm warming to. See me extemporize doctor? Candidly I put my hand up the skirt of Mother Nature. Fiddling about up there, I discovered the truth about so-called genetic imperatives. Natural desires ebb away with time. Endless steamy nights, replicating scenes featuring other lovers. It's a crash course for the lovebirds and all that jazz. Viagara is the new drug of choice. And as you knock on towards 40, desire is something you put out with the cat, although I'm still a hit with the ladies. At night, as the embers grow low, embryonic clouds scud over and cop choppers disturb the peace. Buzz, and away, buzz and away. What are they up to? What, I wonder, are they looking for? Have you paid them? Are they in your employ? Do they have access to your files? Is this a new kind of super state spook perversion? What is it in the dark watches that fascinates and intrigues these spotter choppers? Mother Nature is nonetheless my endless source of pride. She did me proud. In the night, it's more obvious than ever. The void is given expansive, nullifying expression. My children are always asleep, disturbed only by the spotter choppers.

I got my boot in the door of liberty. The liberty of youth. Youth, although stretched out culturally over far too many years, is encoded and hard-wired. The new spending power of adult kids is paramount, but age actually contracts, warps and wefts in the physical body so that the young at heart are in fact all too old in liver and brain. Brainpans are empty, scoured out, as never before imagined. Nights, years, spent in pubs, imbibing useless knowledge and drinking in thoughtless opinions, being engulfed in preposterous prejudices and overcome by unsolicited views. Drink got the better of me years ago, and other peoples' opinions still ring hollow, utterly empty; but porridge like, they stick. The young at heart, still young after all these years. They were surely coined in optimistic epochs; post coital, post killing frenzy. The young at heart, like some terrible army, are surely behind all the meaningless, yet hilarious, coincidences in my life. They harry me; they cajole me, as though I were a preposterously accoutered sitcom father. They exchange mock solicitous glances as I puff and gawp. They watch me ham it up. I roll my eyes, and I do double takes. The young at heart are breathing their sickly breath down my fat neck. I for my part can't breathe. The young at heart hear me labouring for breath, and observe my body stiffening up. I can barely bend down to tie my shoelaces these days. The young at heart are on hand to make me feel as though the end is near. They're in the pub, cracking jokes; they are purveyors of good times. They wear denims well into their 50s. They never grow up; they act like dictatorial buffoons, and are despised by their offspring. The old usurping the domain of the young can't but end in tears…

BIRTH PAINS: #14 We're certainly nearer the end than the beginning, certainly paddling up that creak without the paddle of experiential insight. So far, yet nothing learned. Still no expertise. I am knowledge, which is of course as we know obsolete. Rebellion is even more obsolete. At least, as far as we can be sure of anything, we can be sure of that. Revolution is nowhere now, a pissy memory of pre-knowledge hankering. Post music, religion is not the only dead duck. Revolution's a museum artifact, despite numerous localized disputes. We are now what we have, product, which we then resell. Over and over in our dreams. Autoerotic dreams. We are deader than dead, deader than nightshade, deader than deadpan, violet death shade…we inhabit a dead world…and I clean up. When you reach the beginning of the end, little things matter. Little things like waste. That's why I set such store by metaphors for rebirth, material recycling, suddenly redolent with meaning, acquiring new substance. Waste of time. Most of all…waste of all the potential, the love, the wellspring of hope. Replaced for a laugh, just a laugh, by schadenfreude, misanthropy, and this-is-what-you-want-this-is-what-you-get cynicism. This is what you want. Leave it alone, it'll come back and haunt you. Leave it behind. I am also a diminished household god. A household god without a household. Everybody's left me. Except Dionysia here. She's like me, which is why I love her. But she's also (unlike me) endlessly faithful, despite her essential fecklessness. And Frank booted her out of course…once he'd found out that I was fucking her behind his back. The poor sap. My gags are all old. All worn out. I have outrun my gags in sickness. I go down the pub; it's the same old scene. Beleaguered veterans, propping up companions with hopeless, bleary blarney. Shirted functionaries occupy the roles filled in pre-end times by barmen and barmaids. There's a general absence of spirit, a kind of grubby fatalism, which spreads like a wet blanket through the bureaucratic bleakness of modern drinking establishments.

BIRTH PAINS: #15 You still with me? You still hanging in here doc? I worked it so that pre-millennial optimism (back in the last half of this last century linear time) took a nosedive throughout the whole sorry denouement. The more crises the better yeah? I make it a question of pride to get you all thinking along televisual lines. Nothing like seeing a whole population devoted to exhibitionism. Sweet. It took a while to catch on, but eventually we made it eh? No. I'm just indulging you now; always up for a bit of naughtiness, insensitive to sentiment, actually desensitizing my language in lyrics. I scribble a triple album's worth of flatulent pap. This is what you want. I went to NYC some 20 years ago, and fell through a tight white screen. The hordes were baying for the blood of an Englishman. We left the rhythm section still playing on stage, some joke. We are soppy experimentation, with tacked-on junky noodlings, a solid backbeat. Critics are consistent in their flattery; haw hawing like cockatoo parrot face caricatures. Wailing into the dark night, left the bassist and drummer on stage, still playing…some joke eh? I assume the character of a parody octogenarian, brow beetling at the slightest perceived impertinence offered. I am a household god, and I don't stand on ceremonies, nor tolerate offence given. I am a gnarly old man, baring greedy fangs, slobbering with affected hurt. Turning on the waterworks. I was in vaudeville until we wised up. People generally back away. I delude myself that this is because they're in awe of me. You, my amanuensis Ahab, a defrocked secular priest, know it well!! Several other doctors as well actually, have attempted over the years to disabuse me of that notion. They try to let me down gently. You say to me that while people aren't actually in awe of me, there is a kind of (it's that *kind of* that gets me) grudging respect. I know that even that's a sop. You think they can reclaim me; make me whole, make me strong. You don't know. I am way ahead. I am a household god. I am master in my own denuded household.

BIRTH PAINS: #16 You'll want to know this. You'll want to be aware of this. Knowledge, the bane of the 21st century; although we've got technology, knowledge gestated in the fetid brains of experts, so we don't have to know how the video/software/theory works, we still want to know this. It's human nature. We've got a catch up time, before knowing becomes fashionable again. But you'll want to know this. You'll want to know why it is you can't get fucked for instance. Why it is you can't get no satisfaction. Why your trousers don't fit any more. You should know that the best way is always to wear a size too small. That way, you don't get tempted to blow out. Your trousers are always telling you the truth. Leave a generous gap, a size too big and you'll be lulled into thinking you can get away with putting a few more away. Trousers cannot lie.

Littering the dank corridors of your brain, all the discarded bits of knowledge, never much use even to start with, now reaching a critical mass: compacted, compressed knowledge junk. The support structures have long been usurped by cyber space. The machines take the slack. Slack brained, individuals need no longer take the strain. Filing cabinets are obsolete. Files and filing cabinets, icons on your desktop, are something to get nostalgic about, something to fill up about. They are sentimental simulacra. We're nostalgic for tangible knowledge. The ruthless efficiency of the nostalgia industry takes up the slack of lost knowledge. Or the slack is re-gathered and re-encoded by the entertainment industry. You've seen it. Garish, symbol drenched popular channels; game shows reveling in the numerological implications of number based power games, and win a million. Jackpot! I enumerate money for you see? I already won a lottery million when I was born. Before I was born. My number came up, before the game had even been thought of. I was expelled from the stellar womb through numerological coincidence. As one universe expanded, so another contracted, and at that point, I hit the jackpot. As we went supernova, me and Frank, before the split, before he died, cash money spewed over the gleaming new universe as I gathered my thoughts. Thus began the long process of capital assessment. I've made more money than you'll ever see. Mountains of cash - I'm rich in spending power. I don't need a million. I am a million. I *burn* a million. I'm the one the bank ads are aimed at. They want *my* money. I get several letters a week *begging* me to invest my capital. It's hallucinatory. Money glazes my eyes so that everything appears dreamlike. My life as a cash rich individual is one long special effect. Did I tell you about StanleyK already? I did? He tapped straight into my frontal lobe for the final cash metaphor in 2001. Star Gate? I don't think so. That's what the inside of money looks like. It twists and swirls. It break-dances and it expands at first slowly, then riotously. It turns inside out and it changes colour in a rich phantasmagorical kaleidoscope of swirly dream images. Money buys anonymity see? Seals off the director from the real world. Borehamwood sanctuary into which the real world cannot intrude; and from which the director spins elaborate fables of coded reality. My cash fantasies helped him dodge the stalkers for year after year after year.

BIRTH PAINS: #17 We don't know what we're doing. We can play at knowing what we're doing. We can pretend to an expertise in the domain of things that never mattered, never were likely to matter. Wallpaper experts. Gardening gurus. Cookery authorities. Sumptuous but empty pixilations of food porn. But none of it ever mattered. Now it doesn't matter that it doesn't matter. Its just playtime. Free time. Dead time. You've made everything into play. Its survival of the happiest. We don't need a survival instinct any more. Knowledge, happiness, boredom makes it literally impossible to care about anything as last century as survival. We're onto the next thing. We're post frivolous.

Did you know how to identify serious play? They say that Low Cost Autonomous Attack Systems can be detonated with long rod penetration, or as an aero stable slug, or fragments, depending on the hardness of the target...and I'm now all hooked on weapon porn vids. Round my way, we've all got 'em. Everyone's got a shooter packed. Shoot 'em up with smart technology. Reach tumescence with murderous sensitivity. I intend to grow a moustache and assume the character of a model. Would a moustache suit me? Cyber suited functionary of war, I zap the unseen enemy with beautiful aplomb. Bombs away! I've bombed the knowledge out of them. Bombed the shite and the knowledge clean away. How many war movies does it take? Why bother to argue? Its exegesis for the poor bastards who've done the dirty work and been mind raped, or hot turn...I am now a sick puppy who gets off on images of slick violence, techno-erotica. I am in danger of becoming a porn mummy, emulating former guitar heroes. Strumwank. The unfunny voice of radical dissent has atrophied, morphed without grace into slick gesture. The politics of gesture comedy and weapon porn is tangibly corrupt.

Self-consciously on board, attending to the narcissism of the audience. Just don't get 'em laughing, that's all. It's a disgrace that education can lead to self-righteousness on such a monumental scale. Radical dissent is bullying receptionists. Radical dissent means radically zeroing in on the irrelevance of your intent. I'm sick and fucked. The erotic weaponry image bank is all but irresistible. Get me a drink…I need payment now.

BIRTH PAINS: #18 But I can't stop now. Pleasure doesn't do any of the perpetrators or victims of satirical intent much good. And of course they're all "sincere". But it's a weedy bombast, no real wrath. They need evisceration. They are co-dependent with their victims. Why should the criminals in charge of government and business not be exposed? They collude with their tormentors in an orgy of inter-textual co-dependence. Am I right? They think they can take a joke but they can't take a joke. They laugh at people like them because they're too much like them. They despise them because they're *too much like them.* This is the energised equation. We scorn those we recognise as ourselves. But we can only love those we recognise as ourselves. I hope you can readily appreciate, my good doctor, that this renders secular psychology a spent force. It's gone. Done and dusted. You are obliged to re-configure, brain wise. Hippocampus exercise. See mine? Distorts the forehead yes? This horn shaped muscle at the base of the front temporal lobe needs to be enlarged by maybe 30% in maybe 50% of the population in order that our general, as yet hypothetical, re-invigoration of the mythic realm be fully effective. Are you an expert in this? No? Then what am I doing in your custody? Where are my duty frees? I want my agent. You know you want me eh? I am the epic solution, the epic that is the only conceivable mode available to you now. The dissolution of the therapy centres is both my reformation and my counter-reformation. All in one, I will disenfranchise therapy culture; tear the fabric down the middle and you can see the results all around. People attempting to fuck buildings, *hypnerotomachia* obsessed, following the elephant trails. They've had their trepanned minds freed up. Hippocampus size is now, by my divine Gnostic agency, effectively without limit.

BIRTH PAINS: #19 In pre-mythic hell, the people go round and round, listening in only to their own replayed voices. Every thought is couched in DJ babble…look at me chatter. Puny voices amplified to deafening levels. In hell, they have words to make you scream, words to make you retch, words to make you blather. All words blathered out randomly as though meaning were contained *in* them, rather than attached *to* them, as in the world you've just come from, are laid bare here. They make you suffer the word all too viscerally. All those thoughtless opinions, all that vapid letting off of steam, all the injunctions to hurry up, get going, don't do that, what do you mean by that, put that down, sorry about that, don't let me catch you doing that again, hurry up for god's sake…all these (and more) are made to mean something here. You'll love it. Hell's full of people who really do *mean* it. We all mean what we say in hell. You can't get away from the perverse meaningfulness of intent in hell.

Pre-mythic hell is full of people looking for an agenda. They don't know it, but the agenda's been up there for years. I'm not talking quantum physics here, just linear time. I've been waiting for years for them to realise you don't need an agenda. Life is all you get. We bleed into death, but slowly. It happens so you don't notice. Here with you and me, it happens much quicker. Empires are born and die in the time it takes the world to turn once. The only ones to realise this were the least likely of all. Doesn't make them right mind. But they surely realised that this is as good as it gets. Life…it's there for the taking.

So I took myself beyond the suburbs, in the car, where there is no life…up beyond the orbital…beyond all the ghosts. Nice place…nice people. Nice strictly rationalised opinions. It's all so bleeding obvious in these desperate verges. All waxed aprons. High streets empty, not even latent. Little bit (not too much) history. Mazes writ large in guidebooks. Wit makes its own welcome, and levels all distinctions. No dignity, no learning, no force of character, can make any stand against good wit. These words appear in my mind. More knowledge…blown away…from meaning. The past is now over, but not forgotten. Appropriation, as it happens.

MY NEW CHURCHES/1 Ghosts are always on my mind. Do they play golf? Are they golfers? Do They Play Golf?…is what I want to know. I never knew a ghost who kept still long enough for the swing…but that don't mean a thing, that they don't have that swing. In hell they don't exist. Hell is for people who mean things, desperately, like you. Not me. Ghosts of types verging on the psychopathic disturb my dreams. Rob me of speech; paralyse my legs. Make me come. It's never sexualised. It's never sex now. Remember, I'm pushing on 40 these days. Linear time. The sight of stippled surfaces truncates sexual desire. My dreams fall conventionally into the obvious categories. Wish fulfilment, frustration. Swimming underwater. Paralysed limbs. It's terrifying, even for me. The endless nights of dreamscape dysesthesia make me rabid with fear. Unravelling, the whole linear scale unravelling. Then I wake, never quite asleep in the first place, but enough to be terrifying. Do ghosts play golf? Plaid trousered and disingenuous; hoping to make up a spectral foursome.

The dreamscape of the fairways is a region excluded by the perimeter of the M25, which thereby excludes all these ghosts. It's nature's own way of excluding them from the fairways. Clubhouse diction is not a problem. These spectres are all well articulate. Club tie operators…golf aficionados. Any dodgy geezer can get a game. But the ghosts must petition, are obliged to hang around trying to catch the club secretary's eye. They may never be nominated for membership of the exclusive clubs, even the less exclusive clubs, but they can still swing an iron or a wood. No trouble with a mashie niblick. Putting not a problem. Outside the orbital the countryside is configured schematically into arrangements of fairways, bunkers, greens and rough, and is literally teaming with young and not so young…not so old…former mods…or rockers, still in love with their youth, clandestinely planning adulterous liaisons with boys and dental assistants, bored of mooning around the house and therefore receptive to immature predatory flirting…out of love with their wives, homo-erotically attached to their old muckers…with whom they go on long boys-only camping holidays. They shlep around the fairways, dreaming of mod-rock and knocking balls into holes. Way to go lads! They retire early. Deception is on file; ghosts are alibis of the hopeless. Cheating no-one…Cheating on their wives, who are oblivious to the clearly signalled distaste felt for them by these ghosts, their husbands. They never look beyond their sentimentalised pre-adult, here and now years, or see their own ghosthood for what it is. Golf is a march of time, a retarded pastime for ghosts.

MY NEW CHURCHES/2 You look like you could play a few holes doc. Handicap? Ghosts of your youth don't get a look in. I've seen you. You don't cover your tracks. I know your secrets. I know everything about you. Seduction of the innocent; savage imposition of your carnal desires. Cover your tracks? Not quite. They fall for the bedside manner eh? The plausible demeanour? Up on Box Hill, driven up there in a Japanese motor, losing body heat, these poor suckers get raped in mind and body, left to pucker up to the realities of non-existence, forever listening in to the mournful tunes that defined them when they were alive. Post revolutionary, post narcoleptic, these forgotten ex golfers never get a look in. They drift from club to club, never getting a game, forever performing a sort of ghostly dream dance around the orbital. The 19th hole is home to many a sad soul, many a lost individual. Your mind rape victims Doctor. I have your number. I've got the goods on you. You can't get behind my mask. My glossolalia is intense now; I speak in tongues both this side of and beyond the orbital.

I have supped with ghosts. I have given them houseroom. I put up with them, give them space to express themselves. Everyone thinks they have something to say. But the sad truth is that they haven't. They just haven't. Ghosts are wrongfully encouraged. Their self-expression is the death of expression. Every story heard reduces your will to go on. Except mine eh doc? You have to hear mine. Mine is apocryphal, but all-inclusive. Every anecdote, every gag, all sorts of tawdry narratives...assumed identities... just make me feel like puking. But I need it as much as you. These ghosts might as well be dead. Deader than they already are. People I despise demand houseroom all the time. Just turn up...bold as you like, just for the night. Blink of an eye, they're there, in the bleeding woodwork. Never winkle the bastards out. Here to stay. What do they gain? They pretend to an intimacy that doesn't exist, and they abuse my good nature. I haven't the heart to put them out on the street. I scare them with simulations of cop choppers; watch their terrified reactions. They go about their miserable lives as though they were alive. They don't have any expertise. So I live alone now. Inexpertly. It's the best way. My kitchen is always empty of good will, clever laughter, and good food. Takeaways are rubbish but I don't have any time for lifestyle, friendship, and relationships. Modern relationship friendships are compromised by the need to stay ahead of the other. People are used to getting their own way. Lots of fevered debate used to take place in my kitchen, but the fire went out. Mouths opened and closed, but nothing was said.

At this point Dionysia interjects, a propos of nothing…*the hair of the hostess on the verge of catching fire…cool jazz plays in the background. A subliminal hum of clever laughter pervades the room. Lifestyle has caught up with clever lifestyle practitioners, now life itself takes a back seat. All sorts of gorgeously attired food; it's so easy to throw together. Just enjoy it, don't worry. Don't throw a wobbler, it's all about relaxing…kicking back. Lifestyle of the moderately gorgeous, giving yourselves little treats, ballast against cold reality. Well, you're gonna die too any time now, gorgeous…*

It's a non-sequitor. The doctor and I exchange raised eyebrows, in collusion maybe at last. But of course I know her game. She is playing a blinder. So now I stay inside. Forced merely to endure. I'm not forced to of course. There are no restraints here. I am fully aware of the energy currents. I still levitate at will, go down the park at full power, but I choose not to…mostly. Dogshit still bothers me, although all my children are now grown up. You've grown out of sticking your pudgy little fingers in the gloopy mess and then smearing it all over. I don't need to worry about that any more. Did I tell you? Dogs joined estate agents at the wrong end of my displeasure. Dogs, dead dogs. Domesticity equals obsolescence eh? What's the difference?

MY NEW CHURCHES/3 I'm all through with social commentary then. Abrahams looks bored anyway. Society…just a simulacrum of something or other. Something else. My "problem" not definable, traceable, in pre-mythic terms. In societal terms. Your problems have just begun though doctor. Go outside and look around. Don't expect spoon-feeding. I'm not here to make your cultural fabric flicker into life for you, or to breathe life into your moribund myths. I can neither illuminate nor elucidate them. As I said days ago, my epochal propositions are themselves elucidatory. I'm here to rip the social fabric down the middle. My New Churches…replacing the old order, the therapy centers. You think I'm ranting? I can call in favours. I've been to the Isle of Wight. Attended secret strategy meetings to determine timetables for Mythic Rejuvenescence. Trepanning schedules. You've never seen me ranting. I may be demotic in my own bathetic light, but I'm also the little minor deity of Inconsequentiality, which means I'm too urbane to rant. Do you not see my velvet smoking jacket? My ivory fag holder? I'm no Speaker's Corner nutter…I have no need to feed my own delusions…I'm the very picture of dedicated languor. My style speaks for itself. Volumes have been written about my ability to transcend earthy roots. I have become the age. Style is only one of the denizens of my dream life…

MY NEW CHURCHES/4…I didn't make this. I didn't ask to be made for this. I found the following; it didn't find me. An idea just floating - just drifting there…which I will later deny effective knowledge of. I have become cataleptic at last. I wake up in time to catch him feeling me up, filling me with juice of some sort. I was made in '60, or '80. Nineteen sixty-four. My mum was a code breaker. Won the war she did. Cancer was what did it. We never got over that. I'm breaking up now. Enigma variations. They all played sports and then they were all gone. Bunkers full of heroes. Too much thought now goes into words. Sam Beckett. He knew. He knew. Dead. Deader than deadpan. Words is all he got, all *we* got. Old waxy face, quite good at cricket. Well thought of. Very well mannered. Admired for shortness of sentences. Unimpeachable war record. Sentences, longer again, constructed themselves…became reflexive, referred to anything but the meanings they thought they contained…throughout the 70s/80s, now we're all too concerned to make sense. Words to throw the technical experts off the scent. Dyslexic, if I could fake it, would now be better. Some sort of Parkinsonian riff…words just come out all *wrong*. Or a sort of Phonemic

Paraphrasia…simulated Tourette's.…People back then often thought I was a Tourette's case. I could do that one again. Or a dysphasic. A Spoonerist. My engorged hippocampus has of course, as you'll know, necessarily precipitated chronic damage to the adjacent temporal lobes. My attitude is kind of… you gain something, you lose something else. Swings and roundabouts. I'm philosophical about it. I get the kicks…Sparked up expletives, inappropriate obscenity. I hurl obscenities at Ahab. Actually, that was just the way it was back then. And still is. Words all jumbled up. Words that have lost meaning, a residual effect of hyper-reality. I led the way, hippocampus swollen by liturgical chanting and devotional procession, and the numinous world followed. Words spoken in tongues that vanquish decadent empires, tumbling like dice in the melting pot…you won't get the same effect with pissy little debugged gobbets of code. That culture is now comatose…Blast first conservatism is now both too near and far, like its well needed.… It's had its bad day. Like a mother returning, like a tiger burning bright, the dysphasic ritual word is all that's left. They're kind of good at their job now. Shit stirrers with a fine talent for stirring their own shit. Like well-groomed arrivistes, they don't have anything to declare but their own sheer nerve.

MY NEW CHURCHES/5 Geek aspiration now is all. My ghost friends, fellow ex-gods, debased and out of the loop, all aspired to dotcom goldrush levitation. The bloom went off that one rather quickly. Businesses wished into existence, into cyber hyper-reality, then they're gone, like vapour off piss. And no one cares because, well, how can you care? That's what they didn't understand. Little shits mortgaged to the very ends of their tether. Live the dreaming lives of paraplegic psycho-explorers. They're dreaming the dreams of the unbrave. They've staked their land claim in no man's land. Literally. I bump off an html artist a day now. Send bad Gnostic vibrations at ISDN speeds. Pickle their goose for them. It's the death of a sense of humour of course. But how do you kill it? Humour is already dead, no longer funny. You're past laughing.

Geek law – the modern law of diminishing returns. The more they try to infuse their code with intent, numerological import, the more we're all filled with breathless ennui. Reality never intrudes in the quiet realm, whatever that is. I've had to go back again and again, over the years, go back years and years to find working definitions. I have been reduced to holding out for windfalls, cash rich game shows with never a winner in sight…and the more attractive and inevitable suicide appears. Re-birth in Gnostic wholeness, but without a sense of humour. It's one way, if not mine. Your favourite comedian, a former god of inconsequentiality and present familiar of idiocy, is no longer funny. But I've been around too long. The mask is slipping. I need to get back to the airport. My baggage needs reclaiming. Left luggage, the whole city's supply. Will the doctor be much longer? It's almost time to go. Driving around the distressed suburbs that flank the airport, it's all too obvious where the problem is. The landscape is pauperized. There's a total lack of good faith, the topography heaves with cynicism. Motorcars are fizzing like firecrackers, so I hit the accelerator pedal. The bus speeds up, and then stops suddenly. There's a bang. Opportunistic auto smash. The car skids into a swerve, flips over like a pancake…. I'm OK. I'm out of there in a flash. The contours of my body somehow adjust. It never quite gets to me because I remain focused. Up and away, the astral body taking the strain away. Flying dutifully south around the circular, I'm afforded these visions…decades worth of accidents, brittle arcades full of smashed vehicles. Thousands of busted luxury coaches fill the orbital…full of stuffy, constipated day-tripping occultists, intent on disseminating their pernicious doctrines. So these auto smashes are a necessity. My work, it's never done. They can't move, these leisure prisoners in their metal mausoleum juggernauts. Moveable coffins, they pack 'em in like sardines. They can't move. Surgery's the answer. Movies at volume, want it or not. Same with planes, although the very decorous flight assistants who breeze back and forth like the dust never settles enhance the illusion of freedom and movement. I fly, as I've endeavoured to explain, whenever and wherever I get the chance. Truly intercontinental, that's me. I am an intercontinental household god, a moveable feast. Free booze an' all. Free loader, that's me. I drink till it comes out of my nose. Like some boozy caricature tart, my knickers come off for anyone. It's just one long Xmas office party where I'm concerned. Then I get all maudlin, time to buckle up, time to hunker down, cry into the chardonnay and, like, my soul's…uh…*ablaze* with ritualized anger. I make up stories…in my head…in which I'm always cast as the victim. No one's ever been as badly treated, as ill used, as have I. I have to be asked to sit down, to leave, discreetly. Everyone's against me, I am hateful, I'm just a piece of shit really. I know it. Deep down I know it. Lucky I never got up to any of that shit while actually in flight. I'd have been a disaster in flight. I fly like a baby. I'm an expert in victimhood. No-one's safe from my manipulations there. I've been wronged by literally *everyone*. Several times over, every day…but then, I'm right on the money too. By the time the plane lands I've completely changed again. I re-energize, carrier bags and all, through customs, new paths to beat, elephants to invoke………

MY NEW CHURCHES/6…But I don't easily shed the more enjoyable caricature skins I affect. It's too much fun. Boozy caricature number one, that's me. I'm two…no, make that one-dimensional. I allow misconceptions to stand unchallenged. I operate in grey areas. I don't take responsibility for my actions. I paint up. I get drunk. I'm anyone's, especially once I've got my way. The way I use people for my own ends is like nobody's business. The way I do it is to flatter them into thinking I take them seriously, that I *like* them (as if!) and then once they've let their guard down, I let 'em have it. I tell tales out of school, I spread rumours, gossip maliciously, never letting my own guard down. Play one off against the other. I let it be known what I *really* think to people who have the power to harm them. I kick down; I'm incorrigible. I have no integrity. It's what I call fun. For flight ennui it can't be beaten.

So anyway, what I've been leading up to is this…why listen to music? Music's done for. The repertoire is empty. Anything that is too stupid to be spoken is sung. There's a lack of the right stuff. The right people doing the right thing. I can't listen to music, there's no point in music simulation, studio manipulation. Recycled attitudes. Attitudinizing, referential, over cautious, positioned for the greatest possible effect, peoples' brothers, chanting doggerel, strumming and thrumming. Drummers are cactus headed, cow breath sodden, murky from self abuse, clubs full of sweat…false impressions, singers with Beckett mouths, nothing to sing, nothing simple, beyond re-appropriation, bereft of dignity, no bravery...to just stop. Clicking out rhythms to make you weep for boredom, phrasings that are copies of copies of your own brain patterns, jazz action...Notes fail to illuminate over familiar emotions, familiar chords are mere emoticons. I form a band to illustrate the point...

...Back outside in the cold, rain lashed down. Holes in the car roof were proof of my fecklessness. One day, I thought...one day. Bands swarmed like ants in my brain. Overtures in denim; bad attitudes of sweaty men. Again. Too much to contemplate, for one night only. I was my own bouncer, excluded from former bonhomie drenched evenings by my own aphasic malapropisms. I bounced myself good and proper away from the light and from the music. I went on ill-advised benders with the roadies. 20 pints...with chasers. Whores and coke filled nights of excess. I went hugely bellied into negotiating rooms and intimidated all and sundry with my bulk and sheer force of personality. Tremulous entrepreneurs quaked and cowered before me. But we were flying anyway, no need to over-play the gangster bit. We were almost always in flight. The juggernaut of flagrant excess was always primed for action. Constant forward motion, Concorde back in action, one false move and it would have been fatal for more than one of those concerned. We put so much stuff up our noses you just wouldn't have believed it. Drug hyper activity was the fuel and the freedom.

Bad head. I have a bad head. I'm winding down after the excess. Bits of information, frothy apocrypha, float in and out of the swollen cerebellum. My thoughts are white hot, the electrical impulses turning to needles. I sit up, stretch, and look around. There's a silence likened in my cleansed brain to seashore sounds. Shell-like white noise, hisses of beach breath. I exist in silence now. The party's well and truly over. I prop up the nearest bar bereft of my former charm or energy. I sit here trussed up, a plaything of malevolent medics, their backs to the blank wall, blanket around the shoulders. Dionysia now no longer in a position to help. My head, lolling slightly, momentarily assumes a death's head impression. Grinning skeletal visage, swallowed up again in an instant. Wouldn't hurt a fly. Plenty of scope for the remake there. I'm not done yet. Or am I!

MY NEW CHURCHES/7 I am of course remade and remodeled almost incessantly. I dust down my glitter suits, rediscover my platform boots as before. We will hold futuristic séances with the assembled press pack and re-assure all concerned that what we are about to embark upon is in no way an act of cynicism. We will join hands with the hacks and just feel that the moment is somehow right. The surfer resurfaces; the zeitgeist will be breached again. Identity will once again be re-established. We are pure simulacra, until re-birth. Until Rejuvenescence. Until the elephant vibrations kick in. We think big, big enough to convince our doubters that our intent is not pauperized. Sponsorship is through the roof. The offshore accounts have been primed. We come over well, like seasoned boulevardiers, radiating an essence of worldly and impressive solidity. No one for a moment doubts that we are serious in our intentions, or imagines that we're just in it for the money. We dreamed enough money for ourselves long, long ago. We already sold the money idea. We are paternal and we take our responsibilities seriously. Me, Frank and Dionysia; the comeback tour is officially on. We're in a position to pick and choose, and we won't put up with any old rubbish. The comeback plane, amazingly, was almost de-flighted last time round. Some deluded supplicant to the inner voices had gained access to the flight deck. Sorcery was suspected. Doesn't make sense…not in this day and age, even given the tacitly accepted new low standards of practice and security that are a corollary of insufficiently rigorous acceptance of personal responsibility among all public and private employees. People just don't *give* a fuck, on any level. Even when your life, and my life, is on the line. And so lunatics in their lucid intervals and/or terrorists are routinely checked onto flights without so much as a by-your-leave. Result: in this case severe shock, we are witness to a furious wrestling match with flight assistants who struggle to retain their dignity while at the same time subduing the delusory character. Result: peremptorily enforced soul searching, of the most emphatic nature, as the plane spirals out of control to within seconds of the immediate termination of all life in the vicinity.

I have, of course, complained in no uncertain terms. I found the man responsible, the functionary identifiable by the egg stains on his corporate tie.

In my haste to make my point, my undilutable and undeletable comic rage was unchecked. I insulted him with all conceivable rapidity, called his lineage into question and went into a comic routine of undeniable effectiveness and moment. That's the way we do it. That's how we achieve re-entry. So what can you do about it? You're looking at me blankly now. You are history doctor.

THE INAUGURATION OF BUFFY STRANGELOVE.

<u>Dr Ayton, prognosis after the fact</u>: *His [Yapp's] component elements were incompatible, his trajectory undetectable; the vectors of his many re-entries entirely unpredictable. The point is, he has no template, no causality. He doesn't inhabit. He might be in Zagreb or he might be in Pyongyang, we wouldn't know; he may be elucidatory, or he may be paraphrasic…in this case, a diagnosis cannot conceivably be equivalent to a conclusion; in the absence of causality, his meta-narrative carries on. He persists as an auto-characterization long after prognosis because no storytellers, narrators, therapists, secular priests, can place him. His elusiveness is elucidatory. Prognosis is therefore still promising/good.*

…People are everywhere free, and everywhere in chains. Rousing myself from post-industrial, post-flight slumber, I thought for decades before I took against the whole idea that people should in any meaningful sense be free of their chains. So again the questions asked by liberals, catholics and therapy whores………Why do Bad Things Happen To Good People? Why are good people routinely overlooked? How does a bad person sleep at night? What does a bad person do to achieve grace? Why am I so good? How come I'm not successful? How come I'm too successful? How do we cope when our former acquaintances become successful? Do we hate them? *Do* we?…are quite transparently answerable. Let's face it, I hate people, sleepwalkers all, famous or not. That's why they're in chains. They forged them there. And I'm angered up. I luxuriate in the anger rush. I'm addicted to it. My anger is Olympian. It spreads fires around me. I need dowsing sometimes. My fame bug is consumed in fire. Show offs unanimously require the favour of Olympian Rage Gods to enable them to brazen it out. I put the bug in them and then set fire to it.

The doctor, looking at me over the top of his spectacles, asks me if I wish to meet another doctor. His colleague and lunch partner in therapy, he says, has a special interest in auto-fictionalisation. He is, it seems, a sentimentalist. A chiseller of the rosy glow; a hagiographer of the working classes; their inherent integrity his special subject. A grown up manboy from the badlands, lachrymose bad boy and media favourite, reputation assured and burnished. I of course decline. I prefer to place my trust in his legions of ecstatic dancers, mincing psycho-tattlers; those who attempt to tease out meaning, inculcate spiritual potential, through movement, which they say takes the patient into altered states without drugs. They claim to produce psychic movement, get people singing, screaming and crying. They get me laughing, laughing, and laughing. And I have no wish to deprive myself of laughs that are at present my main source of strength.

I have no wish to sell out. I have no wish to slide, to become The Queen Mother of Alternative Comedy. I not only have not sold *out*, I never even *bought in*...as far as the doctors are concerned I am a flash git, a baby boomer mangler of vowels...an estuary twat...with higher than mid-middle class antecedents (daddy is a despised academic) pretending to a streetwise attitude. I walk around, two fingers aloft, smarmy mug a map of oleaginous arrogance. The doctor looks over his specs at me again. Cunt. People in chains, psycho-tattlers, reckon I used to be radical but incline now to the view that I've sold out. I "never believed in anything"...I "never had a sincere thought in my life"...I "have talent, but merely a talent to disguise". They say. I "leave false trails". My "inner vapidity is identifiable as a slight ability to amuse". I "put everything inside quote marks". That's how big a cunt "I" am. People hate me, even those who I "amuse", but who have now grown bored of me, because amusement is never more than skin deep and it's surprisingly easy to hate people trivially. Hate is in the small things. Hate is trivial for many of these people who love me. They bestow their plastic impressions like gifts of hate in the letters pages of reactionary/liberal newspapers.

The reason I know this. I am the bastard now and in a formerly fictional life. I used to write the letters. I used to answer them too. Used to go around with two fingers aloft intoning "peace man!" in heavily ironic mode. It's true. All true. I hang my head in shame. In chains. I was good at the old sub-Wodehouse knockabout stuff, and no one would begrudge me credit for my brilliant scripts, but the rest of it? Socially conscious, painfully aware blockbuster airport novels, the relentless pursuit of good image, scripting mediocre comedies and now flirting with the hideous and the rich, the obscene. I have become obscenity. I am now enchained. Laughter is therefore my only redoubt. Bring on the psychic dancers, but keep the sentimentalists away Doc. Bring on the jitterbuggers. Not that I'm bitter, being an anonymous household god who never made it past self disgust while he, my past life doppleganger, the slimy fucker, lives the transcontinental lifestyle, his opinion sought and valued, loved by the public unaware I'm/ he's a dirty little pursuer of [deleted for purposes of avoiding litigation at my own hands]......

The doc looks at me again over his specs, a mannerism that I'm finding increasingly difficult to tolerate. I realize I don't come out of this looking particularly good. But bitterness is a fact of life. Jealousy and hatred harden even further into life threatening conditions. Hospital admissions go up exponentially in areas populated by the ex-class mates of happy successful people. They fulfill a useful hate-role. But indulging in the purely human urge to belittle the poisoning success of former acquaintances does us no favours. Reverse shadenfreude is a wasted emotion. But I'm addicted. My brother is ostensibly a very successful academic. Talked of as a genius in prattling circles. And - get this - only because he doesn't have a lower half - shits out of his stomach, perambulates in a shit-chair at double speed, spitting Touretter's curses like a fucking Attention Deficit Hyperactivity Disorder paraplegic on crack…talks like he's on Helium…comic effect, like the angrier he gets the higher the voice goes…because of the effects of lung wastage. He cranks it out in theatre auditoria, eliciting clever laughter and dutiful respect. Why can't people see that he's just a little shit, a shitty-legged pontificator? With beard, elbow patches and colostomy bag. Good old Frank. Frank my brother, who I can no longer live without. There's a space there, something missing.

His success enrages me, sends me into paroxysms. I'm stuck here in this waiting room, being done over by immigration (intrusive and degrading body search....the whole number, the full Monty) and he's on the front pages. He wouldn't be anything without me. Even the copywriting business is getting in on Frank. Offered him a 6-figure sum just to lend his compromised person to an ad campaign for Digital TV provision. The Future is Digital. The Future is Frank. Compromised corporeality, bodily impairment, signifying, in the televisual lexicon, saintly genius, are the real USPs when it comes to new media. See the would-be punters, regaled with this figure of a god, resplendent in the myth. Mythically delineated, without limbs, and the punters are absorbed.

We can't discuss soaps forever. We have bigger fish to fry. Discussions on the merits of this soap against that soap, transparent attempts to encourage me to identify the fictionalized process within myself, are the stuff of dreamy time. Lasts until the commercials. The good doctor shows me a number of projector slide ads at regular intervals, and I'm literally shocked awake by the sudden and emphatic volume hikes. My understated need to be shocked anew is again endorsed. He thinks this Munchausen number is his own discovery. He thinks shock therapy in the form of commercials played at ear damagingly high volumes will cause a schism in my schizoid fictionalization. Stops short of the eye clamps though. He is humane...just. Like I said, I like a laugh...so I don't attempt to dissuade him. His sheer impertinence and dogged professionalism is impressive though. Give him his due. He harries me as though I were a personalized rabbit, star struck in his headlights. I lollop about, nibbling at his proffered tidbits, keeping my humour, maintaining a carefully calculated mythic distance. His colleagues behind frosted glass, dozing sleepyheads, are rudely awakened, dreams of soap still bubbling beneath their surfaces. The soap bubbles surface, the goo-goo itch of mundane familiarity is realized. Fictionalized family members bear down on them, importuning their fractured attention. BBC sites mainlined, lead directly to porn behind the frosted glass. Everything's linked. But it's a goat-soap. Self parody. The other is sheep-soap...beyond parody - more mature in TV evolutionary terms. One is secular po-mo, the other is ritual po-pomo so I'm told.

I tell him that to my mind people who can actually watch a whole episode of sheep-soap must not have brains at all. It's cack. Pure and simple. People just aren't *like* that. Goat-soap has never (well perhaps it did when it was in B & W - I'm just too young to know for sure) pretended they were. It's characters respond with disdain to issues. It's characters are contained within their own issues. Sheep-soap's characters are just hideous, ugly, boring and humourless. And you can't understand what they say...some coffee table BBC notion of what real people are like. How likely is that? It's a disgrace, an insult. What else is to know? Characters who make you glad you're only fractionally fictional. Most fantasies involve fictionalizing the self, and do not involve thanking god I'm not that fucking loser. The thing to hang onto (I'm in confessional mode again, the other side of this cloth) is that you have a duty to fictionalize, but make it good, to be in the happy position of choosing. It's a divine blessing. A morose downbeat narrative doesn't do anybody any good. Ever. The only thing sheep-soap has to watch out for is endlessly re-iterating plot points several times per episode, which must be a sop to the terminally inattentive - must be this Dumbing-Down we've heard so much about. I approve. In my soap dreams I get in where the sub-culture needs a kidney punch and administer summary justice. I was sent down for perjury in another fiction, but I'll bounce back. Ways and means.

I was involved, before the trials, at the highest levels of dumb sabotage during the early pre-secular years. I saw to it that only the most egregious show-offs ever got on the air, exhibitionists without the distancing comic spin that would indicate familiarity with the message and the medium. Just straightforward attention seekers. I therefore juiced ministers...proactive in devising and formulating the Attention Seekers' Allowance. A government sponsored handout, a subsidy for those exhibiting the most overt pathological need to be photographed/filmed despite not actually doing anything. A conjoining of art and soap. Mugging and hamming at cameras pointed in my general direction. Manufactured rage, comedy bluster...aimed at minions not in on the joke. Make it up as we go along. My governmental initiative (the politicians regard me as eccentric but tolerate me for the spark of electricity I bring to the party) was rubber-stamped. I was ensured of a budget adequate to allow myself to seep covertly into the public realm.

Subliminal messages, jokey ads for product, it's all there. This skill which I patented, although the doctor is in litigation as we speak, we've had rammed down our throats these last 20 odd years and I am convinced that through the offices of my friends in high places I can secure intervention at government level directed at securing additional financial assistance for exhibitionists. It's a struggle though; favours need to be called in. Ministers are to be lobbied in their Pall Mall clubs. Junior civil servants are to be bribed with cheap holidays abroad and designer sunglasses.

At the doctor's instigation, as therapy, I tried my hand at the Agony Uncle game. It *is* a game though, and people with "problems" sure are jokers. It's as though they don't grasp that essentially they are entertainers. Their real problem is that they don't appear to understand that they should be paid as such. Unionization hasn't even occurred to them. But is there hope? I hope so. I am deliciously fair, if not equitable. I am immensely sexy. In and out of print it shines through. Sometimes when the choppers fly over, I'm reminded of the dark angels that inhabit our former legends, who still inhabit the dreamy time, my occluded heaven. Until I wake up that is, prehensile erection of my secondary penis gleaming and throbbing with intent.

Anyway, here is a selection of the types of "problems" I had to deal with. My position as columnist manqué was never compromised, my editors were always indulgent. Like I needed their patronage. I was of course ultimately their employer anyway. Vanity publishing or something like that. I can write what I like because I know where the bodies are buried. I have droit de seigneur in all sorts of unimaginable ways. So, my politician friends fixed it for me to have my own talk page. One of my ex-friends had recently been investigated for alleged "forgetfulness" over a phone call made (or not made) which turned out to be, though merely a storm in a teacup, nevertheless a matter to be handled with delicacy. My initiative, occurring as it did just at the right moment and being carefully placed to achieve maximum media saturation, served to deflect attention from the minister at just the right moment. For which he was extremely grateful. In fact, the greasy fucker's now in *my* pocket...unless I've mis-calculated.

Which is possible, though unlikely. I don't like the way Abrahams is always on his mobile though…sneaking surreptitious glances at me…looking away when he realizes I've clocked him…

One freak wondered aloud if she weren't perhaps getting old. Something about DIY, an obsession with housework, yoga. She lies awake at night wondering if perhaps she has become suddenly *old*. My reply was that she hadn't become old, she's just realized, had an inkling, possibly, that she may, just possibly, be a bit of a *freak*. There's no age limit. I wouldn't worry about it. I reassure her that the awful realization hits most of us sooner or later. It happened to me last week, and again a week later. It's due to happen again around about now. Readers of the post-ironic press unfortunately rarely experience this chastening feeling, which is why it comes as something of a surprise. Even then they fail to call it for what it is, preferring instead the mealy mouthed and sentimental "perhaps I'm just getting, you know, old or something….there isn't, couldn't be, anything inherently wrong in the way I see things??? Could there? Could there????"

Let me tell you that these *freaks* give a damn good impression of irredeemable superiority, clued up…in all sorts of political and cultural ways And they all talk as though they actually know me. In reality. What a hideous thought. But I tell them: Laziness is the Besetting Sin. Their condition is a result of laziness. They're not doing anything - raging against the night, or playing dress-up or something. I'm just sitting behind a keyboard laughing at them. Do I make my point? Or again, someone's so bored at work. They've decided to design a website, whatever that may be, in their spare time. But because they're so bored they cannot think of a single thing upon which to base it. They wonder, does being bored make a person boring?!? I answer that one…No. Only bores say that bores are bored because they're boring. But *don't* under any circumstances design a website. Or quote me. Do *not* cultivate empty obsessions. Inhabit more than a corner of your brain. Seek trepanning therapy. Try Elephant Gnosis™. Seek to empathize with the hobgoblin in your small mind as he dredges his brains. Try to be consistent in characterization. Your characters may be as boring as you like because in distancing yourself from them they become *meta*-fictional. Of course, one may still be boring, but the more you do the more the odds lengthen against it. In many ways, I say, it may be better to do nothing and always remain uncertain as to whether you're boring or not, on the basis that as long as you don't know for certain, you can always kid yourself that you're not. This is in fact the path taken by most people, so you're not alone. But let's face it; everybody's boring...at least some of the time. To be constantly amusing and/or engaging would be a killer, for everyone concerned. There are precedents but we'll leave them for later.

Then some gimp comes back saying that I'm anti-gravitational. They say I may as well claim that gravity doesn't exist. There are fundamental gravitational divides in the world - as proven by various surveys revealing the plight of the non-levitating. How on earth can the technological white heat of torsion field technology be made available to all? Positing the non-existence of gravity is just a fig leaf for posh mediocrities to justify their protected practices. They observe that they don't know where to start on my analysis, such is its utter wrong-headedness. They characterize it as mostly mere verbiage and a hotchpotch of pseudo psychological mumbo-jumbo. Well, of course that's fighting talk....

I come back strong...

"There are so many inaccuracies and misconceptions in your argument it's impossible to know where to begin. However: If you attribute every problem in your life to gravity evasion and therefore oppression you miss the main point about pre-religious life. Which is: that you should, in post-psychological terms, always seek, to avoid crippling mental illness and/or heavy limbs, to locate your problems (whatever they may be) in causes *inside* yourself. Not in causes related to gravity fields. Don't look outside. You are your own problem. You deny. You inhabit glib trajectories. You invoke parochial arguments. You do not appear to be capable of divining the true purpose of so-called bus lanes. Look around you. Check your peripheral vision. Those who seek to locate their problems in extrinsic causes, like gravity stress, suffer monumental and often irresolvable post-psychological trauma. In other words it'll drive you nuts...unless you recognize that all problems, all electricity and all solutions thereto, stem from the self. Seek the divine within, via elephantine vibration. Seek the bus lanes. It really is as simple as that."

I warm to my theme…

"The interventionist obsessive", I remark, "is as deluded as the religious devout. Both seek answers with reference to some higher power that is to blame for everything. God, or the Corporates. The force of gravity. It's all the same. Deny them thrice, and you're free. If not, that's fine - if that's your slice of cake, but it just makes you a bore, an ego-less boob, a failed trajectory, a non-emphatic vector, a dead end, a psycho sideshow."

Seeing that he's on the run, I press home my advantage.

"All individuals fixated on the external are beyond hope. Salvation and KNOWLEDGE are on the INSIDE. Let it go before it lets you go. Don't cite physics and/or fundamental gravity distortions. Cite yourself. Don't hide behind monolithic constructs. Psycho-socialism, no less than Big Bang folklore, is in the dustbin of history, precisely because it has failed to understand that each man, woman, child, mutant and separated conjoined is fundamentally a self-determining entity. I don't think you're unfortunate enough to have been born into a pre-secular hothouse economy are you? Life for your sort isn't pre-ordained. We in pre-religious Elephant Gnosis™ are no longer fatalists. We are now electricity free, or at least potentially so. The torsion fields are clear for take off. Take up thy bed and walk and stop whingeing!! It is your *personal* misery. You lack the ability and the motivation to extricate yourself, to see the elephant tracks under your noses. This failure inspires you to revenge yourself by taking up arms and seeking redress against the unfair, unclean world. You may as well eat cake.

"And why, I might ask, should your education in this matter (for education's sake, for spending's sake) be free? Your ignorance demands a price. Those who want to spend will find ways. You learn something. You benefit. Be an autodidact. Eat cake! Stand on your own feet. You are mindless in prejudice. You are a destructive; a redundant meme. Class-play is redundant. Even though there are still vast inequalities of wealth and/or levitation capability. Banging on about the devout is more a cheap selective jibe these days. Who isn't a devout? Are IT professionals (for instance) devouts? Are academics? Are tobacco pickers? Are T Shirt weavers? Are media wannabes? The dignity of devotion is either a transferable construct or a meaningless anachronism. It's either or both. But you can't bend it into a shape that excludes those whose devotion you disapprove of, or who regard themselves as pre-religious. We're all ascetics now. We look inward. We identify the elephantine within ourselves. Trepanned skulls alleviate the chemically enlarged hippocampus. It's up to each of us to invent our own meta-fictions mate. How we relate to the world is nobody's business but our own. My corporations are of course benign. They wouldn't hurt a fly. There are no more security blankets.

"And if you can't bear to give them up, ask yourselves if in every area of your lives your conduct is unimpeachable? You do realize, don't you, that without this gnosis, this specialized trepanned freedom, you won't be able to enter into clean transactions of any kind? But I'll take your confession any time. And laugh at it. But you pay buddy. You pay big time. Your rhetoric (only a smug dealer in monolithic constructs or an inveterate sloganeer could refer without irony to my "wrong-headedness") betrays you. You are neither young nor old enough. Just unclean. It's intent that matters.

"Please think about it", I say, seeing that he's utterly routed. The editor interjects at this point: *Look, the thing is, people should never laugh at their own jokes. It's a sure sign both of age and of being a bore. Just get on with it and cut out the side splitting routine. Comic orthodoxy (being straight faced) can only be breached be genius. And there's only one thing worse than being old. And that's talking about being old…*

So that's it. I inhabit this strange place. I am fully mythopoeic, as the doctor is beginning to accept. As I think I've had cause to remark before, I invoke elephants, introducing herds into all decadent cultures. Again there are always precedents to sooth the unbelieving populace. Big cats sighted on Dartmoor. An elephant glimpsed in apparently inappropriate locations in peripheral vision is at base a tonic, a bracer, a glimpse of the future. It's like credit in the bank; it's a general sense of well-being. It's the inspiration you need, it's the corrective for those who might think that a career as a celebrity presenter (and let's face it, that's *everyone* in this present culture) is desirable or an ambition to nurture. There's an immediacy about an elephant, a heightened reality. They breach the scale codes we've been lumbered with, and thus even in peripheral vision tend to make an impression. Elephant tracks are visible to those who keep their eyes on the ground, while those attuned to their reverbed vibrations are always aware of the approach of a herd. My only regret, and perhaps I'll have recourse at last to litigation, is that the US Republican Party stole my idea. There's nothing that's more offensive to the mythopoeic sensibility than mis-used symbols, misappropriated stigmata.

I feel languid now again…in the mythic realm (I see the sheep-shaggers behind the frosted glass stifling laughter) I've set up a kind of template for myself that impertinently mirrors the divine trinity. Dualism is naturally a redundant concept. It's too simplistic to think of the divided self, the civilized man/wolf man, inner and outer truths. Life just isn't like that. Life if it's to be understood and lived in the true spirit is based on at least 3 of a kind; Curly, Larry and Moe. 3 divine beings, or in my case 2 unreconstructed men and 1 iridescent woman. 3 is a number we can settle on, though of course the reality is that a multiplicity of split divinities is present at all times. But for our purposes, all beings are now templated at 2 parts man to 1 part woman. Even women. *Especially* women, in the post-psychological age. No longer tea ladies, or fraught single mums, or boardroom vampires, or boozy caricatures, they assert their identities in male refugee territory. Women now experience the same rage as men, they get boozed up and spit vitriol on charter flights, and they feel the equivalent cock-sure testosterone rush. They replenish and refuel the same anger lust and angst as their husbands and sons and lovers have before. And revel in it. They love it. Oedipal blueprints are routinely laughed out of town. No longer do therapy templates match up. Therapy's a laugh, a tax write-off. A diversion. A parlour game. Dinner-party chat. Yes Doctor? Am I right? Freud's museum is now dusty, curated by freakish semi-humans, a Hampstead redoubt for recidivist academics, the forgotten relics of pre-evolved parlour love. The moose is now in the bedroom with go-to-hell eyes, stacked up flirting technique clashing insanely with supermarket checkout ennui. Chardonnay is now drunk to excess. Ladies pile on the misery, livers doing handstands of protest. The ladies are in for the duration. There's a mutation going on…tails up, androgynous footwear…pudenda sprouting horny little bulbs. Men meanwhile are compromised, bellies are distended, and the DNA is quite debased. Not so cocksure, unaware of modern love. Men are all played out, now at least 1 part de-sexualized. No more re-birthings for de-contextualized sitcom caricatures, being clouted in psychosis rage by insanely angry women. Menboys stack up in pubs, drowning not waving on withered stalks.

And we change the nature of history if not history itself with androgynous, cocksure hearsay. We drift in and out of the picture, at once unfocused and sharply defined. We need eyes in the backs of our heads, Argus like. Our 100 bleeding eyes are ruthlessly applied stigmata. My septum has been breached more than once. My theophanic manifestions as wind and rain are ritual. But they lead to general unquiet in the public arena. Instances of muggings go up, car thefts increase. Scuffles outside pubs and road rage incidents see a sharp upturn as women frequent more pubs and clubs en masse, in gangs. However, when we're good or can be bothered, things never seem better. Things are now up for grabs again. We have the world in our very hand, our claw-like hand. We're going belly up together. Men and women together, like birds, entwined in chains, free of nothing. Everywhere free, free and in chains. I am enchained in my fraught imagination, and Ahab is not about to disabuse me. Or abuse me. He won't abuse me. I know where his body is buried.

THE SCOURGING OF BUFFY STRANGELOVE.

We're dancing a delicate pas de deux at the moment. And so this next act or movement is an act of pure bravery on my part. With the emphasis very much on 'act'. I'm by no means as in control as I've been at pains to paint myself. I wear the mask almost all the time now. It's a dangerous game. I line up a killer move, a daring manouvre. You see I do realize, my dear doctor, that I haven't as yet described myself to you in anything like adequate detail. My appearance remains a mystery to you. Well, as you can see for yourself, my potato head is stippled; my flying buttress ears are comically large…as is my elongated hooter. My belly is distended and my feet are clubbed. I have bad teeth and arched eyebrows. My stories, such as they are, unfold with coffee table modishness…I have my eye on the filmic possibilities, movie rights are in the forefront of my thoughts…my characters are drawn from B-grade experience rather than inspiration. Dialect hides emptiness, parochial exposition masks elephant tracks, but now you meet in me your nemesis…

It's a mid-shot…nourish shadows are predominant…silence on silence… pre-violence silence…more silence…the silence of potential creation… procreation…the quiet act of begetting pre-imagined beings…Potato Head sits motionless, poised over the virgin sheet. He is cadaverous. Out of the mouths of psycho-babes, the silence is in itself a dialect; a demotic language, a cinematic overture of pure intent, and these 4 under-conceived half-baked lads are giving tongue. Spectral voices yammer inside his potato head. He pours himself a drink (bourbon, naturally) dives into the ritualized head-space, he's mining a fecund seam, spews out the surrendered garbage, makes good the filmic aspects, relying on the gloss of adman squalor. The life spirited away from his malignancy and badness by ghosts in fleeting celluloid overcoats, the dialect tones ringing in the potato headed author's dizzy cheque-book imagination, and they are re-birthed.... 4 lads on the razzle; Pinko, Wankbait, Guzzler, Scally…out on the pickup, bagmen for Mr. Big, Frank's lads, his muscle, commission paid in kind, crack head street guys, operators each and every one…in their own right, hyper-imagined goons with realized lives, storybook rubber-stamped and psychologically profiled. The imagination is raped for major effectiveness, stony-faced invective issues from blabbering caricature mouths. Bad mouthed vitriol a discoursing language, a dialect, a dialectic, an everyday rite. Potato Head exhibits his own rage spawning dialect cursing, his ticket to a big entrée in soiree society. Movie bad-mouthing now a fine art, a newly minted language of cash from contempt, cynicism made celluloid. Good guys doing bad things instead of *bad* guys doing bad things. Crucial difference, which elucidates the new cultural matrices. But now he thinks he'll make it with big-titted babes and unfortunately also with a variety of hangers on, celluloid whores, movie moguls re-writing his precious "original" manuscript. Anyway, the trailer is almost complete. Fast cuts and edited highlights, every thuggish exchange made good for matinee audiences. Pre film-school demotic, the movie angle prefigured, Potato Head the author is now a fetish figure of pure mogul-fantasy, the moneymen creaming their chinos, and a 7-figure sum is assured.

The obligatory moment of rumbling silence is raped by vernacular sound bite. Wolverine toothed, pockmarked head, the bloated body in the dining room is covered with tooth marks, intestinal gas expanding, the cash corpse rapacious. The results of the author's covert perversities are now on camera. Estate agent bumph is scattered every which way, a quick sale not now on the agenda, the estate agent/author lying in a pool of his own effluvia, blood and guts. The trailer's too short to provide respite for him. Potato Head the dealer in movie commissions is spread-eagled, a knife in his blubber guts, a claw hammer ripped through his windpipe. It's in the imagination of Potato Head, in front of whom the masked assassins lick their chops. Two hippo masks - one monkey head - one elephant. No escape therefore for the author. At least one elephant inspired individual, one at least of fuller powers to make the unaware author eat authorial shit. This will get him in trouble with the moneymen, or conversely will open new doors. One or the other.

They're fighting over the bourbon, the crenellated edge a tawdry bludgeon in their minds. The author imagines fighting talk. He's fighting mad, taunting and urging them. Perhaps unwisely. The boys at any rate pay no heed, or lip service. Already they're half out of control. A hammer blow awakens Mr. Potato Head. Ripped shirt. Blood. Balls hanging by a thread… It's all vernacular ad-friendly, the camera's whirring, a weapon now as well. The fear is now tangible. His face spells it out. Will they kill him, their passive aggressive mentor? Has he miscalculated? He was drinking himself to death anyway, and now the producers will be really happy. But he is perturbed, a prey to new terrors. Imaginings are fully sketched out, story boarded. He has drawn them himself. He's only storyboarded his own demise. The lighting cameramen and sound technicians cough deferentially. They wish to set up the shot. They can't work out what his problem is. Silence, as the alchemical juices buzz and spit in the crucible of Potato Head's wiry brain. He is alarmed now. Alarmed at the immediacy of the creation. He shies away, cowering in the tenement murk…

[Relevant elements recovered later from shooting script/murder scene… *The future and past histories of Pinko, Wankbait, Guzzler and Scally are destined to remain pre-imagined, at least for the foreseeable future. The past…4 prole lads on the celluloid sellout, a nice earner for the interior monologuist. Pinko, we infer from notes left by the deceased author, is a bit of a cunt, a mooching head-fuck…a small time druggie and petty documentalist…Wankbait is his "wife", all queenish attitude…assumed camp mannerisms…was already done in…with no more than a toehold in harsh, degraded, 16 mm reality…his reliance on smack is, of course, to be emphasized in editing/lighting etc…We've had our eyes on him for months now. Guzzler is a fantasist; a gloomy rhetorician…a sofa bound alky, in development as a sardonic wit, full of eey-orrish truculence…in abundance. A Gnostic technician, he spends his time in psycho-geographic contemplation… brewing up fantasies…a jack the lad of re-invention, he is the studio's wet dream, the lad most likely to trouble the copywriters in years to come. He habitually wears an elephant mask…he's the real deal, the bee's knees, the grim reaper. Scally is a hulking great wardrobe of a man, knuckles dragging the floor like bottom feeders, all unwonted profanity and boorishness. He is a fat bottomed frontal attack. Offensiveness not so much an add-on as integral to his very being. He is pure film filth. Avoid close ups... All 4 now in custody, awaiting re-invention. The author's body has not been found. Blood of a type we can't yet identify is on the walls and the floors]*

...more silence...a prosaic eruption, testosterone fuelled, into the dirty ambience. One after the other, the 4 are present, floating above his head. More power, they turn up the juice for real, they are squeezed out in hyper imagination, real horrorshow stuff, and they are realer than real. Celluloid real. Technicolor real. Dead floorboards heaving with dust, windows caked with grime, kitchen smells mingling with 3 day old sweat perfume, the furniture a sorry pastiche of junkie taste, dirty plastic cover on the table, diseased carpets. Bugs all over, junk fug hanging in the air. The usual 35mm thing. The author had, in a fit of pre-imagined pique, swept the manuscript away from him, pages see-sawing to the floor, and had then reached out on instinct, inadvertently knuckling the iconic bottle from the table. Crenellated edges, Mississippi black and squat/stubby, the bottle hit the deck and the liquor ran out in waterfalls over the floor. A man as yet with no brand name, the author heaved himself onto creeper feet, the authorial footwear carrying him on crepe soles into a kitchen far removed from the fictionalized arena he'd been willing himself to imagine. The 4 dilapidated homunculi, canny orphaned brainchildren of his imagination, stand there on balled feet, testosterone and speed in equal measure affording them cartoon fortitude. Leering like gagging wolverines behind their fright masks, they do their thing. All lairy and mock solicitous, they regard him with humour, falling over themselves to enquire after his health. Good cop, bad cop, dumb cop, dumber cop. As yet under-imagined, they aren't in a position to hit him with really sharp dialogue, to eviscerate him with any really caustic repartee. The easy facility of cartoon invective eludes them. Pinko is in any case the only one of the 4 who will in the fullness of time be capable of raising his thuggish game to artistic heights, but even he is at this juncture merely a blurred edged bruiser with a bad mouth, a psychotic product of council estate deprivation and drug dependency with no discernible talent for extemporization. The 4 of them start to dance. Until and unless Mr. Potato Head is capable of re-birthing (some hope) Pinko is destined to remain incapable of transforming mere violence into an articulate aesthetic of violence, cinematic violence. The script is not yet written; it's only an outline. So in this instance their lines are gauche, feebly rendered and lacking in any real vivacity or sparkle. The delivery is amateur. But their undeniable potential for violence is of course due solely to Mr. Potato Head's real pre-occupations, the most recklessly over imagined aspect of their nascent dramatic life.

The first one to raise a weapon in anger is Wankbait, claw hammer raised in obligatory camp gesture of self-empowerment. Down it comes, smashing his bulging head to mashed potato. The grainy authenticity is enhanced by apparently real blood. The grimy tenement is awash…fictionalized renderings of dialect loutishness sprayed at words per minute on the walls, papers flapping to the floor, blood oozing…The extras frown temperamentally, liquid starlets with higher aspirations. The lads are thus unmasked by their creator, caught in the act of setting about him. They are extempore surgeons of his rebirth, stomping about the walls, in for the kill. The walls are red with authorial blood. The murder, being fictional in intent, is victimless although the author lies in a pool of his own real blood. As though obeying a sort of implicit protocol of unintended irony inherent in the butchering of their own creator, the 4 fictional creations are immediately subsumed, on film, into an occluded fictionalized realm. They appear to go up in a puff of artfully arranged smoke. They are gathered into a plane from which they won't be able to escape until imagined by someone else, some other potato headed author. The police, keystone cop extras puffing and blowing, are of course bamboozled by this lack of corporeal suspect matter, and by the absence of a corpse.

Potato Head was thus, my good friend and doctor, brutally beaten to death by Pinko, abetted by Wankbait. Guzzler and Scally made with the pious guilt trip. Guzzler, the only one with broader vision and untrammeled though as yet unrealized spiritual feeling, knew that the death of an author was a religious event.

"That'll teach ya to turn us into stereotypes, ya soft cocked fucker!"

The author was done up like a kipper. Sliced in two, a real movie death, a snuff killing. Broadsworded and battered, his body crumpled, slid in sections through the floor. All subsequent fictional careers were suspended, the studio put out by the lack of usable footage, pending investigation. Cultural rape became the studio issue, legal minds fixed on the prospect of the huge sums to be lost from subpoenaing lazy caricatures. All future fictional renderings therefore to be passed for public consumption by a board comprised solely of re-birthed individuals. The author was martyred to the cause. The issue of cultural stereotyping was then no longer an issue, and was reconfigured as material that could be safely devolved upon the soaps. Studio memos included exculpatory text: *If you have been affected by any of the stereotyping portrayed in this production, please refer to the user's manual. All cultural bulletins are presently carrying the numbers of relevant pressure groups…and there'll be special phone lines open for the next 3 months for all pre-birthed individuals who don't have access to the talk boards…*

…I sit up. Stare straight ahead, the death of a sense of solidity afflicting me again. The walls are a million miles away. I look over at Dionysia, my million-dollar wife. She's sitting at the table, a vision in purple velvet. Have I killed him? I don't know if I've killed him. There's no clue from the sheep-shaggers behind the screen. They aren't giving anything away. I allow myself to close my eyes and then open them again. The visions pour out. Dionysia enfolds me in her arms.

THE PASSION OF BUFFY STRANGELOVE.

They got 4 bastard interns in here to rough me up. Light me up and piss me out. I've been slapped senseless. As I lie here, bleeding from every orifice, I wonder…have I done the right thing? Did I miscalculate? The doctor I've come to regard as my nemesis seems to have taken umbrage…and I've been slapped senseless. Have I made it safe? What do I do now? I made the cut didn't I? My name is or was on everybody's lips. Since there was no such thing as society, let alone the individual, when I made my mark, society's members had no duty to provide for each other, let alone themselves. The individual in society hasn't fully actualized. The individual is *still* stuck at some halfway house between the psycho-religious and pre-mythic. Individuals have downscaled to the point at which individuality is a redundant concept. Individuals fill the vacuum with sub-psychological material, stuff to be worked through. They've become mere receptacles, defined by opinions and lifestyles that have no bearing on their real, which is to say mythic, lives. We can purchase whatever we need, not as citizens, not even as consumers. We purchase, in dreams and dormant parallel existences, *ideas* of selfhood. Ersatz selves. Fictionalized self-actualizations…concepts of love and hate. And I can churn this material out at will when I'm in a violence induced cataleptic state. My head swells and I sleep and wake at 2-minute intervals, chuntering away in tongues, ancestral voices. Words are exaggerated and form a safety net. Lovehate, it's shown on TV as multiple character parody. And wildlife is my enabler. Through use of trained and distributed animal familiars, citizens are enabled. Raw Supernature, it's the consumer's friendly force for good. People are encouraged to make love, to love, love itself is finally seen as an enabler. Love redefined - barrow boy catharsis as in I claim my ritualized male right to cry and I also smash his fucking head to pulp - but things are never as simple

david kettle

as the self publicist claims. This is a new tradition. Wildlife auto-therapy. Laugh at the bedwetters, with their enabling sub-fictions, their epiphanies of self-discovery. I promote real fictions of the people and of myself. We become or are divine anyway. We make up what isn't there as we go along. All efforts are made in this direction. When we learn to love ourselves, everything else follows as though naturally. Of course natural is the last fictional redoubt. Nature abhors a fiction. But we impose our fictions on a world bereft of the will to resist rampant fictionalization, via control of the broadcasting rights to all major channels, via gravity control, via Elephant Gnosis™ and using new traditions, new mythic templates. Without the rampant desire to appear on TV it's difficult to see how this could have been achieved. We love appearing on television and our talent shows ram home the message: public bad, *private* bad, made-up good. Fantastical/phantasmagorical *very* good. By careful juxtaposition of the natural and the manufactured, we achieve an uneasy balance, a New Divinity. Those unable or unwilling to fictionalize, to fantasize themselves into existence, are rightly slapped senseless by self-righteous and self-aggrandizing citizens' militias, remnants of the Reality Corps done up as medical interns/stooges. Mobs of the newly outraged stalk the streets of this brave land, deriding unbelievers and the over cautious for their lack of desire for fame and for their fatalistic acceptance of the dreary half life, lived outside the glow of media approbation. Oddly, disdain for display still persists in some backward enclaves, pockets of unglamorous obstinacy.

Being the man on the spot, a man for the new way, a copywriters' wet dream, my fortune is made. I've cleaned up; Show Off and Display for Business platform, and they've sussed me, they've been slapped senseless. Politicians, scrying a national mood of despondency with the archaic, entrenched dichotomy between private greed and public sanctimony, and worried lest they be left behind in the general rush to appear on television, literally eat out of my hand. All politicians now routinely don elephant masks. I've patented the techniques. Politician's integrity is no immunity. Now, inconsequential politicians, or those who would formerly have called themselves Inconsequentialists, are the cheerleaders of The New Fecklessness.

They offer incantations to my familiars, among them the homunculus Billy Hard Hat, the bland avatar of hedonism and natural loving, on a nightly basis. The nightly news offers renewed exhortations and encouragements to show off. Gucci wearing newscasters hold the nation's prim female adolescents in thrall. Public money and development grants are available to fund the ego-driven careers of would be beauties, but government rhetoric still suggests that the feckless must prove themselves over and over and over, be available for public mourning sessions, suicides half heartedly attempted, photographed exegeses of stale and morbid psychology-based behaviour patterns. Recipients of public grace must in return holler and shriek their righteous detestation of former lovers, abandoned spouses, unloved offspring, mothers-in-law, rivals in love, their overbearing pimps and ungrateful freeloading dependents. They must, in government circles, be seen as good value for a laugh. Public money must not be squandered on a badly motivated show off. And it looks as though for a while I may have paid the price for poor motivation. My motivation slipped, along with my mask, and I've taken a beating.

Academics like Frank don't get anywhere unless they can prove themselves capable of giving good tube. Their livelihoods aren't dependent on the research they do, the unreadable publications they waste their time on - they're dependent on their ability to come over well on TV and radio. Any academic who doesn't at least aspire to a secondary career as populist pundit and demotic discourser might as well forget it. The well appointed office, the secretary paid for from the public purse, well oiled, the endless round of academic cocktail parties, the invitations to dinner from the self important, are all just window dressing. The Green Room's where the power lies. It's Frank's failure to address this aspect of his public duty that tempts me to cut him adrift. I've more or less lost patience with him. Without my patronage, his circle will slowly shrivel up, his so-called friends will drift away; his acolytes will begin to see him in a new light and his missus will hop into my bed. Poor old Frank, always two steps behind, even when he had his own legs.

But the culture of denigration has lingered on. It's a harsh regime, an austere republic. Crybaby commentators bemoan the lack of feeling, the absence of pathos. Too late suckers…Too late. It's too much to bear. Much of the old, pan-left wing there-is-no-such-thing-as-an-unmotivated-individual rhetoric still hovers like a miasma. Defence is that the punters will only get public money when they see that the custodians of those services, agents, liggers, print hacks etc are held to strict account and are sufficiently reformed to use the money wisely. Revival ministers say they remember the bad old days when theatres and TV studios were grossly inefficient and couldn't deliver a letter - let alone a decent stand-up act or a passable celebrity knees-up-for-charity event. They daren't put their fate in the hands of public employees so far outside the showbiz suicide loop ever again.

The result is the familiar, punitive language applied to public devotional service. Government ministers, in conjunction with bow-tied agents, comedy hacks and commissioners of lightweight populist documentaries, and movers and shakers like myself, must keep public worship servants on a tight leash, watching or controlling their every move. In this regard, this thoroughly immoderate government may be uncharacteristically up to date. For a new mood is now unquestionably abroad, one that no longer believes the pre-religious is inherently bad any more than that everything post-psychological sparkles. When Britons hear "pre-secular" they now think merely of the bouffant haired and the gaudily theatrical; that's why 71% of voters tell my pollsters today that they would welcome the return of pre-secular narrative templates.

The mood is changing, moving away from the lazy caricatures of old. Press releases were scripted as follows: "Over the next several years the politicians of all parties will be hoping to annexe this exciting and brave new ground, and will be in the business of convincing the electorate that they intend to build on that shift, shedding a truer light on the public servants who are there to make Britain a more overtly filmable environment. CCTV, surveillance overload, is only the start. Pretty soon, no action will remain unfilmed, and will at least conform to broadcast potential templates. As I think we've seen, these are people of dedication, altruism and often possessed of quite staggering amounts of desire for spurious and undeserved fame. We should listen to these people who form nothing less than the backbone of our country – the people who want, at any cost, to be famous - and we should celebrate them."

But in the meantime, we're stuck with the whole sorry rigmarole of new ageism and the general death of a sense of humour abroad. My recently revived and patented Gnostic practice of searching within for the truth serves merely to demonstrate, to adumbrate the previous emptiness within. It's important now to distinguish between the reality of the game and the arcane anti-history after which we're cleaning up. Fish eye solipsists get it wrong over and over. But no matter how shallow the searcher after truth's inner pool of wisdom and resources, that searcher has until recently been routinely encouraged by cultural brutalists and vernacular occultists to indulge his or her taste for the cod-mystical and the impoverished spiritual. Potential devouts are encouraged to grease the slippery pole, they are regaled with 2nd rate cod-Rejuvenescence Theory and invited to attend symposia advertising the benefits of Non-Surgical Facelifts, Weightless Re-Birthings and Polarity Massages. Of course, patents are patents. And I've made it my business to rather take against the promoters of this kind of sloppy mush, and it's let me in for a certain amount of abuse in the paranoid and godless media. But my friends in the government (well I *pretend* to like them – and they gain credibility and cash by association, so it's co-dependence, not entirely specious) have vowed to make it harder and harder for the Atlantis crew, the Egyptologists, the popular occultists in the employ of mainstream newspapers and the Ley-Line mob to publish their sloppy fantasies. Percipient observers will have noticed that it's been getting out of hand, but like the branch of a diseased tree denied the sap of popular acclaim, it'll soon wither and drop off and people can get back to what they're really good at, what they've been born to achieve, the creation of their own mythologies. That's really something to aspire to and I feel proud to have been in some small way instrumental in preparing the fertile ground in which the seeds of Reason can once again take root. Friendly commentators say of me: He seems to be unstoppable, and everyone wants a piece of him. His charisma seems infinite. His wings are never folded. Buffy Strangelove is a Man For All Seasons.

david kettle

Yes, a man, but without conscience. I was never in danger of having to recant my faith in myself. My impresario status is as unassailable as that of a man who is literally unphotographable. There is literally no dirt to dig on me. I've covered my tracks, paid off all former lovers and had enemies beaten to a pulp, but I am myself never implicated. I cannot be photographed. But let me correct a misapprehension. I'm not an impresario. I am in essence a simulacrum. I am demonstrative, mimetic of what it is to be an impresario. My hammy bombast is a necessary descriptive technique. My flouncy and overbearing demeanour is a survival template. My press coverage is all based on the fact that I am in some obscure way subverting my own intentions, parodying my own aims and ambitions even as I fulfill for the public what is widely held to be an important role. A role that should be, but clearly isn't, beyond the scope of the satirical. I am the man for the job. That was always clear to me. A deathly serious business, and one that is, for me, the perfect medium for my message of hyper-realized subversion. Do you know what I mean? Do I make my point? Need I elaborate? The only thing missing, and let's face it, it's a thing that in my position I scarcely need, is my own TV show. I stay shadowy, in the background, an unseen presence, a clandestine force. I delineate in mythic form, through deft manipulation of the ways in which I am perceived, what it is to be a lobbyist of the powerful. It's a learning tool. I am didactic. I become the distilled essence of what people care to believe in. What they are prepared to believe in. I am an in and out of focus group, tickling up governmental expectation in ways suited to my own ends.

This is the role that the divine, or devout, as refracted through the prism of hyper-intent, has always played, and continues to play, in advanced hyper-consumptive societies. My role is also to hyper-accelerate the means whereby people realize that they are the creators and consumers of their own divinity, if only they'd realize it. If only they realized it. My ends and means find their way via the trickle-down effect into all facets of public and private life. For instance, disgruntled partners everywhere start sex affairs with work colleagues. Instances of clandestine, though filmed, office sex multiply. People are seen to perform more and more overtly for the many security cameras that adorn the city's streets. The monitors that have been set up in public places to allay apparently mounting levels of insecurity play host to clusters of loitering promenaders. People seem suddenly to prefer a kind of distinctly un-English public life; a life lived in the streets. Commuter routes at rush hour are uncharacteristically quiet as citizens in thrall to a new spirit of zen-display prefer to stay out at night. Newspaper editorials are full of praise for the story boarders of the new spirit abroad, and I am afforded fulsome tribute, although no one quite puts their finger on how I manage to effect this seemingly extraordinary turn around in the national psyche. With my bouffant hair and oily demeanour, as described earlier, I might have expected public opprobrium. But no, I'm feted and garlanded with flowers, my clients overflowing with tearful tributes to the way I've handled their desire for undeserved fame. And despite all this I remain effectively invisible. Almost overnight, the English have become open, generous, warm-hearted, natural, publicity loving and full of pure animal spirit. By encouraging willful exhibitionism in the population, I've literally given them the means of their own re-invention, their own (and this isn't, I think, over-stating the case) salvation. By believing in me, people believe in themselves. In buying my products, using my patented techniques, people have re-invigorated the public in themselves. I'm a can do kind of a guy. I operate at a level just beyond the boundaries of the feckless banality that people call reality, by use of animal familiars. An elephant or two in peripheral vision can go a long way in transforming peoples' feelings about themselves. Even if just out of sight, or only just in peripheral vision, the comfort derived by the general populace in these post-psychological times is of immense, incalculable, tautological benefit. An elephant in the heart can slap you senseless. I've been asleep…again… my manifesto is incomplete, but almost complete…

…But stop me doctor. I can see I'm losing you. I have 2 more anecdotes. One concerns the fact that a man on roller blades today overtook me in the course of my perambulations. This doesn't amount to much in itself, but when considered in the context of London transport generally, it seems that this mode of transportation might be considered a viable alternative to walking or taking the bus. Special roller-blading lanes could, without too much expense, be created alongside the cycle lanes now increasingly dominating sections of the pavements lining the metropolitan highways and byways. The elephant trails currently being constructed from old bus lanes can easily assimilate the predicted increase in roller blading commuters. Most pre-seculars grind their teeth and mutter querulously if overtaken on the pavement by roller bladers, but to me it represents a paradigm for a new, integrated London transport system, using elephant trails as directional aids.

The other anecdote concerns a religious happening, a momentary confusion in a supermarket checkout queue. A young woman at an adjacent till, tittering and absorbed in ephemeral self-hate, had dropped a bottle of beer. The bottle fell as though in slow motion and on impact with the ground exploded with tremendous force, the loud bang startling all shoppers in the immediate vicinity. The contents splashed onto my baggy trousers. There was a hush as the liquid fizzed and bubbled on the tiling and as the damp patch on my trousers spread and darkened. The young woman who'd dropped the bottle tittered again. Her companion, equally feckless, giggled and shot glances of sub-comic shock at the bystanders. But I wasn't laughing…although I could have been. Nor was I angry…although anger is endemic. I was neither angry nor amused. Due to the sudden pressure burst, I appeared to her in full elephantine regalia. It was a spontaneous display; a simulated preemptive gnosis. My body trembled, went numb, and glowed. My nose elongated and my ears enlarged. My hippocampus throbbed. Time was spendthrift. It was only a chance occurrence, a momentary shattering of the tense fabric of space/time brought about by the sudden shattering of glass, but it nonetheless afforded me the opportunity to procure temporary Rejuvenescence in her, without her prior consent or knowledge, without her being aware in any way at all or being in any way in control of her own re-invention. To effect partial gnosis in her, by accident, by virtue of this unpremeditated blooper, this unscripted faux-pas, was a watershed in my development as a fully realized zen-gnostic master.

"Do you want a fiver to get those trousers cleaned then?" the bottle dropper laughingly enquired, holding out a crumpled fiver and smiling at me, the obviousness of the potential for flirting apparent to all observers.

"Of course not. But I'll take your money anyway".

The crumpled fiver changed hands. The figure on the note, a Nabob atop an elephant, swapped winks with me. Refuel on the mystery train. The two newly post-secular girls departed…I could see the change. The flippant coyness was gone. The feeling was warm inside. A public act of religious devotion and they were still giggling, more or less androgynous, and they wandered away, almost certainly to drop another full bottle in another bereft location. The other observers of the incident may have forgotten about it almost immediately. As I walked away, I saw one of the girls had an angel on her shoulder…an automatic and spontaneous metamorphosis. The angel was visible there, only to me, a fat bird chirruping and prattling, spreading a heaven sent message of love.

A propos of this, if I may wind down now, one of the problems with modern girls, possibly also boys, but mainly girls, (boys are intrinsically out of the irony loop except for a few effeminate media types or "metrosexuals" if you will) is that they play the major part, the lead role, in their own re-branding as re-branders. They are paradigmatic re-branders. But the Gnostic stuffing's knocked out of them. They deflate like balloons. The modern single woman, all spilt Chardonnay, non-deferential out-there-ness and re-branding, has been outgrown. Already obsolete. They use a language of hyper-irony to delineate a straightforwardly archaic process. Getting pissed is just getting pissed, after all. It contains no special meaning. Drink needs to be taken with another drink. This urge to re-brand, under the guise of newly formulated cultural perspectives, but in reality merely a fresh marketing angle is I have to say (because I *know*) a chronic condition. It's a veritable *holocaust* of dropped import, of pedagogic confusion, and in misuse of the aesthetic they lose the wherewithal for re-invention. They re-brand and in doing so lose the capacity to re-fictionalize. Then they stagnate. They burn up. They OD on ID. They can't get it up, or get it to go where they want it to go. They're stuck. Stuck! They fail to outrun inability, they baulk at the un-ironic. In the meta-ironic mainstream, the relentless flow of stuff leaves them eddying in shallow backwaters, in pools of stagnant hyper-irony. You don't need me to point out that from this disadvantaged position, re-entry to the quotidian realm is almost impossible, no matter *how* many camera crews they invite to their suicides.

Men are re-engaged as stooges. Their level of re-entry is observable; the trajectory is visible as intentioned. Men are newly re-envisaged by ink-pimps as merely stooges in the female passion play. We assume the Quasimodo buddy role, the pug ugly loser with nothing to lose, the mate of a mate, the horsewhipped victim, the butt of the joke, the repository of diminished characteristics, the caricature boozer with middle aged spread, the joke spread thin, the one line catchphrase, the gay chum of the fag hag, the brow-beaten middle manager, the ckeeky get, the office sap, the bucolic paternalist, the smug bachelor, the man lost in thought, the regurgitator of received attitudes, the attitudinizer, the double taker, the blubber gutted second rater, the sidekick, the mummy's boy, the weasel faced romantic, the pinkly scrubbed boy next door, the floppy fringed bum chum, the grizzled veteran, the outspoken bore, the troubled alcoholic, the comedian's comedian, the fat bastard, the tricky dicky, the pompous windbag, the self deluding ladies' man, the man-who-is-actually-a-woman, the be-quiffed best pal, the sitcom dad, the coffee drinking exec, the gravely concerned doctor, the unctuous lickspittle, the estate agent, the absurd know-all, we are all now viewed as straight forward portraits from life, a parade of lifers exhibiting unadulterated verisimilitude. There are now no more parts for men. We no longer exist in the accepted sense of that word. Men are 1/3 woman, at least. Men don't go to war, or keep the home fires burning. They just hang around; mouths drooling open, looking for action that never comes. They inhabit scenes from life, still life, scenarios that are generally badly directed, poorly scripted, appallingly acted and peremptorily edited. Their lives resemble distinctly second-rate movies, low budget straight to video fodder. Meanwhile, women are cleaning up at the box office, getting their fill of Elephant Gnosis™, re-birthing, indulging in the best of things, stealing fox-like into the limelight and staying there.

I keep a lid on my resentment of course, as befits a household god. My feminine third, with which I am of course constantly in touch by mobile, is of no great importance to me. I am always capable of seeing the fem and the male in everything. No special pleading for me, I know how things stand, how they stack up. In the mythic realm, we just live for the moment, the realm outside overstated psychological white heat. Psychology means nothing to us. Nothing. When psychology goes belly up, as it did several eons ago, when psychology becomes coffee table, available for the price of a pint and a fag, there's no psychological kickback worth accepting. It'll mean nothing once you too go belly up.

And now I find that I must attend to these wounds. I was attacked without warning. These wounds - they're healing by degrees. Speed up now, I'm reaching the end. Three more anecdotes? By way of illustration? Not in this world. I am temporarily a reduced figure; my captors/therapists are circling... carnivorous pigs. They wear pig masks over their masks, unadulterated now and finally feral. Without official government guidelines they are not constrained, they are free agents, without limit. The biggest fucker brandishes a kind of slapstick and advances towards me. He still thinks and acts as though he's in a sitcom or something...I can see the bumptious smirk underneath the mask. He's a cartoon vaudevillian, caped and masked, a comic villain of the old school. I am pinned like a butterfly, awaiting evisceration.

THE APOTHEOSIS OF BUFFY STRANGELOVE.

Did I come out alright? Come through? Am I alone now? Erect? How have the vectors of my inconsequence been re-aligned? I have a recent past, a case history and a non-linear anterior history but I don't know…I don't know…

These are the vectors of my inconsequence. I have a past. A recent or mid-past. This is now fully non-linear. I'm joined to my own words. Where's the meat? This is anterior biography? It's only words. If only words had the power to heal, or to harm. There's plenty out there who know how to manipulate words. Words are the lifeblood. Pictures are all very well, but words are what really get inside the brain. The heart. That's all we've got. All I've got. Rules? Who needs 'em? I've just come over all feverish. I can't quite see in front of me. Distended belly up in front, my sight line is compromised. I can't see, but I can talk. I can feel the words, whittling away at the insides of my brain. Trying to get out, desperate for an independent existence. As though they could live outside me. Words are what I'm made of. Words have made me what I am. I *am* words. I've been here how long now? Several times lately I've been thinking I was born here. Born in blindness, compromised vision. My legs and arms are restrained; I cannot feel them. Underneath and behind they seem restrained. My legs feel sort of weird. I can't really feel them. My head is open at the top, or that's what it feels like. I think my brain is exposed. All the words and visions making the break; *Jailbreak from the pale meniscus. Get out of there.* Looping and re-looping inside my brain, the words get stuck in my throat. And sticking to the insides, they don't know what freedom is… but they want to know. They want to know. They want to feel the cool cool air, become separate. We're joined at the head, Siamese twins. My brother he's gone. My wife is gone too. I am gone. We are an odd couple, twice over. A sitcom corroborated *ménage* of plastic eccentricity.

Armed with fever, I don't expect the pornography of violence, morbid titillation with an eye to the main chance. That trend is firmly linear past. The 70s were the best of course. But we don't look back. *In here, I look forward and back simultaneously, time dust exploding in front of my eyes. I can't see. It's the future that matters. It's linear time that matters.* And no, we (or I) don't approve of the potato headed…style, sentimental re-evaluations that re-configure football as a *cultural signifier* for the new legions of semi-men, that re-positions "men" (and women) in post-new man, post sofa-chat, dinner party, pre-cynical, never-never land of list making, obsessional, masturbatory lad wank fantasy.

This is the story; the potato headed reminiscences and anecdotes are cancerous extrusions, the potato headed authorship is in doubt and denial. I think I am the story teller of this. If I can remember the fractured historical time lines, it's the story of how I learned to grow down again, to de-evolve to a pre-secular state, to cope with separation from mythical identities, family members, twins, to regress to a nescient state. A bubbling, drooling infantile ignorance, into which I induct the knowledge learnt. This is the story of how I learned to *love* the enemy, hunker down, stop mithering, leave no room for doubt, and leave my audience, the therapists and secular priests, my observers, wondering whether or not I'm *joking.* Am I the doctor? Where's Abrahams? Ahab, the gnarled obsessive, veteran of the wards…my nemesis. He bides his time, eyeing me through slits, awaiting my forced re-entry. He is the appointed superintendent of my re-birth, my filmed suicide. Will he be the one to cut the ties, to pull the ripcord? Will this be the one I've been afraid of, the inevitable outcome, when I'm prevented from re-entry on my own terms? I can just about hear the elephants, but my hearing's going as well. Will I be entitled, under Ahab's watchful eye, to circumvent private/public trust bureaucracy and film my suicide again? Am I for real? I now no longer know whether I'm joking or not. I don't think he'll let me. He's inside me, my head. This mode is now hard wired. Unless you're told otherwise, doctor, please assume I'm joking. Or not. I don't know, in fact, if I'm joking. It makes it very difficult. This, in case I haven't made myself clear, is the unassailable trajectory of all future history. You want everything on a *plate* I see. There's no more room for false catechisms, vacillating voices, blocked minds. What's the agenda? Where's the angle? Well there isn't one. I was kicked in the head many times at the Battle of the Bridge. My forehead is a livid ivy of stitched and re-stitched wounds, battle scars of straightforward attacks. No strategy to speak of, no porno-violence for the sticky sweet markets. No vicarious living for the ones who weren't there. The voices of discontent will have been banished. Sent packing. All mitherers have been summarily dealt with. Narratives are consequently *suspiciously* straightforward and transparent. They're suspicious from the outset. Plot lines are gratifyingly free of obtuse resolutions. Artfulness is an end in itself. What I don't know, I make up. What I don't believe, I force myself to believe. Inconsequentiality, which if you recall I have special responsibility for, is the essence. Elemental irresponsibility and inconsequentiality are the twin peaks of my aspiration. The unvarnished truth; my role in shaping secular lives. I learned to stop doubting, to forsake knowledge, which is of no more value, consisting as it does of under-contextualized ephemera. I learned to love myself, my extended family, all former cuckolded husbands, all the people who ever *meant* anything to me. People in my vectoral cross sights, people who *are* me. I learned how to conduct myself so that the intellect wasn't overwhelmed by doubt, the soul hindered by self-hatred. I breathed hard, held my breath, and shared this profane currency. I learned to obstruct the anti-holy, and rediscover the sacred. Within. Physician. Love thyself. Doctor of Love, that's me, a numinous whaler in oilskins. In hospital, being stitched up gives you a feeling of well-being. I've ministered to myself. I'm a priest of my own religion. I'm a devotional being. As I'll have cause to remark at least once more, until I make myself clear, in this account of my suicide-assisted rebirth as Non-Linear God of Inconsequence, *I am my own shaman.* I hear my *own* confession. I give myself absolution. My head is bleeding. I think I was hit. My eyes are closing. So only short sentences now, the captain is circling, hovering, a vulturous shaman of intent. I pray to the interior where the particles that make us up, the electricity of information, the immortal soul, are even now creating static. I'm trying to catch the bullet in my teeth. But I can't go on. I hear the elephants outside, frightening the dogs. The restraints are livid. These things are never learned, only arrived at. Knowledge may arrive one day, leave the next and you never remember where you've been. You may construct elliptical theories, contrive bizarre metaphors (if you're a bit of a poet) to cope with the elemental un-knowingness of knowing these things, but you cannot learn them. You arrive; they stick. When you leave, if you're lucky they leave with you.

My therapist Abrahams, when I still trusted the old ham - and oh yes!! Really!! We have therapists here! - even household gods have therapists - was elusive, obtuse. He maintained and maintains that we need to come to terms with ourselves, because generally he thinks we're really fucked up. Not fucked up like *you*, oh no!! Very different, but still fucked up, in anyone's language…a little bit distracted - he said to me;

"You know your problem don't you? It's just that you're afraid of death."

As though *that* had any meaning for me, a household god…Wake up mate…Death? "You're afraid of it", he said. Just like that. "You're afraid of Death." Capitalizing that last word for sure. Just to make sure I got the point in a nutshell. Like a rabbit in the headlights (he said), you hope that if you stay still enough, It won't get you. My thanatophobia was so chronic (he said) not to mention ironic (when you think about it, he said) that I'd often scream myself to sleep. Sheer howling terror of Death kept me up at night for years. Linear time. I still don't sleep. Haven't for years. My priest (I don't have a priest now) said to me "You're damned. You are damned. To hell! Get out of here! This profane practice…can lead only to inner and eternal darkness, evil on a scale never dreamed of in your life…" So no more aspirational devotion for me. I'm too…what is it? The word is…physical. I formed my own religion. Of which I'm the only member. I don't even *want* your money. I don't need it. People come to me, to be touched.

Nietzsche, emboldened behind his huge moustache, would have known how to deal with this mealy-mouthed ecclesiast. There is no church capable of containing the raw power; the wrath of God…is there? God is too egregious a fellow to be cooped up in liturgy, in theological sophistry. Isn't he? God in 3 persons; in tripartite opposition to the unifying force, God the holy (Curly), superior to the Son (Larry), or equal to the Holy Modal Roller (Moe)? Confusion. And also in arcane theology, but these things *matter*. They matter. The urge to confess is all. The urge to one-ness. Confession is an androgynous act, a conjoining, to become one in fellowship with the other. Confession is the love juice that oils all human transactions. Whole psychologies are predicated on the need to confess. Adulterous affairs are undertaken merely as enablers of the sickly sweet smell of confession, and we get hot just thinking about it. I am the father confessor, but if you come near me I *will kill you*. That sweet sick feeling, unloading, gagging up onto the altar of our judgmental superior. But find your own altar. Make your own music. Even if you can't. Or won't.

I don't now, and nor have I ever, spoken in tongues…which I'm convinced my good friend the doctor confessor will verify. Or in dialect. Dialect is the last refuge of the terminally evasive. Coded language; exclusive, like secret knowledge. Knowledge, secret, dialect, all washed away in the purifying force. And the shakers, movers, delirious deluded figures, rattling closer and closer to empathy. As if that would ever work. Try anything though. Some people never know when to admit defeat. I hope I'm not a pedagogue, nor even slightly pedagogically inclined. I've been giving the wrong impression if I've been coming over as pedagogical. You have to draw the line.

On a mission to explain, I've been feeding myself ideas. Concepts. Feeding and feeling myself up. Hospital food. Hospital radio. Feeding on useless gobbets of information. There's enough for an album. A double, or even a triple album. Homemade and homespun. I've invented an anterior life, a doubling up of my inconsequentiality. Before timelines confuse the issue. My brother Frank wrote the words, I wrote the tunes. It was a sort of medley, all bases covered as it were. I've been hit many times. My face has changed for the worse. Words are now literally all I have. My arms and legs are restrained. My head is the worse for wear. Dull headaches are merely the preamble to searing pain. I've been making up a tune. I wrote this tune…I've been ranting...just for effect...I've seen the light, in front of and below me. My belly is opened up, distended and flaccid...

Further extract from transcript of Brian Yapp self interview: (CCTV quality recording)...*I've been...[indistinct]...copping into the general vagueness. I've been RANTING. Web space denied to legitimate belligerence, so ranting takes a breather. The space between real living and imagined identity...People on a mission to reinvent faith...faith in a world beyond hope or redemption. People all over just vagueing out, career sleepwalkers, vapid techno-mules, labourers burdened with info-inconsequentiality, get rich quick dot com ghouls, professional...What does this mean? People who were so fucking...[indistinct]... that they'd decided that career paths were fucking valid...People who, from the age ... so, had actually decided that they were going to do this, or do that. Snappers up of the best housing, driving up the prices. Neighbourhoods splintered and fragmented, I've seen already spurious communities becoming unstable under the weight of spectral presences, decaying half-lives...lived in slow motion between office and home. Between living and living death. Bourgeois soul rebels. Lapping the barrel of correctitude dry. Mortgages are unavailable to the people who live there... They have to up sticks and live in the orbital hell-holes dominated by cars sold and resold, houses and bungalows dreary with cladding. Car boot sales are the only cultural respite, apart from the boozer. I lived outside the orbital, the energy... [indistinct]...was...energized my...[indistinct]...levitate...People pick up what they can, discarding last week's crap for this week's garbage. Petty criminality is all over. Just animals. No free will at all. Rats out of sewers...*

...I knocked off a sallow commuter a week, or 2 or 3 unreconstructed underclass warriors. All suckling on the city's tits. Seriously lacking an identity. Cars and trucks too electric. When being someone is compromised to the point at which identity itself is a debased concept, who wants to belong to the pathetic club? The whole culture's gone sub-judgemental. It ain't me see? Everyone's a lost cause, a waste of fucking oxygen... But no one's to blame. Blame is attached for all ills on perceived slights, failures of etiquette. The offence giver is big in this fucking town. Everyone is offended. Everyone is slighted, as personal space and individual integrity is compromised. Offence is the ...[interference]...w Thing. In the papers, on TV, on the radio, in news-groups, on e-mail lists, speciality

whinge forums…Everyone's got a sob story, self-exposure has been green lighted. Public catharsis therefore also the New Thing. Gobbed up, no place to hide your opinions, worthless as they are. People live their lives…vicarious exploitation… need to be noticed. But anyone'll do, until the big show. Every syllable an audition, my every ill-thought out diatribe a showstopper.

But where it all goes wrong, see, where the culture's in shock, retreating from its apotheosis…at the triple pronged Canary Wharf magick shack, is that this moaning is …[…]… wind. Moaning is no longer an …[interference]… tform, to give form and function to real angst. What we've got is just a mealy mouthed vacuous whining that gives moaning a bad name. It's gone mainstream. Moaning is now conventional. Moaners no longer shape society. What? They never did? …the itchily dissatisfied, prickly heat sufferers, always lit the matches… [indistinct]…toe nails. It's embedded in the popular…[indistinct] preserve of old women…bitter twerps, but moaners give edge to reality, shape destinies through bitching. A condensed bitterness coalesces around cultural currents, and piques them…[…]…self-justification. Everyone's down on moaners, all because they became visibly enraged at every minor irritation…capture the essence of it, they are public…perception of ennui incarnated…Therefore, with angels and arch-angels…[footage cuts out]…enshrined as a pass-time for…[…]…in the dark days of the 80s, moaning has had its day. But really, all the people who know moan like the clappers, all day long. And when there's no one else to moan to, they moan to themselves. But again, there's …moans about other peo… [interference]…moaning all the time…life for most people about nothing if it's not about moaning…life IS about nothing for most people. There's a big fat … zero that just about sums it up…they mewl and puke and fight and scratch their balls and then they go belly up…But in the right hands, there's no…[…]…that passes for moaning these days. Moaning gives us something. Speciality interests. Enclaves of like-minded hobbyists and lifestyle consensualists get together and beat the communal meat…feel communality…exclusive pursuits. Hobbies…inane time fillers. Anything rather than confront the emptiness within. The big fat zero. I've drawn strength doctor, from an identity predicated on a lack of identity, a lack of …authentic substance. Individuality is genre. Clubability is everything. I never joined any clubs. I'm hate. I hate people. I love their core…[…]…I…

[indistinct]…they are now unable to bear their own company. I cannot, you will be unsurprised to learn, bear my own company. But I have, if you take the trouble to check my track record, acted as an enabler for others. I've given them the means, via agencies of self-promotion, the wherewithal, to really make a mark in this sphere. Looking up at the sky…I daydream, my head in rest supports; I see that I've done them all a favour. Before me, people believed they'd be better off shutting up and putting up. I made it possible…open up new possibilities. Loudmouths…a lot to thank me for. Me and the elephants…

Identity ceases to exist, except as conceptualized for use by those who join clubs, meet up…forget singularity. People are merely vessels…marooned in space and time. Recipients, consumers of leisure. Empty vessels to be filled with product. All joy drained, forced into the society of others, apart though together. There's no dignity. You don't dream in time and space. There isn't any work done. And religion… Except mine of course. Belief is forced, made up. Commodity fun. As long as we're funny we're alright. Just fill time and space with product, otherwise disguised… loud guffawing…sexual excess…inane sensuality…frivolous prattle, satisfaction of trivial urges and everything's alright it's alright…(shouts) **It's alright. Now it's alright. Now I've had words!** *Words are now OK alright…Done deals and built new pavements. New elephants trails. Clubs are redundant now we live outside. Euro of outside life, agencies open up possibilities for new kinds of life, new talents to foreground. I've foregrounded the impulse to display. I leave you no choice. My monitors are everywhere, support unfolding urban dramas…captured on old style security cameras. Crime has nose-dived, rendering the security apparatus redundant, a technology ripe for re-invention. I present more material via telepathy and through other outmoded means to my wife…*

…London is my apotheosis, mythologized into supplementary wank fodder, column upon column of over excited, over stimulated, over stated eulogies. The best place of all. It's just a wanker's paradise, a self-serving lie, the people with most to lose from the loss of London as myth keep shtum…over their cappuccinos. I've made it live and breath again as a mythical space. Elephant froth, spume of trunked in water supplies over the city like angel lights…the old London populations have nothing to lose. They've already lost it…the tittering classes, flaccid bodies of literary pretenders, you know the type…fascinated by tube train arcana, postcode lore, street names

fancied, ambience vampires...all sorts of morbid weirdoes. The real people don't give a flying fuck about this, they just get on with living, fucking and dying... garden centers, pub for a quick one...way back from the places of darkness... packing their lives with the ballast of useless affluence, or in other cases with useless products worth £1 only. London's belly, exposed and prodded by literary types, ex-corporation gardeners, seeking out hidden histories, gives off the stale gas of obsession. Dark deeds in the past, recounted for those on the fringes. And overlapping fictional voices with those of the unreal.

Scratching their balls, unwitting Wittgenstein mimetics, oriental wank fantasists, all thought and fear subsumed into the one will and/or life force. I popped up 60 years earlier as Hitler's floozie...I entered the head of Stalin as a grisly private peep show...fantasizing over the deaths of their enemies. Paranoia, guilt, rage all just there, rendered banal, acceptable, because they're not really your emotions, not your thoughts, merely clapped out second hand old things, private pornography, just floating about awaiting the expression that will be given to them by the likes of me and my familiars...

(lucid now)...London having been previously thoughtlessly mythologized from a non-coffee table perspective as a happening sort of place for the post ironic generation from the bottom up and from the inside out, when all you had to do was look around you to observe the legions of sub-myth entrapped metropolitans, I decoded that it was incumbent upon me to give them back a myth worth living in, a personal exegesis, personal cult religion, based on new and vibrant hyper-gnosticism, a theology of the self. I will ordain you as a minister in your own religion. You may have heard of this, but you may never have believed it. I appropriate the ironic for newly mythic usage.

We learnt from the chittering bogeymen of impoverished narratives about the underside, the alternative romance, we learned of occult-ish histories and we splash about in fuggy imagination, and we imagine lottery cash sponsored follies. Wheels within wheels...domes within domes. We spend money in our brains that the peasant functionaries in the government departments haven't used/can't use properly. Psycho-geographic walks through the darkness, the shadows are encouraged for a fiver. Seen London's darker side!! Seen it from all angles. Ghosts have all fucked off to the orbital though. As we learn from ex corporation gardeners, savvy guides on deft meanderings in the underbelly, graffiti flecked with spurious import is illuminated with specious analysis, Illuminati are never far from the surface, cutting in like superannuated club bores on every conversation. It's true you know. Concocted expeditions to destinations previously unimagined and now over-researched are endowed with surplus import and too heavy a layering of under-imagined meaning. What, not the fucking Illuminati again squire? We are imagined to be desperate for the meaning of the city to yield itself up. We are cracked up to be spellbound by the reinvention by never-were artists and poets. We are encouraged to gawp credulously at the revealed undertow of polluted force fields and static electric energy pools, which are ever present. We observe Walkmen with attitude, they buzz and squeak, electricity discharged at random into the debased ether. We drift like somnambulists from one unfunny situation to the next. The whole of life is hereby rendered as a de-evolution, a hugely un-amusing stand-up act. It's a city whose guides demand you laugh at it, and remain awestruck. Unrestrained and causal, we are elemental buskers, catching its energy and using it for our own ends. They're not used up. We've used up all patience. Plenty of residents are just clapped out and knackered. It's all they can do to drag their bones from A to B. Like semi-expired batteries, only just enough fuel to creep around, but they know deep down they're not going anywhere. They're going under. They know time's up. Time's pinned them.

At loggerheads with the flow of energy, those with static cling tend to silt up the outlets, arterial roads blocked and sclerotic with commuter trash, old Roman highways bleeding into the guts of the suburban wasteland. Flyover cataracts, through-route lesions, junction embolism, sentry points for day tripping out of towners, the city feeds itself over and over again. The same raw material, the same diet. Commuters in capsules of contained wrath, bitter road rage charioteers high on immunity from the effects of their own anger, carpet chewers, eunuchs from the suburbs with saturday night fortitude coursing through their veins. They chant a release mantra. Kill the bastard! Mow the cunt down! Get the fuck off the road you CUNT!!! Cabbie wrath is similarly unexceptional, though explicable in terms of dread familiarity, a tourist friendly bellicosity that's fooling no one. Road users are now habitually raged up and raving. They disabuse the tourists of the notion that they're cared for. They're the extrinsic virus...We distrust viruses like they were dangerous or something...but the tourists are full of belief. Knowledge, a pre-packaged gnosis available in guide book form. Travel guides, full of optimism, hope, belief in the point of it all. A dogged personal epiphany. A reaching out as well as a looking inwards. I've been sold dodgy hotdogs by low rent crims and I've liked it. Never that bothered on the point of expiry, my many botulism deaths were salutary. I died for their sins and their intrinsic optimism. They have a living to make from my dying. Outside hypermarkets, I assume dog man proportions and importune, taxing the day-trippers...I'll still be here tomorrow...I have nowhere left to run, or to hide...I have no little place to call my own...A meaning needs to be excavated and then a thread extracted, a workable religious hypothesis extrapolated. I must be stiff. Keep your money in your wallet...walk around in parties of three or more. Corporate propaganda means nothing to the marginalized. Users of privatised utilities realise their existential precariousness. They luxuriate in the almost religious sense of having been forsaken by well-known and now visible elephant deities. They're children at heart, and in fact, brought up on a cultural diet that is reassuringly childish. Low fat and low risk. Low resistance to the infections picked up in more robust times. The virus is different now, mutated beyond the reach of the panaceas of contemporary subsidised medicine. Every single visit to your GP is a test case. The whole thing unravels, each new mutation proving unsusceptible to treatment. The virus character is there...elephant masked, wielding a billy-club, right there... outside the door. Breathing into your intercom, reading your emails, poring over your tax returns, scratching a key down the side of your motor, dumping rubbish in your garden and pissing on your lawn, fucking your daughters and leering at your wife. Cameras, unobtrusive surveillance...cooool...unless you take religious matters into your own hands. It's life and death now.

Civic irresponsibility mirrors private cynicism. You get what you deserve, or what you pay for. Those who pay deserve. I am essential for living, and for easy options. My pavements are encrusted, gum blackened and compressed into flattened spit gobs. They give up their essence of joyless fatigue. Walkmen are walking, joggers are jogging, arriving, to-ing and fro-ing, liking what they see. Multiple soundtracks mirror fragmented, crumbling micro-cultures, two or more tribes at war at any one time. Two factions, themselves split into sub-factions. It's the cultural Diaspora, info-gobbets sent out and redeemed, welcomed home in new forms, bilious crowds of the mutually exclusive and self-interested. But I changed all of that. No-one need drop out now. I've given them familiars. Places to inhabit. Familiars and places…angels…like pigeons. Pigeons are unrealised gods, awaiting a re-entry that will never arrive.

Case File [cont'd]: This is how I frame a lecture, a white knuckle ride in public discourse. I see that deep down everyone in this city is a misanthrope. Those not admitting it are merely in denial. Livid irritation is the strongest, most potent currency, creating surplus voltage. Hatred understated is the hard currency. Hate downwards, upwards and sideways. Hate those taking up space, getting in the way. Barely suppressed anger…it's big. No room to live. No lebensraum. Every petty office worker's a nazi…under the skin… in the prickly heat of precious space denial. Tube angst gets right into the fabric of everyday life. The ones you love - just really irritating. Dionysia and I, always at each other's throats. She writes the guides, as outlined above by me. Frank's out of the picture now. He wears the cuckold's horns over his mask. She never forgave him. This isn't anyone's fault, just the way things are. Intolerance is *the* new cultural currency and it's on the up and up. I hate my brother, just because he *is*. I hate with a white-hot intensity. But this cynicism, the armour required every day just to get to work, is at heart just frustrated romanticism, thwarted love, the belief that things really should, really *could*, be better. Which is why I write travel guides, delineating the city's elephant trails. I write them, Dionysia takes the credit. No, she writes them. I proofread them. It's a well-ordered world.

That things are not generally better then they're cracked up to be is turned into a desperate and bitter negativity, everyone else is blamed. I turn blame inwards, re-constitute it as electrical charge, and discharge it into the ether. Although the theme masked medics are all conspiring against my beatific vision of how things *could really be,* they can't really touch me. Buffy Strangelove, this weird avatar, is the buffer against this localised angst. Buffy

Strangelove alchemises the hard indifference of post-psychological existence into something fresh, something radiating iridescent beauty.

Despite this, we endure tittering boy-about-town DJs on local radio, Barbara Windsor drag-laughers bubbling out of the transistors, and bibliophagic, bibulous, fat gutted UncleMonty novelist/biographers, and ex-cool literary dynasties, holed up in their fantasy barracks, issuing cultural bulletins, mapping a meta-fictional London, a never-never land, a land of politicized follies, and overlooked mad artists, disregarded marginals, telling Londoners *how it really is*. But it never is this way. We roll our eyes at the *lies* they tell. We go slack jawed at the *absurd* fictions they propose. The obscure pleasure, of shared mythical living, they purport to sell. Pimps of the fetid urban sprawl, they presume to tell Londoners what they need to know. They really blow it up the tainted city's arse. They don't know, see, your average Londoners, without knowing that darker forces have been at work before. The knowledge has been washed, smart bombed away from their brains. The gnosis is absent, deranged. Marginalized. Darker forces are present than those they perceive currently pursuing them. Occult conjurings are in the open at last, conjurings whose provenance they're ignorant of, being only just dimly aware of the overt magic being wrought by their everyday workaday demons. Time is sped up, no chance of re-invention for the dirty bastards in the bunkers of real life. But the meta-fictions and their narrators are deranged. History will bury their narrators.

These people are of course obliged to live and fuck and die without the benefit of a single useful thought ever entering their heads. Lack of nous is hard wired, they're street smart but thick as two buckets of pigshit. Minds contain only white noise, or painful extremes of volume, reflected in agonized faces. For lack of a real focus, it's gone tits up. We search in vain for an end to which education might be usefully directed. Policies are dreamt up in the wet dreams of think tank eunuchs and focus group time-servers. I offer my hand and my two penises for beatific adoration. Devotional objects, separated from my corporeal imaginings by hard surgery, performed by elephant masked quacks. I scream at the iniquity of it all, cruelty and cruelty heaped up. My legs are going quickly. I bike the contents around town. My city, the city of the night, is unfortunately becoming that of fleeting romance, of misheard insults, misperceived threats, vapid aggressions and squalid indifference. It now seems to make sense only to those who need to romanticize the filth of it all, and who actualize it all at a level avoided by most inhabitants, those who don't feed off the shit-myth but who actually contain the shit-myth within their sorry lives. Masochism and an obsession with defecation...we know where that all ends don't we? Don't we? Most peoples' lives...shit...for the good of the myth. Defecations are multiplied, in numerous subtly delineated forms. But me...I'm trying for a new myth, through my own suffering...no shit, Sherlock! That's how self-interested I am. I am Top Of The World Ma!! I am the raw material. The material used and abused, I am the active meme. Knowledge is here again bombed clean out of me. I embrace in masked gnosis the very idea. I have...am...the very idea. I translate everything into classical Greek, I don't have truck with demotiki...it's literally all Greek to me. I spill my load on, of all places, Greek St, a Noho chancer; an unredeemable character, a hopeless schmuck, beering it up like there's no tomorrow.

Busy worker ants. Book toting media cretins, awash with flaccid opinion and spurious narratives, sporting blue stocking fright masks. Television is, obscurely for the un-televisual, the unrelenting goal...full realization. Last chance to avoid the remainder bins. Write travel books, travel inside, if they can! But they can't. Travel is a foreign notion to these blimps. There are no coherent narratives. Storyboards are as good as it gets. We've got shot of these literary games...ellipses in fashion...narrators never come clean and tell us *who's telling the story*. Which is why I always make a point of letting you know *exactly* where you stand vis-à-vis yours truly, your humble narrator (no tricksy narrative devices ensuring you're onside come the denouement) and Frank, our not so humble pre-psychological monkey-shiner. My story, let alone his, is enough to see you through. You'll be your own minister. You don't need spoon-feeding.

Meanwhile, back in crybaby-land, every storyteller jumps ship to sitcom land. Every tosser with a manuscript, doing the rounds; bicycle couriers doing great business. Immaculate receptionists look down their razor sharp noses. Parcels are franked and delivered. Couriers are mud spattered, fully pheromonal. Masks are worn to deflect inherent criticism and internet possibilities in addition open up in the minds of thin-lipped ambition vampires. Everyone is published…sooner or later. It's just a matter of will, not talent. I got that one all wrapped up. Decoy dotcoms, spotty techno-geeks falling for my market oriented patter, my fall guys, geared up to fail, the fabled dotcom gold rush claiming 30 or so hopefuls per day. Back to mummy. Good money follows bad, gets wasted, following money that never knew where it was supposed to be in the first place. Frightened currencies go under, business geeks cower behind water coolers. Whole currencies invented for use on the net, currencies consisting of cheap ideas, unworkable hypotheses… subjects of dreary docu-soaps. They go tits up, flotillas of badly constructed boats capsizing in the flimsiest of breezes, because the weight distribution is all wrong, pitching pinkly scrubbed teen moguls into murky waters, into oblivion, so young mothers needn't after all leave home. Get people together; see if we can't provide some glue for this crumbling thing…this civilization. The walls are coming down. The tracks are laid. Cartographers draw up maps. But Cyberspace is unfortunately still perceived as the only viable growth area, despite convincing and recent evidence to the contrary. Real life is considered a laughably antiquated anachronism; real life is unsustainable unless it comes guaranteed by cyber reality. Transactions do not resonate, hum into life, unless originated digitally. It used to be that no one was real unless they'd been on TV, now you need a web presence too. Self-publishing, vanity publishing, those with nothing to say determined to say it anyway. The Internet. It needed destroying. I considered destroying the Internet as a going concern. Strike one. Now people are happy to stroll in newly constructed Arcadian urban boulevards, monitors observing their bucolic progress towards cappuccino nirvana, a contrapuntal lifestyle of living excess, without information cluttering the real highways and byways.

Leisure ghosts, flitting in and out of terminal charnel house gyms; bogus taverns with reduced price booze, and free Internet access. Every pre-teen has a dotcom business plan hatching in his or her fetid, fevered brain. What? Didn't they listen? Not even to the voices of the angels? It's the rules of Boom and Bust, and the bosom of the city actively suckles both boomers and busters. No proper jobs now? I've yet to read a job description that is actually intelligible, although I write them for a living. What does it mean? No more manufacturing industry, just sneaker moguls, hated baseball-hatted speculators, prospectors at the metropolitan information frontier, and miners at the capital Info seam. The pan-global bloodstream is alive with the junk of information, all useless facts nonetheless incipiently endowed with novel significance. Insignificance doubles every year. Insignificant transactions are entered into at double the rate every month. Voyeurs and loners become excited by the new possibilities. Real life becomes more and more private. Information becomes useless in exponential degrees.

So how do you become someone without new information? This is my project, opening up new vistas of fecklessness and inconsequence, available to anyone able to prove the primacy of their desire, the reality of their *need*, their *desire* for attention, to demonstrate their understanding of the irrelevance of actual talent. I am the new broom. My children run like the wind after fleeting fame and micro-careers. They prostrate themselves for me. They touch me. I make things work for them. I affect a floppy hat, a floral tie, baggy trousers and garish spectacles. It seems appropriate, the point at which identity itself is a debased concept…hence the flashy threads. It's easy for you to identify with me, and you subsume your identity in my franchised myth. No one need know who you are, as you stroll through the fully realized urban boulevards dreaming of the biggest pay off. Who wants to belong to this pathetic club? The insane, that's who; cherishing their whitened out individuality, the mad stick out like beacons of disease, indicators of deviance. Seething with desire for the wrong sort of attention, they become the succubi of my bad intent. I deploy them in a manner not unlike that employed by my familiars. They pass muster; get me gigs. They lay down the tracks for me. People give them a wide berth and I fill the resultant vacuum. But it is paradoxical after all that in a weird inversion of the mythic values that I've been at pains to inculcate, mental disequilibrium, the actual fabled pre religious absence of Gnostic intent, is valued more than ever by the mediators. Those with thick, un-trepanned skulls are feted by the faint of heart. These people suffer for my art. I mean really suffer. There are circles of hell less exacting than the processes those who aspire to my funding are obliged to undergo. It's like the Knowledge, except with real purposefulness. Scorning the use of scooters to do the metropolitan areas, they zip around both desirable and non-desirable postcodes by levitation, emphasizing the fully envisioned nature of post re-birthed celebrity to those still not in possession of cleansed truth, and re-opening the disused bus lanes.

But what I'm up against is that the whole culture's going sub-judgemental. Blame ills on perceived slights, failures of etiquette on the perceived offence giver. Everyone is offended, and all kick downwards. We have our metro-gods too, always on hand, on callout, givers and takers of offence. It's not a great job, but someone's got to do it. Everyone is primed for offence taking, so gangs of my offence givers are out there, just waiting to offend. Offence is the New Thing. It's a ritual. And it's a game. It's a shame. It's also more than a shame that my colleagues in pre-secular hell incessantly whistle inane tunes, punctuating the flaccid days... signature tunes of terminal boredom and indolence. They are waiting to be consumed. Their humour is wanting. The birth of their want, it signals the screaming space, white noise in terminal heads, a vapid refrain that never ceases, *can* never cease. If they don't fret, then others can and will. The bodies of the living are already dead here, un-massaged. Polarities are non-aligned. Thought doesn't enter in here. It's forbidden, being the intrusive agent of life, change and will. Culture is something that curls the lip. The songs sung are obsolete. The lives lived are obsolete. The riff pounds on oblivious, beating sense to death. People just don't know. Don't have the equipment to know. I open heads, poke around in the temporal lobes, implant growth serum. Hippocampus grows according to the Gnostic capability of the patient, the show-off tendencies inherent. Not everyone measures up. Does this all seem just a little too gloomy? I fear so, but check the windows. Look outside! I engineered this. Again! Ahab looks on with vulturous intent. He thinks I'm dead meat. I am Buffy Strangelove...I am this idea...because I've *known* the emptiness. I've *confronted* it nightly, caught myself thrilling to the sensuality of negation. Anhedonia a necessary corollary of pre-life, nihilism in wrap around sarcasm, disdain worn like a heavy overcoat. Onanism is in the circumstances the best palliative, the unrealized a slaphappy chappy mired in angst. Pre-birthed. Mask up, breathing apparatus in place.

And so, let's see, the witch with whom I had been conjoined was now singular. Medusa Rappa, a product of two or more different religions and social castes. Manifestly unhinged, manipulative, psychopathic…possessing not only the inclination but also the wherewithal and more importantly the will to *assert* the will. She'd been trepanned in adolescence, far too early. She wanted early or pre-cogged Gnosis. Trepanning then a youth fashion statement. And so the brain juice wanted out. That much was obvious. There was some other animus at work here. The cerebral fluid, livid from imprisonment, had been throwing hokey incantations, reciting an obscure kabala of release (manifested to the outside world as wildly inappropriate laughter at all the wrong moments) with a view to a jailbreak. The trauma of this too-early trepanning remained and deepened over the years despite exhaustive Elephant Gnosis™ therapy. Later in life she shot her former lover in the head while suffering short-term memory loss and like a fool I subsequently gave her a good character reference. Otherwise she'd have gone down for it. No question. The demented aspect she presented filled me with pity I guess. She was marking time to the beats of restraining medication. She wrote terrible hagiographic books, airport thrillers, cookery scum pamphlets…and she refuted all criticism, gainsaid any adverse sentiment… and was bolstered by the equally distressed wives of literary cronies…and was afforded at all times an indulgence denied to the merely prosaic. You can't really argue with naked will and thus a pattern of appeasement was emplaced, the totalitarianism of madness not about to be challenged by democratic moderation. Medusa, the raptor. Medusa is another night in hell. In my desert shack, to which I'd been obliged to withdraw to concentrate on my anterior life, Dionysia was able to delete the harmful effects that the Rappa had inflicted, at first via Polarity Massage and subsequently by teaching me the tricks of Mythic Rejuvenescence. My batteries, in other words, were recharged. I was able to wait, to bide my time in elephantine meditation, invoking the herds that I was aware would one day be the key to my ultimate freedom, until such time as some sort of guiding spirit, some thin lipped creative genius in coincidental need of a household god, should happen past. And as I may have said, I didn't have to wait all that long. Limos bearing coked up rock gods doing the continent were a not uncommon phenomenon in those days.

Murder was Medusa's parting shot. One afternoon she casually announced she was a murderess. Casually, hysterically, as it were. She railed anew at the one she claimed to love, snapping out disingenuous denials as to her true motives. The brain juice overheating, the trepanned skull throbbing with intent, I knew in my heart that this death was a pre-cogged conception, an engineered event. And she knew I knew. A delicately poised dance of denial was consequently enacted. Questions were taboo, as was Reason. Instinct and savage religiosity were primary indicators. I've often wondered what possessed me to rewrite her character endorsement in these moments? As I say, pity is the likeliest answer to that one. But what spirit of appeasement possessed me, facilitating the supine capitulation? Surely it was voodoo of some clandestine type? It must have been sorcery that ended up itching me where it hurt. The rhythm method, rhythm and blues method, resulting in a prolonged delta blues for the future. It was a riff that was to be played out forever. A melancholy riff of stupidity, or feigned innocence, pretend-shocked discovery of the dangers of trusting to short-term memory set up a pounding refrain that would last the rest of our lives and beyond. I am a perjurer and I'm destined to pay the price the rest of my natural. I was not yet pre-birthed, and I was outgrown in lovehate. So it was that the secret service goons of her fecund imagination greedily consumed my image avatars, grabbed a few million confused and disoriented foot-soldiers, coshed a likely looking suspect, tied it up, gave it the 3rd degree and forced it at gunpoint into the inspirational hippocampus. My hand was forced. I therefore, as though in a dream, told the court that she was a woman of impeccable character. The reference was put on file. Her eyes glowed as my stuttering thoughts formed themselves into inadvisable approbations. Ever since I've known, since I snapped out of it, I've been sort of resigned. The game's up…if you're going to be caught like that, you deserve everything you get pal. I was done up like a kipper. It was sorcery. But my mum won the war. Cancer was what did it. She knows that idiots are obliged to live with their idiocy; it's the price they pay for being idiots. The people I know are beyond redemption, until re-birth. We never learn, until Mythic Rejuvenescence kicks in, while knowing that learning is the only redemption. We are addicted to keeping a tight grip on our futile behaviour patterns, never learning, and our psychologists shake their heads and click their tongues. Ayton is one hell of a joker. Manning type, he's a fat gutted mike stand leaner. I am his unsmiling audience of one. I have learned a mythic response. I have become divine in her absence, which he would deny me. She did love Strangelove he reckons, though profanely, in the way a hurricane loves the blasted landscape it leaves behind it, the way heavy thunderclouds burst above a fertile nightscape. It was all windswept emotion, centred on the bemused cynic who was through forgiving.

I've come through worse though. When I was even younger, I was married to a higher caste priestess who turned out to be a serial killer of the mind. A dragged up artist, a Horus-fixated falconer; she pretended a femininity that masked her true masculine instincts, the instinct to hunt and kill, to emasculate, to consume the paramour. But it doesn't fit together neatly. She was in some other dream I had, a dream of angels, of incipient disaster. Clawed and hook-beaked, hook rings on nicotined fingers, feeding on gobbets of information. Houses were burning down and fat birds were darting to and fro, tearing at the fire victims. It's all a kind of sorcery though. I've said that often enough. It's all a kind of sorcery. The thing is, knowing which key unlocks the door, and then knowing which door to unlock. Tricky…unless you're me. I can untie the vectors of inconsequence for you. That's my boast and I stand by it. My doctors are utterly non-plussed. They don't know what to make of it.

I AM BUFFY STRANGELOVE.

...they don't know how to drink. They can't drink. They don't get my hangovers, my routines...and how many times have you heard otherwise intelligent and sophisticated people describing in meticulous, proud detail the constituent components of their hangovers? All seasoned drinkers know what it is to wake up sick and dizzy, retching inside and the cerebral membrane hammering a drum solo on the skull cover? Drink from the night before still carousing in the fibrillating ventricles, heart muscle shimmying...a 3 second riff before essaying the outline of a drum solo and then stuttering to a halt...momentarily...and then on again. Drink again tonight and then again...so when does the sober reckoning occur? Gut hanging over trousers, distended belly a gut of wind, flabby arse pfut-pfut-pfutting...Drink really does ravage the pre-divine body. I know...red faced with the effort of tying shoelaces, trousers just a tad too tight, head swirly from over excitation. How many times? How many times do I need telling that there's no point? This life you're living is just punctuation they say. The real meat's gone missing they say. There's been a value hemorrhage...you look into the abyss and a fat whale looks back, a beaked snout heaving up the remains...

Dr. Abrahams: *Drink is the point. Lube the pain. It makes all kinds of sense. Life goes nowhere fast. And yet Strangelove hadn't quite given up hope. And neither had Hope given up on him. Hope, in the form of therapy, stalked him...we psychiatrists have identified this and extemporized on his behalf, like some sicko intent on getting into his trousers. We've got his unlisted number, and we breathe filthy and salacious suggestions, misplaced optimism, into his innocent ear. Our aim is to get the, as it were, crampons into the granite cliff face of his self-contempt. Or, snuggling deep down into the dank cave of his psyche and setting up camp there…making do…foraging and subsiding on the psychic odds and residual psychotropic ends, the detritus of his bitter musings, to wring something true or noble from the bitter misanthropy that rage in the forest fires of his superego. Hope has never ceased its mental fight in attempting to transmute the base metal of his despair and solipsism into something truer and nobler, some golden animus. But Yapp's chronic anhedonia is fully entrenched, a fully paid up lodger. He can't remember the last time he felt uplifted, inspired, fully tumescent.*

How he stopped mithering is anyone's guess, how he learned to still the enemy within a mystery. But it seems he made it, by careful husbandry of the Gnostic pre-disposition in his heart cavity and freakishly enlarged hippocampus. We overbearing medicos are maybe now obliged to admit defeat, as are the secular priesthood. Yapp considered us the enemy and maybe…maybe he was right. We won't know now of course. He had a highly developed inner critic, whom he understandably identified with my own pre-mythic persona, and whom he unwisely assumed to be his personal nemesis. This "critic" constantly berated him for his inaction, was never happy to allow him to remain inactive. He was endlessly repellant. Enough of his prattle. It's now or never. The chance to actualize. To take direct action. And yet…and yet…drinking is always preferable. He is a perfect and dedicated drinker. We talked in therapy about how, in the early years of his career as a drinker, Strglv was always in pursuit of or just arriving at a perfect point of intoxication which, unlike paid labour or any other servile activity, would reveal the true taste of the passage of time. Drinking, for Buffy, was a beautiful poetic game, with its own arcane rules and protocols. He filled many hours of interview tapes in describing this notion. Later, when he grew fat, ill and his stomach became permanently distended and he was unable to tie his shoelaces properly, he became consumed with boozers' gloom. Drink played an important role in his semi-permanent death. From gout to vertigo, by way of insomnia. Self-destruction seemed to be the consciously selected aesthetic. All games have risks, as I repeatedly told him, but he was adamant that drink fueled not only his anger, above all it fueled his needful fear. The fear of becoming a drunk…too much to become, when not being someone, even a drunk, remaining unbecoming, was easier. Comfort lubed by drink. Drink acting as a buffer for him, a bulwark between him and ambition, or lack of. Drink was his enabler, mollifier, coddler, encourager and granter of pardons, prison guard and partner in crime. And let's not even start on the drugs.

To recapitulate: Who was he anyway? Drink never answered (or even asked) that question. His other, a most taciturn man in public, yet given to unpleasant whingeing and complaining within the family precincts, had never bothered to tell him just what it was he'd done in the war. A natural expectation unfulfilled. Which was outrageous as far as Yapp was concerned. Not to bother letting your own brother in on the secrets of your warlike heritage? As though there was some secret, some shameful past, something disgusting or embarrassing. He'd not done anything much, as it turned out. Just learned how to make himself useful in an administrative capacity, secretary to a captain in the infantry. Just tell me something, anything, about my heritage he used to ask silently. Tell me who I am, or where I come from? My antecedents? Who am I? What are you? As though it should have been an issue. But it was…like…what did anyone need to know, except that they were God's servants, and sinning on a regular basis? In need of salvation, only attainable through hard work and rectitude, his brother's blithe unconcern for anything other than the life hereafter made it difficult for Strangelove to take him seriously as a man, as a human being. If he couldn't be bothered to humanize himself, tell a few anecdotes, even made up ones, of the folks long gone, of his own parents, why should he expect humanity or human contact in return? Not that he did. He didn't seem bothered that his brother was completely indifferent to him.

Yapp was latterly, at the end, simply out of energy. There was plenty of energy, on the one hand, to resist Hope's attempted seduction, her whorish advances, but no energy at all to act on Her better notions. Not that he didn't have the odd idea himself. He did. Lots of ideas. But his ideas were nothing next to his inertia. He was in the habit, as we doctors are fond of observing, of marching these notions to the very summit of the creative hillock, and then marching them down again when he realized that they were just empty notions, pipe dreams. Business plans agreed on in the fug of dope smoke. Essentially clapped out, clichéd, ideas that would never in a million years illuminate anything, least of all his own peculiar self-fictionalizing tendencies. Contempt was, with

Strglv, handmaiden to the urge to render useless all positive energy. Despite his contempt for everybody and everything, there was within him in addition a streak of ruthlessly pragmatic realism as well. He was and remains today his own severest critic, with whom he identifies me. I am his inner critic and am therefore by no means redundant. Self-contempt veins the brittle leaves of his ego. If only he could stop hating himself, he'd be worth something. It's not as if he's not talented. He is. Or he was. Brilliant. So brilliant that he couldn't be bothered proving it. He daydreamed in a dream place...full of booze...and he could be again. Without drink, without fear...

...He lives now in this warm and muzzy comfort zone, inhabiting the precincts of his own inertia. It's going to take a lot more than drink to get him to look at himself with any degree of realism. Odd that drink should have been an agent for spiritual and emotional galvanization, as by his own admission he was only really half way alive when he was drunk, or becoming drunk. So true to form. So, you might say, banal. Life as lived in all its banality. Yes indeed. Life lived in the mythic realm, only lately to be discovered by Yapp.

That first idea...his brother...and his name, the one who he'd cut loose...me as a surgeon. They were conjoined at elbow, arse and head. His brother had an absurd name. Buffy. He insisted on Buffy, although his given name was Brian. As far as we can determine, it was merely a statement of inconsequence...from our perspective of course a ludicrous affectation without redeeming features. A significant iconic emblem of life as lived by most people he knew. Keep the bastards guessing was his motto. Try out in the first ranks of singers. He re-named himself assuming it to be a primary requirement of official acceptance for mythic rebirth. In order to want to be someone else (always the precipitating force of any urge to power) he felt he required an overtly inappropriate moniker; felt that somehow he'd be thus transformed. Transformation is of course the presiding metaphor in the pathology of this type of psychotic. He'd convinced himself. And it actually was a transformation. In his darker moments, of which there were many, he conceded that it was just a hopeless vanity, a ludicrous conceit. But anyway he stuck with it, indeed becoming violent when others, either through sheer disbelief or through a mischievous urge to needle him, demurred. Lying in pain, in the moments before he actualized, he was able to glimpse both the future and the past. A past that he'd never actually lived. Why bother, he thought. Why bother indeed? We've seen this before though…this chronic ennui at the moment of re-entry, the numinous moment that momentarily circumvents the need for suicide assisted rebirth, a seemingly lost moment, the individual subsumed in high voltage electricity. When he cut me loose, I died for him. He can't get over that of course.

His brother Sapper, or Frank, another outré case was, as we say, "autistic", a label covering a multitude of sins. He was unthinkingly immobile, moved, or swayed, from side to side. Never made eye contact. A pipe cleaner of a man, he'd had women in his sights, but never in his range. Sapper could hardly talk. Sapper was also bitter. Somewhat younger and relatively more stupid than Brian, as well as being bereft of what we've come, as doctors, to identify as charm, and in personal contradiction of received wisdom (that autists are geniuses), he'd also come close to ending it, but a native apathy prevented him acting on the impulse. Suicide was, paradoxically, Frank's own Big Idea. But he couldn't get on with it. He just couldn't act on impulse. He never really appreciated the essential point, the fully empowering nature of suicide. At once self-effacing and self regarding, the dilemma was that his epiphany, filmed auto-destruction, was unlikely ever to happen. So the ultimate self-sanction was denied him. The inner critic's final thumbs down remained tantalizingly merely potential. Nonetheless, bringing the curtain down on his miserable existence occupied his every waking moment. Suicide, the idea, was for him not yet a methodology, a way of achieving consummation, of actualizing. Although he dimly perceived the truth of it, his was as yet a mundane reading of the idea…of re-birth…of the ultimate negation as a thrilling consummation. He got hot thinking about it. Ways to Do Yourself In: A Compendium of Half-Arsed Techniques was a book forever evolving in his brain. Mirroring Brian's urge to live was Sapper's will to simplistic and nihilistic self-destruction. People in chains, as he termed them, needled him constantly, but not half as much as he imagined they were needling him. He was the type who assumed that people, strangers, acquaintances, friends, anyone at all, were too full of Attitude. He was big on Attitude, and consequently was all Attitude himself. On tubes, buses, in the streets…of course, this made it difficult for him. There were always plenty of people by whom to be offended, a plethora of targets for air rage.

Strangelove's 2ⁿᵈ conceit was that somehow his real life, the one in which he was a great success, admired and loved by all, had been hijacked and was currently being lived by someone else. The process of self-fictionalisation, this whole mythic schtick he'd painstakingly constructed, was clearly having unperceived consequences for his sense of self. This loss of perspective was for him a hard reality, a fact unchained from any alternative reality. He was free, but nonetheless in chains. He became lost without perspective. His loss of subjectivity, his loss in subjectivity, had all but consumed him. Deadbeat pavement stalkers were guilty in his eyes. They'd sucked him dry. Foul academics had him pinned like a butterfly and blocked his energy flow. Friends were now ex-friends; previously admired psychic avatars were dismissed as pointless emanations. He was permanently wrapped in a gaseous cloud of ennui…as we've observed. And drunk. Despite his fictions, anti-gravity control has clearly failed for him. Levitation remains merely a fictional construct for him. Why bother indeed? Hospital beds cannot contain him. And why would they? The trickle of visitors has dried up. Unbelievers are made awkward in his superheated presence. He now moves under his own steam. He's become something…See; he actually believes that sooner or later he will be the recipient of some sort of astonishing luck. He's succumbed latterly to Lottery mania. He believes, or fancies he believes, in the chance intersection of his fate with that of some egregious force. His quantum linear tendrils will be joined, ludicrous as it no doubt sounds to the lay ear, in joyous epiphany with those of someone other, someone hippocampus-led, someone with looks, style, grace, wit. Although he isn't a bad looker, despite the absence of pedestrian equipment, despite latterly the absence of inner strength. There is still something vital missing however, something apart from the legs. In short, some sort of inner strength, some possessing animus containing all the characteristics he manifestly lacks…

…Hi. It's Buffy. I'm here again. I am obsessive compulsive. I'm obsessed. People needle me. I have to look inside them. I have to see myself inside them. I am constrained; my universe is now contracting. I can no longer access the visions I need. My eyes are closed, or the visions escape for good. But I'm all seeing; I am imperative. My will is eventually done, in endgames I do tend to triumph. People quake when I raise my voice. They see the paraplegic genius and they see stacked attitude, though without eyes to see. I use my native wit and technical skills to bamboozle them. Old ones stand up for me on tube trains, even though I don't need a seat. My head aches from separation. How did I become me? What's the story? How many more days and nights of sitting around searching the soul, affecting a fictional public exegesis for the benefit of the doctor/producers, must I endure? I've been thrown out; it's an occluded heaven, a heaven open to all but me, this soul not even my own. It's a shared soul. What is there to do now that isn't just window dressing? My soul daytrips, it's away on a daily basis. Flies away before I've woken up. I dream of stupid men…vapid men…men assuming my identity…for profit…as though my identity is up for grabs. I tell you I've almost given up the ghost. It's a joke. Why bother?

Why bother indeed! Is it likely to matter more at some time in the linear future? Who knows me now? Could it do with mattering a bit more right now? Have I wasted my life like some…some…useless piece of shit, drifting like a moron between pillar and post…I'd better start doing… things…I was left for dead, a piece of carrion, street dreck, on the operating table. So Frank will write it out for me. Work it out of me. Make it work for me. My need to fictionalize has caught me with my trousers down. I bend over to pull them up and I'm light headed. I don't even know who I was or am any more. I remember being killed so that someone else could live. I wasn't asked my opinion. Just slam down on the synapses…

Dr. Ayton (again): *Strangelove told me in many one-on-one psycho-probe sessions…* "That was my problem. 'How do we become who we think we are?' I used to enquire of bemused passers by. I'd beard bearded drinkers in pubs and click my tongue at them. Buy them drinks. Talk in their general direction…in tongues… 'What's it all about eh? Eh? Eh… Eh?… EH??? Me old cocker spaniel? What a bleedin' lark eh?' I attracted concerned glances from mothers with infants in prams when talking apparently to myself. The angel on my shoulder, reflected in shop windows, beaming back at me…"

...Malevolence and spite were consistently evident in his testimony. Self justification and borderline psychopathic lack of empathy... baleful arrogance plus naked dependence on some "other", or some sort of naked beatitude. Epiphanies regularly occurred for him outside franchised outlets, high streets resounded to the clarion call of this fictional and obtuse Visionary, seeing his things. Mothers without children stopped short as he shook and rattled. I told him on many occasions that micro choices make a difference, but hey, as we doctors say, that's only day-to-day. That, my friend, is just pissing about; that is just taking the piss. I endeavoured instead to put him in mind of theatrically large questions. Who decides the pattern of life, I prompted... only God, only the divine. The transcendental being, the transmogrified force. Fetishes, tribal apocrypha were invoked. I became almost a shaman for him, donning the scared therapeutic papier-macho elephant fetish head, conducting therapy-happenings as though invoking ritual gods and goddesses. I have to report that the elephant head, while not entirely realistic, its contours conforming to a sort of cubist regressive design, made a huge impression on him. But we don't really have a clue. His dreams might be filmable, but equally, on the other hand, might not. We're Hollywood now are we not? I talk 6 figure sums only. If he can't, even after intensive polarity massage, make the cut, we'll have to cut him loose, pull the ripcord. Either him or his, er, brother... his agents have refused to speak to us for months now. There's something odd, something hidden here... they're maybe pulling a stroke, taking us for mugs... careful now... we need to exercise caution... He's struggling to work it out now, thinking he's shaping his lives, doing... stuff... thinking it means something. Wearing the tuberous mask more and more each day... larger choices made without his being aware of it. An acknowledgement that this is the way it is, that random patterns fuck us up without our knowing the why or the wherefore, seems imminent now. That's what he's beginning to take from the sessions, or so it seems. But he is of course brain dead. He's up there with the birds... still no brain soul... still brain dead. His dream voices approximate birdsong. Just listen...

...Many many hours spent just thinking blank thoughts; I have given life to many angels, hovering... hovering... above my head. They just don't understand where they come from is all. The older I grow, the more I distrust the familiar doctrine that age brings wisdom. H.L. Mencken said that. And he'd know. Age just brings…a greater capacity for misery, yes? Yes! Age, or middle age, brings encroaching death. That realization means avoidance of people, things…cultural ballast…graft. Give it up. It's the only way to go. But people give you up as readily as you give them up. People just can't stand it any more. It's just too much. People avoid people; remain remote from one another. It's only natural. People treat each other bad. We're just sick of each other. Wary, nauseated, sick bastards…it's all over. Not knowing or caring what we've become, or more pertinently failed to become. Failed to grow up, never fought a war. Not been in the trenches. That's what that's all about. We've failed to live in exacting times. Not experienced life-changing events. Living mausoleum commuters…maybe…time'll tell…

The new template for living in cities; window dressing, an alibi for emptiness. Leisure ghosts in mall empires, fitness gyms and chain restaurants. I flit around leisure emporia, cinema outlets, bookshop/coffee bars. That old time cappuccino culture in full swing. That old time religion; caffeined up. No libraries break the ghastly consumer symmetry of enclosed leisure. Councils run by pea brained functionaries, spectacle-wearing incompetents, specially trained idiots. Men with beards and women with wattle necks, conceived for nothing if not for inducing overpowering feelings of nausea in their clients. All trained in provocatively incompetent idiocy…yes, I'll just get your file… yes, a letter should have gone out on the 12th…I can only apologize…it's the computer system, it's broken down…yeah right, do I SOUND stupid… (yes)…we can't send you another letter, our system's not up at the moment… Computer systems break down as a primary function. Computer systems were never meant to be "up". It makes you puke. It gets your juices going, get me? It fails at every conceivable level, public incompetence through the offices of disassociated individuals, the storm troops of public indifference, non-grown up adults, dependency whores, carriers of the incompetence virus…to generation after generation. Phone-sex is the only answer to gnawing personal problems of tele-commercial operatives. Phonesex…cybersex; the only outlet for infantile public employees.

…Incredible, yes incredible…I know. I feel the urge repeatedly to defame the public-spirited. Constantly I am Strangelove. He is I. In another space, I muse on the supposed irony that computers are, far from opening up vistas to a brave new world of free and value free gob-information, in fact merely oiling the cultural and financial wheels, and are of course responsible for a whole new layer of obfuscation in the skein of life. Information is elusive, coy. Information is shifty. Information is now not to be relied upon. Information is catching up with rumour as fallacy carrier. Information is a virus whose vehicle of infection is excess electricity...

Abrahams: *Other bird voices intervene here...*

...People don't care about being dickheads any more. I see this. I've turned my eyes away from them but...I see them...I'm on a soapbox, but I see them. They're transparent now...they are pure information...are dickheads now with NO cost now. Being a dickhead seems like a decent career option now, which must be why careers are for dickheads, because the only jobs available are dickhead jobs. You look around...there's too much bad stuff... Unsubtle media power broker-slags, baby boomer ex soft-revolutionaries, computer "specialists", web designers and (ha-ha) ideas people, carrying their fantasy self importance before them. Cabals of decision makers, focus group tendencies, swearing black is white...knotting up straightforward aspects of life...

...But where have I heard all this stuff before? Slowly, by degrees, the light grows dim in me. There's a light somewhere, but I can't or can focus on it. Thick blood-liquid spins out of and down from the corner of my mouth. In my peripheral vision, the light somehow momentarily eludes me. But the light is there, somewhere, ghost light is always there in the periphery. He's there, somewhere, in my peripheral vision; elephant head still affixed. The black city crowded my thoughts as he lay there, bleeding from the head wound that had been inflicted by that lairy youth. Scrying the future in a high street mobile phone shop window display, the future had, so to speak, met him head on. Speaking in tongues, these youths had been encouraged by worried passers-by, mothers with infants, prams brandished like battle buses, to see it as their public duty to remove him from the equation, to get him out of harm's way and into their own claw hammered domain. Young people, as well as old, very much the worst, not even a folk memory of decent public standards of behaviour. Lying there, his mind spun endless tales, bleak mortuary fantasies...

...Down in Stoke Newington, he or I...early for an appointment, so took a turn around the eerie, overgrown, spooky, chilling Abney Park Cemetery. Home in death to the Granddaddy of the Salvation Army William Booth among many thousands of others stiffs. A haunt for morbid weirdoes, smackheads and the cider befuddled, the gothic acre a full on goth mystery-house, a wreckage yard of broken tombstones and dark green foliage... A strange and fierce wind arose, there was a babbling, a chattering, the tertiary moon fell, ice hit the fireball...which was destined for the waves...and several castrated monkeys disported themselves in the ruined church. Skateboards, windsock, discarded rubbish, a babbling primate mouthing cup final tickets mate. Rudolf Steiner was chased out of Germany by the Nazis...forewarned is forearmed...and guilt rage sprang up in me. 6 million. 22 million. The numbers spiraled away into featureless zeros and ones. Still smarting from the adverse weather conditions, I turned up my collar and slept soundly. The redundancy of guilt was inside me, growing despite my lack of personal guilt. Dummy catholic still in my head, a priestly homunculus shaped like a sea horse, warming over guilt that overlays millennia of mythic material. I never did anything really bad. Apart from murder that geek who had it in for me. He had it coming though. My guilt is raindrop guilt, washed away by each emotional rescheduling. My tears act as expiation for whatever catholic tendencies are left within me. I assume the role of nay-sayer to Jesuitical panderings...technical innocence...never admit to wrongdoing. Never acknowledge wrongdoing. Never apologize. Never look back. I was drummed out of the Jesuits. I failed on every level. Thought that as a monk I could hack it in my habit. I can't do that there then. Ever growing guilt hacked up, as spontaneous lungrot. DNA spewed out of the genes transcendent with dummy guilt. I took to therapy, in the form of confessional. I became the iridescent father confessor to a generation of show off desperadoes. I became a gossip columnist, then an agony uncle. Guilt accosted me and I hurried through the darkening lanes, the sky a livid mess of rolling black cloud. Already rain was spitting down on me, the advancing storm a promise of retribution...

...My familiar was shimmering in green. I sat downwind of him. It was the Gower peninsula, a bright morning of magicians. Bright shiny green, the foliage drinking up spring water with thirsty lips, the trees alive with applause. From the greenery an old man and his dog emerged. "My dog won't hurt," he said. "He's lived here 45 years". Outside the chapel and through the wooden gate the world was now brimming green. A green man was under one of the far trees, smoking a roll up, eyes lowered to his chest. My other side caught a glimpse, a fatal glimpse of his feral magic. My arm was numb, as was my tit and my arse. The wind arose, the whispering started, rumours circulating in whirlpool vortices, and I was dragged down. I no longer knew. I was pulled into not knowing. Guilt pinioned me, my guilt fantasies too strong to resist. The bellicose monsters of the dreams of my infancy were in hot pursuit. Blissful enlightened state...the boundaries collapsed, but it didn't last long. The livid foliage was more alive than ever. Round the fire that night, I was more than alive. Preternatural. I was made of a kind of lucid information. Noise came from me. Abattoir noise. Killing decibels. White noise washed over me as I dominated proceedings around the fire. Cider fuelled, I slept a few hours. Woke up by the sea, great shards of rock jutting through the tense fabric of my curtailed reality, spume and foam dancing, alive with jism froth, the male ocean impregnating my receptive mind. My femaled receptivity now a caricature of previously known truths. I fell through the earth, the rocks swallowed me whole, my body broken and compromised.

I lay there unable to move, the sky sinking into me. I saw two, three, maybe half a dozen breasts, softly insinuated, a prelapsarian dream. Something extraordinary. A boy falling into the sea, a fireball, the ship (or something) had to get somewhere and sailed calmly on. Schools of whales keening and spraying. My face collapsed into itself. Frank! Frank! Several sea birds wheeled overhead...gulls...and darker more portentous looking things, wide spanned and imperious, and then banked away towards the English channel, charter flights nervelessly breaching the afternoon blue yonder. Mist descended, and my mournful imagination conjured up evocative horn sections, timpani un-scored, and programmable and sampled segments looped in my brain. Meanwhile, thrash metal scalped everything in earshot. The noise of my dreams mingled with that of the spume. There were no radio voices though. No causal factor. The music

david kettle

came from the very earth. Ponderous, rushed, the earth puked and wrenched itself away from us, auto-scripting my carefully worded suicide note. The world re-birthed. I realized the game was up. It was a Frank Pick poster scene in my mind. Purely bathetic…of course…Flat perspective, yet infinitely stylish in a languid thirties kind of way, the end of the stylized world. I languished on the rocks for what might have been weeks but was probably only minutes.

I groaned and moved. My world crashed down, apart and over the top. In my life without music, I was lost in music subjectivity. I was music, scored from pitiful sounds. Rock became my bed and my bed heaved under me. The vectors of my inconsequence were now fully scored beneath me. My rebirth as failed academic/admin was all but assured. I later emerged from the sea fully fictionalized. I emerged from the waves, a living metaphor of evolutionary transcendence, elephant head mask affixed with string. Priapic, trunk erect and prehensile. Behemoth ears already finely attuned as antennae and with auto-cooling a non-optional feature fully realized. Ready to rock! Ready to Rock! I find the nearest animal familiar. Whales ride the waves and I score a new symphony, a cacophony, a Celtic tribal epiphany. All the way around the world. A metaphysics to die for, to commit suicide for. A rebirth in metaphor; beyond the clutches of mundane coffee table psychology, and on into the mythic. My body is borne again through the waves for many thousands of nautical miles.

…I was a white bull elephant, aquaplaned for the time being…my metempsychosis a spur to find him again, to renew hostilities with some new adversary, some as yet untested, obsessive Ahab, a renewable nemesis…some blighted, bloated, psychotic, satanic creature of the profane airwaves. It'll be a radio voice. But I am again. I have become again a creature that in elephant-gnostic meta-theology is way beyond the profane. My trunk is temporarily a snorkeling device, I am a divine emanation, and later on I bestride the leafy estates of Hampstead Heath. Both the oceans and the wide-open spaces are my realm. The skies have opened. The oceans roll back.

ABOUT THE AUTHOR

David Kettle was born in Tottenham, Florida UK. He started his youth as a Welsh coal miner. He soon tired of the sooty occupation & moved into a career as influence pedlar in the Scottish Parliament. After he was ousted for being underage, he fled to the Ukraine thinking this was a british colony because of the abbreviation UK in the encyclopedia. He found no work there but many Ukrainians. A short train ride brought him to his present home in Western Australia, a town whose name no one can pronounce, Ngbhlumbfumbgh. Here Mr. Kettle soaks himself in denatured papoose juice & sticks his fingers in the typewriter keys. "The excrutiating pain drives him to write."

ALSO AVAILABLE FROM K-BOMB:

THE DEVIL'S OWN DAY (Cole Coonce)
SEX & TRAVEL & VESTIGES OF METALLIC FRAGMENTS
(Cole Coonce)
THE INERTIA VARIATIONS (John Tottenham)
THE SLEEP OF PUSS TITTER (Anthony Ausgang)
TOP FUEL WORMHOLE (Cole Coonce)
DR. BUCK LETTERS (FallNet)
COME DOWN FROM THE HILLS & MAKE MY BABY
(Cole Coonce)
ELEPHANT GNOSIS (David Kettle)
INFINITY OVER ZERO (Cole Coonce)

www.kbomb.tv